Julianna wore an el~~abo~~**mask over the top h**~~alf of her face but~~ **it only enhanced her beauty, making her look mysterious. But even the mask couldn't hide the brilliant blue of her eyes. Or that enticing mouth.**

Mine. The word thrummed through Ben's blood, just as a voice near the front shouted out, 'Five thousand dollars!'

Something went tight inside Ben as the bidding started to escalate. *Ten thousand…fifteen…twenty.* There were gasps now, people looking around. And then a booming voice called out, 'Fifty thousand dollars!'

The auctioneer held his gavel up and asked if anyone wanted to contest this latest bid. No one moved. The thought of that man getting anywhere near Julianna made Ben feel a level of violence he hadn't experienced in a long time.

The auctioneer brought the gavel down once, twice…

Just before he could bring it down again Ben spoke authoritatively into the silence. 'One million dollars.'

Everyone gasped and turned to look at him. He walked forward, the crowd parting to let him through.

When he was near the dais, he stopped and said, 'But I want more than a kiss. For a million dollars I want a *weekend* with Julianna Ford.'

Brides for Billionaires

Meet the world's ultimate unattainable men...

Four titans of industry and power—Benjamin Carter, Dante Mancini, Zayn Al-Ghamdi and Xander Trakas— are in complete control of every aspect of their exclusive world... Until one catastrophic newspaper article forces them to take drastic action!

Now these gorgeous billionaires need one thing: willing women on their arms and wearing their rings! Women falling at their feet is normal, but these bachelors need the *right* women to stand by their sides. And for that they need billionaire matchmaker Elizabeth Young.

This is the opportunity of a lifetime for Elizabeth, so she won't turn down the challenge of finding just the right match for these formidable tycoons. But Elizabeth has a secret that could complicate things for *one* of the bachelors...

Find out what happens in:

Married for the Tycoon's Empire by Abby Green

Married for the Italian's Heir by Rachael Thomas

Married for the Sheikh's Duty by Tara Pammi

Married for the Greek's Convenience by Michelle Smart

MARRIED FOR THE TYCOON'S EMPIRE

BY
ABBY GREEN

First Published in Great Britain 2016
By Mills & Boon, an imprint of HarperCollins*Publishers*
1 London Bridge Street, London, SE1 9GF

© 2016 Harlequin Books S.A.

Special thanks and acknowledgement are given to Abby Green for her contribution to the Brides for Billionaires series.

ISBN: 978-0-263-92132-8

Printed and bound in Spain
by CPI, Barcelona

Irish author **Abby Green** threw in a very glamorous career in film and TV—which really consisted of a lot of standing in the rain outside actors' trailers—to pursue her love of romance. After she'd bombarded Mills & Boon with manuscripts they kindly accepted one, and an author was born. She lives in Dublin, Ireland, and loves any excuse for distraction. Visit abby-green.com or e-mail abbygreenauthor@gmail.com.

Books by Abby Green

Mills & Boon Modern Romance

Awakened by Her Desert Captor
Forgiven but not Forgotten?
Exquisite Revenge
One Night with the Enemy
The Legend of De Marco
The Call of the Desert
The Sultan's Choice
Secrets of the Oasis
In Christofides' Keeping

One Night With Consequences

An Heir to Make a Marriage
An Heir Fit for a King

The Chatsfield

Delucca's Marriage Contract

Billionaire Brothers

The Bride Fonseca Needs
Fonseca's Fury

Blood Brothers

When Falcone's World Stops Turning
When Christakos Meets His Match
When Da Silva Breaks the Rules

Visit the Author Profile page at millsandboon.co.uk for more titles.

I'd like to dedicate this book
to the Mills & Boon authors who inspired me
from the very beginning: Susan Napier, Emma Darcy,
Robyn Donald, Sara Craven, Helen Bianchin,
Penny Jordan, Sally Wentworth, Sara Wood,
Kate Proctor and Stacy Absalom, whose book
Ishbel's Party is still my touchstone for the high-stakes
high emotion these books promise. Thank you!

PROLOGUE

BENJAMIN CARTER SAT in a high-backed leather chair in a corner of the private members-only club. The lighting was artfully dim, and the atmosphere was hushed and exclusive. Warm golden lights and flickering candles added to the sense of rarefied privacy. Cigar smoke curled into the air from another dark corner, adding an exotic aroma and diffusing the light.

The club promised absolute discretion, which was specifically why he'd chosen it. And now Ben looked, one by one, at each of the other three men who had joined him at his table. At his request.

Sheikh Zayn Al-Ghamdi—the ruler of a desert kingdom rich in oil and minerals, whose wealth was astonishing and control absolute.

Dante Mancini—an Italian renewable energies mogul whose charming, handsome exterior hid a rapier-sharp intellect, business acumen and a sarcastic tongue that could strip paint from a wall—as Ben had discovered during one particularly acrimonious deal years before. Right now he wasn't exuding charm; he was glowering darkly in Ben's direction.

And, last but not least, Xander Trakas—the Greek billionaire CEO of a global luxury goods conglomerate. He was cool and aloof, with strong features that gave nothing away. Ben had once told him grudgingly that he should play poker if he ever lost his vast fortune and needed to win it back. Which was about as likely as a snowstorm in hell.

Ben might not rule over a desert kingdom, or half of Europe, but he ruled over Manhattan with his towering cranes and the deep pits he forged out of the ground in order to build new and impossibly ambitious buildings.

The tension around the table was palpable. These men had been his nemeses for so long—and each other's— that it was truly surreal to be sitting here now. What had started out as minor infractions during various deals over the years had escalated into entrenched warfare, with each recognising in the others formidable adversaries to be defeated and vanquished. The only problem being that each one was as successfully ruthless and stubborn as the other, so all they'd ever achieved was a series of tense stalemates.

Ben sensed that Dante Mancini in particular was about ready to bolt, so he sat forward. It was time to talk.

'Thank you all for coming here.'

Sheikh Zayn Al-Ghamdi's dark eyes were hard. 'I don't appreciate being summoned like a recalcitrant child, Carter.'

'And yet,' Ben pointed out, 'you're here.' He looked around. 'You all are.'

Dante Mancini drawled, 'And the prize for stating the obvious goes to Benjamin Carter.' He lifted his heavy crystal glass in Ben's direction and the dark liquid inside shimmered with golden opulence, reflecting the decadent luxury of the club around them. He downed his drink in one and simultaneously gestured for the waiter. He caught Ben's look. 'Tempted to drink something stronger than *water*, Carter?'

Ben fought down the urge to rise to Dante's jibe. He was the only one of them not indulging in the finest single malt whisky one could buy outside of Ireland and Scotland.

He looked pointedly at the others. 'Gentlemen, as fun as it's been over the last decade, squaring up to each of you, I think you'll agree that the time has come for us to stop giving the press an excuse to pit us against each other.'

Xander Trakas looked from Ben to the other men and sighed. 'He's right. The press have targeted us all, one by one, and what started out as a few salacious gossipy pieces in that rag *Celebrity Spy!* have turned into something much more serious. While I believe we're responsible for the stories that end up in those rags due to our own lax PR, I draw the line at spurious claims of excessive partying, revolving bedroom doors and, most damaging of all, conspicuous absences at the office.'

The Greek tycoon's face hardened with displeasure. 'The fact that I've been pulling all-nighters in the office when they say I'm out partying is infuriating. I lost out on a lucrative contract last week because of doubts about my competence. It's gone too far.'

Dante Mancini made a sound of grudging agreement. '*I'm* about to lose out on a deal because they want someone with "family values"—whatever that is.' He took a healthy sip of his refreshed drink.

The fact that Dante Mancini and Xander Trakas were still here and agreeing with each other told Ben more effectively than anything that he'd done the right thing in asking them here this evening—and also that they had a very real threat on their hands.

He said, 'We're being reduced to caricatures, and these exaggerations of our private exploits are becoming too damaging to ignore. I can handle walking onto my construction sites and having my men rib me about a kiss and tell, but when gossip and innuendo starts to affect share prices and my professional reputation that's unacceptable.'

Trakas looked at him and there was an unmistakable gleam of mockery in his eyes. 'You're not trying to imply that your ex-lover made it all up, Carter, are you?'

Memories of lurid headlines—*The hard man of construction is just as hard in bed!*—made Ben snap back, 'Her story was as real as *your* infamous little black book that divulges the names and numbers of most of the world's most beautiful women. What was it they said, Trakas? Still waters run deep?'

Trakas scowled and Mancini scoffed, 'As if Trakas has the monopoly on the most beautiful women. Everyone knows that I—'

A cool voice cut them off, 'If we're quite finished with the dissing contest, perhaps we can discuss how to get ourselves out of this mess. I agree with Carter: it's gone too far. This adverse attention is not only affecting confidence in my leadership, but also my business concerns. It's even affecting my little sister's chances of the marriage she wants, and that is unacceptable.'

They all looked at Sheikh Zayn Al-Ghamdi, who had sat forward. The dim lighting made the lines of his boldly handsome face stand out harshly. They were all dressed in classic black tuxedos except for Mancini, who was bucking the trend in a white jacket with his bow tie rakishly undone.

It reminded Ben of the function they'd just come from and he said grimly, 'It's not just our business concerns... or our families.'

Mancini sat forward too, frowning. 'What do you mean?'

Ben glanced at him, and at the others. 'The director of the charity came to me this evening and told me that if this media furore doesn't disappear she'll have to remove us all as patrons. She's noticed an adverse effect, with less tickets sold and people not showing up.'

Dante Mancini cursed colourfully in Italian.

The Sheikh said ruminatively, 'So that's why you asked us to come and meet you?'

Ben nodded. 'I think we can all agree that the last thing we want is for the charity to suffer because of us.'

The charity in question was the only thing that linked them all, outside of pitting their wits against each other during business deals, and its function was the only time of year when they were all in the same room at the same time, which invariably caused much media interest.

The Hope Foundation focused on giving funds to young kids—girls and boys who were from disadvantaged backgrounds and showed an aptitude for business and enterprise.

Dante said now, 'Carter's right. We can't bring the charity into this mess.'

For the first time Ben had to recognise a sense of kinship. They all genuinely cared about the same thing, and it was slightly disconcerting when he'd depended solely on himself for so long. It wasn't entirely unwelcome— almost as if a burden had suddenly been lightened.

And then Sheikh Zayn's cool voice said, 'So what the hell is the solution?'

Ben looked at him, and glanced at the others. 'I'm guessing that, like me, you've consulted with your legal teams and realised that it isn't worth the added publicity to sue *Celebrity Spy!*?'

They all nodded.

Ben went on, his voice as grim as the faces around him. 'Issuing a statement will also get us nowhere; we've gone beyond that point. If we do that it'll look like we're backtracking, trying to defend ourselves.' He sighed volubly. 'The only solution is for us to be seen to be cleaning up our acts—comprehensively and for the long term. Unless we do, I don't think it's going to go away. If anything, they'll only start to dig deeper, and I can assure you that I for one have no desire to invite further scrutiny.'

Dante's gaze narrowed on Ben. 'You don't want people being reminded that your rags to riches story isn't entirely accurate?'

Ben's whole body tensed and he glared at the man. 'I've never hidden my origins, Mancini. Let's just say I've no desire to have old history raked over again. Just as I'm sure you'd prefer not to invite a spotlight onto your own family background?'

Ben was referring to the way Dante was so zealous about guarding his family's privacy—which could only mean he had something to hide.

After a tense moment the ghost of a hard smile touched Dante's mouth and he lifted his almost empty glass in the air. '*Touché*, Carter.'

Sheikh Zayn interrupted tautly, 'I think we can all appreciate not wanting to attract even more attention, for whatever reasons we may have.'

Ben was aware of Xander Trakas shifting uncomfortably to his right, evidently ruminating on the skeletons in his own closet.

A brooding silence descended on the group for a moment and then the Sheikh said with a grimace, 'I agree with Carter that cleaning up our personal lives seems to be the only viable solution. As much as I've tried to avoid it, I know the only thing that will restore my people's faith in me will be a strategic marriage and producing an heir to the throne.'

Ben was aware of the collective shudder that seemed to go through all of them. With the utmost reluctance, he had to admit, 'After discussions with my PR advisor and my solicitor, I've come to a similar conclusion.'

Dante said, with evident horror, '*Marriage?* Do we really need to take such drastic action?'

Ben looked at him. 'Even I can see the benefit in marrying someone suitable. It will restore confidence and get the press off our backs. It'll also restore trust. I've found myself in numerous social situations where clients' wives have made their interest all too obvious, much to the anger of their spouses. It's only a matter of time before a deal falls through because of petty jealousy—or, worse, the belief that something happened.' Ben looked around the other men. 'We're being seen as threats, in more ways than one. And that's not good.'

Dante's irritation was obvious. 'You said someone suitable—what is *suitable*? Is there such a woman?'

Sheikh Zayn answered, with all the confidence of a man who came from a society where arranged marriages were commonplace. 'Of course there is. A woman who is happy to complement your life...a woman who will be discreet and loyal above all.'

Dante raised a brow. 'So, genius, where do we find this paragon of virtue?'

For a moment there was silence, and Ben tensed again, suspecting that Dante Mancini had gone too far. Sheikh Zayn was a head of state, and used to far more reverential exchanges.

But then the Sheikh threw his head back and laughed, long and hard. When he looked at them all again he said, 'Do you know how refreshing it is when someone speaks to me like this?'

The tension that had been pulled taut between them ever since they'd all sat down seemed to relax perceptibly.

Dante smiled and gestured with his glass towards the Sheikh. 'If you would finally agree to discuss alternative energies with me, I'll disrespect you as much as you want.'

Sheikh Zayn's eyes flashed with rare humour. 'Now, *that* is an offer I could consider.'

Ben cut in. 'As warm and fuzzy as this cessation in hostilities is, we need to focus on the fact that we've agreed that promoting a more settled front is the way to deal with this situation. And for that we need to find women who are happy to marry us quickly and conveniently. As Sheikh Zayn said, women we can trust, who will be discreet. Loyal.'

Dante Mancini's smile faded and he said darkly, 'You'd have more luck finding a leprechaun riding a unicorn down Fifth Avenue.'

They contemplated that silently for a few seconds, and then Xander Trakas said quietly, 'I know someone.'

They all looked at the man who, Ben realised, had been suspiciously quiet up till now. 'Who?' he asked, intrigued.

'A woman. She runs a very discreet dating agency aimed specifically at people like us. She knows our world inside out—'

'Who is she to you?' cut in Dante. 'An ex-lover?'

Xander glared at him, not looking so aloof now. 'That's none of your business, Mancini. Just trust me when I say that if anyone can set us up with the right women, she can.'

The Italian mogul held up a hand. 'Fine—keep your pants on.'

Ben, who'd been absorbing all this, looked to Sheikh Zayn. 'Well?'

The Sheikh looked as if he'd prefer to sign up to a knitting class, but he finally said heavily, 'I think it might be the best option... If we're doing this, time is of the essence—for all of us.' He punctuated that with an expressive look at each of them.

Dante eventually said, with palpable reluctance, 'Fine. I'll take her details but I'm not promising anything.'

Ben held out his phone to Xander Trakas and tried to ignore the sensation of his collar tightening around his neck. 'Put her number in there. I'll call her next week.'

As Xander added the contact details to Ben's phone Sheikh Zayn sat forward and said, with another glimmer of wry humour, 'Do you know, I've actually forgotten what it was that set us off against each other in the first place…?'

Ben quirked a rueful smile. 'I think we have to admit that perhaps we liked being adversaries too much to give it up.'

Xander put Ben's phone down on the table. He held up his glass. 'Well, then, maybe it's time to concede a mutual defeat for the benefit of a bigger victory. Restoring faith in our reputations, which in turn will restore confidence in our businesses and profit margins. Because, as we all know, that's what's most important.'

Dante Mancini lifted his glass and drawled, 'Hear, hear. To the start of a beautiful friendship, gentlemen.'

Ben looked around at each of the men and thought that in spite of the slightly mocking tone of Mancini's words something *had* shifted here tonight. These men were not foes any more. They were allies and, yes, possibly even friends.

Ben raised his glass to join the others. Nothing was going to get in their way now. Not even the women they would take as their convenient wives.

CHAPTER ONE

BEN CARTER STOOD near the main window in his office, with its impressive views over downtown Manhattan. The thing that usually pleased him most when he took in this view was seeing his construction cranes high in the sky, dotted around the island. Right now, though, he had his back to the view and every line of his body was in defence mode, from his crossed arms to his tense stance.

'So, I think that about covers it.'

He bit back the urge to ask snarkily if she wanted to know what colour underwear he was wearing today.

The woman seated by his desk glanced at him and observed wryly, 'You don't like answering personal questions, do you?'

Ben bared his teeth in a forced smile. 'Whatever gave you that impression?'

Elizabeth Young, the matchmaker, shrugged nonchalantly as she tapped something into her palm tablet. 'I think the fact that you look about ready to jump out of the window gives it away.'

Ben scowled and walked back over to his desk. With every question she'd asked—from innocuous ones like, *What's your favourite holiday destination?* to more edgy ones like *What is it you want from a relationship?*—he'd put more and more space between them. As much as he recognised his need for a convenient wife, the quantum leap from a life of no-strings encounters with beautiful women to a committed relationship—albeit for convenience's sake—was making Ben's skin prickle uncomfortably.

After witnessing the collapse of his parents' marriage, which had fallen like a deck of cards at the first sign of trouble, Ben had never entertained notions of domestic bliss.

The matchmaker was right: if he could have jumped from the window he might just have tried it.

He scowled harder as he sat down—who the hell's idea had this been again? *Xander Trakas*. Recalling the Greek man's reaction that night, when Mancini had asked if this woman was an ex-lover, made Ben assess the slim and elegant blonde on the other side of his desk.

Hair that looked as if it tended towards being curly was tied back in a low bun. She was casually dressed, yet smart, in tailored trousers and a loose unstructured top under a fitted soft leather jacket. She oozed elegant style and, he had to admit, discretion and professionalism. Xander had been right.

As she looked at him now, he noticed that her eyes were an unusual shade of amber. Ben waited a beat to see if he had any reaction to her on a physical level. *Nothing.* He told himself that was good—the last thing he needed now was the distraction of someone he actually desired. Which brought him neatly back to why she was here.

He said, 'So, now that you've mined my soul for every tiny detail, who do you suggest is my best prospect for a partner?'

He saw the unmistakable flash of cynicism in her eyes, and a small smile tipped up her mouth at one side.

'Oh, don't worry,' Elizabeth said. 'I'm under no illusions. I know that you've told me only as much as you want to reveal. I know men like you, Mr Carter, that's why I'm good at my job.'

Ben decided to ignore the urge to ask exactly what she meant about knowing *men like him*. If it helped him to achieve what he needed to survive this crisis then what of it? He steepled his hands under his chin and admitted to a grudging respect for the way she wasn't intimidated by him, as so many were.

'Xander Trakas recommended you.'

And just like that this woman's composure slipped slightly, just as Xander's had that night in the bar, almost a week ago. She wasn't so sanguine now.

She avoided Ben's eye, fussing with the tablet. 'I have lots of connections, he's just one of them.'

Ben was intrigued by the button he'd obviously just pushed, but not intrigued enough to lose sight of his own goal. He became businesslike and sat forward again. 'Forget I mentioned it. So, do you have anyone specific in mind?'

She turned her tablet around to face him, laying it flat on the desk, and pushed it towards him. 'There are some possibilities here. Look through them and see if anyone piques your interest.'

Ben took the tablet and did as she had bid, scrolling through the pictures of women along with a few lines of their bios. They were all stunning in their own ways, and obviously accomplished. He scrolled past a human rights lawyer, the CEO of a software company, a UN interpreter, a supermodel...but none of them jumped out at him. He was about to hand the device back when one last woman appeared on the screen and something inside him went very still.

He didn't even look at her bio. He was transfixed by her. In the picture her shoulder-length dark brown hair was being blown around her shoulders and face by a breeze and she was laughing into the camera, revealing two dimples. She had high cheekbones and a lush mouth.

He couldn't recall the last time he'd noticed dimples on a woman. Dark blue eyes, long-lashed. She was innocent and sensual all at once. And exquisitely, vibrantly beautiful.

For a second Ben found it hard to breathe. He also had a sense that she was somehow familiar.

Elizabeth obviously sensed his interest. 'Ah, that's Julianna Ford. Stunning, isn't she? She's British, and based in London, so that could prove a bit of a challenge, but as luck would have it she's actually in New York this week for a charity benefit.'

Ben frowned sharply and looked up. '*Ford*? As in Louis Ford's daughter?'

Elizabeth cocked her head. 'Do you know her?'

He glanced at her picture again before pushing the tablet back towards Elizabeth. 'I know *of* her. I met with her father a few years ago. I tried to persuade him to sell his business to me. He spoke of her, and I saw her pictures around his house, but she wasn't there at the time.'

Ben struggled to remember. She'd been away on holiday…skiing? Whatever her father had said about her, it had reinforced the impression he'd formed of her at the time: she was the spoiled and pampered only daughter of a doting billionaire father.

Ben had experienced that scene while in London, where the rich partied alongside royalty and to excess. He'd hated it. It had been a forcible reminder of the fact that if his father hadn't been so corrupt Ben would have still been part of that world too. Still living a blinkered life, blind to harsh reality. The harsh reality that had reshaped him into the man he was today. Answerable to no one and with his astronomical success bedded so firmly into the earth that he would never suffer the same fate as his parents—being at the mercy of volatile markets with no solid investments to speak of.

Ben diverted his mind from old and painful memories and focused on the matchmaker. And the future. Not the past. What she was handing him here was an opportunity not to be missed. The Ford construction company, with its solid black font signage against a dark green background, was a ubiquitous sight on construction hoardings in Britain.

Ben knew what a coup it would be to gain a foothold in Europe by acquiring one of its most respected companies—which was why he'd gone after it once before. Louis Ford had resisted his advances then, in spite of his rumoured ill health, but Ben had been keeping an eye on him ever since, and he realised now that Ford had gone quiet in recent months. *Very* quiet.

And now the man's daughter was here. Looking for a date.

Suddenly Ben realised that Julianna Ford represented the solution to all his problems. If he was to take the drastic step of committing to one woman for the sake of his reputation and business, then why not pursue a marriage that came with solid potential for business expansion? If she agreed to marry him Ben's empire would extend into Europe and he would have reached the very pinnacle of everything he'd set out to achieve. All with a stunningly beautiful wife by his side.

He looked at Elizabeth and a sense of delicious anticipation coiled through his gut. He said, 'She's the one I want to meet. You can set up the date.'

Lia Ford was trying to curb her mounting anger, but it was hard. Her stiletto heels clacked sharply along the wide Manhattan pavement, as if to underscore her volatile mood.

First she was angry with her father for his meddling ways, even if his heart *was* in the right place. And then she was angry with her father's secretary, for following her father's instructions to give all of Lia's information to Leviathan Solutions. She was even angry about the photo that had been given to the agency—one her father had taken, catching Lia off-guard during a happy sailing trip. A far too personal memento for a dating website!

As the Leviathan agency's global operations were based in New York, Lia had gone to Elizabeth Young's Manhattan office earlier that day, as soon as she'd found out—thanks to her father presenting it to her as a fait accompli over the phone. *'See, my darling? I've done it all for you! Now all you have to do is meet some nice young man!'* Lia had been ready to demand that all her details be removed…only to be informed that someone had already signalled his interest in dating her.

And Elizabeth Young had surprised Lia. She'd been expecting… Actually, she hadn't been sure what she'd been expecting of a billionaire matchmaker, but it hadn't been a beautiful young woman of around her own age, whose style reflected Lia's preferred classic relaxed elegance. Elizabeth Young had also personified professional discretion, which Lia had responded to in spite of herself.

And somehow, while acknowledging Lia's reluctance to accept the date, Elizabeth had somehow skilfully managed to persuade her to give this one date a chance. And then she'd shown Lia a picture of the man in question.

It had taken Lia a few long seconds to look past the piercing blue eyes and the boldly handsome and very masculine features. With his thick dark hair, he oozed sexy confidence and virility. Exactly the kind of man that Lia instinctively shied away from—because a personality like that brought up all her most secret vulnerabilities. And a reminder of another too confident personality who'd had no time for Lia's innate shyness—her mother, who had walked out on Lia and her father when Lia was just ten years old.

And yet she'd felt a disconcerting flutter of very feminine awareness at the man's sheer masculinity. It was most unwelcome. She wasn't interested in dating. She'd tried to please her father before—even going so far as to consider marriage, becoming engaged—but that had ended in abject humiliation when she'd surprised her fiancé in his office one day and found him with his face buried between his secretary's spread legs as she'd lain back across his desk, moaning loudly, her hands locked in his hair.

'You're frigid, Lia,' he'd hurled at her afterwards. *'I can't marry a woman who doesn't like sex!'*

That experience had only reinforced her insecurities, and she'd vowed since then to focus on her career and prove to her father that she could stand on her own two feet. Unfortunately his habitual ill health meant that she'd spent more time shoring up the family business than focusing on her own ambitions...

Elizabeth Young had brought Lia back to the present with a bump, though, when she'd revealed who the mysterious man was and recognition of his name had made Lia's gaze narrow on the woman on the opposite side of the desk. *'Benjamin Carter?* As in Carter Construction?'

Elizabeth Young had nodded. 'Yes, he said he knew of you, actually, even though he's never met you. He had some business with your father a while ago?'

Every protective hackle inside Lia had risen. It had been a couple of years ago when Benjamin Carter had come to the UK and tried to take over Ford Construction. Her family business. Her father had rebuffed Carter and his very generous offer, but his health, which had always been weak, and particularly weakened at that time, thanks to a nasty bout of pneumonia, had worsened.

If she'd met Benjamin Carter then she would have told him where to go and saved her father that relapse. Louis Ford was so proud, though, that he would have died before he'd let anyone see how frail he really was. Especially someone like the American construction mogul whom her father had described as 'formidable'.

And now Benjamin Carter wanted to meet her for a date? If this was mere coincidence then she was the Sugar Plum Fairy.

Lia stopped at a pedestrian crossing and forced herself to regulate her breath. She knew she could have just called the date off—instructed Elizabeth Young to inform Benjamin Carter that she wasn't available for any dates while she was in New York as she didn't live there—but she'd felt the compelling urge to inform the man emphatically and in person that there would be no route for him to get to her father. And certainly not through *her*.

On the other side of the street the majestic *beaux arts* Algonquin Hotel soared into the sky. They were due to meet in the darkly seductive Algonquin bar. And now all she could seem to think of was his boldly handsome features and those blue eyes. She found herself feeling slightly breathless, wondering how tall he would be. How big.

The pedestrian lights said *Walk* and Lia stepped into the road, assuring herself fiercely that Benjamin Carter would undoubtedly prove to be a disappointment in the flesh, as so many public figures did. *Not*, she hurriedly assured herself, that she was going to be hanging around long enough to check him out. No, she was going to waste no time informing him that—

Smack!

Lia's thoughts were scattered to pieces as she ran into a brick wall just outside the hotel. Gasping for air, she looked up to find that this particular brick wall was actually a very tall human. And very male. And very broad. With piercing blue eyes.

So not a wall at all. Dimly she registered that Benjamin Carter wasn't a disappointment in the flesh. Far from it. He was...*more*. He smiled, and she noticed the sculpted sensuality of his lips.

'I'm sorry, I hadn't planned on a collision as our introduction. I saw you crossing the street and recognised you from your photo, so I thought I'd wait for you. Are you okay?'

His voice was rich and deep enough to impact on her on a physical level. Lia felt a bit stupid, and put it down to the momentary shock and lack of breath. She nodded and managed to get out, 'Fine...just fine.'

She'd been so preoccupied with meeting him that she'd walked right into him. She realised then that her hands were wrapped around his arms to steady herself, obviously having landed there instinctively. She could feel hard biceps, even through the material of his overcoat, and she snatched her hands back as if they were burning.

He looked at her for a long moment and then stood back, indicating with a hand. 'Please—ladies first.'

Irritated that the wind had been knocked out of her— literally—Lia had no choice but to proceed to the front door, where a doorman was waiting, holding the door open, tipping his hat to her as she entered.

She heard him say to the man behind her, 'Welcome back, Mr Carter.'

'Thank you, Tom, always a pleasure.'

Lia felt like scowling at his smooth delivery, even though she had to acknowledge that her first cataclysmic encounter with the man didn't make her think of smooth at all. It had brought to mind lots of things—none of which were smooth. *Big, powerful, strong.* Immovable. That was what came to mind.

He was behind her now and she could smell his scent—as masculine as he was, and evocative more than overpowering.

The *maître d'* came forward to greet them at the entrance to the dark and lushly decorated bar, clicking his fingers for a staff member to come and divest them of their coats. Lia wanted to protest that she wasn't staying long, but before she could speak their coats had expertly been taken and she was being led further into the seductive space, to an intimate table for two at the back.

Giving in to the inevitability of at least explaining herself to this man, she slid into the velvet banquette seat at the wall and watched as Benjamin Carter folded his tall frame into a seat opposite her. She sucked in as much oxygen as she could, desperately hoping that her sense of equilibrium would return after the shock of that impact.

Now his coat was gone she saw that he wore a three-piece suit. Dark grey tie. She also recognised with a disturbing flash of heat, that in spite of his very suave exterior there was an unmistakable edge of something dangerous and uncivilised about the man. It was in the way his muscles pushed against the fabric of his jacket. As if he was more warrior than urbane businessman.

That realisation sent a shard of panic to her gut, and with a rush Lia started to speak. 'Look, Mr Carter—'

The words dried up when he held out his hand and smiled, drawing her gaze helplessly to his mouth. A full lower lip and a slightly thinner upper lip—diminishing any prettiness and giving him that sensual edge that made her aware of him in a way that no man had ever made her feel before. Certainly not her ex-fiancé.

'Forgive me. I never introduced myself properly, I'm Benjamin Carter.'

A lifetime of manners being drummed into her by her father and strict boarding schools couldn't let her ignore his hand. She reached out, intending it to be a sterile and quick transaction, but the first thing that registered when his hand encompassed hers was a surprising roughness, which only reinforced her impression of him being less civilised than he looked.

She felt a pulse throb between her legs…her intimate flesh reacting to his touch. It was so powerful that she pressed her thighs together, and her fingers tightened reflexively around his in reaction as she said faintly, 'I'm Julianna—Julianna Ford.'

As slim, feminine fingers tightened around his all Ben could think about was how it would feel when other, more intimate muscles would tighten around a more sensitive part of his anatomy. He'd never had such an immediately carnal response to a woman, but the feel of her slimly curvaceous body colliding with his outside the hotel had had an impact he couldn't ignore.

He'd seen her from across the street, an intent look on her face, a small frown between her eyes. And then, as her long legs had closed the distance between them, he'd been too mesmerised by her graceful movements to budge an inch.

And then she'd cannoned straight into him.

The lush imprint of her soft breasts against his chest was still vivid. As soon as their bodies had collided lust had hit him like an injection of adrenalin to his heart. And it hadn't been one-sided; he'd seen the effect on her too. Those widening shocked eyes. Her cheeks flooding with colour. Her hands tightening around his arms. She was tall enough for him to have just dipped his head down slightly to claim that provocative mouth, if he'd so wished.

And now he was drowning in dark blue eyes, glossy dark brown hair, pale ivory skin and that mouth, so sweetly curved it was all he could do not to sweep the table to one side and devour her right here.

She was stunning. Exquisite.

And she was pulling her hand back from his now with a little tug. He let her go, reluctantly.

A waiter came to take their drinks order. Julianna appeared flustered for a moment, and then quickly ordered a bourbon on the rocks. Ben ordered a soda water.

When they were alone again Ben dragged his mind out of the carnal gutter and said, 'Thank you for agreeing to meet with me.'

She looked at him and his blood surged south and his flesh hardened. Ben cursed the rush of rogue hormones. It wasn't even as if she was wearing anything overtly provocative. A pale silk shirt that was buttoned to her throat and a dark pencil skirt. Discreet make-up and jewellery. High heels. Classic. Elegant. But as far as his libido was concerned she might as well be naked.

'Look—' she said, but was cut off when the waiter returned with their drinks, setting them down.

Ben noticed that she took a swift sip of the amber liquid before putting the glass down again.

She appeared edgy all of a sudden, and he made allowances for the fact that she was nervous, saying, 'I believe you're only here for a week? You're based in London?'

She swallowed and his eyes followed the movement. Even that small movement was graceful. Her refined elegance was impacting upon him somewhere deep. And it surprised him. He'd long ago rejected the cool upper-class beauties who thronged around him—drawn by the hard shell he knew he wore, hewn over years of hard graft as he'd remoulded himself into something much more durable. He knew they were attracted to the rough edges he'd acquired. They didn't want to know he'd once been one of them. They only wanted the thrill of thinking they were with someone vaguely *dangerous*. Rough. Someone whose industry was gritty. Base.

He took pleasure in rejecting them because he rejected that world—and yet here he was, sitting mere inches away from a woman who could put all those other society bitches in the shade with a mere arching of her elegant brow. And his blood was pumping so hard and so hot he could hardly think straight.

She looked at him and dark tendrils of hair trailed over her shoulders like silk. 'I...yes, I'm based in London. So, to be perfectly honest, I think this date is pretty redundant.'

It took a second for her cut-glass English accent to sink in—and her words. And then they did...along with the very cool expression on her face.

Ben blinked. 'So why agree to a date if it's redundant?'

Her gaze narrowed and she took a deep breath, and despite the sudden chill in the air Ben's gaze helplessly dropped down to take in the press of those luscious breasts against the thin silk of her blouse.

'Because I wanted to meet you face to face and tell you that I know you met my father before, when you tried to take him over.'

Ben's gaze snapped back to her dark blue one. The heat in his blood simmered, not diminishing under the positively frosty vibes she was sending his way now. He hid his surprise that she'd registered the connection and shrugged nonchalantly. 'It's a small world.'

She sounded bitter. 'Evidently *too* small.' She took another sip of her drink, her fingers pale around the heavy glass.

Ben tensed. 'What exactly are you saying?'

Now she looked almost angry, with two spots of colour coming into her pale cheeks. 'What I'm saying, Mr Carter—' she put heavy emphasis on his name, as if he might still be under any illusion that things weren't deteriorating rapidly '—is that, based on your previous history with my father, you can't seriously expect me to believe that this date is pure coincidence?'

Ben thought of how mesmerised he'd been by that photo of her and felt exposed. Her cynicism shouldn't have surprised him, but somehow it did. He was on high alert now. Carefully, he said, 'I can't say that it's pure coincidence, no. I am aware of who you are—who your father is.'

She smiled, but it was hard. 'And so you saw an opportunity and grabbed it?'

Ben forced a smile too, in some kind of an effort to try and relieve the tension. 'Evidently you joined the Leviathan agency because you're interested in dating, I would have thought the fact that we have something in common is a good conversation-starter.'

Julianna's eyes glittered like dark sapphire jewels. 'Well,' she said coolly, 'I'm afraid I have no interest in starting any kind of conversation with you, Mr Carter. I came here merely to inform you of that, in case you'd be left in any doubt.'

With that, she downed the rest of her drink in one go and gathered up her bag, which was on the seat beside her.

She stood up and looked down at him. 'And as for my father—his position has not changed, so I suggest you seek your opportunities elsewhere. Thank you for the drink, Mr Carter, I'll see myself out.'

Before Ben could fully process what was happening she was hitching her bag strap onto her shoulder and walking away from the table.

Ben finally stood up, his reflexes dulled, thanks to shock, and was just in time to see the anxious-looking *maître d'* helping her with her overcoat. Then she was walking out of the bar without a backward glance.

Ben looked at his watch incredulously. The date had lasted less than fifteen minutes.

He sat down again, her haughty accent reverberating in his head. *'I suggest you seek your opportunities elsewhere.'* If it wasn't so disturbing it would be funny, but the fact was that her father had been the furthest thing from his mind until she'd brought him up.

Julianna Ford, with her glacial dark blue eyes and her upper crust accent, had just pulled the rug out from under Ben's feet. And it was only now that he fully registered that last look she'd sent him—disdainful and dismissive. As if he wasn't fit to clean her shoes.

Ben signalled for the bill. It had been a long time since anyone had looked at him like that and, even though he knew he should be writing Julianna Ford off as a spoilt rich bitch, his blood still ran hot. Hot with lingering lust, and hot with irritation that she'd lodged herself so neatly under his skin so quickly.

To say this date had morphed into something out of all expectations was an understatement.

Ben was grim as he walked out just seconds later. No one took him by surprise—certainly not a woman. And definitely not a woman he wanted.

Lia was still trembling from an overload of adrenalin as the yellow cab took her to her Central Park hotel. And her head felt light with the effects of the alcohol she'd drunk too quickly. It had provided the Dutch courage she'd needed, though, to say what she'd had to say to the most intimidating man she'd ever met.

Even now she could picture him lounging on the other side of the table, all sleek hard muscle and broad shoulders, sheathed in that suit that had done nothing to disguise his crackling virile energy. That sexy smile playing around his mouth.

She couldn't really believe she'd found the where-withal to stand and look down at him and deliver those parting words, or that she'd managed to walk out on rubbery legs. She'd been terrified they'd buckle underneath her before she could make it to the door.

She knew she could project an icy veneer of confidence when she needed to—it was a skill she'd honed after her mother had left, when Lia had overheard her saying cuttingly, 'Of course I'm not taking Lia with me. What can I do with a child who stutters and stammers and blushes every time someone looks at her?'

Even now, all these years later, Lia still felt the faint burn of shame mixed with humiliation. Her father's sub-sequent over-lavishing of attention and love upon her hadn't been able to remove the scar of that rejection, but Lia had never stuttered or stammered again from that day on. The blushing, though... She put a hand to her cheek and it felt hot. Seemingly she still had little con-trol over that.

At least Benjamin Carter had stayed in his seat. The thought of having to say those words to him if he'd un-coiled to his full intimidating height made her throat go dry.

She might—hopefully—have convinced him that he was less interesting than the fungus growing under a rock, but her throbbing pulse told her that he was far from uninteresting to *her*. And, as successfully as she might have delivered her put-down, that was the real rea-son why she'd all but run from the hotel, stumbling to a stop outside in the cool autumn air, gulping for breath as if she'd just run a marathon, her heart still pounding.

Thankfully the doorman had hailed her a cab straight away and they were pulling up outside her hotel now.

Lia paid and tried not to run into the hotel, feeling irrationally as if a large hand might land on her shoulder at any moment.

The fact that the whole encounter with the construction mogul had veered way out of her control was not something she was going to dwell on. If she had had any tiny doubt that his request to meet her had been entirely innocent, it had been blasted apart by his poker-faced reaction when she'd told him she knew who he was and about his previous encounter with her father. He'd been unapologetic, that incisive gaze reading her reaction like a hawk.

So she was glad she'd gone there and met him. She'd done what she'd set out to do, leaving him in no doubt as to what she thought of any plan he might have to pursue her father.

Or her.

Lia ignored the weirdly hollow feeling in her belly and stepped into a blessedly empty lift. And as for her very unwelcome physical reaction...? The way she still felt jittery, as if her skin was too tight, too hot...? That was just the lingering after-effects of adrenalin.

A sense of futility rose up inside her, a hint of remembered humiliation. After all, she was frigid, wasn't she? She'd been told that in no uncertain language by the only man she'd ever slept with. And she had the memories of how her body had failed miserably to respond to his love-making to back it up. So he must be right.

The lift doors opened and Lia stepped out into the plushly carpeted corridor. As she let herself into her room she ruthlessly pushed down a very alien sense of something that felt awfully like...yearning.

Ben was back in his vast loft-style apartment a short time later. Sirens pierced the air from far below in the vibrant Meatpacking District, but he was oblivious. Pacing the floor. He'd taken off his jacket and tie, feeling constricted. His head was still full of Julianna Ford, and her cooler than cool aristocratic beauty. The memory of that haughty accent and the way she'd so icily dismissed him made him want to see her come undone, hear her voice hoarse from screaming his name.

Dammit. Since when had he grown such an active imagination?

But something else niggled at him—her hostility, and her immediate leaping to the conclusion that his motivation to date her had something to do with her father. Ben's conscience niggled, but he pushed it down—he hadn't tried to pretend to Julianna that he was unaware of who she was. He just hadn't mentioned it up front.

He thought again of how absent her father had been from view in the last few months and Julianna Ford's actions took on a much more intriguing light. She'd been... protective—and why would she feel the need to be protective unless her father was ill...weak?

Just then his phone vibrated in his pocket and he took it out, scowling when he saw the name *Elizabeth Young* on the screen.

When he answered she spoke straight away, sounding disapproving, 'I don't know what happened between you and Julianna Ford but she's instructed me that she doesn't want to meet with you again and to take her profile out of my portfolio.'

That made Ben feel simultaneously annoyed at the confirmation that she didn't want to see him again, and pleased that she obviously wasn't eager for a date with any other man. Also, it confirmed his suspicion that she had something to hide...some vulnerability. Because she perceived him to be a threat.

The unmistakable instinct to take up a challenge

coursed through his blood. 'It's unfortunate that the date didn't go well, but I'll take it from here.'

Elizabeth Young was sharp. 'This is not how I conduct my business, Mr Carter. You can't pursue her if she's specifically requested not to see you again.'

Irritation prickled at this reiteration that she didn't want to see him again—*and* at the implication that anyone could tell him what to do. But Ben realised that he couldn't afford to alienate this woman. She was the key to all their futures. Except right now he was determined to take his future into his own hands.

'You can rest assured, Miss Young. I won't pursue her again through your agency.'

There was silence for a moment, and then Elizabeth Young said, 'Thank you. If and when you're ready to date again we can set up another appointment. But, Mr Carter, I have to warn you that I won't tolerate anyone alienating my clientele.'

Once again Ben had to admit to a grudging sense of respect for the straight-talking matchmaker. Intimidated by powerful men she obviously was not. He said, 'Julianna Ford and I had a clash of personality—that's all. It happens from time to time. If I need you again I'll call you. Goodbye, Miss Young.'

Ben terminated the call, filled with resolve. A clash of personality it might have been, between him and the lustrous dark-haired British beauty, but electricity had sizzled between them, no matter how icy her demeanour. He knew Julianna Ford was here for a charity function, and New York could be a surprisingly small place when you moved in certain circles. If they happened to meet again it wouldn't be via Elizabeth Young, as he'd assured her.

Ben made a call on his phone, issuing curt instructions to his assistant on the other end. He told himself that the spiking of anticipation in his blood had more to do with the fact that Julianna Ford represented a chance to achieve his public and professional redemption and less to do with the fact that she'd intrigued the hell out of him with her frosty attitude—or the fact that he wanted her more than he'd ever wanted another woman.

CHAPTER TWO

THE FOLLOWING EVENING Lia surveyed herself critically in the full-length mirror of her hotel suite. The long evening dress was far more revealing than she liked, with its sleeveless plunging neckline and thigh-high slit, and also, if that wasn't enough, the vibrant blood-red colour.

But, as much as she squirmed to show so much flesh, she knew that it would be effective as a means of deflecting attention from the fact that her father was conspicuous by his absence at the charity auction he'd been due to attend in one of Manhattan's glitziest hotels.

She was also due to attend on her own behalf, because the charity—which helped crisis-stricken regions to begin rebuilding—was close to her heart.

She'd spoken to her father briefly and had been somewhat reassured. He was sounding a little perkier than he had in recent days. But this last stroke, albeit mild, had given them both a fright.

She'd told him that she'd gone on a date, and he'd been so delighted that she'd felt bad when she hadn't revealed who her date had been. The last thing he needed was to hear Benjamin Carter's name. Like her, he'd inevitably jump to the conclusion that he had ulterior motives—because the vultures were circling, just waiting for their chance to step in and make the most of Louis Ford's weakness.

Lia had confirmed it for herself when she'd done an

internet search on Benjamin Carter late last night—unable to sleep because a leanly handsome face with piercing blue eyes had kept her awake.

She'd come across a recent paparazzi photo of Benjamin Carter together with three of the world's most notorious playboy tycoons and renowned business rivals. Xander Trakas, Dante Mancini and Sheikh Zayn Al-Ghamdi—all names that were indelibly linked to vast fortunes, beautiful women and an aversion to commitment.

The accompanying article had pointed out that they'd all suffered adverse press in recent months and speculation was rife as to why they were suddenly joining forces.

And that was when Lia knew she'd made a huge tactical error in showing Benjamin Carter such obvious antipathy. He was not becoming bosom buddies with his old enemies for no reason, nor asking her for a date for the good of his health—not when he could date any number of more beautiful and accessible women.

He was definitely up to something.

Curiously reluctant to leave her search there, though, she'd also learnt that he was a self-made legend who'd come from the most adverse of backgrounds, growing up in foster homes in Queens before working his way up through the construction hierarchy on sites all over New York. That had reminded her disturbingly of that air of something untamed about him in spite of his suave appearance.

Within just a decade he'd risen to the top of the industry—literally. His company was currently responsible for constructing what would become the tallest skyscraper in Manhattan.

He was ruthless and single-minded, and women only featured in his workaholic life as very momentary diversions—as brutally evidenced by a recent 'kiss and tell' Lia had found during the online search. Usually she abhorred gossip, but she'd found herself avidly reading about the way his ruthlessness extended beyond the bedroom once he was tired with seduction and conquest—which seemed to happen after only one or two dates at the most.

Yet that information hadn't stopped Lia having a very illicit and dangerously wistful daydream that when she'd bumped into him in the street perhaps Benjamin Carter might have been just a random gorgeous stranger. Because for the first time since the humiliating aftermath of her broken engagement, a year before, she realised that a man had managed to break through the high wall she'd built around herself.

Lia quickly shut down that evocative image. So, she'd reacted to him? All that proved was that she was as dismayingly susceptible to his charms as the next woman. In spite of her frigidity. Benjamin Carter's particular brand of virile masculinity was obviously potent enough to break through the thickest ice.

She glared balefully now at the extravagant vase of flowers on the antique side table, set there by a conscientious staff member. The accompanying note lay torn up in the bin, but she didn't need to take it out to reread the arrogant slashing handwriting. She'd memorised it all too easily and annoyingly.

Till we meet again, Julianna. Ben.

The fact that he knew where she was staying caused little surprise. It wasn't as if she was using an alias, and a man like Benjamin Carter would have minions aplenty to do his dirty work.

She'd almost been tempted to call Elizabeth Young again, to tell her to reinforce the message that she had no interest in him, but she'd realised she was being ridiculous. As rough as Benjamin Carter's edges might be, she couldn't see him stooping so low as to actually *chase* a woman. And in a few days Lia would be gone—safely back on the other side of the Atlantic Ocean.

She turned her attention to her reflection again and took a deep breath, picking up an elaborately feathered black lace mask and fitting it to her face. She was relieved the charity auction had a masquerade theme, because she was feeling exposed enough as it was.

Firmly pushing disturbing memories back down where they belonged, along with thoughts of dark, handsome, annoying men, Lia gathered her things and left her suite.

Less than an hour later Lia had to stop herself from pulling the bodice of her dress up higher. She knew she was being silly, because there were women there in far more revealing dresses, but if one more man nearly tripped over his own tongue as he drooled at her chest she was going to scream.

Just then the three men who had been making more eye contact with her chest than her face seemed to melt back into the throng, and she sucked in a deep sigh of relief.

She turned away to look for a waiter and get a drink and found herself being jostled from behind. She was pitching forward helplessly into thin air when two hands caught her and stopped her fall. She looked up, heart hammering, to see a man—a very tall man, with broad shoulders. He was dressed in a white tuxedo jacket, white shirt and black bow tie.

His face, like most of the crowd's, was obscured by a mask. Except his was more ornate and covered his whole face. She could see thick dark hair... For a heart-stopping moment Lia almost suspected— But then she told herself she was being ridiculous if she was letting

Benjamin Carter get to her so much that she suspected this man could be him, when it was far more likely to be a stranger.

The man spoke, his voice slightly distorted under the mask. 'Are you all right?'

Something inside Lia relaxed when she realised she didn't immediately recognise the voice. His hands felt hot on the bare skin of her upper arms and she realised he was still holding on to her. Feeling flustered, she took a step back. 'I'm fine, thank you... Sorry. I was just looking for a waiter to get a drink.'

'Let me.'

As if by magic a waiter appeared by his side and the man handed her a glass of Champagne. She noticed that he didn't take a drink. She sipped at the cool sparkling wine and felt some equilibrium return. Lia assured herself that if this *was* Benjamin Carter alarm bells would be ringing loudly.

She pushed all thoughts of that man aside and observed, 'You're not drinking?'

He shook his head. 'I like to keep my wits about me—and my mask isn't exactly conducive to drinking. I'd have to reveal my identity, which would defeat the object of the evening.'

His voice was cool, sardonic. And deep.

Something skated over Lia's skin. Excitement. She couldn't see his eyes, they were obscured, so she didn't know what colour they were. The realisation that she didn't even know where his eyes rested on her, or if he liked what he saw, made her skin heat with awareness. Before, she'd felt exposed, violated. Now she felt...aware of herself in a way that was very unlike her.

She almost had to suppress a slightly hysterical urge to giggle—maybe there was something in the water here in New York that was having an adverse effect on her?

'You could have chosen a less restrictive mask,' she pointed out to the stranger.

'I could have,' he agreed, leaving the words *But I didn't* hanging silently between them.

Bizarrely, she got the distinct impression that this stranger would bend for no one. A crazy thought to have about someone she'd only met for mere seconds. Someone whose face she couldn't even see. And crazy that it should send another shiver of excitement down her spine.

A hum of electricity infused her blood. Yesterday evening, when Benjamin Carter had precipitated similar sensations, she'd escaped as fast as she could. And now she was feeling all those things again. It was almost a relief—proof that his effect on her wasn't exclusive.

The crowd seemed to be pressing in around them, pushing them closer together. Heat prickled over Lia's skin in earnest now. A little panicked by her strong reactions, she said, 'It's getting claustrophobic in here, don't you think?'

'Would you like to get some air?'

Lia nodded, heart hammering. He expertly divested her of her half-empty glass and put a hand under her elbow. She found herself trying to assess if his palms were smooth or callused, but the crowd was jostling them too much. Then he was opening the French doors and leading her outside. It was late autumn, not quite yet winter, and the air was fresh. She moved away from him and gulped in deep breaths, her head feeling light. She put it down to the sparkling wine and the sudden rush of oxygen.

She went and put her hands on the stone wall, aware of the man coming to stand beside her, but keeping a distance that she appreciated. The lights of Manhattan sparkled around them, and Central Park was a dark shadow in the distance. There was silence between them for a moment, but it wasn't awkward. This unexpected encounter was taking on an unreal quality.

'I could never get tired of this view even if I lived here,' Lia said.

The man turned towards her. 'Where *do* you live?'

She glanced at him, finding the mask disconcerting but also a little…thrilling. Not knowing who she was speaking to was freeing, in some way. As if the normal social niceties could be ignored. The sheer breadth of his chest under his shirt made her hands itch. She felt very feminine next to his tall, broad body.

'I live just outside London, in Richmond.'

The man made an appreciative sound.

Lia smiled. 'You know it?'

She heard an answering smile in his voice. 'It's a nice place. Expensive.'

Lia commented dryly, 'The tickets for this event start at a cool six thousand dollars, so I'm guessing that you're no stranger to the more salubrious end of the property scale.'

Now he shrugged lightly. 'I can't deny that.'

Lia thought she saw the glitter of light eyes behind the mask and her heart beat a little faster. This felt risky… dangerous. But still thrilling.

She had never felt comfortable flirting, not having had her mother to guide her. She'd been so young when her mother had left them, and the all-girls weekly boarding school she'd attended hadn't done much to help her grow more comfortable around boys and men.

But at least by the time she'd left school the acute shyness that had blighted her earlier years had been largely a thing of the past. Although even now that awkward stuttering girl still lurked deep within Lia, reminding her of the fact that a lot of what she projected was an elaborate act.

It was an act so effective that her ex-fiancé had been incredulous to discover that she was a virgin when they'd had sex for the first time, which had only added to the mortification she'd felt when the experience had proved to be painful and generally underwhelming.

But now she felt confident, and a little reckless. 'So, is your role tonight to be as enigmatic and unrecognisable as possible?'

'Is it working?'

His tone was light, but Lia could sense an edge. It added to the air of illicit danger and excitement.

'Well, you've got the unrecognisable part down to a T.'

'Ouch,' he said softly. 'Clearly I have to work on being an enigma.'

Once again Lia had the distinct impression that being enigmatic came all too easily to this stranger. And he knew it. Even without seeing his face she could sense his sheer command and charisma. He was *somebody*.

She felt even more reckless as she said, 'Are we going to exchange names?'

'Do you want to?'

Lia nodded, and then shivered lightly. It was as if she could *feel* his gaze on her now, even though she couldn't see his eyes. It was like a caress across her skin.

Obviously misreading her shiver, he took off his jacket and settled it around her shoulders before she could protest. The heat from his body felt absurdly intimate, and she was acutely aware of his fingers brushing the bare skin of her shoulders.

Was it her imagination, or had they lingered a moment? 'Thank you.' Her voice was husky.

He was closer now—close enough that she could see his stubbled jaw under the mask. It looked strong, defined. His scent was masculine, woody and musky.

To her surprise she felt her lower body clench in reaction, and a rush of damp heat between her legs. That very physical reaction sent a dose of reality rushing back. This wasn't her. This wasn't a usual state for her to be in... For a second she wondered what had changed inside her. How could she be reacting so wantonly to two men in the space of two nights?

The stranger cut into her thoughts with his deep voice. 'Are you sure you want to exchange names?'

Lia wasn't so sure now. That slap of reality had reminded her that she was out of her depth here. But she wasn't ready to burst this sensual bubble yet. She was pretending to be something she wasn't—confident. Experienced.

Feeling absurdly regretful, she said, 'I'm not sure if I do...but we can't hide for ever...'

She heard the smile in his voice again. 'It's tempting, though, isn't it?'

She nodded, feeling something melting inside her at the sense of kinship she felt. She desperately wanted to keep pretending to be someone else for another small moment, and helplessly she found her feet moving closer.

He seemed to reach for her at the same time, and his hands cupped her jaw, thumbs caressing her cheeks. 'You're exquisite—do you know that?'

Lia shook her head, embarrassed. She knew without false modesty that she was pleasant enough to look at, but she'd never felt truly beautiful. She looked at women sometimes and saw that they owned their innate sensuality in such a way that she envied them. And it had nothing to do with being the perfect size or having a pretty face.

But right now...even though half her face was obscured by a mask...she felt an inkling of it. For the first time. Her mouth tingled and she imagined his gaze on her there. Her lips parted and his hands tightened on her

face. An urgency seemed to infuse the air around them…
the atmosphere grew thick and heavy.

Excitement rushed through her. Lia reached up one
hand, to touch his mask. Her heart thumping so hard
she wondered if he could hear it, she started pushing it
up, desperately wanting to see him, wanting his mouth
to touch hers.

She caught a glimpse of his lower lip and then one
hand wrapped around her wrist, stopping her. His voice
sounded rough. 'You might not like what you see.'

Lia shook her head. She *knew*, just knew that she
needed to see who he was more than she needed to draw
breath. She pulled her hand free and was about to tip
his mask up again when a voice broke through the thick
tension.

'*Lia!* There you are. I've been looking everywhere
for you! I'm having a total crisis—you have to help me.'

The mood snapped instantly. The man stepped back
and Lia's hand dropped to her side. Her heart was racing as if they had just kissed, and she realised she was
trembling.

She tore her eyes away from that impassive mask that
hid so much and she wanted to shout her frustration. She
could see now that the person interrupting them was the
charity auction event manager—an English ex-pat called
Sarah, who had become a friend of sorts. They met whenever Lia came to New York.

'What's wrong, Sarah?' Lia was relieved that her voice
sounded calmer than she felt.

The attractive blonde woman looked panicked. 'Stacy
Somers, the supermodel, was supposed to be here for the
charity auction, which is due to start in ten minutes. The
deal was that she'd auction a kiss, and now we're stuck.'

Lia's eyes widened at her friend's expressive look, and
she spluttered, 'But…but you can't mean for *me* to fill

in?' All her old insecurities flooded back. 'I'm hardly supermodel-replacement material—and hardly anyone here even knows me!'

Her friend's eyes were wild and panicked. 'Please, Lia. You look amazing tonight, and no one will care who you are. It's for charity, and it's a fun item, and it's in the auction brochure and my boss is going crazy at the thought of the schedule getting messed up...'

Lia felt cornered. Just the thought of everyone staring at her made her skin break out in a cold sweat.

And then a deep voice from beside her said, *I'd* pay for a kiss from you.'

She looked up at the man—she'd almost forgotten he was there in her moment of panic. And now she felt hot all over. At the thought of his eyes on her. At the thought of him claiming her in front of everyone. *Lord.* New York was warping her brain completely.

'I'm sorry, but who are you?'

The question came from Sarah, and Lia's attention snapped to her suddenly very curious-looking friend. The thought of him revealing who he was here and now threatened to burst the intimate bubble that had cocooned them.

Lia made a split-second decision and said, 'I'll do it.'

Her friend looked at her and her relief was palpable. Lia shrugged off the jacket and handed it back to the stranger. Their hands touched and she felt a zing of electricity. She felt jittery, as she had last night. Had she just sent him a challenge? Would he bid for a kiss and reveal himself?

Before she could think about it any further Sarah was taking her by the arm and all but hauling her back into the thronged room, gabbling about what she needed Lia to do. Lia barely heard a word.

She glanced back once before she was sucked into

the crowd, but when she did the patio was empty and she wondered for a crazy, panicky moment if she'd just dreamed up the whole encounter with the enigmatic stranger. And, if she'd ever see him again.

'Now, who is going to start the bidding for a kiss with our lovely English rose, Julianna Ford?' said the smooth-voiced auctioneer behind the tall lectern.

Benjamin stood at the side of the room with his arms folded and his hands tucked under his arms. Because he was afraid he might reach out and throttle anyone who dared to attempt to kiss the woman standing on the dais, situated in the centre of the vast room.

She looked far too enticing with her hair pulled back, exposing her long neck, but also strangely vulnerable. He would have thought that someone from her background and particular social scene would be accustomed to showing off in such a manner. She'd certainly shown an authoritative side when they'd met the previous evening.

And yet he recalled her wide-eyed look of shock just after they'd collided. The way colour had washed into her cheeks. Most women he knew would have made the most of such an encounter, but she'd appeared slightly awkward. Unsettled.

She wore an elaborate black lace mask over the top half of her face and it only enhanced her beauty, making her look mysterious. But even the mask couldn't hide the brilliant blue of her eyes. Or that enticing mouth.

He could sense other men's interest and a surge of something completely alien rushed up inside him. It took him a moment to recognise that it was possessiveness, because he'd never felt it before for a woman.

Mine. The word thrummed through Ben's blood, just as a voice near the front shouted out, 'Five thousand dollars!'

Something went tight inside Ben as the bidding started to escalate... *Ten thousand, fifteen...twenty...* There were gasps now, people were looking around.

And then a booming voice called out, 'Fifty thousand dollars!'

Ben knew who it was immediately. An old foe of his— someone who had tried to stamp out Ben's company before it had even got started. He saw the man pushing through the crowd now, small and squat, eyes bulging, perspiration beading on his brow.

He also saw, even from where he was, how Julianna's eyes widened behind the mask as she took him in.

The auctioneer held up his gavel and asked if anyone wanted to contest this latest bid. No one moved. The thought of that man getting anywhere near Julianna made Ben feel a level of violence he hadn't experienced in a long time.

The auctioneer brought the gavel down once, twice... And just before he could bring it down again Ben spoke authoritatively into the silence. 'One million dollars.'

Everyone gasped and turned to look at him. He walked forward, the crowd parting to let him through.

When he was near the dais he stopped and said, 'But I want more than a kiss. For a million dollars I want a weekend with Julianna Ford.'

It was him. She hadn't imagined him. She'd looked for him in the crowd as people had bid for the kiss, squirming with embarrassment but trying not to let it show. All the confidence and bravado she'd felt out on the terrace had faded under the glare of lights and hundreds of people.

But he was here. Still in the mask, like so many others. *Who was he?*

As if reading her thoughts, he said, 'If you agree to the bid I'll reveal myself.'

Her heart palpitated. She'd wanted this, hadn't she? She'd never felt so exposed in her life, and yet so tempted to throw caution to the wind and act completely out of character. Apart from anything else, the promise of a million dollars as a donation to her favourite charity was mind-boggling.

There was a discreet cough from nearby and the auctioneer said, 'Miss Ford? Do you accept this bid? It's a little unorthodox...'

Feeling as if she was taking a giant leap off a cliff and into the unknown, she nodded her head jerkily before she could lose her nerve. She was barely aware of the auctioneer wrapping up the bidding—because who on earth would bid more than a million dollars? It was crazy, outrageous.

Romantic, said a small voice that she quickly shut down. Since when had she been interested in *romantic*? Certainly not after seeing the devastating effects of her mother leaving her father...

And now the auctioneer was saying, 'I think we'd all like to know who our mysterious benefactor is—not least Miss Ford, who has to spend a weekend with you.'

Slightly nervous laughter rippled through the crowd as the man reached up to pull his mask off. Just before he did, Lia caught a flash of light blue eyes and a shiver of foreboding skated down her spine.

No. It wouldn't be. It couldn't be.

But the mask came off and there seemed to be a collective sigh of female appreciation as Benjamin Carter was revealed in all his dark masculine beauty. All his dark, masculine, *smug* beauty.

Lia felt as if she'd been punched in the belly. The fact that it had been *him* all along was something she couldn't quite assimilate yet. Or didn't want to. It was too huge.

And now she was being ushered off the dais so that they could get to the next item on the auction list.

The charity's CEO approached Lia with suspiciously bright eyes, pumping her hand, telling her she had no idea what this would mean for them, and all Lia could think was, *I'm going to kill him.*

However embarrassed she'd been, standing up in front of that crowd, she writhed with mortification inside to think of the ridiculous flight of fancy she'd taken for a moment, that some enigmatic stranger wanted her enough to bid a million dollars for her company.

Just then a large, warm, *callused* hand curled around her elbow and she went rigid as sensation shot through her—and the galling confirmation that it was *his* touch alone that seemed to affect her, and not some general awakening of latent desires.

She tried to tug her arm free but his grip tightened and another shiver went through her—not entirely unpleasant. She refused to look at him, though, even as the CEO of the charity was gushing all over him.

He said smoothly, 'I was inspired by Miss Ford's dedication—offering herself up for the good of the charity—and as you know this cause is close to my heart.'

Lia just bet it was. *Not*. She wanted nothing more than to round on Benjamin Carter and tell him exactly what she thought of his outrageous stunt, but she couldn't. Not after such a public display of largesse.

Finally he was moving away from the CEO and taking Lia with him, walking out of the function room. People looked and whispered. Lia caught more than a few envious glances and felt like saying, *You're welcome to him!* But she gritted her jaw and kept moving.

As soon as they were outside the room, Benjamin Carter walked her over to a secluded corner of the lobby, where tall plants shielded them from general view. Lia finally managed to pull free and turned on him, steeling herself not to react to his sheer magnetism.

For a second she couldn't get a word out, she was so incensed. She plucked at the ribbons of her mask behind her head and pulled it off. She felt very bare without its protection, but ignored it.

Benjamin Carter's gaze had lowered to where her chest was heaving with indignation and shock. She folded her arms pointedly. 'What the *hell* do you think you're doing?'

He raised his gaze and put his hands in his pockets, supremely at ease. He drawled, 'Apart from displaying immense generosity, I would have thought the rest was fairly obvious.'

'*That,*' Lia spat out, 'was the most ostentatious, crass demonstration of wealth I've ever seen in my life.'

Something tightened in his expression, but Julianna didn't feel regret.

'You didn't look especially enthralled at the thought of kissing Saul Goldstein.'

She fought not to shudder at the image in her head of the other man's fleshy mouth. She tipped up her chin. 'I would choose to be kissed by him any day of the week rather than spend a minute in your company.'

He made a mocking sound. 'Such strong feelings, Lia...'

She cursed her out-of-control emotions, feeling heat climb into her cheeks at the thought that she was behaving far beneath her usual levels of decorum. Even so, she said, 'Only friends and family call me Lia—and you're neither.'

He put a hand to his chest. 'I'm wounded...'

Lia all but snorted. She couldn't imagine *anything* wounding this man. He was like a force of nature. Immune to any kind of threat. And certainly immune to her sustained animosity, which she was very afraid stemmed from a place that had nothing to do with the threat to her father's business and everything to do with a far more personal threat.

'You didn't have to accept the bid,' he pointed out. Annoyingly.

Lia unfolded her arms to put her hands on her hips. 'You didn't reveal your identity until *after* I'd accepted the bid. How could I then turn down a million dollars for the charity?' She shook her head, desperate not to let him guess for a second what deeper desires had led her to accept the bid. 'You painted me into a corner, Mr Carter. I had no choice.'

His eyes gleamed bright blue against the olive tones of his skin. 'We always have a choice, *Lia.*'

His insistence on goading her seemed to get lost for a second in the way he said her name, making her think of how intimate it had felt to talk to him out on that terrace. She decided that his calling her Lia was a lesser battle and not to be fought right now.

She started to pace, feeling edgy. So much for believing earlier that her antipathy would have somehow magically signalled to her who she was dealing with. She stopped and looked at him accusingly. 'You completely tricked me from the moment you came up to me, hiding behind your mask. Why didn't you tell me who you were?'

'Why didn't *you*?' he riposted.

Lia made a sound of frustration and her hands became fists at her sides. 'You had an unfair advantage with your mask. Obviously you don't experience many women walking out on dates with you, but if this is just because your pride is dented then—'

'Don't be ridiculous.'

The steel underlying his deep voice stopped Lia.

'You really think I'd be so petty that I'd pay an extortionate amount of money just to buy a weekend with a woman who walked out on a date?'

The man in front of her bristled with lots of things... none of which was pettiness. Lia was suddenly aware that she wasn't sure if she wanted to know exactly why Carter *had* paid all that money for her.

'There's not going to *be* a weekend,' she said tightly. 'It's ridiculous to think that I would go off with a complete stranger. Everyone will appreciate that it was just a stunt.'

He shook his head and came closer to Lia. She fought to stand her ground and not back away. He was so close now that the disparity in their sizes was apparent again. It brought back the memory of standing on the patio and looking up...aching to feel his mouth on hers...reaching up to take his mask off and having his hand close around her wrist... It was as if she'd blocked it out at the time, but she realised now that she *had* felt the rough skin of his palms on her skin. But she'd ignored it.

The fact that less than an hour ago she'd been reaching up to kiss him made her feel exposed all over again. She couldn't even contemplate the suspicion that on some level she'd known who he was all along.

Lia was aware that her reactions to this man were completely out of her control, but she couldn't seem to rein herself in. This close to him, she couldn't focus. All she could feel was the threat to her equilibrium and the desire to get away from him. Far away.

'Look,' she said, purposely making her voice as chilly as possible, 'I don't know how things work here in America, but in England we don't really go in for such crass displays of wealth. I appreciate that you've undertaken to donate a lot of money to the charity, but there is simply no way that I am going to go *anywhere* with you—a million dollars or not.'

She folded her arms again and regarded Benjamin Carter as best she could from several inches less in height.

Benjamin Carter, damn him, just smiled.

'There's no need to be patronising, sweetheart.'

Heat washed up over her chest and neck. She'd never usually descend to such rudeness, but this man, under his guise as a stranger, had seen her react in a way that made her want to crawl under a rock and hide.

'And, yes' he said now, 'you *are* coming with me. Because if you don't I will tell the charity's CEO that contrary to your public acceptance of the bet, you're not actually willing to fulfil your end of the bargain and therefore I will be withdrawing my funds.'

All the heat left Lia's body as her blood rushed south. 'You wouldn't dare. Not when everyone knows how much you donated.'

He took his hands out of his pockets and folded his arms across his chest. 'Do you really want to test me?'

Right now he looked as immovable as a mountain. And Lia had serious doubts about what he would do if she *did* test him. Clearly a man like this, who could make such obscenely huge gestures, was beholden to no one and wouldn't hesitate to prove his point.

Feeling utterly cornered and trapped, Lia said, 'Why are you doing this...? If it's not for spite...then what?'

He looked at her for a long moment and she couldn't read his expression.

Then he said, 'It's very simple, Lia. I want you.'

CHAPTER THREE

THE AIR SIZZLED between them and Ben's very direct words seemed to hang between them like a dare. What was it about this woman that seemed to arouse the beast in him? That made him do crazy things like pretend to be a stranger? And make outrageous public bids?

Her eyes were huge, as if she was still absorbing what he'd said, and then she responded, with a frigid tone to her voice. 'You want me enough to pay one million dollars for the pleasure? I don't know who you're used to consorting with, or who you think I am, but I'm not some kind of high-class—'

'I know *exactly* who you are,' he said curtly, cutting her off, surprised at the rapid surge of anger her insinuation had provoked.

It had been a long time since he'd felt the need to justify himself to anyone—much less to someone who came from the same part of society that had turned its back on him and left him to fend for himself. In that respect England and America were one and the same.

Nevertheless, he couldn't stop himself saying stiffly, 'I've never paid for a woman in my life. I don't need to.'

Intriguingly, she blushed, and suddenly she didn't look so confident. 'What do you mean, you know exactly who I am?'

The nerve she'd struck, however inadvertently, made him say, 'You might not be royalty but you're a princess.

Someone who has probably been denied nothing in her whole life. You don't like me because I turn you on, and you don't like being turned on by someone you consider beneath you.' He continued, 'Out on that terrace, before my identity was revealed, you had no prejudices holding you back because evidently you had judged that I was someone a little more...*refined*.'

The play of reactions across her face was mesmerising. Shock. Anger. Insult. And then fire. 'You played with me like a cat with a mouse. And, in light of your opinion, I fail to see why you'd want to subject yourself to spending a whole weekend with me.'

Lia went to move around him, to get away, but he stopped her with a hand on her arm. Her skin was silky smooth and warm, her arm slender under his hand. He felt crass then, and boorish. Not fit to touch someone as exquisite as her. But he held on and she swung around to face him, eyes flashing.

'Let me go, *damn you*. And for the record, you don't turn me on—not in the slightest.'

A challenge to disprove her rose hot and urgent through his body and Ben put both hands on her arms. But then, through the obvious anger she displayed, he caught a glimpse of something else in those stunning eyes...something almost like *hurt*. Hurt that he'd been accurate in his assessment of her and she wasn't used to hearing the bald truth? Or because he'd got it wrong?

He forced a modicum of civility back into his overheated brain. 'I didn't mean what I said as a personal attack. You're a product of your upbringing, that's all, and I was merely pointing out that I'm well aware that you're the furthest thing imaginable from a high-class hooker.'

That curious expression faded from her eyes, making Ben feel foolish for suspecting for a second that he'd hurt her because he'd got her wrong, and then she tensed under his hands, as if to leave again, and everything in him rejected it. The urge to disprove her assertion that she didn't want him was calling to the most primitive part of him.

'But I'm afraid I can't accept the lie.'

'What lie?' Now she looked wary.

'*This* lie.' And then he hauled her right into his body and covered her mouth with his.

Everything that had just passed between them was forgotten as the world seemed to combust into white heat. All Ben could feel was the press of that soft lush mouth and her body, moulding to his as if made for him alone.

All Lia could feel at first was steel, and then she realised it was the sheer hard-muscled strength of Benjamin Carter's body against hers, his hands tight on her arms. Her body was pressed so closely to his that her breasts were flattened against his chest, her nipples tingling from the contact.

And then, as if encouraged by the fact that she wasn't pulling away, his hold gentled minutely and his mouth became less of a searing brand and started to move on hers. Lia knew that she should be using this as an opportunity to pull free, stand back, demand to know what the hell he thought he was doing—especially after that heated exchange... But, treacherously, she didn't. Or couldn't.

One of his arms was sliding around her back now, pulling her in closer. And before she could stop herself she was responding to his kiss, her mouth softening and opening, and at the first touch of his tongue to hers she had no hope of remaining sane. Lia realised she was clutching at something to stay standing and that it was his arms, his biceps bulging under the material of his jacket, reminding her of the awesome power of his body.

There was something about this evidence of his sheer unadulterated masculinity that made her feel very feminine. It was seriously addictive. Yet the fact that she found his very masculine differences so attractive was unexpected and disorientating.

Certainly her ex-fiancé had never made her feel this... hot, or this desperate. This was wholly new and all too treacherously exhilarating.

Benjamin Carter's hand was cradling the back of her head now, and his other hand was on her hip, fingers digging into her flesh. She could feel his erection against her and it didn't shock her—it made her want to move against him. She wanted to feel him notch it against her, between her legs where she felt slick and swollen. She felt a curious hollowness, a desire to be filled...

His kiss was rough and smooth all at once. And it was only when his mouth left hers and he started to press kisses along her jaw, when her head fell back in weak supplication, that she seemed to come to her senses. A voice screamed at her. *What the hell are you doing?*

She jerked away from him abruptly and took a shaky step back, staring at him, aghast. Her mouth felt swollen and she realised the top of her dress was dislodged, revealing the swell of her breast. She pulled it back up with a jerk. Her hair was half undone and she noticed the black mask she'd been wearing lying on the ground nearby. She was unravelling. And she'd just betrayed herself, spectacularly.

In a thready voice she said, 'I don't know what that was...'

'I do.'

Carter was grim, and Lia hated it that he looked as if he hadn't just fallen apart—not like her.

'That was me proving that I *do* turn you on—and unfortunately proving it to the rest of the world too.'

Lia went still. 'What do you mean?'

Carter glanced back at something she couldn't see and then looked at her again. 'I think we've been papped.'

She went cold. The thought of someone witnessing that intensely private moment when she'd been so vulnerable made her want to squirm. It was too much exposure in one night—especially on the heels of how deeply his words had cut when he'd told her exactly what he thought of her: *'You might not be royalty but you're a princess.'* She knew that she hadn't helped matters by reacting so defensively to him, but she was far from some pampered princess, and the fact that his opinion somehow mattered was even more infuriating.

She glared at him. 'This is all your fault. If you hadn't pursued me and made that ridiculous bid this wouldn't have happened.'

He had the gall to shrug one shoulder, and a devilishly sexy smile tipped his mouth up at one side. 'Sweetheart, I just proved there's enough electricity between us to power a small nation, so it was inevitable.'

Lia started to pace again, as much to convince herself that her legs were still working as anything else. Then she stopped and looked at him. 'I'm not your sweetheart, and I've had enough. I'm leaving.'

This time he didn't try to restrain her, he just said with deadly efficiency from behind her, 'I really wouldn't do that if I were you.'

Something in his voice made Lia stop. She looked longingly at the entrance to the hotel and felt her neck prickle under his gaze. With the utmost reluctance she turned around and said, as nonchalantly as she could, 'And why would that be?'

He folded his arms and said, 'You've agreed to the terms of a very public auction and I'm really not joking when I say that I'll renege on my bid if you don't fulfil your end of the agreement. You'll be followed and mercilessly tracked by the paparazzi.'

He took a step closer to Lia and she fought against his physical magnetism. The memory of his tongue, thrusting into her mouth with a kind of possessive intensity was still vivid, and she hated it that it was.

'And,' he continued, 'I know you're here till after the weekend, and that you have nothing else on your schedule—except presumably shopping. So you have no reason to refuse to take a trip with me.'

His sheer obduracy made Lia want to stamp her foot. As did his casual judgement of her—again. *Shopping!* Clearly he'd checked up on her—but only at the most superficial level—and the thought of the lengths to which he was prepared to go caught her in her solar plexus before she crushed it. No doubt he'd laugh his head off if she told him that she'd actually planned to go to a series of lectures at NYU on advances in sustainable temporary emergency structures.

This was all just the means to some nefarious end, chemistry or no chemistry. She could see that under his devastating charisma there was a merciless streak, and a sense of futility filled her. Look at what he'd done so far! She didn't doubt any more that if she walked away then he *would* take back his one million dollars.

Something about the fact that he thought he had her so neatly squared away in a little box was actually somewhat comforting; he wasn't anywhere close to seeing the real her. If she had to put up with his overbearing and cocky arrogance for a weekend for the sake of a greater good, then she could do it.

She just wouldn't be so susceptible again. And she certainly wouldn't be kissing him again.

Hitching up her chin, she said as icily as she could, 'It

would appear that you leave me no choice in the matter. When do we leave and where are we going?'

Something that looked awfully like triumph flashed in Benjamin Carter's eyes as he strode towards her and took her arm in his hand again, propelling her forward and saying, 'There's no time like the present. We'll go to your hotel first, so you can pick up some essentials and your passport.'

Lia stopped in her tracks, forcing him to stop too, and he looked back at her, clearly impatient. Mindful of the people around them in the lobby, Lia hissed, *sotto voce*, 'Passport? Where on earth are you taking me?'

There was a definite glint of devilry in his eye as he said, 'Now, that would take all the fun out of it, don't you think? Don't worry, Lia, you'll be quite safe with me.'

She shivered minutely. She was afraid that she'd never been less safe—and it had nothing to do with physical safety...it was the sensual threat he posed and her own weakness to it. She was terrified of the way he made her feel so off balance. Out of control.

Fiercely, she said, 'Nothing is going to happen this weekend, Mr Carter. No matter what you believe. That kiss was a mistake.'

He smiled, and it was distinctly wolfish. 'I've never had to force a woman into my bed and I'm not about to start. Whatever happens will be completely mutual, I assure you.'

And then, before she knew what was happening, she was being handed her wrap and they were at the entrance of the hotel, where Carter opened the passenger door of a sleek dark grey sports car.

Holding herself rigid as she passed him, she got in with as much dignity as she could and in her head called him every name under the sun as he slammed her door shut and walked around the front of the car with lithe animal grace.

When he slid in beside her, bringing with him that tantalising musky scent, Lia held herself even more rigid. She could feel him glance at her and she stared straight ahead, vowing that with every fibre of her being she would resist this man and keep the vulnerable core of herself intact.

Whatever his game was, she wasn't interested in playing.

There had been nothing but a frosty silence interspersed with the barest of monosyllabic answers from the woman who was now curled up in a seat on the opposite side of Ben's private plane, looking out of the window, with her wrap pulled tightly around her, her hair down around her shoulders. Tousled dark silkiness...

Irritation and something more indefinable lay under Ben's skin at the thought that she wouldn't be here if he hadn't publicly paid a million dollars for the pleasure. But he pushed that aside. She was here now—that was all that mattered.

They'd taken off from a private airfield near Newark about an hour ago, after they'd gone to her hotel suite so that she could collect her passport and some essentials. She'd been about to go into the bathroom to change out of her dress when something perverse had made Ben say, 'We don't have time for that.'

She'd looked at him, blue eyes sending a flash of dark icy fire, and then, to give her her due, she'd merely stalked out of the suite, leaving her bags for him to pick up.

She was playing the role of princess to the hilt, and he had no one to blame but himself after he'd called her one. That enigmatic look in her eyes came back to him, the sense that she'd been hurt. His conscience pricked, even as he told himself that the women he knew from her kind of world were hardened.

But he had to admit that she was an intriguing mass of contradictions. Not least of which was the contradiction he'd met while they'd been wearing their masks. He had to acknowledge a little uncomfortably that he *had* had an advantage, having recognised her from the first moment. He'd intended to tell her who he was, but then she'd been so surprisingly sweet. And flirtatious. *Hot.* It had been a stark contrast to their first meeting—confirming that he'd never really stood a chance, because she'd gone there only to warn him off.

But then, when she hadn't realised who he was, he'd been loath to ruin the mood by revealing his identity. Ben scowled now. It wasn't like him to give in to weak impulses. The whole object of this exercise was to seduce her, and ultimately—possibly—marry her.

Although right now the idea of this woman submitting to a life of domestic bliss with Ben seemed to be a stretch too far, even for his imagination. Surely this was the point when he decided she wasn't worth the trouble? There was any number of ex-lovers who'd made no attempt to hide their desire to become Mrs Carter...and yet Ben found he was curiously reluctant to let Lia go.

He wanted her. And the thought of taming her sharp tongue and making her acquiescent and pliant with desire was more arousing than anything he could remember.

He finally looked away from the disturbing provocation of the woman on the other side of the aisle and yanked at his bow tie, undoing it. He felt petty now, for not letting her change earlier. It wasn't exactly helping to douse his desire, knowing that just under the slimmest of coverings that tantalising body was—

'There were no paparazzi, were there?'

Ben jerked his head round to find those cool blue eyes narrowed on him, and saw that her arms were folded. Some of the tension inside him loosened and he turned towards her, seeing how her gaze involuntarily darted down and then back up.

She wanted him. And he would prove it to her.

Feeling only the tiniest prick of his conscience, Ben said, 'If you remember, I said I *thought* we'd been papped.'

Her eyes flashed. 'I can't believe I fell for it.'

Ben shrugged and took a sip of his coffee. 'You still wouldn't have had a choice in the end.'

That lush mouth tightened and Ben had to restrain himself from reaching across to touch it, make it soften. He thought of something then, and said, 'I like that you're called Lia. It's less...rigid.'

Those ivory cheeks flushed. 'Like I said, that's for friends and family.'

Ben smiled, enjoying her discomfiture more than he should. 'I think we're definitely more than friends now, *Lia.* I don't know what you're used to, but in my world friends don't kiss the way we did earlier. Lovers...now, that's a different matter.'

Lia darted a glance behind her, to where the discreet staff were, and then hissed across the aisle, 'We will never be lovers, Mr Carter.'

Ben ignored that and sat back, extending his legs, making himself comfortable even though the last thing he was feeling was relaxed. 'There's a bedroom at the back of the cabin. You should slip into something more comfortable and get some rest. We'll be in the air for another seven hours at least.'

'You're still insisting on not telling me where we're going?'

Ben glanced at her with mock innocence. 'And ruin the surprise?'

Her jaw clenched. 'I don't like surprises, Mr Carter.'

'Please, Lia,' he purred, enjoying himself immensely, 'call me Ben.'

After a long moment, when she looked as if she was seriously tempted to do him some physical violence, she undid her seat belt and stood up, saying, 'You're impossible. *This* is impossible.'

She took her bag from an overhead locker and the wrap over her dress fell to the floor. Ben let his gaze roam freely over her curves, in particular her pert behind.

She whirled around and he looked up. She grabbed the wrap from him as he picked it up and held it out to her, and said tersely, 'I'm going to get some sleep. And I don't want to be disturbed.'

Ben smiled. 'Please, be my guest.'

Lia walked to the back of the plane, her red dress swirling about her body and those long slim legs. She went into the bedroom and the door was shut forcefully enough behind her to make Ben wince slightly. Then he heard the distinct *click* of the lock being turned.

His smile slipped from his face as he had to shift his body to accommodate his erection. He felt feral enough to be tempted to go and kick open the door and prove to Lia right now that they were more than *friends*. But he reminded himself that he was civilised.

After all, he had to acknowledge bitterly, for the first twelve years of his life Ben had been exceedingly civilised. Until everything had changed and the real world had been revealed, like in *The Wizard of Oz*, when the curtain had been pulled back to expose the truth.

Just then Ben's phone vibrated and he welcomed the distraction. He took it out of his pocket to see a name flashing on the screen. He smiled mirthlessly and answered, 'Trakas. Are you missing me and our new friends already?'

'Hardly,' came the dry response. 'The internet is buzzing about you making some outrageous bid at a charity auction and absconding with a British society princess for the weekend. I thought we were trying to improve our reputations, not make them worse.'

Ben looked pointedly at the closed door of the bedroom and said through a tight jaw, 'Don't worry, it's all part of the plan. Elizabeth Young set us up on a date. Was there something in particular you wanted or did you just call to gossip?'

Xander Trakas was silent for a moment, and then he said, 'And...? How was she?'

Ben frowned. 'Who? The matchmaker?'

Trakas sounded impatient. 'Of course.'

Ben felt another pang of his conscience when he thought of what she'd think of his pursuing Lia in spite of her warning. 'She was fine. Why the hell do you care anyway?'

'No reason,' came the swift response, and then the other man said, 'Later, Carter,' and hung up.

Ben shook his head and put his phone down, glancing at the shut door again and scowling. He had no idea what was going on between Xander Trakas and the Leviathan Solutions director, but if it was anything close to what he was currently engaged in, then he wished the man luck. From what he'd seen of Elizabeth Young, and her quiet but steely self-possession, he'd need it.

'Let me show you around.'

Lia looked suspiciously at Benjamin Carter, who had no right to look so fresh and gorgeous after sleeping in his seat on the plane. He'd changed out of his tuxedo into dark trousers and a black short-sleeved polo shirt, and she was acutely aware of the bunching of his biceps where his arms were folded. He was even more powerful than she'd thought.

Stalling for time, to let her disorientated brain catch up with events, she said, 'Where exactly are we?'

They'd landed at Salvador International Airport in Bahia, Brazil, about an hour before, and to find out how far they'd come had blown her mind. Then Carter had collected an open-top Jeep and driven them out of the city and along the coast for about thirty minutes. Lia didn't like to admit that she'd been captivated by the Atlantic sea frothing against miles and miles of pristine beaches.

'We're at my private villa, north of Salvador.'

His blue gaze dropped momentarily down her body and Lia regretted not changing when she'd had the chance on the plane. But after pacing in the spacious bedroom for long minutes she'd given in to fatigue and had lain down on the bed, still in the dress. Then, when a peremptory knock on the door had woken her, and a too-familiar deep voice had told her they'd be landing soon, something petty in her had refused to make him feel more comfortable about what he'd done, so she'd emerged still wearing the dress.

But now she felt silly. And self-conscious. It made her say defiantly, 'What's to stop me from taking that Jeep and driving back down to Salvador to take the next flight home?'

Her host didn't look remotely perturbed. 'Well, I'd have to report it as stolen, and the *policia* here are very efficient. So there's really no point.'

The same sense of futility she'd felt in New York sank into Lia's bones as she had to come to terms with the truth smacking her in the face—she was here for the weekend.

As if reading her mind, her host unfolded his arms

and held a hand out, gesturing eloquently for her to take his invitation to look around.

Capitulation wasn't easy, but after a few seconds of inner struggle she bent down to slip off her shoes—which were now officially killing her. When she straightened, holding the shoes in her hand, she said tightly, 'As it appears that I have no choice, lead the way.'

Ignoring the fact that she felt a lot more fragile without the added height of her shoes, she followed him deeper into the villa and tried to avert her gaze from that broad back, tapering down to lean hips and tight buttocks.

It was almost a relief to focus on the furnishings, and with some surprise she took in polished wooden floors and open white shutters allowing the warm breeze to circulate. The rooms flowed into each other, the spaces generous and open.

It was casual, yet elegant without being ostentatious. She noted valuable works of art dotted around the rooms and on the walls. Everything complemented each other. The décor was very much to her own pared-down tastes, which was something she had not expected.

A spacious den was comfortable and inviting, with low coffee tables and a media centre. Huge art and photography books looked well-thumbed, and one wall was shelved and full of books. Her hands itched to explore what was there.

'Your interior designer is very talented,' Lia remarked.

A dry-sounding, 'Thank you,' made her look at Carter, who had a small smile playing around his mouth. She saw the glint in his eye and then said disbelievingly, 'No... *You* designed this?'

'It's amazing the amount of taste money can buy.'

His tone was even drier now, and there was something else—an edge she'd noticed before, when she'd accused him of being crass. Now she felt uncomfortable. It was disconcerting to feel for the first time as if she was on the back foot.

'It's lovely.'

Wide open French doors led out to the beach. Lia explored a little and her feet sank into deliciously warm and soft sand. The waves of the Atlantic lapped gently and rhythmically against the shore. In spite of herself, something inside her loosened. It had been so long since she'd just...relaxed. Her father's weak health was such a worry, and he depended on her so much...

'Careful,' drawled Benjamin Carter, from too close, 'or I might think you like it here.'

Immediately any sense of relaxation went out of the window and Lia glared at his back as he led her inside again, through a central open courtyard with a pool that was shaded by palm trees.

He showed her a large kitchen, gleamingly pristine with sparkling utensils and a marble worktop. Placing his hands on the counter, where they looked very large and tanned, he said, 'This is Esmé's domain. She's my local housekeeper and chef. She takes care of the place when I'm not here and opens it up for me. She'll be in later to cook dinner.'

Lia dragged her gaze up from those hands and ignored the illicit flutter in her abdomen at the sudden image of a romantic candlelit dinner on the beach. She was silent as she followed him through the villa again and upstairs. Several bedrooms lay off a wide corridor there, with a luxurious runner carpet, and then he walked across a balconied atrium. He opened a door and said, 'This is your room.'

She looked at him suspiciously, and he said with a wide-eyed innocence that she didn't trust for a second, 'What? Did you not think I would be civilised enough to give you your own room? I've told you already—whatever happens will be mutual.'

Lia slipped into the room before he could see her discomfiture. She wasn't used to men being so...up-front. And on some level she wasn't sure *what* she'd expected. One thing she had to admit was that she felt in no danger at all. Her prevailing feeling was that any danger would come from her own reactions.

She dropped her shoes to the floor and walked over to where huge open doors led out to a balcony that looked out on the beach and the sea, just yards away. It was stunning. Just then a small bird flew past, with an iridescent flash of exotic colours. She realised with a sense of irony that the man wouldn't have to resort to any kind of force—this place could seduce a woman all on its own.

When she turned around he gestured. 'There's an en suite bathroom through there, and a dressing room.'

Curious, Lia looked into the massive bathroom. It was gorgeous—with a wet room shower and a huge claw-footed bath. A very feminine part of her sighed in appreciation.

And then through an adjoining door she saw what must be the dressing room. She walked in and gasped when she saw that it was full of clothes, all brand-new, with designer tags still dangling from the expensive fabrics.

Other doors that led back to the main bedroom were pulled open and Benjamin Carter leant nonchalantly against the doorframe, with a faint smile on his face that smacked irritatingly of a man watching a woman having the desired reaction when she saw a closet full of beautiful clothes.

She folded her arms and narrowed her eyes on him, bristling at that look. 'So this is your seduction routine for the women you bring here? Frankly, it takes more than a closet full of expensive clothes to get *my* interest. I'm not that shallow or spoilt—no matter what you might believe.'

Something flashed in his eyes and for a second Lia thought he'd taken offence. He didn't move, but she could sense his tension.

'Actually, I've never brought a woman here before. But I do loan the villa to friends and business acquaintances. I keep the two master suites stocked with clothes because the nearest boutique is in Salvador. A stylist I employ checks the stock after each visit and removes the clothes that have been worn, which are then given to a local charity.'

Lia felt ashamed of her quick judgement. This wasn't like her... But he pushed her buttons like no one else. And had he really never brought a woman here? She tried to read his now expressionless face and had to admit that a man like him wouldn't lie about that. Why would he need to?

The realisation that it must be some sort of sanctuary for him made her feel even more vulnerable. She weakly chose deflection to avoid acknowledging the revelation that she was the first woman he'd brought here.

'Well,' she said stiffly, 'that's very generous of you, but I've brought my own clothes.' She belatedly realised that her autumn/winter clothes would obviously be totally unsuitable in this climate.

Ben straightened from the door now, and for the first time since she'd met him Lia sensed a slight chill in the air. Contrary to the way she would have expected to feel, she didn't like it.

He glanced at his watch. 'It's my first time here this year, so I have a few maintenance things to catch up on. Make yourself at home. There's plenty of food in the kitchen if you'd like a snack. And you've seen where the beach is—it's entirely private, so you won't be disturbed.'

And then he turned to walk out. A veritable cauldron of emotions rendered Lia immobile and speechless for a moment as she watched him leave. There was anger that he'd all but kidnapped her, but that was fading in light of these all too seductive surroundings and the fact that he was giving her space.

And then she castigated herself for being so easily duped—because he *had* to have an agenda. And she needed to remember that. Because something was shifting, and if she wasn't careful she'd be falling under a spell she might not be able to resist.

She hurried to the door of the bedroom in her bare feet and saw his broad back descending the stairs. 'If this is all just to get to my father then you might as well send me back to New York right now,' she blurted out. 'Because I would never let someone seduce me to get to him.'

Ben stopped in his tracks. Frustration still coursed through his blood. Never had a woman so comprehensively stonewalled him. And certainly not one who wanted him. And never had a woman had such an obviously low opinion of him. To his utter chagrin, when usually he couldn't care less what people thought of him, he found himself caring about her opinion.

She looked at him as if he was something stuck on the bottom of her shoe, even as that pulse beat hectically under her skin at her neck, every time he came close.

Slowly he turned around, jaw tight, teetering on the edge of telling her that he'd arrange for her to be taken back to Salvador, but then he saw her hovering by the doorway, and that compulsion died a death when he saw the expression on her face. There was still defiance, but there was also something he hadn't seen before—a kind of wary uncertainty. A hint of vulnerability. It made him think of the fleeting look of hurt he thought he'd seen when he'd called her a princess. And the moment of sheer terror on her face when her friend had asked her to step in for the model at the charity auction.

In bare feet, and still wearing that decadent dress which was badly creased by now, with her hair loose and mussed around her shoulders after the long journey, she looked more beautiful than anything he'd ever seen in his life.

And he wanted her.

Ben slowly came back up the stairs, seeing how her eyes widened. She was tense, too, and it wasn't just from anger at his commandeering of this situation. She was tense because of him, because she wanted him, and suddenly Ben knew that there was no way he was letting her go.

He stopped a few feet away from her. 'I won't stand here and insult your intelligence by denying that I have an interest in your father's business...but right now I'm not concerned with that.'

Ben was surprised to find that he really wasn't. Right now all his interest was focused on one thing. *Lia.* And making her acquiesce to him.

She swallowed and his eyes tracked the movement down the slim column of her throat.

Finally she said, in those cut-glass tones, 'You won't get anywhere with me, Mr Carter, so I think it would be best if we just kept ourselves to ourselves until it's time to go home.'

Ben almost felt sorry for her as he answered, 'You really shouldn't issue a challenge like that, Lia...'

CHAPTER FOUR

'YOU REALLY SHOULDN'T issue a challenge like that...'

That evening, Benjamin Carter's words still resounded in Lia's head. Damn the man.

After pacing her sumptuous room for a couple of hours that morning, she'd finally explored the dressing room. Determined to make the most of this situation, she'd kitted herself out in a modest bathing suit and some beach attire. After helping herself to a light lunch in the kitchen she'd headed to the beach.

There had been no sign of Benjamin Carter, much to her relief, but she had heard some noises that sounded as if they were coming from the front of the house. Not wanting to face him in a diaphanous beach cover-up, she'd found an idyllic spot on the beach under the shade of a palm tree, out of immediate sight of the villa.

For a few hours she had almost fooled herself that she was on a vacation she'd chosen willingly. She'd dozed, swum, and read a book that she'd pulled off the shelf in the comfortable den.

She'd returned to the villa as dusk was falling and had nearly tripped over her own feet when she'd seen a half-naked Ben Carter perched precariously on the terra-cotta rooftop of the villa. Her eyes had been immediately drawn to the sleek muscles of his broad back, moving sinuously under his skin as he'd hammered something into a slate.

The fact that he had been laughing and joking with another man, whose ebony skin had also been gleaming with exertion, had gone largely unnoticed. Carter had been wearing nothing but a faded pair of board shorts and battered-looking sneakers.

Lia had almost jumped out of her skin when a melodious and mischievous-sounding voice had said near her ear, 'Not a bad sight at the end of a hot day, hmm?'

She'd looked to her left to see a startlingly pretty young woman, with skin the colour of warm chocolate, eyes to match and a huge smile. With a colourful scarf on her head, she had blended into the exotic background perfectly.

The woman had introduced herself as Esmé, and after explaining that the other man was her husband had said, 'I was just coming to find you. Ben sends his apologies for being busy all afternoon but says he'll look forward to you joining him for dinner at eight.'

Lia had been about to demur when she'd realised she was being ridiculous, and that this nice woman didn't deserve to be put out just because the last person she wanted to have dinner with was her host.

Are you so sure about that? a little voice had crowed.

In any event, Lia had made her escape from the provocative view of a far less civilised Benjamin Carter before he'd been able to turn around and see her reaction, which was confusing to her on so many levels. Since when had she found men doing manual labour particularly enticing? And why did the sight of him doing something so earthy appeal to her so much?

She cursed her revolving thoughts now, as she debated what to wear after her shower. A part of her wanted to wear jeans and a shirt, but then she thought of the mocking look in Carter's eyes when he registered that she was obviously trying *not* to make an effort. So instead she picked out a simple black silk dress that had a scooped neckline and a gathered waist. It fell to her knees. Positively nun-like. Perfect.

After applying a minimum of make-up, and pulling her hair back into a low bun, she slid on her own kitten heel shoes and made her way downstairs, noticing that she was just on time. She was just grumbling to herself that she was pathologically incapable of being late, even if she wanted to be, when Carter appeared in the lobby below, with a bottle of wine in one hand and a glass in the other.

He'd been transformed from manual labourer back to suave, elegant businessman, in dark charcoal-coloured trousers and a light grey shirt. Lia could see that his normally unruly hair looked damp, and was bombarded with an X-rated image of him in a shower, with water sluicing down over those impressive muscles.

'Esmé told me she'd found you. I apologise again for leaving you to your own devices but after Joao—Esmé's husband—offered his services for the afternoon, we managed to get all the maintenance jobs done at once.'

Lia wasn't quite sure how she'd made it down the stairs, but now she was standing only a few feet away from him. Something about his easy manner and her sense of this villa feeling far too familiar, even after such a short time, was very disconcerting.

Her voice was husky. 'I wasn't expecting you to entertain me. I had a lovely afternoon on the beach.'

His voice had a faintly disbelieving tone. 'You weren't bored?'

Lia shook her head, realising that the afternoon had been far more pleasant than she'd even admitted to herself. And if she *had* felt a tiny sense of loneliness it hadn't been for the company of this man, she assured herself fiercely, and got a grip on her wayward emotions. She put it down to the after-effects of the sun.

'I swam and read a book. I haven't had a chance to do that for a long time.'

He didn't respond, but Lia could imagine that Carter believed she meant since her last luxury holiday. She bit back the urge to disabuse him of that notion. She didn't care what his opinion of her was... All that mattered was putting up with this weekend for the sake of his charitable donation.

Lia followed him into the salon, where the lights had been dimmed and candles flickered invitingly. The air was still warm after the day, and it was heavenly after the biting breeze of autumn in New York.

Carter turned from where he was opening some wine at a drinks cabinet. 'Would you like a glass? It's from a good friend's vineyard in Argentina.'

Lia was about to say no, but then something stopped her. A rogue desire to give in to this seductive relaxation. So she nodded and took the glass of chilled white wine, noticing that Ben Carter had picked up a glass of what looked like water. She recalled that he hadn't ordered alcohol on their date—or *non*-date. And he hadn't been drinking at the charity auction.

'You don't drink?' she heard herself asking, before she could stop the words.

He shook his head and gestured for her to take a seat on the couch behind her. He sat on another couch, on the other side of the coffee table, his arm spread across the back, his big body dominating the space easily.

Lia looked away and took a sip of wine. It slid down her throat like cool silk, its bouquet flooding her senses and making her head instantly light. And even though she wasn't looking at him his image was burned into her retinas. He reminded Lia of a lounging pasha she'd seen once in a painting, surrounded by a bevy of exotic beauties. The civilised surroundings didn't diminish his robust masculinity at all. And that provocative memory of him half-naked wasn't helping.

He eventually supplied, 'I don't drink. At all.'

She couldn't keep averting her gaze, so she looked back to see that his expression was almost challenging. She just shrugged, as if her curiosity wasn't as piqued as it was. 'I don't drink much myself…a couple of glasses is usually my limit.'

Some of the tension seemed to go out of his shoulders. The thought of him having had a drink problem… She just couldn't see it. He was way too in control. Perhaps it had something to do with his upbringing?

Just then Esmé appeared at the entrance of the room and told them dinner was served. Ben stood and let Lia precede him out of the room to the dining room next door, similarly dimly lit, with candles flickering.

A table was set with a white tablecloth and silver. It was very romantic. And that, along with her sudden curiosity to know more about this man, made Lia say stiffly, 'You really shouldn't have gone to this trouble.'

He held out Lia's chair and she had to sit down, very aware of him behind her.

As he came around and took his own seat he drawled, 'It took an eight-hour plane journey and a two-hour time difference to get you to have dinner with me, so a little effort is worth it, I think.'

Lia looked at him and had to figure that most men wouldn't have bothered pursuing her this far—or they would be resenting the trouble they'd gone to. A man she'd dated briefly before her ex-fiancé had turned nasty when she'd been less than eager to jump into bed after their first date. It was one of the reasons she'd liked Simon—because he'd respected her boundaries. Little had she known that he was being respectful because he was eyeing up a chance to get a permanent foothold in the legal team who represented her father's company, and because his 'needs' were being met elsewhere.

But Carter was still here, and it felt as if he had stormed into her life, blasting apart the cynicism she'd built around herself after her parents' break-up and her disastrous engagement.

The consequences if she was to unbend even slightly and give in to his seduction were suddenly terrifying to contemplate—because Lia knew now that he'd already slid under her skin enough to make an impact that she really didn't want to acknowledge.

For him this was just about a conquest—personal and professional. Of that she had no doubt.

She leaned forward slightly. 'Look, Mr Carter...I know that this is about my father as much as you say it's about me—'

But she had to stop as Esmé appeared with their starters—beautifully prepared individual ravioli in a cream and mushroom sauce. Lia didn't miss the all-too-interested look the woman sent to each of them.

When they were alone again he responded. 'First of all, my name is Ben. Second of all, the fact that I have a professional interest in your father is common knowledge. Many others have—not just me. Your father has never had a problem protecting his interests, so unless something has changed he is perfectly safe, no matter what happens between us. And thirdly...when I saw your photo in the matchmaker's portfolio I wanted you before I knew who you were.'

The words sat between them in the thick silence. Fatally, all Lia registered was that he'd wanted her before he'd known who she was. And, God help her, that struck deep. It was like when she'd been standing on that dais and someone had wanted her enough to bid a small fortune for her…an elusive stranger she'd thought she wanted. Who was *him*. The man sitting across from her now, blue eyes glinting. Handsome as sin.

This man was dangerous to her because he made her yearn for things she'd thought she could live without—for deeply personal desires to be fulfilled. For a man to touch her and make her come alive. Prove to her that she wasn't defective in some way…

And then she thought of what he'd said about her father. The truth was that her father *was* vulnerable—he needed to retire and there was no one he trusted enough to take over the business. Lia realised that she was leading Carter to question her father's robustness when she should be taking the opportunity to deflect it.

She had to give a little…or he'd smell blood.

She forced herself to relax slightly and sucked in a breath. 'Fine. Ben it is.' Her heart thumped as she said his name. It felt ridiculously intimate.

He held out his hand across the table, over their fragrant starters. 'Truce?'

Lia reluctantly held out her own hand. 'Truce.'

His hand enveloped hers and she had a flashback to seeing him on the roof, skin gleaming with exertion, those muscles bunching and moving. She tried to pull her hand back but his fingers tightened and an unmistakable fire in his eyes mesmerised her.

'I'm glad you're here, Lia,' he said. 'I look forward to getting to know you better.'

Ben didn't fool himself for a second that Lia's apparent acquiescence had anything to do with *him*, per se. Oh, she wanted him—that was obvious. But she was still determined to fight it. Still, after he'd declared that truce, and resisted the urge to pull her over the table towards him so he could kiss her, they'd actually had a cordial meal and conversed. Albeit about completely superficial subjects.

On one level it infuriated Ben, because he knew now that he'd underestimated her hugely, and yet she seemed to be determined to close him off, not let him see beneath the surface. And he only had himself to blame. For a man not used to failure—in anything—it was disconcerting.

They'd finished dinner now, and she'd joined him back in the living area for coffee. She was walking around the room, looking at pictures and books, cradling her coffee cup in her hand.

Without that direct blue gaze assessing his every movement, Ben could look his fill. The dress she wore was lovely, but it comprehensively covered her body. He guessed she'd chosen it for that very reason, and once again he found her reluctance to give in to the chemistry between them slightly mystifying.

He didn't think that any of her reluctance to come with him had been feigned, so he knew she wasn't the kind of woman who would play hard to get. And yet he'd never expend this much effort on a woman who didn't want him, so it made him wonder about her, about her experience. Maybe he'd underestimated her in more ways than one?

He asked carefully, 'So, in light of the fact that you'd signed up with Leviathan Solutions, I'm a little curious as to why you seemed so eager to leave it after your first date?'

He saw how her whole body stiffened at that question. She turned around slowly, after putting the book she'd been looking at back on the shelf. He saw her clear reluctance to speak on her face and it fascinated him—he was used to women who had injected so much filler that they couldn't emote more than a tense smile.

After a long moment when he thought she was going

to deflect his question, she said tightly, 'The truth is that I had no desire to join a dating agency. Someone decided to do it on my behalf.'

Ben's curiosity shot up, but he schooled his expression. 'Who would do such a thing?'

She sighed and came and sat down. Every move she made exuded that effortless casual elegance, even when she was tense.

She put her cup down and looked at Ben. 'It was my father's idea. He's old-fashioned, and he's determined to see me settled.'

She shut her mouth, as if she'd said too much. Ben could see that she was tempted to fold her arms, shut him out completely. It suddenly occurred to him as he took in her vaguely tortured expression...and when he recalled her reaction to, and subsequent tension during the charity auction...that she might actually be *shy*.

He leant forward. 'I know you're not gay—not after that kiss we shared... So what is it, Lia? Why don't you want to date?'

She stood up again, agitated, and moved back over to the shelves, turning to face him. 'Is it so hard to believe that a woman might not want her life to revolve around a man? That she might have ambitions of her own? In case you hadn't heard, a revolution was fought and won a long time ago.'

Ben sat back, more and more intrigued by these buttons he was pushing. He drawled, 'I'm no misogynist, Lia, and some would say there's still a fight to be fought. But people—women in particular—can multitask, dating and working at the same time.'

Now she flushed. 'I know that.' She wrapped her arms around herself. 'I just... My father shouldn't have done that. Not after—'

She broke off abruptly and Ben sat forward again. 'After what?'

She glanced away, her jaw tight. When she looked at him again after a moment, she said, 'Well, it's not as if you couldn't find out easily enough.' She lifted her chin. 'I was engaged briefly. A year ago.'

'Who was he?' Ben asked sharply, hackles rising.

Lia came back around the couch and sat down, picking up her coffee again. 'I met him at one of my father's parties. He was a solicitor with a firm that my father's legal team uses sometimes to take on extra work.'

Ben felt a surge of that same possessiveness he'd experienced when he'd seen Lia standing on that dais in front of everyone. 'I wouldn't have had you down as the wife of a mere lackey.'

Lia's eyes sparked. 'No? That just shows how much you don't know about me, doesn't it?'

Ben shrugged a shoulder. 'I hardly know you, Lia, but I know you're more than just corporate wife material. He would have stifled you to death.' It surprised him that he *did* know this. And it made him wonder what on earth kind of marriage of convenience *he* had in mind, if not corporate.

He noticed then how she'd gone still. 'That's some leap to make when you hardly know me...'

Ben grimaced. 'I owe you an apology. I was wrong about you. You're not a princess, Lia. If you were you'd have been screaming and begging to get back to civilisation hours ago, and yet you've been perfectly happy here all day, looking after yourself. Esmé told me you made your lunch and cleaned up after yourself.'

She responded with a touch of wry defensiveness. 'Making lunch and cleaning up hardly merits special congratulations. I've still had a more privileged upbringing than most people ever see in their lifetimes.'

'But you're not spoilt. Far from it.'

For a long time she said nothing, biting her lip. And then, finally, 'No, not as you might have imagined at first. It's been just my father and I since my parents divorced. I became his hostess from a young age and…and I think he overcompensated to make up for the separation. But I was never really comfortable with lavish gifts or things like that. Once he was happy, *I* was happy.'

Ben absorbed this nugget, acknowledging uncomfortably that he'd misjudged her again. He'd known Louis Ford was divorced, but not the particulars. He asked, 'Where's your mother now?'

Lia shrugged minutely and her face was carefully expressionless. Ben recognised it because he used that defence mechanism himself when someone asked too many questions about his past.

'I think she's in a Swiss château with husband number four. It's hard to pin Estella down. I don't see her often. When I was a teenager she would summon me periodically to whatever luxurious resort she was residing in at the time, usually when she was between husbands and in need of distraction.'

Ben felt a surge of irritation at this faceless woman, but he said lightly, 'She sounds charming.'

Lia blinked at Ben and then put down her cup and stood up abruptly, taking him by surprise. He'd not even noticed that they'd got into a personal discussion, and he usually did his utmost to avoid straying into such territory with women.

He stood up too, just as she said, 'It's been a long day. I think I'll go to bed.'

'Of course.' His gaze tracked her as she turned to leave the room, and then he made a split-second decision and said, 'I thought that perhaps tomorrow I could give you a tour of Salvador. It's a stunning city, and I'd like to make it up to you for leaving you to your own devices today.'

She stopped, and the lines of her body were tense. For a moment Ben had a premonition that she was going to turn around and say enough was enough, that she wanted to go home tomorrow... And in all conscience he realised that he couldn't really say no if she wanted to. Even as everything in him rejected the thought.

But she turned quickly and just said, 'Okay—fine.'

And then she was disappearing from view and Ben let out a long breath, more relieved by that small concession than anything he could recall in a long time.

As soon as Lia made it back to her room she closed the door and leant back against it, breathing deeply to calm her racing heart. What the hell had just happened down there? She'd been moments away from curling up on the couch and spilling her entire guts to Benjamin Carter, as if he was some kind of confidant she could trust.

It had only been when he'd responded to what she'd revealed about her mother, and she'd had the distinct impression that he was angry on her behalf, that she'd snapped back to reality. First of all, she never spoke about her mother to anyone—the old wound of rejection still smarted, and she usually avoided being drawn into any discussion about it. *Usually.*

And what about telling him that she wasn't interested in dating? And letting him provoke her into talking about her failed engagement?

Lia groaned and kicked off her shoes, walking over to the French doors that led out to the balcony.

The air was still deliciously warm and balmy, caressing her bare skin. She couldn't see anything in the inky darkness but she could hear the gentle lap of waves against the shore and it soothed her jittery nerves a little, and her sense of exposure.

She thought of his apologising for calling her a princess, and his observation that she was more than corporate wife material, and something inside her felt weak. And yet hadn't she almost settled for that? Because after yet another stroke, her concern for her father's health had been so great that she'd given in to his plea that she give Simon Barnes—the nice but dull solicitor—a chance.

When she'd started dating him and they'd had a frank discussion he'd admitted that he'd pursued her to get into her father's good graces, thus potentially securing a job on his legal team. Simon had then assured her that he would not stand in the way of her ambitions, and so— foolishly, maybe—Lia had seen a way to keep her father happy, and also to forge a life for herself within a marriage that wouldn't confine her.

After all, she'd never entertained romantic notions of a happy-ever-after marriage—not after witnessing her own parents' disastrous marriage and her father's subsequent heartbreak. Lia had vowed from an early age never to be so destroyed by giving someone else that control over her.

But then her chest grew tight when she recalled that oh, so vivid image of her fiancé's head buried between his secretary's legs, and the humiliation washed over her again. It hadn't been his infidelity that had hurt her— after all, they hadn't been in love—it had been the stark knowledge of the fact that *she* hadn't been able to rouse that passion in him.

Lia curled her hands around the balcony railings as if that would centre her again. The truth was that as much as she wished she could find it easy to dismiss Benjamin Carter...she couldn't.

Something about this place, about *him*, was making her loosen up. Dangerously so. She'd all but accused him of being boorish and she had outright accused him of being crass. But this beautiful house didn't belong to a crass man, and a boorish man didn't climb up to hammer slates into a roof with his housekeeper's husband. And, an overly arrogant man who had made no bones about the fact that he wanted to take her to bed wouldn't exercise such restraint that he'd actually let her go to bed. Alone.

Lia hadn't mistaken the heat in his eyes… It was one of the reasons, apart from her over-sharing, that she'd practically run from the room.

She had to remind herself that the man was a consummate playboy; he knew exactly what he was doing. He was like a big jungle cat playing with a tiny helpless mouse—letting it believe that it could get away when all he had to do was bring down a big paw and that would be that. Game over.

She'd been here less than twenty-four hours and the man was already playing her like a fiddle. Lia was very tempted to go back downstairs and demand that he take her home immediately.

Funnily enough, she suspected that if she insisted he would let her go. But, perversely, she didn't want to give him the satisfaction, or let him suspect for a second that she was perturbed by all that she'd revealed to him. One more day in his company… She could keep her mouth zipped and keep him at a distance. She could. She had to.

Lia sat beside Ben in the open-top Jeep as they drove down the main route to Salvador from his villa. Her dark hair was pulled back into a practical ponytail and the warm breeze made it look like skeins of silk behind her head. He was finding it hard to maintain some semblance of control. It was as if he'd never seen a woman dressed in a sleeveless T-shirt and shorts before. But he'd never seen *this* woman dressed like that before, and it was all he could do not to stop and ogle her slender pale limbs.

She seemed ethereal and delicate beside him. Even though he knew he shouldn't be thinking of her as delicate at all. When she'd arrived in the kitchen earlier she'd had a determined look on her face and had kept up a general patter of inane conversation. No doubt signalling to Ben that the little confidences of the previous evening wouldn't be happening again.

And that the sooner this weekend was over the better.

In fact—and his jaw clenched when he thought of it now—she seemed to be determined to treat him as if he was just a hired tour guide. Bestowing bright smiles upon him and sticking to annoyingly trite and inconsequential conversation.

Determined to crack through that cheerfully icy veneer, Ben asked, 'So, did you sleep well?'

The dark glasses she wore hid her eyes, and when Ben glanced at her she was smiling brightly. 'I slept like a log, thank you. All this fresh sea air makes such a change from muggy city pollution.'

His jaw clenched again. Time to ruffle her feathers a little. 'Aren't you going to ask how *I* slept?'

She looked at him, and he could sense the glare behind those protective shades. 'I hadn't planned on it, no.'

'Well, if you must know,' he said, 'I didn't sleep well at all. Lots of tossing and turning.' He grimaced. 'And I had to take a shower during the night.'

Because every time he'd closed his eyes all he'd been able to envisage was an image of her, standing in her long red evening dress, looking crumpled but sexily dishevelled, and he'd wondered what it would have been like to go and pick her up and bring her into his bedroom—

'Well,' she said stiffly now, her faux brightness gone, 'we didn't *have* to do this today. You know, if you're too tired, you can always drop me off at the airport and I can get a flight home. That way you can get as much rest as you need.'

His mouth quirked. 'Not a chance. And I didn't say I was tired. I don't sleep much, as a general rule.'

She was practically bristling beside him now.

He continued, 'So, tell me about these ambitions of yours…the ones you mentioned last night when you were assuring me that a woman's life doesn't have to revolve around a man.'

She crossed her arms and stared straight ahead. 'I don't think that's any business of yours.'

'Maybe not,' he agreed, glancing across at her, his eye instantly caught by the lush curve of her mouth. 'But humour me?'

Damn the man, Lia thought churlishly. She'd bet money he was just trying to rile her. And her sense of complacency had gone out of the window as soon as he'd revealed that he'd taken a shower during the night.

It had been hard enough to maintain a cool front as soon as she'd walked into the kitchen and seen him sprawled in a chair, wearing faded worn jeans and a dark polo shirt, with bare feet.

His hair had still been wet and he'd looked at her over his coffee cup and said, 'You should have joined me for a swim in the sea this morning. It was magnificent.'

Instantly Lia had been bombarded with an image of their wet bodies entwined as waves crashed around them.

She'd forced a sunny smile and sat down, helping herself to coffee and ignoring his comment. 'It's almost hard to believe we were in New York this time yesterday, isn't it?'

Until now she'd kept up her valiant façade.

'Tell me about these ambitions of yours…'

Lia thought about his question for a long moment. This was exactly what she'd reassured herself she'd do last night—keep him at a distance. Get on a plane and go home. And yet…there was something inside her that felt as if it wanted to break free.

It might be the sun-drenched exotic surroundings and the sense of being out of her comfort zone, thanks to having been literally transported to another country. Or it might be the effort it was taking to resist this man's natural charm. Or, more dangerously, it might be the desire to reveal herself. Somehow along the way his opinion had come to matter to her—just a tiny bit.

She sighed volubly and Ben said cajolingly from beside her, 'It's another thirty minutes to Salvador…'

Treacherously, she felt resistance give way inside her. Angry with herself for giving in she said almost accusingly, 'If you must know, I studied Architectural Engineering at university.'

It was almost worth saying that to see the way his head snapped around.

Lia smiled sweetly. 'Didn't expect that, did you?'

Ben had the grace to look slightly sheepish and he said, 'When I met with your father at your house a few years ago he said you were on a skiing trip…'

Lia rolled her eyes. 'I've never skied in my life. I was in college. My father never liked to admit to anyone—or himself—that his daughter had ambitions and wanted a career. He preferred people to think I was a harmless socialite.'

Ben's jaw clenched and Lia saw his hands tighten on the steering wheel.

'I have to confess that I did assume you were part of a certain social set…'

Something tightened in Lia's chest. 'I guess that's understandable. Most people aren't interested in my qualifications.'

He glanced at her before looking back at the road. Lia was glad his eyes were covered. She wasn't sure if she wanted to see what was in them.

'So, what do you plan to do with your degree?'

She hesitated for a moment, and then said, 'I have a specific interest in crisis zones—in being the first on the ground to help with the rebuild.'

'Hence your interest in the charity whose benefit we were attending? They're renowned for the work they do in desperate situations.'

She nodded. 'I volunteered with them after an earthquake in South East Asia, and that's when I became really committed. I persuaded my father to support the charity too.'

Ben cast her another quick look, a wry tilt to his mouth. 'You weren't planning on shopping this weekend, were you?'

Lia shook her head, her heart tripping at the thought that she was telling him this. 'No, I had planned to go to a series of lectures at NYU.'

He said with a devilish grin, 'I'd be lying if I said I was sorry for upsetting your plans.'

Lia felt breathless again as something hot moved through her. Then Ben made a small whistling sound.

'Intelligent, noble *and* beautiful? If you're trying to turn me off, it's not working.'

Lia felt a rush of pride and berated herself for being so weak as to seek his regard. But still... The fact that he seemed to be so accepting of this more secret side to her meant something.

In a bid to deflect attention from her, she said, 'The CEO of that charity appeared to know you?'

He nodded. 'Believe it or not, I'm also interested in

what it takes to make disaster areas stable again. I've taken equipment and some of my men into crisis zones to help them stabilise buildings, the infrastructure. The truth is I'm one of the patrons of that charity.'

His words sank in and Lia turned in her seat to face him, shocked. Instant humiliation washed over her, because she'd believed he'd pursued her there for no other reason than to get her to agree to date him. *Because he'd wanted her so badly.* Now she felt like an abject fool—because he would have been there anyway.

Had he simply seen her there and made the most of the opportunity? More humiliation flooded her when she thought of how she'd just been laying out her accomplishments, seeking his approval. Lord, she had it bad.

Fury strangled her words, but eventually she got out, 'Stop the car—*now.*'

She had her hand on the door handle even before Ben pulled the car into a layby. As soon as it stopped she jumped out and faced him when he got out too and stood beside the bonnet. She pushed her sunglasses on top of her head and put her hands on her hips, not even sure why she was so angry...just that she was.

'So everyone there must have known exactly who you were, and yet you let me make a complete fool of myself—standing on that podium with no clue as to who on earth you were—'

He came towards her, cutting her off. 'My aim was never to make a fool of you, Lia. I hadn't intended on hiding my identity for as long as I did.'

He muttered something that sounded like a curse and pushed his own sunglasses to his head. His eyes were intense on her, making her regret reacting so forcefully.

Ben went on. 'The opportunity to talk to you without you knowing who I was too tempting. Especially after that date. And the truth is that I didn't want to see your reaction when you realised who you'd been talking to.'

Lia forced down the weak way she wanted to seize on that and folded her arms. 'That doesn't change the fact that you saw me and made the most of an opportunity. Were you bored? Was that it? You thought you'd have some fun at my expense?'

Ben frowned and shook his head. 'No, it wasn't like that at all. I had no plans to go to that particular function, Lia. I went because I found out that was where you'd be.'

The fire drained out of Lia's anger like a stealthy traitor. She believed him. He looked almost angry, as if he hadn't wanted to admit this to her. A muscle pulsed in his jaw.

Lia was embarrassed by the emotion she'd shown even as she began to feel mollified. She'd revealed far too much. So she just said, 'Okay,' and walked back to the car and got in.

Ben looked at her for a long moment as she buckled up, and then he got in too. For the remainder of their journey to Salvador they only spoke when Ben pointed out things of interest to Lia.

The fact that they *did* share a common interest in a cause very close to Lia's heart was something that she'd never expected, and it wasn't doing much to help her resolve to keep him at a distance.

CHAPTER FIVE

'THIS IS ONE of the earliest squares in Salvador, laid out by the then governor. And that is the Catedral Basílica de São Salvador—one of the most ornately decorated baroque churches in Brazil.'

Lia had thought she couldn't be more impressed than she already was, but as she followed Ben into the huge church off the beautiful square and saw how everything gleamed with gold—literally—her jaw dropped. She had to hand it to him for keeping this till last.

It was a fitting end to what she had to admit had been a very enjoyable day—after that skirmish by the side of the road.

Almost against her will Lia had found herself relaxing bit by bit as Ben showed her around the stunning city which had once been next in importance to Lisbon in the Portuguese colony. It was vibrantly colourful, with hilly cobbled streets and baroque architecture everywhere, and she'd been charmed from the start.

Everyone seemed to smile all the time, and the mix of cultures and nationalities—many of the population were descended from African slaves—added to the melting pot atmosphere. There was music everywhere, calling to a side of Lia that she didn't indulge often.

Just as she'd relaxed when she'd sunk her feet into the sand outside Ben's villa yesterday, something seemed to be unwinding inside her today. Everything about this place called on her to settle into a different rhythm. It was intoxicating. And Ben, surprisingly, was a brilliant guide. A natural storyteller.

He'd also proved himself to be a consummate gentleman. If he'd touched her at all it had been only fleetingly, to draw her attention to something—like when they'd stood on a bluff overlooking the city and the impressive bay. Perversely, that had seemed to have more of an effect on her than if he'd touched her with more intent.

He'd taken her to lunch to an admittedly dubious-looking restaurant on the seafront earlier. Catching her expression, he had chided softly, 'Don't let its exterior fool you—the owner keeps it looking like this to scare the tourists away. This place serves the best fish in Brazil, and it's for locals only.'

He'd been right. To Lia's surprise it had been pristine inside, and the fish had indeed been the best she'd ever tasted, served on a beautiful rooftop with trellised vines keeping the harshness of the sun at bay. The smell of the sea had only added to the taste.

She was acutely aware of Ben now, as he walked close behind her as they looked around the cathedral.

Lia stopped at the wooden altar, which was covered in a thin layer of gold. She shook her head. 'This is totally over the top, but it's beautiful.'

'I know.'

She glanced up to see Ben had come to stand beside her and was looking up at the ceiling. He said, 'They brought the stone for a lot of these buildings all the way from Portugal, on ships. The sheer industry involved is breathtaking.'

Lia hardly heard what he said. She was mesmerised by the strong column of his throat and that proud profile. The sensual curve of his fuller lower lip. She wondered about his early life. Where exactly had he dragged himself from to become such a titan of industry?

Just then someone bumped into her from behind, making her pitch forward into thin air, but within a split-second strong arms were around her and she was pressed close to Ben's side as he accepted someone's profuse apology over her head.

Lia's breasts were crushed against hard muscle, and every curve she had and even some she hadn't been aware of melted into Ben's form as if they'd just been waiting for this opportunity. Her hands were splayed across his chest and she was very aware of the thin material of his T-shirt. She'd noticed how it had moulded to those defined muscles whenever the breeze had caught it during the day. And the way his faded jeans clung lovingly to powerful thighs and tight buttocks.

For someone who up till now hadn't considered herself very sexual, some switch seemed to have been well and truly turned to *on*.

The tour group behind them moved on but Ben didn't release her. She was filled with lassitude and a reluctance to break free. Slowly she looked up—and fell straight into those bluer-than-blue eyes.

The memory of that hot kiss in New York emblazoned itself on her mind…she wanted to reach up and feel his mouth on hers again. Feel the slick slide of his tongue against hers. Something sizzled.

'I'm okay…' Lia finally managed to get out, pulling herself back from the brink of humiliating herself again. 'You can let me go now.'

For a moment Ben didn't, and Lia's heart spasmed with anticipation in the flickering glow of a thousand candles, and then he did, saying with a little grimace, 'As my thoughts are decidedly *un*holy right now, I think it's for the best.'

By the time they'd reached the entrance again and walked out, with Lia keeping a careful few steps behind Ben, she'd almost got herself under control. She'd just had a glimpse of how much he'd lulled her into a false sense of security, but instead of making her angry, she felt excited.

The setting sun was burnishing everything with blazing orange and pink, and some musicians nearby were infusing the air with a contagious tropical beat. An old Bahian couple danced together and for a moment Lia felt reckless, giddy. Just as she had on the dais at the auction... *Dangerous.* Maybe the intense smell of incense had got to her inside the cathedral? Maybe it was all part of this man's plan to break down her defences until she was just a weak, pliable mess?

Then he turned to look at her and every coherent thought left her head. She already was a weak mess. Pathetic.

Ben frowned then and plucked his phone out of his jeans pocket, looking at the screen. Lia hadn't heard a sound, so it must be on silent, and she only realised then how much attention he'd devoted to her all day, rarely looking at his phone at all—which, in this day of digital over-connectivity, was pretty amazing. Especially for an important CEO of his own company.

Her ex-fiancé, who'd had a far less important job, had always been glued to his *two* phones.

Ben looked at her. 'That was from a friend of mine who lives here in town. He's heard that I'm here and he's invited me to a party in his house tonight.'

Lia felt an acute sense of disappointment that their day was at an end and, terrified by that reaction, said quickly, 'Oh...of course you should go. I'm sure I can take a bus or a taxi back to the villa...'

He shook his head at her and his eyes gleamed. 'I don't intend to go alone.'

Lia flushed with a mix of pleasure and trepidation. Her feelings for this man had undergone a seismic change in just one day—helped by the seductive surroundings, yes, but also because he was proving to be far more enticing than she'd expected.

She'd thought it would be easy to dismiss him. To maintain her aloofness. But right now she was hot and sticky on the outside, and inside, in secret places. Although she had the sense to know that she was no real match for a man like Ben Carter, connoisseur of women. Playboy.

'I couldn't intrude, but you should go.'

Ben shook his head and asked softly, 'When was the last time you did something spontaneous and had fun?'

The question was so unexpected that Lia blinked for a moment. A kind of cold horror swept through her as she realised that she'd couldn't remember the last really spontaneous thing she'd done. If she'd ever done anything. And as for fun…? She'd had fun with her father on their sailing trips, but they hadn't done one of those for a long time.

As Louis Ford's daughter, not a lot of her colleagues saw her as someone to have fun with when she was keeping an eye on things for her father—no doubt afraid she'd report back to the boss. And, her relationship with Simon certainly hadn't been fun.

Absurdly, she felt her throat grow tight as the pathetic reality sank in. And through it all Ben just watched her with those bright blue eyes, seeing all the way through to where she was most vulnerable.

Lia fought to regain her composure and swallowed the lump in her throat. 'Well, if you're sure he won't mind…'

'He won't.'

Ben smiled, and it knocked the breath from Lia's chest.

'You'll see how things work here—it's much more relaxed. It's not just Luis, it's his husband, Ricardo, too. They love being surrounded by beauty—including beautiful women, so I'll soon be relegated to the sidelines.'

Something inside her contracted at his easy mention of these friends. And the truth was that she wanted to know more about Ben Carter—she couldn't deny it, much as she might want to.

She pointed vaguely at her attire, dusty and wrinkled after the long day, and said ruefully, 'I'm hardly dressed for polite company.'

'I know a place that'll look after us.'

Ben held out his hand. Lia looked at it for a long moment, and then an overwhelming sense of *rightness* made her put her hand in his. He held it as they left the square behind and walked back to the car. And Lia tried to ignore the sensation that she'd just turned a corner and she'd never find her way back.

But she couldn't. It sat in her belly like a fizzing time bomb.

Ben had taken Lia to a friend's boutique after she'd put her hand in his and let him lead her back to the car. Her agreement to go to the party with him had left him buoyant. Crazy how each tiny concession from this woman felt like a ridiculous triumph.

When they'd got to the boutique Ben had tensed, waiting for Lia to turn up her nose at the discreet name over the door, but she'd gone in, oblivious to his tension, showing him yet another facet of her personality—she obviously wasn't defined by designer labels.

Within minutes he'd explained what they needed to Gaby, Esmé's cousin and the shop's owner, and she'd handed Ben some clothes and whisked Lia out of sight behind a swathe of velvet material. Ben waited now, having changed into smart black trousers and a shirt.

When he heard a noise behind him he turned around and for a second his brain froze. Lia stood before him in bare feet, her hair tumbling around her shoulders. And her dress...her dress took his breath away.

It was a long silk wraparound dress in a deep royal blue colour that made her eyes pop like two gems. He could see a tantalising slit in the material that revealed one long shapely leg. He could see even from where he stood that in the space of two days her skin had taken on a faint golden glow, and he knew that there was already a spread of light freckles across her nose.

He felt robbed of breath. As if someone had punched him.

The vee neckline of the dress was a tantalising enticement to pull the material aside. It would be so easy to expose a lush breast and then cup its weight—

Lia started to turn away, saying, 'I knew it. It's too—'

Her voice cut through the haze in his brain. 'No!' His voice sounded too harsh to his ears.

She turned around again, slowly. Amazingly, she looked unsure.

'It's perfect,' he managed to say, sounding only half coherent.

Gaby appeared then, and caught the end of their conversation. 'Ben's right! It's just perfect for one of Ricardo and Luis's parties. And on you, my darling, it is *perfeito*. Come, let's find you some shoes to wear.'

Ben was glad of a moment alone to gather his wits again. What the hell was wrong with him? He'd seen plenty of women in far less clothing and it had never made him feel as if he was teetering on the brink of some kind of meltdown. And usually seeing women in clothes he'd bought them came *after* he'd slept with them.

So far his relationship with Lia was the most chaste he'd ever indulged in. He wasn't necessarily proud to admit that, for him, relationships with women were less about really getting to know them and more about slaking the desire he felt for them, which was usually fleeting.

He had a sense that where Lia was concerned his lust wouldn't be so easily slaked.

For the first time he had to wonder if he'd done the right thing, bringing her here... But then she emerged again, wearing strappy silver sandals, and that last thought was blasted apart by another surge of desire.

He instructed Gaby to put all the items on his tab and took the bag she gave him containing the clothes they'd been wearing earlier. Outside, Ben opened the car door for Lia to get in. He could see her biting her lip, looking concerned.

She stopped with her hand on the door and looked at him. 'I'll pay you back for the clothes.'

Confirmation of the fact that she wasn't spoilt. Another blow to Ben's misconceptions.

'Don't worry about it,' he said gruffly.

Lia slid into the passenger seat, her dress gaping slightly as she did so, affording him a glimpse of the curve of one perfectly rounded breast encased in delicate lace.

Gritting his jaw, Ben closed the door and strode around the other side of the car, praying for the strength to restrain himself. He'd never needed it more than right now.

Ben's friends were an exuberant couple who swept Lia into their embraces and their stunning baroque mansion, high on a hill overlooking the entire city, within seconds. Much to her amusement, Ben had predicted their reaction accurately: he was all but ignored as they grilled her.

'But where have you been all our lives?'

'This is a scandal! You can't live in cold, grey England—move here! We need more beautiful women!'

In truth, they were a little overwhelming, both at once, and soon Ben took advantage of more guests arriving, skilfully manoeuvring them to where long tables covered in pristine white linen groaned under the weight of more food than Lia had ever seen in her life.

Every delicacy was available. and she found herself gravitating towards the local fare, much to the chef's obvious pleasure, as he explained exactly what everything was.

Ben took their plates and Lia picked up their drinks. He guided her over to one of the many small round tables laid out for guests to eat at with ease. It was idyllic, with hundreds of candles flickering and the sparkling lights of the city below them. A jazz band played on a dais in the corner.

After they'd eaten a little, Ben sat back. 'You can admit it—you won't self-combust, I promise.'

She looked at him and knew instantly what he meant. A small, slightly smug smile was playing around that far too gorgeous mouth and something inside her just... *melted*. Also, far more disturbingly, that giddy reckless feeling was back. In the white shirt, open at the neck, he was astonishingly handsome. And the fact that he hadn't pushed her was working in his favour. Damn him.

She picked up a small morsel of cheese from her plate and threw it at him, saying grudgingly, 'Fine. Yes, I'll admit it. I'm glad I came to the party and I'm enjoying myself.'

He flicked the cheese off his shoulder and leaned towards her. 'It's polite to say thank you, you know.'

She could read very well in his expression how he might suggest being thanked, and for a second Lia desperately wished she had the confidence to pull him closer, so she could explore that mouth… She snapped her gaze back up to his, feeling hot. The thought made a spike of pleasure arrow between her legs, and she said, far too breathily, 'Don't push it, Ben.'

He just looked at her for a long moment. 'I won't… for now.'

And right then Lia's belly swooped, because in all honesty she wasn't sure if she could hold him back for much longer. Or if she wanted to.

'He's quite a specimen, isn't he?'

Lia jumped, and blushed when she realised that she'd been spotted ogling Ben—who was standing head and shoulders above everyone else in the crowd—by one of their hosts, Ricardo. The impressive sight of Ben had stalled her momentarily.

The handsome grey-haired Italian who she'd discovered owned several of Brazil's most luxurious hotels was looking at her now, assessingly.

'I…yes, I guess he's handsome,' Lia said weakly.

The other man snorted inelegantly. '*Cara*, he's certifiably one of the sexiest men on the planet, and right now I am jealous of *you*.'

Lia hid her discomfiture and smiled. 'Better not let Luis hear you say that.'

Ricardo waved a dismissive hand. 'Lusting after someone isn't a crime.'

Lia was curious now. 'How do you two know Ben?'

'Oh, we've known Ben since he started out, more or less. When he first set up his company we were among his first clients. We've always been interested in fresh new talent, and we'd seen some of his work in Manhattan. It's really amazing what he's achieved, considering the fact that he was once heir to one of America's biggest fortunes.'

Lia frowned. 'What do you mean?'

He looked at her, incredulous. 'You don't know?'

'Know what?'

Ricardo looked at her as if she'd grown two heads. 'Ben was born into American royalty—more or less. His father was Jonathan Carter, the man who practically owned Wall Street until it was revealed that he'd been defrauding clients and the market for years. Ben went from living in a mansion on the Upper East Side to a one-bedroomed shack in Queens overnight.'

Shock and disbelief reverberated through Lia as she looked across the crowd again at that broad back. Of course she knew who Jonathan Carter was—his name was synonymous with the global financial crisis, and much of the blame had been apportioned to him.

Just then Ben turned around, and his blue gaze lasered straight onto her. She felt the pull all the way across the room.

From beside her, Ricardo said mournfully, 'What I wouldn't give for him to look at me like that.'

Lia forced a smile and made her way back across the room, feeling seriously confused after Ricardo's revelation. She thought back to when it had happened and figured that Ben must have been only in his early teens—if that.

When she got closer, she saw that a very glamorous woman beside Ben had a hand on his arm. She embodied dark-eyed sultry Brazilian sexiness, with generous curves that defied gravity. Immediately Lia felt a surge of something almost violent, and when Ben pulled her close to him with his free arm she found herself revelling in the proprietorial gesture.

The other woman's eyes flashed with displeasure, but she blasted Lia with a fake smile and walked away. Suddenly aware that she was acting very much out of character, Lia tried to pull away—but Ben wouldn't let her, turning so that she was pressed to his front.

'What are you doing?' She looked up at him. What Ricardo had told her was making her feel off-centre. He really had built himself up from nothing. After having had everything.

'I'm thinking that it's time to go home.'

Lia looked around, momentarily disorientated, and re-alised that the crowd had thinned out substantially. It was a lot later than she'd realised. She looked back to Ben, feeling hot when she noticed the growth of stubble on his jaw. He was so masculine. And there was so much more to him than she'd ever given him credit for. He wasn't the only one who was guilty of prejudice.

'Okay.' Her voice was husky. 'Let's go.'

He took her hand to lead her out, and as they said goodbye to their hosts Lia felt genuine emotion at the thought that she probably wouldn't meet them again. She'd enjoyed herself more than she'd expected. She'd had *fun*.

Once back in Ben's Jeep, she kicked off her sandals and stretched out her feet. She couldn't help sneaking glances at his profile, stern in the shadows of the car.

As they left the city behind them, Ben asked lightly, 'So, what were you and Ricardo talking about?'

Lia tensed, feeling guilty even though she knew it was irrational. She could have found out about his past if she'd dug a little deeper. Her own innate sense of hon-esty made her say, 'I didn't know that your father was Jonathan Carter.'

Ben's hand on the steering wheel tightened, his knuck-les showing white. 'I should have guessed Ricardo wouldn't pass up the opportunity to gossip.'

Lia turned in her seat and rushed to defend the man. 'It wasn't like that. I asked him how he knew you and he happened to mention—' She stopped, recalling the exact words. Maybe Ben's friend *had* been a little gossipy.

Ben said dryly, 'Do go on.'

Lia swallowed. 'He just mentioned that he thought it was amazing, all you'd achieved, considering how your family had lost everything.' When Ben didn't respond, Lia said, 'It's not exactly common knowledge.'

He glanced at her. 'You mean because it didn't come up when you did an internet search on me?'

She turned back to face the front and said hotly, 'That's hardly fair. You knew exactly who *I* was when you asked the matchmaker to set us up.'

Tension thickened in the intimate space of the car, and then Ben said with evident reluctance, 'The reason why my past doesn't always come up is because people choose to forget what's not relevant any more. It's old news.' His lips twisted. 'Especially after my father had the temerity to die in relative squalor and solitude with my mother following him a year later. I guess they figured he'd paid his dues.'

Sensing he wouldn't appreciate platitudes, Lia just asked, 'How did they die?'

'My father drank himself to death. He'd always been a heavy drinker—albeit of fine whiskies, when he could afford them. The cheaper stuff didn't suit his system so well. And my mother had a heart attack. She couldn't come to terms with what the real world looked like.'

Lia was silent, absorbing the enormity of what he'd just revealed. 'That's why you don't drink?'

He nodded, the lines of his face stern. Lia figured it was no surprise, after seeing his father poison himself. She knew enough about him now to know that he would consider that an immense failing in personal control.

She could imagine him as a young boy—handsome and privileged, no doubt attending the best schools, with his future mapped out. The world at his feet. Only to have it ripped apart and the grim reality of how things really were revealed. No wonder he'd thought he had her all summed up.

Sensing he'd appreciate a change in subject, she asked, 'So why Brazil? Do you have a special connection to here?'

Ben glanced at her again and she caught the gleam of something wry in his expression. 'Did Ricardo stop gossiping long enough to answer your actual question?'

Lia frowned. 'He said that he'd seen some of your work in Manhattan…'

'Yes, and then he approached me with an offer to bid for the work on one of his hotels in Brazil. It was just when my company was starting to break even.'

'How old were you?' Lia asked.

Ben shrugged minutely. 'About twenty-five.'

Lia held in her shock. Some achievement, indeed. Clearly he'd been very driven, and questions abounded in her head as to what had happened after his mother had died. She knew what everyone else knew, about the foster homes, but how had he crawled out of that to achieve such meteoric success?

Ben continued. 'I went down to Bahia to see the site, and after a meeting Ricardo signed me up then and there. After completing the job I realised I'd come to love the place—it was like a breath of fresh air. Different, vibrant. Unstuffy. So I decided that I'd build a holiday home there. My family used to have a house in North Shore on Long Island. The community there, who had once been like family, completely ostracised us when my father lost everything. But as soon as I started to make a name for myself, some of my father's old cronies came out of the woodwork, as if nothing had happened. The last place I wanted to be was back in that stuffy environment.'

Lia could hear the bitterness in Ben's voice and read between the lines. Where had those 'friends' been when he'd been alone and defenceless?

Lia said lightly, 'Sounds like you made the right decision.'

She could feel him looking at her, but she didn't want him to see the mix of emotions she was trying to hide. She'd felt off-kilter from the moment she'd laid eyes on this man, and now it was even worse.

When Ben drove through the gates leading to his villa a short while later, Lia realised she'd been engrossed in her own circling thoughts. Ben got out of the driver's side and came around to help Lia out—the perfect gentleman. She only realised her feet were still bare when they hit the sharp gravel and she let out a squeak.

Before she knew what was happening she was being lifted into Ben's arms and he was striding into the villa as if she weighed nothing.

'You don't have to carry me,' she said, but it was too late. They were inside, and he was putting her down.

Her head was whirling. She couldn't look at him, overwhelmed with some nameless emotion.

But Ben caught her chin with a finger and tipped her face up. He frowned. 'What is it?'

The fact that she felt absurdly close to tears was horrifying. She bit her lip, and then said, 'I don't know... I'm just...I'm sorry for what you went through. I can't imagine how awful it must have been.'

Ben's expression became shuttered in an instant, and he let her go so fast that she almost lurched forward.

He backed away, his lip curling. 'What? You're feeling sorry for me now because the poor little rich boy lost everything and had to slum it? Suddenly everything's more palatable now that you know I was born with a silver spoon in my mouth?'

Horror that he could think such a thing, and hurt, made Lia put out a hand. '*No!* I didn't mean it like that at all—'

But he cut her off, saying harshly, 'It was the best thing that could have happened to me. It woke me up to reality before I could get too cushioned by life. I knew not to take anything for granted, as my father had done. Not to grow complacent. I learnt the value of hard work and building something with your own hands—something that won't collapse.'

'I can understand that,' Lia said quietly, hating it that he'd misunderstood her.

Ben looked at the woman in front of him, her hair tousled and that glorious dress falling to the floor where her bare feet peeped out. She was all slender curves and pale skin.

He knew he was wrong about her—that she wasn't a snob. And he knew what he'd just said hadn't been fair. But right now he was filled with something that was threatening to push him over the edge. He'd never revealed so much to anyone. Never spoken about his past like that. About his father's drinking. His mother's weakness.

Lia stepped forward, her hand out, her eyes wide and full of something Ben didn't want to decipher.

'Ben, I'm sorry, please let me explain—'

He tipped over that edge. '*No,*' he said harshly. 'You don't need to explain anything because I'm not interested in talking any more. All I'm interested in is *this...*'

Before she could say another word Ben had closed the distance between them, taken her face in his hands and was kissing her. Kissing her the way he'd been aching to kiss her again. For a long second she was frozen in his arms, and then she was moving closer and reaching up. Pressing her body against his.

Everything was forgotten as she twined her arms

around his neck. Their angry words were decimated in the heat of this passion. Their mouths fused for a long moment, as if the intensity was too much to break, and then subtly Ben coaxed her to open her mouth to him. When his tongue touched hers he was lost, drowning in a sea of sensation and growing lust as he demanded a response, which she gave willingly.

He moved his hands down her back and settled them on her hips, hauling her closer. Close enough so she could feel what she was doing to him, where he ached most of all. Lia gasped into his mouth but he didn't let her break away. He never wanted to let her go again...

Between Lia's legs she felt damp and hot. Her breasts ached, pressed tight against his chest. But somehow a tiny sliver of sanity returned and she tore her mouth away from Ben's, breathing as if she'd just run a marathon.

They'd combusted. That was the only word for it. She'd never felt anything like it. She hadn't even known she was capable of this much feeling.

'I can't—' she gasped incoherently, too far gone to be embarrassed. 'This is too...too much.'

The look in Ben's eyes was hot and feral. 'It's not nearly enough.'

He caught her hand and led her deeper into the living room. Lia's body throbbed in time with the blood pumping to every erogenous zone. Ben took her over to one of the couches and made her sit down. She was glad, because her legs were shaking.

He stood above her, looking down with a kind of intensity that scared and excited her in equal measure.

'You're so beautiful...'

She went to pull the edges of her dress together, feeling exposed, thinking of that buxom Brazilian beauty earlier. 'I'm not...'

He came down on his knees before her then, taking her by surprise. He put his hands on her thighs and gently pushed her legs apart, moving between them. His eyes burned into hers.

'Yes, you are. And I'm sorry for lashing out just now... you didn't deserve that.'

His apology struck at the heart of her. 'That's okay...'

He put his hands on her hips and pulled her towards him so that she lay back on the couch. She whispered through her erratic heartbeat. 'What are you doing?'

He smiled, but it was the smile of the devil. Dark and decadent. Sexy. 'Something I've wanted to do from the moment I saw you in this dress.'

He leant forward, putting delicious pressure on her between her legs, and slowly but methodically pushed her hands out of the way so that he could pull apart the neckline of her dress, all too easily. Lia remembered his look in the shop, and instead of feeling self-conscious, something scarily exultant moved through her.

Her delicate underwired blue lace bra opened very conveniently from the front. Ben undid the catch and pushed the lace material aside. He cupped one full breast with his hand, making it pout upwards. Lia's breath stalled as shards of pleasure raced through her body. Excitement fizzed in her veins. And then Ben bent his head and tongued her nipple, bringing it to tingling hardness before he sucked it into his mouth.

Lia had a moment of sheer disbelief that this man could possibly want her this much before sensations she'd never felt before swamped her and removed her ability to think. Without even registering the movement, she found her hands were in Ben's hair and she was clutching him to her breast. Eyes shut, heart pounding...

He was reaching right down inside her and unlocking the door to all the insecurities she'd buried deep. And she couldn't stop him. Because the pleasure was eclipsing any fear she might be feeling—if she was even capable of being rational right now.

When Ben finally lifted his head from her tender flesh she opened her eyes, and it took her a second to focus and realise that she held his head in a death grip.

She let go immediately, horrified. But Ben just smiled. He lifted a hand and brushed some hair back off her cheek in a surprisingly tender move, even as she felt the hard length of his erection near the apex of her legs. She was aware that if she moved slightly it would create the friction she suddenly needed.

Who *was* she? What had she become?

'You look deliciously…undone.'

Ben's voice was gravelly. Lia looked at him, feeling twin desires: to move and pull her dress around her again, and also just to lie there and offer herself up to him.

He started to press kisses down her torso, his hands reaching around and finding where the dress was tied, undoing it easily, the silk like water in his hands. Soon he had her dress pushed apart completely, and he looked down at her blue lace panties.

Immediately Lia had a memory of her ex-fiancé, recoiling in horror when he'd first seen that she didn't shave all over, and she tried to sit up awkwardly, putting a hand down to cover herself.

Ben caught her, though, stopping her hand with his, looking at her. 'What is it?'

Now she felt horribly rational, and exposed and sane. Her ex-fiancé wasn't remotely in the same league as Ben, and if *he* had found that part of her a turn-off…

She looked away. 'I'm not…' She forced herself to look at him. 'I'm probably not like your usual lovers…'

Ben looked down between her legs and then back up, incredulous. 'Because you don't shave?'

Lia gulped. *God, this was excruciating.* She nodded. His face flushed and he took her hand and brought it down until he could place it over the bulge between his legs. The very hard bulge. Now she flushed.

'Sweetheart,' he growled, 'when I make love to a woman I like to know she's a woman. And right now I need to taste you, more than I've ever wanted to do anything else. Will you let me taste you?'

Something scarily exultant ripped through Lia. He wasn't turned off. He wanted to taste her. Did that mean he wanted to do what she'd seen Simon doing to his secretary when she'd walked in on them that day? The thought sent her mind reeling. It had looked so decadent to her at the time. And she'd never got over the jealousy that he'd been moved to do that to this lover, not to *her*… And now this man was asking her—

Before she could lose her nerve, Lia said huskily, 'Okay.'

Ben reached for the sides of her panties, expertly pulling them down and dropping them near her feet. She was bared completely now, the silk of the dress falling away as he pushed her thighs apart even more.

Lia closed her eyes and bit into her fist as Ben's head dropped and she felt his mouth on her soft inner thigh, pressing kisses and nipping at her skin gently. She was in danger of hyperventilating again, especially when his mouth moved higher, closer to the apex of her legs.

She didn't think he could spread her any wider but then he did, his big hands high on her thighs.

As if reading her mind, he commanded, 'Look at me.'

Reluctantly she opened her eyes. Ben had taken off his shirt and his chest was bare and massive. She couldn't breathe as he bent forward and pressed his mouth to her, his tongue hot and wet as he dragged it up the secret folds of her body.

Lia's breath returned and she hitched in big gulps as that dark head bobbed and moved between her legs. His hands looked massive on her pale skin.

Ben looked up, 'Touch your breast.'

Feeling dizzy, even though she was all but lying down, Lia brought a hand to her breast, trapping a nipple between her fingers.

'Now, squeeze...' Ben instructed softly.

She did, and gasped as an arrow of pleasure went straight to her groin. Ben smiled and it was wicked as he bent his head again and tortured her with his mouth and tongue.

When he pushed a finger deep into the heart of her she arched her back off the couch, and then it became two fingers, thrusting in and out as his mouth and tongue lapped at her with fierce intensity.

Lia couldn't hold on. The coil of tension inside her snapped and she cried out as pleasure exploded her into tiny pieces. Waves of after-shocks rocked through her body for long moments, and she only became aware of her surroundings again when she could open her eyes and blink to focus, realising that Ben had lapped all that pleasure from her body and was now pressing lazy kisses to her inner thighs.

She felt undone. Turned inside out. Totally exposed but too spent to do anything about it. She realised that she was still squeezing her breast, almost painfully, and let go.

CHAPTER SIX

WHEN BEN FINALLY straightened up, tearing himself away from Lia's intoxicating taste and scent he was not prepared for the glorious sight of her looking so shocked. Her hair was a dark cloud around her head. The blue silk dress was crumpled beside those lush curves.

The realisation that she looked so stunned stopped him from automatically moving his hands to his belt to seek his own relief. He ignored the insistent ache in his pants and rested his hands on her knees. 'Are you okay?'

After a moment her eyes seemed to clear and she nodded. But he noticed that she reached for her dress with visibly shaking hands, pulling it over her as much as she could. The heat in Ben's blood cooled a little and he moved back so that she could pull her dress down, concealing that glorious body from view.

'What is it, Lia?'

She looked at him for a moment, almost accusingly, but he just looked right back. Making a little huffing sound, Lia scooted back on the couch until she was sitting upright. She bit her lip, but then eventually said, 'One day I walked into my ex-fiancé's office and found him with his secretary. He was doing what you just did to me to her...' She trailed off.

Ben tried to make sense of what she was saying. 'That's why you broke it off? He was unfaithful?'

She nodded jerkily, her face crimson now. 'Yes, but the thing is I've only ever slept with Simon…'

Ben would have never envisaged this scenario in a million years. In one fell swoop any remaining misconceptions he might have had about Julianna Ford were blasted apart. She was inexperienced, and she was achingly vulnerable right now, even though he could tell she hated it from the way her hands held her dress together in a white-knuckled grip.

And instead of feeling the urge to get up and run in the opposite direction Ben got up and sat on the couch beside her, feeling something close to protective.

Lia looked at him. 'I'm sorry. I'm not very experienced.'

Ben felt something dark rise up. 'What happened with this ex-fiancé?'

Now she went pale. 'When we made love for the first time…it hurt. A lot. After that I didn't really want to… to make love.' She grimaced. 'It wasn't as if we were in love. We'd both agreed to the marriage for our own reasons. But he told me that I was frigid, and that was why he was sleeping with his secretary. I couldn't…didn't want to get married after that.'

Ben reeled. He wanted to find that man and punch him for betraying this woman, for leaving her confidence in tatters. Never in Ben's life had he been remotely interested in the notion of taking a woman's virginity, but now he felt a ridiculous sense of loss, just imagining the way her rutting fiancé had probably not even realised the jewel he'd had in his hands. This woman was *not* frigid. Not remotely.

Then he thought of what else she'd just said. 'Why did you agree to a marriage of convenience?'

As if the questions were probing too deeply, Lia got up off the couch, still graceful even while she was deliciously dishevelled. She turned her back to Ben and pulled the dress around her, tying it in front.

When she turned around again it was all Ben could do not to yank her back down onto his lap.

She folded her arms over her chest, as if she could hear his lusty thoughts. 'It was primarily for my father. I told you…he's traditional. He believes I'll only be secure if I'm settled. He was sick a while back and I got a fright… He begged me to give Simon a chance—he knew he'd been asking me out on a regular basis.'

She shrugged and looked down, scuffing the floor with her toes. 'I went out with him and it turned out that we were both happy enough to agree to something more…clinical than a romantic relationship.' She looked back at Ben, almost defiant. 'At the time it seemed like a good idea.'

'You don't need to convince me,' Ben said with a bitter edge to his voice. 'After seeing how little there was to hold my parents' marriage together when the crisis hit, I'm under no illusions about the myth of a romantic ideal.'

For a long moment neither said anything else and then Lia took a step back.

Ben stood up. 'Where are you going?'

Middle Earth, hopefully.

Lia had been ready for the ground to open up and swallow her right from when she hadn't been able to stop the verbal equivalent of *This is My Life* from spilling out. She blamed Ben, and the fact that he'd wrung a response from her body that she'd never believed she'd feel.

He was looking at her now as if she had two heads, and the thought that he might pity her after what she'd just told him was making her burn with mortification. Of anything she might have expected from this man, she'd never expected that. Nor wanted it.

She struggled to look cool and calm, even though she was in tatters. 'I'm going to bed.'

Ben shook his head. 'We're not done here.'

Excitement and trepidation warred in Lia's chest. Ben was unmistakably alpha. Maybe he saw her as some kind of challenge?

'Look,' she said, 'I know this isn't what you expected when you thought of indulging in a weekend fling. I think we've established that I'm not exactly cast from the same mould as your usual women.'

She went to walk past him, instinctively seeking a place where she could be alone and deal with her sense of exposure without that incisive gaze watching her every move. He'd laid her bare—completely. She'd been right to resist him.

A hand on her arm stopped her. She looked up.

Ben pulled her around in front of him. 'There are no other women. There's only you. Are you saying you don't want this?'

Lia flushed at his words. *'There's only you.'* And how could she deny she wanted this when she'd just been writhing and moaning under his expert touch?

She said tightly, 'You really don't owe me anything, Ben. If you just feel sorry for—'

His hands tightened on her arms so much she stopped talking. He looked incredulous. 'Feel *sorry* for you? Believe me…that's the last thing I'm feeling right now. I want you, Lia. Because you make me feel like I'll combust if I don't have you. And that's not pity. That's desire.'

Suddenly she didn't have anything to hide behind. He was calling her out.

She felt nervous. 'I'm not experienced enough for you… I'll disappoint you.'

He speared her with that bright blue gaze, like two flames. 'You couldn't disappoint me if you tried, Lia.

And there's no such thing as inexperience—there's just how two people fit together. You're not frigid—not remotely. That man was an idiot, and he couldn't recognise a brilliant precious gem when it was right in front of him.'

Ben's words reached deep inside her and melted the insecurity Lia had been carrying around like a weight.

He moved closer, as if sensing her vacillation. 'I want you, Lia, more than I've ever wanted another woman. But if you can say that you truly don't want this, then I'll let you go.'

He took her elbows in his hands and pulled her gently to him until they were touching. If she'd had any doubts about how much he wanted her, or thoughts that he just pitied her, they fled when she felt the hard, thrusting evidence of his desire against her soft belly.

Her heart started to pound and her blood heated. Her defences were annihilated. And then she felt a spike of anger. Anger that he'd brought her here and laid her bare, forced her to delve deep inside herself to where she ached and wanted…so much. Where she wanted *him*. Forcing her to admit it.

She felt fierce. 'I can't tell you that.'

Ben was intense. 'What can't you tell me?'

She looked up into his eyes and drowned. 'That I don't want you.'

Lia didn't care any more how or why she'd got here, just that she was, and she didn't want to be anywhere else. She desperately wanted Ben to show her again how she could respond to a man. That she wasn't frigid.

As if reading her mind, Ben bent and lifted her into his arms. And then he was carrying her up the stairs.

She was mesmerised by his jaw, by the play of the powerful muscles of his chest under her arm. Breathless at the thought of what she was doing, and so far out of her comfort zone that it wasn't funny, she pushed all her trepidation down.

Ben shouldered his way into his room, and Lia was vaguely aware that it was just as palatial as hers but more masculine in tones and colours. And then her gaze fell on the massive bed in the middle of the room and her mouth dried completely.

A part of her wanted to leap from Ben's arms and run away fast, but a stronger part realised that she wanted to be strong—for this, for herself. Her confidence had been eroded when she was a young child, when her own mother had rejected her, forcing her to shut away a part of herself for fear of rejection. Then she'd let Simon decimate her confidence as a sexual woman. It was time to restore the balance.

Ben put her down near the bottom of the bed. His voice was deep, rumbling in the silence. 'You can let your dress go.'

Lia looked down and saw her almost white-knuckled grip on her dress. She uncurled her fingers, undid the tie and let it go. It swung open, catching on the slopes of her breasts.

She heard a sharp intake of breath and looked up to see Ben's eyes on her.

'So beautiful,' he muttered as he brought his hands to her shoulders and pulled her dress off them and down over her arms, until it fell to the floor in a sibilant *whoosh* of silk. Her undone bra followed.

Now she was naked, the ends of her hair tickling the bare skin of her shoulders. Ben's eyes had darkened and Lia gritted her jaw to kill the instinct to cover herself with her arms; she didn't want him to see how vulnerable she really felt. No doubt he was used to women parading themselves in front of him.

Instead, just to do something to break the almost overwhelming tension, she reached out and touched his chest tentatively. It was muscled perfection, broad and strong. Defined pectorals with a dusting of dark curling hair led down to the ridges of a six-pack and his flat belly, with its single line of dark hair dissecting the muscles and disappearing under his trousers.

Ben sucked in a breath and, emboldened, Lia explored further, spreading her hands across his chest. They looked tiny and pale next to that burnished skin. She could feel his heart thumping solidly, and some nameless emotion gripped her tight. But she ignored it. Now was not the time for emotion.

She raked her nails over him experimentally, catching a nipple, making him take another sharp intake of breath. He caught the back of her head, his fingers tangling in her hair. She looked up and felt drugged.

Not taking her gaze off his, she let her hands feel their way to his lean waist and found where his belt was buckled. She looked down and undid it, and then her hands were on his button and the zip. She could feel the insistent thrust of his erection through his clothes, and a wave of heat scorched her from the inside out and between her legs, where she felt damp again. Hot.

She pushed his trousers down over his hips and he stepped out of them, letting her go momentarily. Then he pulled down his briefs until he too was gloriously naked. She'd never been more aware of herself as a woman. There was something very elemental about this moment, with everything stripped away.

Unable to resist, and not even recognising herself any more, Lia reached out and encircled his hard flesh with her hand, stroking him up and down, mesmerised by the vulnerability of his erection and also the steely strength. The velvet texture of his skin. She touched the bead of moisture at its head and spread it with her thumb.

At that Ben took her hand from him and she looked up. 'I won't last if you keep touching me like that.'

He caught her hand and brought her around the side of the bed, urged her down onto it, following her. He looked massive from where she lay, all wide shoulders and chest and long, lean body.

Every nerve in her body was tingling. She could feel Ben's erection against her thigh, hard and heavy. *Big.* She felt a shiver of trepidation, remembering the discomfort she'd felt with her fiancé and how she'd failed to excite him, but again, as if reading her mind, Ben distracted her by moving between her legs, spreading them wide.

With his elbows trapping her, he cupped both her breasts and teased her tingling nipples with his thumbs, before lowering his head and sucking first one and then the other into his hot mouth, torturing her with his wicked tongue.

As the flames of lust licked higher and higher Lia moaned softly. She wanted to squirm, to arch her back, but her movements were restricted by Ben's big body holding hers down. It was an exquisite form of torture, and as he lavished attention on her breasts he moved subtly against her, notching his hips higher, until she could feel the blunt head of his erection move against her where she was slick with desire.

She widened her legs even more and tried to move her hips up, wanting him to fill the part of her that ached. Then she heard a muttered curse and Ben suddenly rolled away.

Lia lifted her head. She realised she was panting. 'What's wrong?'

For an awful second she went cold, imagining that he'd realised she wasn't enough for him... But then she saw him extract something from a drawer beside the bed, heard foil tear, and then he was rolling protection onto his thick length.

Relief flooded her and she lay back. Ben knelt between her legs. Lia was all but splayed before him, like some kind of offering. But then, instead of coming over her again as she'd expected—*as she wanted*—he reached out a hand and touched her where she ached most. Where she was embarrassingly wet for him.

He circled her with his thumb, ratcheting up the tension inside her. Dipping inside, and out again, lubricating her with her own juices.

'You want me.'

She wondered how on earth he could doubt it. Then she gasped and her back arched as he slid two fingers into her. She said jerkily, 'I told you I did.'

Lia could feel her muscles tighten around his fingers. Heard him curse softly. She felt too exposed. She didn't want him to make her come like this, while he watched.

She reached out and wrapped her hands around his arms. 'Please... Ben, I need...' Her back arched again as he thrust his fingers deeper, playing her like a violin. She lifted her head, hating the power he had over her right now, and said fiercely, 'I need *you*.'

Ben finally took his hand away, and then he loomed over her, his thighs pushing hers apart, and she slid her hands up to his shoulders.

'Look at me,' he said roughly. 'Don't *ever* doubt that you are a very desirable woman, Lia.'

She looked down and saw him take himself in his hand as he guided himself towards her, and then he fed himself into her body, slowly, inch by inch, making her draw her breath in on one long inhale as he impaled her...*utterly*.

He was big...bringing her almost to the edge of discomfort. But he held himself still for a long moment, letting her body adjust to him. And then, when she took another breath, he started to move, and everything in Lia's world was reduced to the here and now. This moment. This man. And the exquisite sensations rushing through her body.

She'd never felt anything like it as a wholly new tension built inside her with every movement of Ben's body in and out of hers. She wrapped her legs around his back, heels digging into his taut muscles. His hand gripped her thigh and his movements became less careful, a little rougher.

He came closer, moved down over her, making his chest hair abrade her still sensitive nipples. She reached up and found his mouth, and as everything inside her coiled to a point of excruciating pleasure/pain she pressed a desperate kiss to his mouth until finally she was broken apart into a million shattering pieces.

She was barely aware of Ben's own shout as his body tensed over hers for a long moment, muscles locked and taut as a paroxysm of pleasure held him in its grip too.

When Lia woke she felt completely disorientated, recognising that she wasn't in her own bed, or room. And then she felt the unfamiliar aches in her body and memory came rushing back.

Dawn was breaking outside, bathing Ben's room in a pink pearlescent hue that didn't diminish the masculine tones one bit. Gingerly, Lia moved her head, and sucked in a breath when she saw the unashamedly male and indolent sprawl of a very naked Benjamin Carter beside her.

Even like this, in repose, he was magnificent... Dark stubble lined his jaw, making him look rakish. Long lashes should have prettified the stark and strong lines of his face but they didn't. He looked marginally less fierce, especially when those blue eyes weren't watching her and gauging her reaction to every little thing. She might hate him for that if she wasn't feeling so...*sated*.

Her gaze travelled down over hard muscles and her face grew hot when she saw that most masculine and potent part of him—no less impressive at rest.

They'd made love again last night, after that first cataclysmic time. The second time had been slower, more luxurious, but no less intense. A surge of emotion made her throat tight. She wasn't frigid. *At all*. In fact the woman revealed under Ben's expert tutelage was sensual and voracious...and he had shown her that. As easily as flicking a switch to let light into a dark room.

Lia sucked in a breath. That was exactly what he'd done. He'd shone light into the dark corners of her soul, where she'd felt closed-off. Deficient.

His expert dismantling of her defences had started yesterday. By the time they'd gone to his friends' party they'd already been crumbling, thanks to their idyllic day spent walking around one of the most beautiful cities in the world, with surely one of its most charismatic and charming guides...

A voice mocked her: who was she kidding? Her defences had been crumbling from the moment she'd bumped into him outside the Algonquin Hotel in New York.

And then something cold flickered down Lia's spine as she registered the full magnitude of just how easily and completely she'd capitulated. It really hadn't taken much at all, in the end. She'd proved no less susceptible than any other woman to this man. Finding out about his troubled past had only added another layer of depth to a man who was fast becoming far too complex and fascinating.

And now there was this—the ultimate intimate exposure. She'd slept with him because he'd made love to her mind as much as to her body. He'd delved deep and she'd let him in, far more than anyone else.

Emotions she'd never felt before rushed around her in a sickening mix…fear, exultation, hope.

It was the hope that brought her back to earth with a bang. Hope…for *what*? The kind of thing she'd always told herself didn't exist? Hope that she wouldn't face the excruciating lash of rejection if she opened herself up to someone?

As Ben had said himself the previous evening: *'I'm under no illusions about the myth of a romantic ideal.'* And neither was she, she assured herself, but for a dizzying moment there she'd felt hope—and that was dangerous.

The thought of Ben waking, and of herself trying to act blasé when she had no idea how to navigate this kind of situation, made her go cold all over. She had nowhere left to hide.

Her mother's abandonment had not only devastated her father—it had devastated Lia. The knowledge that she hadn't been lovable enough to make her stay had been indelibly inked into her skin from a young age, and Lia knew now that that was at the heart of why she'd avoided intimacy for so long, and why she'd agreed to a marriage of convenience.

She'd found it easy to dissociate, not to engage, because no one had ever broken down the walls she'd erected…until now. The galling reality that she could be as susceptible to heartbreak as her father after years of avoiding it made her feel nauseous.

Ben would see through her in an instant—see all her weaknesses. And, worse, possibly even see that flicker of hope. The part of her that wasn't half as cool and collected as she'd always thought she was. Impervious to fickle emotions.

Lia slid out of the bed, making not a sound. Ben moved minutely, frowning in his sleep, but then he relaxed again, and her heart pounded with a mixture of panic and desperation.

Benjamin Carter had somehow managed to slide under her skin enough to make her realise that all the foundations she'd worked so hard to build up were far shakier than she liked to admit. And that was enough to drive Lia as far away from this man as she could go.

The following morning Ben padded through the villa in a pair of hastily pulled on shorts with an uncomfortable feeling of foreboding prickling along his skin. He'd woken shortly before to find the space beside him in bed empty. And Lia hadn't been in the bathroom.

When he'd woken, at first he'd registered a deeper feeling of satisfaction than he'd ever felt before. A memory had surfaced: after they'd made love again last night Lia had been draped over his body, her head in the crook between his head and neck, her body a deliciously curved and pliant weight on his.

He'd stroked his hand up and down her back and said gruffly, 'See? I told you… It's nothing to do with experience. We *fit*.'

She'd made a huffing noise into his skin, clearly too exhausted to speak. And Ben had smiled…before falling asleep and waking to find her gone.

Ben didn't usually wake with the expectation of finding a woman in his bed—he preferred to keep that boundary firmly intact—but it hadn't even entered his head with Lia.

He frowned now, when he saw she wasn't in the main living area, but still wasn't unduly concerned. She had to be here somewhere.

For the first time in days, since he'd first laid eyes on

her, Ben's head was feeling clear again. He'd known he wanted her, but he hadn't expected their chemistry to be so explosive. And when he found her he was going to convince her to stay another day… He was going to woo her and persuade her to consider marriage—because if she'd considered it once before she'd have to be open to the option again—in spite of the way it had turned out. Clearly it meant a lot to her father, and he obviously meant a lot to her.

Lia Ford was not the one-dimensional person he had believed her to be at the very start. She was bright, sharp, compassionate, *passionate*.

He thought about how he'd felt claustrophobic when the idea of taking a wife had first been mentioned to him…how he'd felt when he'd sat down to discuss it with the Sheikh and the others. But now the prospect of making Lia Ford his wife appealed to Ben in a way that he hadn't ever thought it would.

He realised that he'd seriously underestimated how much a woman like Lia could contribute to his life. They had ideals and goals in common. The more he thought about it, the less he felt inclined to take a wife who would just be meek and biddable. He wanted someone with fire, and Lia had that in spades. She was spirited and unafraid to stand up to him, and he liked that.

And for the first time he even found himself thinking of children. Of what it would be like to have a son or a daughter. Something in Ben's chest grew tight at the thought of a small dark-haired child with sparkling blue eyes running around.

He'd never allowed himself to contemplate it before, because his own experience of watching his parents crumble so catastrophically under the strain of their lives self-destructing had scarred him enough to never want to risk subjecting any child of his to that.

But now he felt he could consider it for the first time. A woman like Lia would never crumble. She would get up and start again. Their marriage would be nothing like his parents'—falling apart like a flimsy structure at the first inkling of trouble.

Ben was in the kitchen now, but that too was empty. He ignored his growing unease and the fact that the villa was too quiet. As much as he admired Lia's independence, and the fact that she obviously wasn't one of those women who liked to cling like an octopus the morning after, he just wanted to find her now.

A sense of relief hit him when he thought of the beach—of course she'd be there. But when he walked out onto the pristine sand, he saw that his stretch of private beach was empty. No supple pale body was lying out under an umbrella.

He heard a sound and whirled around, but it was just Esmé, carrying flowers into the villa. She called out sunnily, 'Morning, Boss. You slept late—not like you at all.'

Ben felt like scowling at the reminder that last night had made its mark, but he forced a smile, following Esmé back into the villa. 'Have you seen Lia?'

She whirled around, frowning. 'You don't know?'

Ben was seriously struggling to hold his irritation in. 'Know what?'

Esmé put the exotic blooms carefully on a table, her face a picture of quizzical innocence. 'She left early this morning. When Joao dropped me off, she got a lift with him back into Salvador. She said she had to take the first flight to New York today, then get back to the UK. I presumed you knew... She said she didn't want to wake you and left you a note. I put it in your office.'

As Ben watched Esmé start to put the blooms in a large vase on the table in the centre of the hall he felt something wide and uncomfortable open up in his chest.

And sheer incomprehension. No woman *ever* walked away from him. But this one had. Twice now.

He turned before Esmé could make anything of his reaction, went to his office and saw the folded-over note with *'Ben'* written on it in a very feminine script. He opened it to read.

> *Dear Ben,*
> *Thank you again for your kind donation to the charity. I think after last night the terms of the bid are well and truly fulfilled. After all, this was never going to go beyond the weekend, was it?*
> *I've enjoyed my time here in Bahia—thank you. I doubt I'll run into you again.*
> *Best wishes,*
> *Lia Ford.*

The chasm opening up in Ben's chest snapped shut suddenly and became a hard, heavy weight. The insinuation that she'd slept with him more to fulfil the terms of the bid and less because she'd wanted to was not welcome.

He crushed the piece of paper in his hands as something broke the heavy weight apart—anger.

He'd underestimated her—*again*. But she'd underestimated him if she thought that she wouldn't run into him again. He was going to make very sure that she did run into him again—and this time she would not be running away. Because she was perfect for him. And no way was he letting her, or this opportunity, slip out of his grasp.

CHAPTER SEVEN

'WHERE'S YOUR FATHER, LIA? Not ill again, I hope?'

Lia felt like hitting the smug smile off the face of one of her father's biggest competitors, who was making it very obvious that he *did* hope her father was ill, but instead she smiled beatifically and said, 'Of course he's not ill, George.' Her smile stayed fixed as she went on, 'He's actually too busy to be here this evening—which is why I have to say I'm surprised to see *you* here. Didn't you know that this evening is the construction union's annual winter party?'

The man's already florid face grew redder as he blustered, 'Well, yes, of course I did…but I wouldn't normally think of going to one of those events—'

Which is why you're only a fraction as successful as my father, she thought to herself privately, even as she said a placatory, 'No, of course not. Most people don't. He will insist on going, though—every year—and his employees seem to love him for it.'

The man was backpedalling away from Lia so fast that she nearly laughed out loud. It was a little mean of her, she knew, to tease him like that. But in fairness her father *had* put in an appearance at the union party largely because it wouldn't be filled with vultures ready to pick him apart to see just how robust he was.

She'd just been informed that he was back, via one of his usual slightly ham-fisted texts, which was all in caps.

I'M HOME NOW. DON'T WORRY. HOLD THE FORT
FOR ME, DARLING. DAD. XX

Lia sighed. That was what she felt as if she'd been
doing all her life. Holding the fort for her father, who had
never really recovered after her mother's abandonment of
them both. But she pushed that moment of uncharacteristic self-pity out of her mind now. She didn't want anyone
here at this exclusive London charity bash to suspect for
a second that everything wasn't absolutely fine.

So she pasted on another bright smile when she saw
two more of her father's biggest rivals bearing down on
her, with glints in their eyes. But just before they reached
her something in her peripheral vision made her look to
her left and her heart stopped beating. Almost literally
stopped.

It was Benjamin Carter, standing at the main doorway,
dressed in a classic black tuxedo, scanning the room as
if looking for something. Or some*one*. His bright blue
gaze—visible even from where she stood—landed on her
and stopped. Lia felt its impact immediately, deep in her
body, like an electrical shock.

Everything dropped away. She was aware of voices
from nearby, aware that she was meant to be responding
to something, but had no idea to what.

It felt as if seconds had passed since she'd seen him,
but it had actually been a week.

A week since she'd left this man lying on his bed
amongst tangled sheets, with her heart pounding so
hard she'd been able to feel it. It started again now, as
he walked towards her, and she drank him in helplessly.
He looked taller, darker, and more handsome against the
backdrop of this much paler British crowd.

For an awful second she wondered if she was hallucinating—she'd believed she'd never see him again, and

had done her best all week to repress the memories and images. But at night her subconscious hadn't been able to stem the tide, and each morning she'd woken hot and sweaty, with the sheets tangled around her body after X-rated dreams.

He closed the distance between them with long strides, the crowd parting like water and hushed whispers following his progress. He reached Lia and she was struck mute.

Without taking his eyes off hers, he said, 'Gentlemen, please excuse the interruption, but I have some unfinished business with Miss Ford.'

And then he reached for Lia's hand, taking it in a firm grip, and started walking back out of the room, taking her with him. The lust that flooded her body at the touch of his hand told her that she wasn't hallucinating—as did the excitement mixed with shock in her blood.

Lia had to lift her long black silk dress in one hand, afraid of tripping. She caught sight of herself and Ben in a long mirror and saw that she looked tiny behind him, her shoulders bare in the long strapless dress, her hair upswept into a rough chignon.

Panic flooded her system as the reality sank in that he was really here. If he guessed for a second how deep he'd sneaked under her skin... The panic intensified. She dug her heels in and tried to pull her hand free, but his only tightened.

He stopped and turned around, a fierce expression on his face. Gone was the civil, suave man she'd first met. He was angry. But instead of feeling intimidated she found her anger matched his. Anger at him for coming into her world like this. For upsetting her equilibrium again.

'What the hell do you think you're doing?' she snapped. 'You're on my turf now.'

Ben arched a brow. 'Oh, forgive me, Lady Ford, do you own this hotel?'

She flushed. 'No, of course not.' Then she arched her own brow. 'Do you have a private plane stashed on the lawn at the back? Are you planning another little kidnap stunt?'

He kept her hand firmly in his and faced her fully, his free arm snaking around her waist and pulling her close. She went on fire when she felt his burgeoning erection between them. His eyes gleamed when he saw her reaction. Lia was acutely aware of the audience around them, and cursed herself for not waiting to confront him until they were somewhere more private.

'You asked me a question.'

Lia frowned. 'What question?'

'In that kind note you left, you said—and I quote— *"This was never going to go beyond the weekend, was it?"'*

Lia flushed hotter. 'That was a rhetorical question.'

Ben shook his head. 'Not any more—because I believe I've just answered it.'

'How?'

He moved against her subtly, explicitly, leaving her in no doubt as to what he meant. Then he said throatily, 'I suggest you come with me right now—unless you want to treat your peers to the kind of show they'd prefer to watch in private or on pay per view.'

Some emotion Lia didn't want to name surged through her as the knowledge sank in—*she wasn't dreaming.* He was here and he still wanted her. And, heaven help her, she wanted him too... She'd run scared in Brazil, but right now she couldn't exactly recall why it had been so imperative to get away from him.

Displaying his uncanny ability to read her mind, Ben was making the most of her hesitation and continuing on

ABBY GREEN 135

his journey out of the room, leading her into the hushed lobby of the very exclusive London hotel.

A lift door opened nearby and Ben diverted suddenly, pulling her in with him just as the doors closed again, almost catching Lia's dress. The lift started to ascend. And suddenly in the confined space, with Ben taking up most of the room with his big body, the panic returned. He really was here. And now she really had nowhere to hide.

'This is crazy, Ben! You can't just remove me to wherever you like, whenever you like.'

She watched as he hit a button with the palm of his hand and the lift shuddered to a halt. Between floors. He finally let her hand go, and caged her in with a hand on either side of her head.

'I have issues with your note,' he said, in a low, deep drawl that impacted Lia right between her legs.

The panic was draining away, to be replaced by something hot and illicit in her blood. And, more dangerously, the memories she'd been repressing all week were starting to break free of their moorings, flooding her brain with images and rising desire.

'Primarily,' he continued, oblivious to her inner turmoil, 'the bit where you assumed that our...liaison wouldn't last beyond the weekend.'

Lia was feeling breathless. Was it her imagination or were the mirrors in the elevator starting to steam up? She struggled to recall what he'd just said, and then asked, 'Is that what it was? A liaison?'

Again, as if she hadn't spoken, Ben said, 'Do you really think I spent all that money just to get you into my bed?'

Lia wanted to squirm. Of course she didn't. Not any more. But that was where the danger lay...in thinking about what he wanted from her outside of this insane heat. Or, worse, what *she* wanted. When she'd protected herself for so long—even going so far as to agree to a marriage of convenience.

She shook her head now. 'No, I don't think that.'

A slow, sexy grin spread across Ben's face and Lia's legs immediately felt weak. The tension thickened between them. He wasn't going anywhere.

The giddy recklessness she'd felt in New York came back. Maybe he was here to finish what they'd started in Brazil. One more night? Two? And then he'd go back to his own life. After all, she reminded herself through the gathering heat in her brain, Ben didn't *do* relationships, did he?

And neither did she. She shouldn't have panicked in Brazil—it could have burnt out there. But she had. And now he was here. So maybe it would be okay to just… let it burn out. Here, as opposed to there. Did the geographics matter?

The fevered circling thoughts all led to one conclusion: Lia giving herself permission to stop fighting the inevitable. Resistance melted and she dived into the fever growing in her blood.

'Kiss me, Ben.'

Stop the chatter in my head, a small voice begged.

He smiled, wickedly accepting her capitulation—*again*—and then he cupped her face in his hands, tilted it up to his, and kissed her, stroking his tongue into her mouth, deep. Reminding her of the exquisite pleasure he'd given her, and the gift of the knowledge that she wasn't cold inside.

That alone made emotion surge again, and Lia wrapped her arms tight around his neck as if that would contain it. He'd flown all the way across the world to kiss her like this, deep and hot and wicked. And she would take it—because this was finite.

She arched her body into his, her blood throbbing in

time with her heart when she felt the very masculine evidence of his arousal against her. His hands moved down her sides to her buttocks, where he cupped her through the slippery material of the dress.

He pulled back long enough to speak as he lifted her up, instructing, 'Wrap your legs around my hips.'

She did it mindlessly, her dress sliding high on her thighs as he lifted her effortlessly. She hooked her legs around his waist. Kissing her again, Ben slipped a hand underneath the dress and explored between the lace of her panties and her bottom, caressing her bare skin. She moaned into his mouth, dizzy.

Her bare upper back was against one mirrored wall of the lift, and Ben angled his hips so that the bulge of his erection pressed against her, between her legs, where she was wet and hot.

Her dress felt too tight. But even as she was thinking that Ben was sliding his fingers under the top of it and pulling it down, so that one of her breasts was freed. He pulled back from the kiss, and stared at her. He looked drunk, dazed.

Lia was vaguely aware that the only things holding her up were the wall and Ben's hand on her bottom. Because now he was thumbing her nipple and she was biting her lip.

'Please…' she begged.

He looked at her, and some hair flopped forward onto his forehead.

She brushed it back, feeling inordinately tender. 'Touch me…like you did before.'

He smiled, and it was wicked. He lowered his head and flicked his tongue against her straining nipple. He looked back up, all innocence. 'Like this?'

'Yes…' Lia growled, feeling even needier now. 'Damn you…*more.*'

His eyes flashed and he lowered his head to her breast and took her nipple deep into his mouth. Lia tensed, to try and hold off falling over the edge, but Ben was remorseless and his hips were making thrusting movements against her... All he'd have to do would be to slide her panties aside and free himself and he'd be inside her, where she needed him so badly.

Shocked at the completely wanton direction of her thoughts, and at how desperate her desire was, Lia's eyes snapped open.

In the reflection of the mirror behind Ben she saw her long pale legs, wrapped around his slim hips, and his dark head at her breast. She saw her own flushed face, blue eyes glittering fiercely. Her hair was mussed and her mouth was swollen. And they were in a lift.

She tensed even more and gripped Ben's hair, pulling his head up. 'We can't make love here—in a lift.'

Ben looked about ready to refute that statement, but then he seemed to come to his senses and straightened up, removing the delicious friction of his body from Lia's. She immediately felt bereft.

'Actually,' she said, feeling reckless and changing her mind abruptly, 'I've never made love in a lift...the idea is growing on me.'

Ben looked stubborn. 'No way. You're right. I'm not going to be the crass American caught *in flagrante delicto* in one of London's most exclusive hotels.'

Lia felt a little shard pierce her. He was not crass—at all. Ben unhooked her legs from his hips and helped her stand again. She was wobbly on her feet and only belatedly realised her breast was still exposed when the lift started moving again. Ben efficiently covered her up, his fingers brushing against her sensitive skin.

Just in time, too, because the doors opened and an older couple with severe expressions got in, muttering about how long they'd had to wait for the lift. Lia had to stifle her giggles and Ben took her hand, gripping it tight.

The lift came to a halt again and she followed him out, not having a clue where they were going until he stopped outside a door and unlocked it with a hotel key. The fact that he'd booked a room at the hotel made something bloom in her chest—something she hadn't allowed room to breathe since she'd taken that flight from Salvador, back to New York and then home.

Hope.

The door shut behind them and Ben had her lifted against it with her legs around his hips before she could take another breath.

'Now,' he said throatily, 'where were we?'

Dawn was breaking outside when Lia awoke. For a few seconds she lay there, blinking, taking stock of all the pleasurable aches in her body. She was aware that her dress was hanging precariously off the end of the bed, and that there was a trail of destruction along the floor from the doorway to the bed, of her underwear.

She blushed when she thought of the urgency of their lovemaking against the door of the suite…and then the much more languid second time…and the third.

She turned her head to see Ben sprawled in unashamedly masculine splendour. Déjà vu made her feel momentarily dizzy and her heart hitched. Instinctively she started to move, but those blue eyes snapped open and before she could take another breath he had her trapped under one powerful thigh, a hand on her breast. Lia's blood leapt, and her sleepy body was awake and humming in seconds.

'Where do you think you're going?'

His voice was deliciously rough. Lia could feel her nipple peaking under his palm and he moved it so that he could flick it with his thumb, rousing it to a sharp point. She almost groaned, but forced herself to put her hand over his—which didn't really help.

All her bravado, and the justifications she'd used in order to acquiesce to Ben's lovemaking last night, felt flimsy in the cold morning light. Her emotions were too raw all of a sudden.

'I should go.'

Ben ignored her hand on his and continued torturing her breast. He also subtly moved his thigh, so that his erection nestled close to the juncture of Lia's legs.

'I think that's a very bad idea.'

Ben bent his head and started to press kisses along the exposed shoulder nearest to him. His hand deftly dislodged hers and he pinched her nipple between his fingers, just as his hot mouth found and started torturing her other breast.

Not able to hold back the groan this time, Lia felt all resistance fade as Ben's hand smoothed its way down over her belly to between her legs, pushing them apart so his questing fingers could seek and discover for himself how much she wanted him—again. Already.

He lifted his head and smiled smugly. A surge of irritation at her own weakness galvanised Lia to move and she took him by surprise, coming up to straddle him, her hands holding his arms back behind his head. She knew he could break free easily, but it was still momentarily heady to have him at her mercy, however illusory.

She moved her body back until she could feel the head of his erection against her and, keeping it between them, slowly started to move up and down, sliding her body along his thick length, seeing his face flush and his pupils dilate.

'Witch,' he ground out, and she could feel him lengthen and grow harder under her.

Their breathing became more laboured as Lia obeyed the dictates of her body to go faster, press down harder. Ben lifted his head and captured her nipple, biting gently with his teeth. It sent a shudder all the way down to between Lia's legs.

And then, proving how little control she really wielded over him, Ben moved and she was flat on her back, trapped under him again. He reached for protection and expertly rolled it over his erection, and then, before Lia could take another breath, he was sinking deep inside her, his eyes on hers, not letting her escape for a moment.

The climax that broke over them came swiftly and was brutal in its power, washing everything else away. And in the shuddering aftermath, when Ben pulled Lia close and wrapped his arms and legs around her, something inside her just…melted.

Lia was feeling marginally restored as she belted a thick robe around herself after taking a quick shower. When she'd woken again Ben hadn't been in the bed and she'd spied him in the living area, dressed in dark trousers and a long-sleeved thin grey jumper that did nothing to disguise his muscles. He was pacing up and down while talking on his mobile phone, so she'd taken quick advantage, locking herself in the bathroom.

She'd avoided looking at herself in the mirror, not wanting to see the aftermath of their cataclysmic night and morning. She'd also avoided letting her mind stray to dangerous thoughts like, *Why did he come here really?* And, *What happens now?* She'd decided she was just going to nip it in the bud now because sleeping with Ben again had only reinforced her fears about not being as emotionally detached as she'd like to be. As he undoubtedly was.

When she padded into the living area of the plush

suite, Ben was seated at the table, reading a newspaper. He put it down as she approached and that blue gaze swept her up and down. Even under the thick robe she could feel herself respond.

'I've ordered some clothes for you to change into.'

For a second she felt inordinately touched at his consideration *and* relief for the fact that she wouldn't have to do the walk of shame out of the hotel, into the glaring London daylight. 'Thanks, I'll pay you back.'

His eyes flashed at that, but he let it go as she sat down and looked at the array of breakfast/brunch items laid out. 'I wasn't sure what you'd like, so I ordered a selection.'

Lia slid into a chair, avoiding his eye. Her pitifully few experiences of morning-after situations with her ex-fiancé had been sterile, dispassionate affairs—she'd never experienced this intense level of awareness before.

'Coffee will do for now.'

Ben reached for a tall slender pot and poured fragrant coffee into a cup. She couldn't take her eyes off his hands: large and masculine, yet elegant, too. She fought back a blush as she thought of how they'd felt on her skin, and took a quick sip of coffee to try and dislodge her lurid memories.

When she felt able, she looked at him. 'So...what's your plan while you're here in London?'

Ben looked at her and a small smile played around his sensual mouth. '*You*, Lia. You're my plan.'

To hear him confirm that he really was here just because of her was seriously disarming—and overwhelming. Emotion swelled and it made her want to push him back.

She put down her cup with a jarring clatter of porcelain. 'You can't expect me just to drop everything to accommodate you. I have a life here...work.'

Ben's eyes narrowed on her. 'Work for your father? Like you were doing last night...being his emissary?'

Lia felt immediately defensive. 'It's a family business.'

'But what about your plans for your own work?'

She immediately regretted telling him all that she had. 'I don't think you're here to discuss my career options.'

Ben inclined his head slightly in concession. 'Not really, no. But as it happens I have an office here in London. I'm taking advantage of the trip to check in with my team on the ground. We've got several projects in development, and they're setting up some meetings for me while I'm here.'

Lia cursed herself for not guessing that he had an office in London, or checking.

He leaned forward then. 'But, more importantly, I want to get to know you better, Lia. That's really why I'm here.'

Her silly heart hitched as trepidation warred with that illicit sense of hope. She'd run from this in Bahia and he'd chased her down. She was afraid that she wasn't strong enough to walk away again. And he knew it.

Ben felt a surge of triumph when Lia didn't immediately jump up from the table at his declaration that he wanted to spend time with her, and tried to hide it from his expression.

Even though she'd acquiesced to him last night, he'd known she'd be prickly in the morning—no doubt lambasting herself for her weakness. And he knew that a large part of why she'd succumbed had been because he'd all but ambushed her.

He was still reeling from the effects of seeing her again after a week. He had intended to come to London, find Lia at the charity function where he knew she'd be, and woo her. Show her how determined he was to get to know her. But he'd taken one look at her across that crowded room and something inside him had turned feral.

He'd *had* to have her. And then he'd morphed into some kind of caveman, all but dragging her into that lift, and if she hadn't stopped them when she had...

But he could see now that her expression was closing off, becoming shuttered. Those beautiful eyes becoming unreadable.

He shook his head, 'Don't do that, Lia.'

She looked slightly alarmed. 'Do what?'

'Retreat behind that prim wall you put up.'

He reached for her, taking her hand and pulling her out of her seat and over to him before she could object. He tugged her down into his lap and stifled a groan when she came into contact with a still sensitive part of his anatomy. The hunger he felt for her was alarming...he was used to it diminishing with a lover. But what he felt for Lia was getting stronger.

Ben knew that if he hadn't been there because he wanted to woo her into considering a very long-term arrangement with him, then he would most likely be running from the intensity he felt when he was around her.

He assured himself that it was all part of the plan. Lia was important to him because of what she represented. The fact that they were combustible in bed was a bonus he had every intention of exploiting to its full potential.

She looked at him, with a wary expression on her face that made Ben wonder if she was reading his mind.

'What are we doing here, Ben?'

If any other woman had asked him that question Ben would definitely be running. But right now the last thing he felt was an urge to leave.

'Well, for a start, we're not leaving this hotel room for the whole weekend.' He could see Lia's immediate reaction to that—rejection—and he said quickly, 'Look, neither of us is what the other expected—would you agree?'

Slowly, she nodded her head. 'I guess so.'

Ben started moving his hand in small circles on her back. His other hand was on her thigh and he exerted slight pressure, seeing how her eyes flared with heat. He would use everything in his arsenal if he had to—unashamedly.

'I want to know more about you. And there's too much heat between us to walk away yet. Spend the weekend with me.' Ben mentally assured himself that by the end of the weekend Lia would be his—in more ways than one. Didn't women find whirlwind affairs romantic?

His hand explored underneath her robe to find the silky skin of her bare thigh. He felt the immediate reaction of her body.

She put her hands on his chest. When she spoke again, her voice was breathy. 'Look, I—'

She stopped and bit her lip when Ben's hand delved between her thighs, opening them slightly. She tried to glare at him, but it didn't entirely work as her cheeks had gone pink.

'Damn you, Ben.'

He smiled, feeling wicked. 'So, what do you say?'

His hand was moving higher now, closer to the hot juncture between her legs. He was ruthless—but she wasn't stopping him from pushing her legs further apart.

He could feel her heat and smell her sweet, musky arousal, and the friction against her pert bottom only made things more acute. He shifted slightly, so that she could feel what she was doing to him.

By now her breath was choppy. He could feel the tension in her body as she fought not to give in to him. 'Just the weekend, you say?'

Ben wanted to growl at her insistence on putting boundaries in place, but he resisted the urge. In another couple of days all those boundaries would be gone.

'Yes, just the weekend.' He ignored his conscience.

He'd seduced this woman into his bed—he could seduce her into marriage.

She looked at him for a long moment, with such intensity that Ben almost wanted to hide from her searing gaze, and then, abruptly, she moved. For a second Ben thought she was getting up to leave, but then she was lifting a leg over his lap and coming back down to straddle him.

Her robe had parted marginally and she moved her hips against him in a small undulating movement that made him bite back a curse as he felt her naked flesh press hotly against the erection straining against his trousers.

She cocked her head. 'Well, for starters, you're way too overdressed for a weekend of debauchery...'

And with that she reached for the hem of his top, pulling it up so that he had to raise his arms, and then it was off, landing on the floor.

She'd taken him by surprise again. Ben was so taken aback at her capitulation that he could only sit there for a moment, and then she grinned at him, bright and sudden, and he felt it like a punch in his gut. He also felt something constrict in his chest but he pushed it down, focusing on the physical.

He dislodged her hands with ease and pulled at the rest of her robe, baring those beautiful breasts to his gaze. He cupped them, dragging his thumbs across her stiffening nipples, and heard her sharp intake of breath.

By the time he'd licked and sucked those peaks to sharp wet points Lia was lifting herself up from his lap and fumbling with his trousers, freeing his aching arousal from its confinement. By the time he was sheathed with protection and embedded in her snug embrace they were both breathing as if they'd run a marathon, a glow of perspiration coating their skin.

Lia's robe was off, on the floor behind her, and Ben didn't even have any recollection of pushing it to the ground, the conflagration between them had been so swift and sudden. He surged up into her body, over and over, his arms welded tight across her back.

Lia pushed him right to the edge, and over, every time. Her face was flushed, she was biting her lip, and her eyes were glazed with passion... Ben realised with satisfaction that he was seeing her come undone, exactly as he'd imagined when he'd looked at her that first evening they'd met.

Except his sense of satisfaction was short-lived. Nothing in his imagination could have prepared him for this reality, or the sheer strength and awesome power of the climax that ripped through them within minutes of their bodies joining.

For a long moment in the aftermath Ben's head rested helplessly on Lia's breasts. She had her hands on his head, fingers funnelled deep into his hair, holding him there. He was still embedded deep in her body and he could feel the rhythmic post-orgasmic flutters of her body along his length.

He realised that even if he'd wanted to pull away from the embrace he couldn't.

When he finally was able to move he lifted his head and looked at her. The fact that she seemed similarly shattered was absurdly satisfying, but that was almost immediately followed by a sensation of uneasiness as Ben realised that whenever he'd believed he had her where he wanted her before, she'd eluded him.

He was a man who exerted control in all things, and he would make sure that didn't happen again. There was no room for failure here. Lia was an acquisition he couldn't afford to lose now.

* * *

'What day is it?' Lia said sleepily into the pillow as she felt a finger trace the bones of her spine.

Amazingly, her body tingled and she groaned. She heard a deep chuckle and wanted to scowl, but she didn't have the energy.

Mustering all the strength she did have, she turned over, dislodging Ben's hand and pulling the sheet up over her body. She glared at him balefully.

He held up his hand, his face a picture of innocence. Well, if you could call his stubbled gorgeousness innocent. Which, of course, he wasn't—remotely. He was wicked, and he had made her do unspeakably wanton things for hours and hours; night had melted into dawn and then day, and then dusk and then night... And now it was getting dark outside again. The world might have ended and Lia wouldn't know.

'You didn't answer my question.'

Ben put his hands on either side of her body and leant over her, his chest broad and bare. 'It's Sunday evening— and I don't think I can take another Room Service meal.'

Lia reeled. She'd known what day it was—of course she had. But still... To hear him confirm that they'd passed almost three full days gorging on each other in a feast of the senses was overwhelming. She now knew, indelibly, that under Ben's expert touch she'd discovered her own sensuality and had learnt to revel in it. For that alone she'd lost a part of her soul to him.

She seized on his words, glad of an excuse to get out of this far too intimate space. 'I know a place near here...'

Ben smiled, and before Lia could stop him he'd whipped the sheet from her body. She squealed as he effortlessly lifted her into his arms. He strode into the bathroom and put her down to switch on the shower. She shivered with anticipation, unable to help herself.

Under the powerful spray of the water moments later, as Ben lathered shampoo into her hair and massaged her skull, Lia was glad she was facing away from him so he couldn't see her face. Because suddenly she felt bereft. It was Sunday evening and their weekend was almost over.

She'd left him behind in Bahia because she'd known that he'd slid under her skin...and now? Lia closed her eyes, as if that could help block out the suspicion that sliding under her skin was only the half of it. She was afraid she'd lost a whole lot more than a piece of her soul to Ben Carter.

He turned her around then and she kept her eyes closed, desperately telling herself, as his clever hands explored her slick body, that this was just lust clouding her brain and making her think crazy things.

For a moment she felt almost angry—that he'd managed to seduce her soul as well as her body so easily. Damn the man. She'd never wanted to go the way of her father—crippled by rejection. Not that Ben would even reject Lia—oh, no, she couldn't imagine him being so crass. He would do it with a silky touch and a devastating kiss and leave her reeling, wondering what had just happened...

But now Ben was sliding his hands between her legs, finding where her body was her ultimate betrayer and saying, 'Look at me, Lia.'

So, even though it was the last thing she wanted to do, she welcomed the distraction from her whirling, dangerous thoughts and assured herself that she would be fine. And she opened her eyes and kept them on him even as he tipped her over the edge and she screamed out her release...even as she was afraid that her worst fears would manifest in spite of everything.

CHAPTER EIGHT

LIA MIGHT HAVE regretted bringing Ben to her favourite restaurant if she hadn't been so hungry and in a physically weakened state from an overload of pleasure.

She took in the exposed stone walls covered with sepia-toned pictures of Italian scenes, slightly mottled with age. The small tables covered with checked tablecloths and the small vases filled with fake posies of flowers.

Feeling defensive, even though he looked remarkably at ease and delicious, dressed casually in faded jeans and a light woollen jumper, Lia said, 'I'm sure you're used to more salubrious establishments…but it's unpretentious and the food is to die for.'

Ben looked at her and smiled that wicked smile. It was as if he'd reached out and stroked her skin with his finger.

'If I'd known you were such a cheap date I'd have taken you to Jersey shore instead of Bahia.'

Lia's pulse tripped at his teasing.

And then he leaned forward and said conspiratorially, 'I'll have you know that I spent many a weekend serving margherita pizzas, and lasagne, to hungry New Yorkers while I worked my way through college.'

Lia seized on the opening he'd given her. 'How did you get to college?'

'As a kid from a foster home?'

She half shrugged and nodded. He knew she wasn't a

snob, that she hadn't meant it like that. But she *was* curious to know how he'd begun his climb to the top.

Their starters had been served, and Ben took a bite from his *calamari fritti*, and wiped his mouth. 'After my parents died I was sent to my first foster home in Queens.'

Lia frowned. 'There were no friends or family who could take you in?'

A hard gleam came into Ben's eyes, turning them cold. Lia repressed a shiver and remembered what he'd said about people turning their backs on his parents after the scandal.

'My parents were both only children, and their own parents were dead. My mother had trouble conceiving. I was the result of years of IVF treatment.'

Lia took some of her soup but didn't taste it. Her whole attention was on Ben. She put down her spoon. 'What was it like…after they died?'

He looked at her. Strong, formidable. It was hard to imagine this man ever being vulnerable.

'It was tough…but it was almost a relief. They'd both fallen to pieces in the aftermath of the scandal. My father had become a bitter drunk. I used to come home from school, after another beating for my accent and different mannerisms and the fact that I was way ahead of everyone else in my class, to find him passed out on the couch. My mother was totally helpless. A Long Island princess living a nightmare. I had to do everything for them.' His jaw tightened. 'But that wasn't what bothered me the most—it was the fact that they gave up so easily.'

Lia tried to ignore the tightening in her chest. 'You got beaten up for your accent?'

He nodded. 'Every day. Until I realised that I had to fight back. And I did. I learned to blend in. By the time my parents died no one from my previous school would have recognised me.' He looked at her with a warning light in his eyes. 'It's not a pretty story, Lia.'

'If you think I'm looking for pretty stories then you still don't have a clue who I am,' she fired back.

Ben shook his head, an enigmatic look in his eyes. 'Tell me again why it is that you're not sunning yourself on some millionaire's yacht and worrying about tan lines?'

She arched a brow. 'That's the only choice open to me, is it? I could ask the same of you—you've surely earned enough by now...'

Ben lifted his glass, mouth quirking, 'I deserve that. *Touché.*'

When he stayed silent, though, still waiting for an answer, Lia said, 'I told you—it's never been what interests me. I was always nerdy at school—more interested in studying than in gossip or clothes—which didn't exactly earn me lots of friends.'

Ben tilted his head to one side, with a look in his eyes that she didn't quite like. 'Why is it that I get the impression that you were a shy kid? You were shy that evening up on the podium at the auction too.'

Lia sucked in a breath. Was she so awfully transparent to him? His perspicacity made her feel vulnerable.

He was waiting for her answer, and she was tempted to laugh it off, but then she found herself admitting, 'I *was* shy as a child. Cripplingly so. I had a stammer. And I used to blush all the time.' She desisted from revealing her mother's intolerance of that.

'But you got over it,' Ben said, and she heard the admiration in his voice.

Lia shrugged. 'I had to. I couldn't let it blight me.'

Their main courses arrived, and Lia seized the opportunity to divert his far too perceptive gaze from her, saying, 'You still haven't told me how you got to college.'

He gave her a look that told her explicitly that he didn't normally accept this level of grilling from anyone, but she just raised her brow again. He'd grilled *her*, and he'd comprehensively upended her life—this was the least she deserved.

Eventually he sighed and said, 'It started with a cop—an Irish/American called Clancy. He picked a bunch of us up one day. By the age of sixteen I was in a gang. We were on our way to becoming serious delinquents—cutting school, shoplifting. I hadn't come on his radar before, so he looked into my background. When he found out where I'd come from he took me aside and laid it on the line. He told me that I'd already had more of a chance than any of those other kids, and that I was squandering the legacy my parents had given me.'

Ben shook his head.

'I was hard work by then—seriously angry and bitter with the world. He almost didn't get through to me...but he persuaded me to take part in a mentoring programme where local businessmen took on kids for internships. I ended up working as an intern for a local construction guy, and that was the start of it. I got out of the gang... stayed out of trouble as much as I could. It helped that I'd got moved to a more stable foster family. When I graduated from high school my mentor helped me get a scholarship to college and I did my basic degree. From that moment on I spent every minute either waiting tables or working on construction sites all over New York, and as soon as I got an opportunity I took it and didn't look back.'

Lia absorbed this and tried not to let herself picture the young angry teen at war with the world around him and grieving for so much. She knew instinctively that Ben wouldn't appreciate it. So instead she forked up a piece of her *carpaccio* and said lightly, 'Is *that* all?'

Ben just looked at her—and then he threw back his head and let out a sharp laugh. When he looked back at her there was something like grudging respect in his eyes and her chest expanded with a rush of emotion. *Dangerous.*

He shook his head. 'You never fail to surprise me, Miss Ford.'

She smiled back, even though the realisation of how happy it made her to make him laugh scared the life out of her. 'I try.'

His eyes narrowed on her then, and he said, 'So, why do you protect your father so much?'

Lia put down her fork, immediately feeling defensive. 'It's always been just the two of us…' She hesitated, and then said, 'After my mother left he never really recovered. For years he's suffered ill health, and I've always suspected it's mental as much as physical.'

'You can't take up the slack for him for ever.'

'I know that,' Lia said, the habitual weight of her father's expectations resting on her shoulders.

Ben was looking at her, and for a second she allowed herself a very illicit daydream of what it would be like to lean on someone else… But she ruthlessly shut it down.

The waiter appeared beside them, breaking the tension, and without looking at the man Ben said, 'We'll take the cheque, please.'

Lia felt relieved that Ben wasn't going to say any more about her father. Emotions she never usually allowed room to breathe were rising inside her, and when Ben held his hand out for hers, after leaving money on the table, she gave it without hesitation.

The cold air outside the restaurant didn't help with restoring her sense of equilibrium. It was as if Ben had unlocked a box and now everything was spilling out—everything she'd kept locked up for years. For ever.

He turned to her, his face lean and beautifully stark in the early-evening light. 'Lia—'

She reached up and put her hand over his mouth. His breath was warm against her palm. 'Just kiss me, Ben.'

She was afraid that if she said any more she would want more than he was offering. He put his hand over hers and pressed a kiss to her palm, and then he pulled her in close, right into his body, and kissed her deeply and thoroughly. It was as effective a way as any to block out the thoughts and feelings she wasn't prepared to inspect. *Yet.*

Ben seemed perfectly happy to avoid talking too, bundling her into a taxi before things got too heated in the middle of the busy street. The atmosphere in the back of the taxi was thick with sexual tension, and by the time they eventually reached the hotel suite again they couldn't even make it to the bedroom, stopping at the first soft surface, their urgency so frantic that when it was over Lia realised that they were both still partially dressed.

By the time they did make it to the bedroom, and Ben took off the rest of her clothes as reverently as if she was made of china, Lia knew that she was in serious trouble. No amount of distracting sex was going to keep the emotions and thoughts bubbling just under the surface at bay.

Lia was luxuriating in a hot bath early the following morning, while Ben was taking some calls on his phone, dressed fetchingly in nothing but a towel. She could get used to this decadent lifestyle, she thought to herself, as long as the Pandora's Box of emotions she'd been avoiding dealing with since the previous evening stayed locked away.

But it was too late for that.

Lia wanted to submerge herself under the water, block everything out, make it muffled. But she couldn't. Despite the warm water and luxurious oils she was tense, and her belly was tight.

It was as if a Benjamin Carter–shaped whirlwind had stormed into her life and ripped everything apart, throwing it all in the air, and now Lia wasn't sure where she fitted any more. Or even who she was.

Reluctantly she got out of the bath, her skin already wrinkling like a prune. Wiping the mirror clear, she sucked in a breath at her pink-cheeked reflection. She almost didn't recognise herself.

Her hair was tied up and long tendrils clung to her cheeks and forehead. Her eyes were wide and troubled-looking, but also suspiciously dreamy. She could see marks on her pale skin from where Ben had touched her with his mouth or his hands, and it automatically sent a carnal thrill through her blood.

Her hand curled around the edge of the sink, as if that might stop her flying apart when she thought properly of just how comprehensively Ben Carter had seduced her.

After this weekend she couldn't keep on fooling herself that it was purely physical for her…but what about for Ben?

Just then a knock on the door made her jump. She called out, 'Yes?'

'I'm going to run out to that French patisserie we spotted last night—do you want anything?'

Lia's heart was pounding. 'Just a croissant, thanks.'

'Okay—back in ten.'

Lia waited till she heard the faint sound of the main suite door closing and then she emerged and dressed quickly in the jeans and silk shirt that Ben had ordered for her on that first morning-after.

A little desperate now, she tried to count all the mornings-after—and couldn't. It was as if time had stopped and they were locked in this bubble.

Lia began pacing up and down, trying to calm herself. She couldn't seem to stop thinking about the fact that perhaps there was more for Ben too. He'd told her so much last night, and his reluctance had revealed that he didn't usually let people in.

He wasn't following his usual pattern with lovers, if the gossip was to be believed. Did a man who just wanted a brief fling cross the Atlantic to find out more about a woman?

Against all Lia's most hardened instincts, she felt a flutter of illicit excitement in her gut. Perhaps…just perhaps…this was *more*. And perhaps Ben wouldn't just jet off back to New York. Then something sank inside her. And yet how could it work when they lived on different continents? How could she leave her father?

Her thoughts were racing so much that Lia put her hands to her cheeks and they were hot. A semi-hysterical giddiness rose up inside her. And hope. And a kind of euphoria. She was falling for Ben…

After the weekend they'd just shared, she couldn't believe that what he felt for her was purely physical…and she couldn't believe that she was even thinking about risking her worst fears. But right now, with Ben's taste still on her lips and his touch like a brand on her skin, she felt absurdly confident and a little invincible.

Just then there was a sound at the suite door and Lia went to investigate, finding that a selection of the day's newspapers had been pushed underneath. Ben must have requested them. Automatically she bent to pick them up, only half taking in the headlines—until one jumped out at her and the rest of the papers dropped to the floor, unnoticed.

American construction tycoon follows construction heiress back to England after million-dollar

weekend in Brazil! Can Julianna Ford be the one
to tame Ben Carter's wild ways?

Under the headline was a grainy picture of Ben and
Lia, kissing in the street the previous evening. It was just
before they'd got into the cab. They hadn't even noticed.
There were also fuzzy shots of them eating dinner. Immediately the memory was tarnished.

Lia felt sick and walked back into the living area and
sat on the edge of a chair. It was only to be expected that
someone as high-profile as Ben Carter would be tracked
and followed, but for Lia, who'd never fallen foul of the
tabloids, it was a shock to see her name in print like this.

She kept reading even though she didn't want to,
frowning when she saw another picture that was familiar because she'd seen it before. It was of Ben and the
three other tycoons, emerging from that private club in
Manhattan some weeks before.

There was renewed speculation as to why the men
had met up in Manhattan that night, and if it had something to do with reversing the negative press attention
they'd all been receiving. And there was a lewd sug-
gestion that Ben Carter was hoping to swap more than
just bodily fluids with Lia, considering her own family background.

Lia thought of her father seeing this paper and barely
managed to keep from rushing to the bathroom to be
sick. The thought was literally nauseating.

Just then Lia heard a chiming noise and looked to see
her mobile phone on a nearby table. Her gut clenched with
dread at the thought that it would be her father because
he'd seen the article, but she frowned when she saw the
name at the top of the text: Dante Mancini. He was the
Italian tycoon Ben had been meeting that night in Man-

hattan, along with Xander Trakas and Sheikh Zayn Al-
Ghamdi. Why would he be texting her? And how did he
even have her number?

The words of the message jumped out at her.

Have you seen the papers, Carter? Looks like your million-dollar gamble is paying off. You might just beat the
rest of us to the altar—

The rest of the message was hidden unless she unlocked the phone, and it was only when she tried to do
so and it wouldn't unlock that the significance of the
fact that it was addressed to Ben finally sank in—this
wasn't her phone. It was exactly the same model, but it
was Ben's.

The implication of the message was too confusing and
potentially huge to take in at first. Words reverberated
in Lia's head: *gamble...altar...beat the rest of us.* That
picture of them emerging from the club loomed in her
mind's eye now. Almost accusatory.

She recalled her initial meeting with Ben and how
suspicious she'd been, and how somehow along the way
she'd forgotten about that. Her conscience mocked her.
Somehow? Her suspicion had been forgotten in a blaze
of heat so intense she still felt scorched.

She looked at that photo again, a sick kind of dread
churning in her belly. They all looked so grim and intent.

The fledgling tender emotions Lia had been feeling seemed to shrivel inside her. She had the very sick
suspicion that she was the most monumental fool in
the world.

She, of all people, who had seen how cruel and ruthless people could be. Even those who were meant to love
you the most. She who had learnt her lesson, but had

been all too ready to forget everything and believe in an illusion.

And just then she heard the sounds heralding Ben's return from the bakery.

When Ben walked into the suite's main foyer he saw the newspapers on the floor, where they'd fallen. He sensed instantly that something was wrong—like in Bahia, when he'd woken to find Lia gone. He stepped over them and his mouth tightened. If she'd run out on him again, like she had before...

But he came to a halt in the doorway of the living area when he saw her standing with her back to him at the main window. The relief that rushed through him would be worrying if he hadn't still been feeling uneasy.

'Hey, I've got some pastries and croissants.'

Lia didn't turn around straight away, and when she did he saw her face was set. Pale. Her arms were crossed in a clearly defensive gesture. A million miles from the sleep-flushed woman who had smiled as he'd kissed her awake earlier...

Ben put down the bag on a nearby table. The way Lia was looking at him made him feel more wary than concerned. 'Did something happen?'

'You could say that,' she answered tonelessly.

Ben frowned, but before he could respond to ask her *What?* she spoke again.

'What is this, Ben? What are we doing here?'

A million carnal images came into his mind, but he desisted from making any facetious comment. An awful suspicion was entering his head—*she knows...somehow she knows*.

'What do you think this is, Lia?'

She looked at him for a long moment. 'To be perfectly honest, I'm not sure. It's an elaborate seduction—that much I do know. For someone who up till just weeks ago was a perennial bachelor with a tarnished playboy status.'

Now Ben flushed, and gritted his jaw. 'You didn't seem interested in analysing things before now.'

'No.' Lia sounded bitter. 'More fool me.'

His gut clenched in rejection of that. 'You're not a fool, Lia.'

She arched a brow. 'No?'

Then she reached down for the newspaper on the couch near her and lobbed it over to Ben, who caught it on a reflex. He saw the headline and felt inordinately relieved.

Barely skimming the article and photo, he looked at her. 'Is this all?' It was just the tabloids...if anything this would work in Ben's favour.

'No, that's not all.' Lia's tone was even cooler now. 'You got a text message from a friend. I mistakenly read some of it because I thought it was my phone. But I'm not sorry I read it. I found it quite illuminating.'

Ben saw his phone on a table nearby and picked it up. When he saw the message he unlocked his phone to read it all the way to the end.

You might just beat the rest of us to the altar, so enjoy your freedom while you can. Ciao. Mancini.

Ben could almost hear the man's drawling, sarcastic tone and he had to restrain himself from hurling the phone against something solid.

When he looked at Lia she was even paler, and her eyes were like two stark blue sapphires. Swirling with anger and other things he couldn't decipher.

'Why did he call it a million-dollar gamble?'

Something solid and heavy settled in Ben's chest. He really hadn't wanted it to go like this, but perhaps it was better just to be completely brutally honest. He threw the paper and his phone down.

He funnelled a hand through his hair and looked at Lia. 'I initiated a meeting with the others after the press seemed to have become intent on decimating our reputations. There's a charity we're all involved in, and it was beginning to be adversely affected. That was the breaking point for me. I figured that if Trakas, Mancini and Sheikh Al-Ghamdi would agree to join forces with me, we could beat the press at their own game.'

Lia's voice was tight. 'So you had your meeting and what…? Discussed strategies?'

Ben felt grim. 'Something like that.'

She said nothing for a moment, but Ben could almost hear her brain whirring. She was a smart woman. It wouldn't take her long. And it didn't. Her eyes grew wider and her face was leached of the little colour that had come into it.

'You set up that date with me a week after your meeting. What's the betting that if I was to call Elizabeth Young now she'd tell me that you all signed up with her?'

Ben had to admit it. 'She would tell you that, yes. We did all sign up with her. And we signed up with her because we decided that our best course of action would be to clean up our reputations by…settling down.'

Lia gaped at him. Her eyes were huge. Faintly she said, 'I can't believe it… You made some sort of sick pact to find women and get married to prove that you're all moving on from your playboy images?'

Feeling tight all over, Ben said, 'People get married for less every day of the week.'

Lia's eyes blazed at him now. He wasn't even sure if she'd heard what he'd said.

'No wonder he called your million-dollar bid a gamble. Were you hoping I'd become completely infatuated with you? Or were you just going to pop the question after testing out our physical compatibility?'

Something on Ben's face must have given him away, because Lia stepped back, shaking her head. There was a light in her eyes that skewered Ben to the spot, all at once accusatory and something more ambiguous.

'To think that I suspected you had an agenda right from the start... But even I could never have guessed you'd go so far.'

The only thing anchoring Lia to the ground was the intense anger she felt. She told herself it wasn't hurt and betrayal. She told herself the feelings she'd believed were real just a short while before had been just a flight of fancy and brought on by sex hormones. How could she have fallen for this man?

She cursed herself for not having trusted her gut at the start. For letting Ben fool her into thinking... Her heart stuttered—thinking what? That he cared for her? What a travesty! Clearly all he cared about was his precious business and his reputation.

Where had her healthy sense of cynicism gone? Melted, she thought disgustedly, along with her will power as soon as he'd touched her... But worse than anything else at that moment was the hurt she felt that he'd lied to her when he'd told her in Brazil that he'd wanted her after just looking at her photo, before he'd even known who she was. And she hated herself for being so weak.

Ben just looked at her, assessing her reaction. He seemed remote, a million miles from the seductive lover who had sent her to heaven and back more times than she cared to admit.

'You were prepared to marry once before for convenience,' Ben pointed out.

Lia felt even sicker now, when she thought of all she'd revealed to him. When all along he'd been playing her like a virtuoso. She lifted her chin and tried to ignore the sensation of something cracking apart in her chest. It was anger, she told herself desperately. ·

'Yes, I was. But I was misguided and doing it for all the wrong reasons.'

'We have more going for us than you ever did with your ex-fiancé. We have insane chemistry. We have ambitions and goals in common. We could build a good life together.'

To hear him so baldly laying out exactly what he'd had in mind all along was like a body-blow. And Lia realised for the first time that she'd changed. She might have agreed to a marriage of convenience before, for her father's sake and on a subconscious level to protect herself from the pain of intimacy, but she'd never do it again. She knew she was worth more than that now. And the fact that it was this man who'd given her that sense of self was galling.

Ben continued, 'I can take care of you and your father. You've admitted his health is failing, Lia. It's only a matter of time before he has to step down. You can't go on protecting him for ever. You can't go on sacrificing your own ambitions for his.'

Lia hated him even more for being able to strike at the very heart of her. She'd given him that power. This was what happened when you let people in. They knew where your weak points were and she'd all but given Ben a map and directions. She had no one but herself to blame. She shouldn't have stopped listening to her suspicions.

She bristled at the implication that she needed taking care of. 'Wow, you must have *really* thought you had it all sorted when you spotted me in the Leviathan port-folio. Not only could you get your convenient wife, you could also be assured of further expansion into Europe.'

Colour scored along Ben's cheeks, but Lia didn't feel triumphant to have scored a hit—she felt worse...disap-pointed. Betrayed. She couldn't keep denying it.

He said, 'I'd make sure that your father's business thrives, that his name survives. You'd want for nothing.'

Lia tightened her arms around herself as if that might hold her together. 'What you're describing is a business merger—and were you not listening when I told you that wealth and all its trappings mean nothing to me?'

Ben's jaw clenched. 'That's easy to say when you haven't had it all ripped away and seen the effect on your family.'

Lia was momentarily rendered speechless. He was right, in one way. Even if she knew that she could sur-vive, she knew something like what had happened to his parents would kill her father. And she hated it that even now her heart ached a little for what had happened to Ben... She hated that she wanted to ask him if he'd felt anything at all beyond this absurd plan. But she wouldn't. She wasn't a complete masochist. And he'd just revealed a level of ruthlessness that took her breath away.

'I'm not interested in a marriage of convenience with you, Benjamin Carter.'

A muscle ticked in his jaw. 'And yet you were pre-pared to live a lie of a life with a man who left you com-pletely cold?'

Terrified he'd guess what a personal revelation she'd had, she fired back, 'I'd rather have *that* life than one with a man who would seduce his way to getting what he wants...lying with his body and his touch. You dis-gust me.'

* * *

You disgust me.

Something snapped inside Ben—some control he'd been clinging to. Something that had made him feel impotent in the face of her accusations. She was right...he *had* set out to woo her with marriage in mind...but she didn't know that he'd almost forgotten that objective, that he'd found it so much more preferable to lose himself in her. Over and over again.

'You still want me,' he ground out, feeling feral. Feeling desperate.

She shook her head, eyes wide, icy. 'No.'

Her denial pushed Ben over the edge of his control. He closed the distance between them in two long strides and reached for her, wrapping his hands around her arms and tugging her towards him. She tipped up her chin mutinously, her arms still locked across her chest, pushing up the tantalising swells of her breasts under the silk shirt.

There was a hint of panic in her voice. 'This means nothing, Ben. Just because I might react—'

He stopped the rest of her words with his mouth, crushing all that tart sweetness, hauling her close to his chest. They were locked for long seconds in a tense embrace and then Ben gentled his hold. His hand reached for her head, fingers tangling in her hair. His other hand slid down her arm, and then to her waist.

For a long second she did nothing, and Ben expected her to pull away, but then, with something that sounded halfway between a sob and a moan, she softened and opened her mouth.

Exultation rose swiftly in Ben's blood, drowning out the self-recrimination and guilt. He knew only this...her delicious curves melting into him...her tongue touching his.

They kissed frantically, passionately. Angrily. Her

arms slid around his neck and her body bowed into his. Ben's hands cupped her buttocks through her jeans and he notched his body against the juncture of her legs.

He was about to lift her up and hook her legs around his waist, so he could take her into the bedroom, when suddenly she stiffened and then pulled out of his arms. They were both breathing harshly and she was looking at him as if he'd just kicked a puppy.

She shook her head and said harshly, 'No, I don't want this, Ben. I want more than just a convenient marriage and a mutual lust which will inevitably burn itself out. And then where would that leave us? It's all a lie.'

Blood was pumping to Ben's erogenous zones and away from his brain. It was hard to think straight. He had to exert extreme control over his body. 'It's not a lie. It's the most honesty I've ever felt in my life.'

Lia shook her head again and started to walk away, into the bedroom. The fact that she seemed to be unsteady on her feet, which showed how much he'd affected her, was no comfort. He wasn't sure he was so steady himself.

She emerged minutes later, carrying the big designer bag that had come with the clothes he'd ordered. She walked quickly to the door, avoiding his eye.

An awful mix of panic and desperation made Ben say, 'So? What? You're saying that you want more now? After everything you've experienced?'

She stopped at the door, her hand on the knob. She turned around and something gripped Ben. She looked very young and delicate, her mouth swollen after his kiss. He wanted to feel it under his again. *For ever.*

She lifted her chin and in that moment she looked almost regal. 'Maybe I do. Maybe I'm not as cynical as I thought. I'm certainly not as cynical as you. And, apart from anything else, I could never trust you.' Then she said, 'I'd appreciate it if you wouldn't go after my father.'

It took a second for her words to register, and then Ben felt like snarling. Clearly her opinion of him was still low, no matter what confidences they'd shared, or these recent revelations.

Tautly he assured her, 'Your father won't be hearing from me. But that doesn't mean he won't be a target for others.'

'Maybe,' she said. 'But we'll deal with that if and when it happens.'

Ben felt an almost violent surge of protectiveness—*he* wanted to deal with it if it happened. He didn't want Lia to be the one standing between her father and some unscrupulous shark. And then he realised that she believed that shark was him.

She was opening the door before he could react and then she was gone…only the faintest perfume lingering behind her. Ben felt numb, in spite of the residual hum of arousal in his blood. The taste of her mouth was still on his tongue.

For a second he couldn't breathe. He turned around and went to the window, his gaze latching on to the soaring buildings, reminding him of what was important. What was solid.

He would be true to his word. He wouldn't go after her father. Ben's mouth firmed. There were others he could target; he wouldn't let this stand in his way. And as for the original plan to find a bride…? Nothing had changed.

The sooner he put Lia Ford into the past and got his life back on track, the better.

He waited until he was on his way to the airport a little later that morning before he made the call. When Elizabeth Young answered and realised who it was, she wasted no time in telling Ben what she thought of him going behind her back to pursue Lia anyway.

When she'd stopped speaking, Ben delivered his piece and then bit out, 'Can you set me up on another date? Please?'

After a long moment she said, 'You have one more chance, Mr Carter, but only because I know how hard it is for men like you to admit you were wrong and to say *please*.'

CHAPTER NINE

'Wow, YOU'RE ACTUALLY admitting you want a marriage of convenience—that's pretty cold.' The woman Ben had had three very chaste dates with over the past two weeks—because he couldn't bring himself to even think about kissing her—seemed to absorb that for a moment and then said, 'I'd have to consider it—and see the pre-nuptial agreement, of course—but it's certainly a possibility.'

Ben wasn't even surprised that she wasn't running away as if he was a two-headed monster. He'd dated enough hard-nosed and cynical women in New York to know that many wouldn't balk at a proposal like this. To some it would be positively romantic.

The woman who sat on the opposite side of the dinner table to Ben, in one of Manhattan's most exclusive restaurants, was stunningly beautiful. Blonde, and groomed to within an inch of her life. A UN interpreter.

She'd make a perfect wife—on paper, at least. But the fact that the union he sought was potentially within his grasp left him utterly unmoved. Because he knew it wasn't going to happen.

He was haunted by someone else. *Lia.* He'd thought he could excise her from his life, move on. The reality was somewhat less…facile. It was downright impossible, in fact, and as the days passed it got worse. Not better. Even now he burned. For *her.* He would have her over any amount of suitable women and she could walk out on him as much as she liked…he'd always go after her.

A sense of bleak futility gripped him and he put down his napkin, saying, 'I'm sorry about wasting your time, but actually this isn't going to work.'

A look of alarm came over his date's face. 'Look, I'm willing to think it over.'

Ben felt grim. 'I'm sorry, but, no.'

She put down her napkin too, and exasperation was evident on her face. She stood up and looked down at him. 'If you want my advice, go and deal with whatever or whoever has you tied up in knots. If you still want to talk then, give me a call. I won't wait around for ever, though,' she added warningly, just before she walked out.

Ben threw down some money on the table, disgusted with himself, and left too, walking out into the cool night air, hands deep in the pockets of his overcoat.

He walked for block after block, until he found himself down near the wrecking site of an old building he'd just acquired. They'd knocked it down just that day. A hoarding emblazoned with his name blocked the view of the mound of rubble. The building had been two hundred years old and crumbling. But for the first time in his life he felt a pang. It had had history—people had lived and died there. It had witnessed lives. And now it was gone, reduced to nothing.

It would be replaced by something new, modern. A skyscraper, making the most out of a small space. Progress. Development. Moving on. So why did Ben feel so damn empty when at this point he usually felt nothing but satisfaction flowing through his veins?

He turned around, emitting something like a growl, making a couple passing near him look at him warily.

Oblivious to their reaction, Ben looked around him at all the darkened buildings, empty but for a few cleaners.

They were solid—shining symbols of the resurrection and success he'd always strived to achieve, something he could literally reach out and touch—but ultimately they were no safer than the building he'd had demolished today. They were just as fragile, susceptible to being destroyed.

From here he could see the twin beams of light marking Ground Zero. If anything signified the fragility of structures and life, that did. But it also symbolised strength and fortitude and survival. A contradiction.

For the first time in his life Ben had a sense that even if he lost everything tomorrow he would be able to get back up and build it all again. After all, he'd started from nothing. He wasn't his father—he would never collapse and disappear as he had done. Or his mother.

He felt something lift off his shoulders…some weight he hadn't even noticed. He faced back the way he'd come, filled with a sense of resolve.

He knew he'd made a pact with Mancini, Trakas and Sheikh Al-Ghamdi, but suddenly what had mattered all those weeks ago didn't any more. Ben knew now that he could only go one way and suffer the consequences…no matter what they might be.

A week later

Lia was standing at the window in her office, looking out over London broodingly. The weather matched her mood: grey and wet. She imagined Ben Carter in his beautiful villa in Bahia, seducing his latest possible wife, the stunning blonde she'd seen in pictures alongside breathless speculation that this woman might be the one to tame the mercurial tycoon.

A knife twisted in her guts and Lia sucked in a breath. She couldn't deny it any more. She couldn't keep telling herself that she hadn't really been falling for him. That it had just been hormones.

She was in love with the man. Deeply. Irrevocably. But she didn't regret walking away from him. No wonder she'd agreed to a marriage of convenience with Simon—it had been eminently safe! But a marriage of convenience with a man she had feelings for…? That would be pure torture. He only wanted her for the advancement she could offer to his reputation and business. Once again his sheer ruthlessness made her suck in a painful breath.

She scowled at her reflection in the glass, hating it that she looked wan and tired after sleepless nights full of X-rated dreams. She loved him—but she hated him for his betrayal and ruthless calculation.

Just then her mobile rang and she turned around, sighing deeply. She saw the name on the display and picked it up, forcing a smile so she didn't sound as miserable as she felt.

'Dad! Is everything okay?'

He'd been instructed to work from home this past week, to help his rehabilitation, but Lia knew he'd been impatient to get back into his office in town, where she worked too. Thankfully he'd never mentioned the tabloid splash about her and Ben, so he couldn't have seen it.

They chatted for a few minutes and then he said, 'Actually, I had a visitor this morning.'

Lia asked idly, 'You did? Who?'

Her father cleared his throat and said, 'Benjamin Carter, the American construction mogul…'

Lia went very still. She could feel her hand tightening on the phone and her blood draining south.

Her father was still talking, and she interrupted him in shock. 'He did *what?*'

'He asked for your hand in marriage. And we spoke about a possible merger… He's right, you know, Lia. I'm not getting any younger or healthier. You have your own ambitions. I need to be practical...'

Lia sat down heavily in a chair, as shocked to hear him mention her ambitions as to hear about his visitor. 'I'm so sorry, Dad. It's all my fault... We met in New York and he pursued me... But he only ever wanted me because of your company, and he needs a wife, and—' Lia closed her mouth abruptly before she said too much. She could feel the shock wearing off, to be replaced by hot, molten emotion. Ben had gone behind her back and done what she'd expressly asked him not to.

'I see...' said her father. 'And how do you feel about him?'

'I hate him,' Lia said quickly, even as a voice said, *Liar, liar, pants on fire.*

'Lia, look, I don't think you really understand—'

'No, Dad.' She cut him off. 'Listen, this is all my fault. I'm going to take care of it.'

She cut the connection before her father could say anything else. Then reached for her office phone and asked her PA to get her Ben's UK office address.

No way was Ben Carter going to get away with this. The fact that she felt butterflies at the thought of seeing him again was as irritating as hell, but she ignored it.

Lia wasn't quite prepared to see Ben striding towards her in the lobby of his very modern steel office building in central London. He looked fierce and intent, but stopped in his tracks as soon as he saw her.

'*Lia.*'

For a bizarre second he looked at her as if she was a ghost. But then he blinked and said, 'I was just coming to see you.'

She folded her arms over her chest and tried to ignore

the pounding of her heart. 'Well, I've saved you a trip. Did you seriously think I'd let this go?'

Ben frowned, and Lia noticed for the first time that he looked a little more unkempt than usual. And tired. Lines she hadn't noticed before had appeared around his mouth.

Churlishly she figured it must be hard work, vetting a new wife. Even if he wasn't in Bahia right now. A skewer pierced deep to remind her of how easy she'd been to seduce.

'What did your father tell you?'

'All I needed to know—which is that you came to him talking about mergers and acquisitions. And that you asked for my hand in marriage.'

Anger and renewed betrayal boiled over when she thought of revealing to him how much her father wanted her to settle down.

She stepped closer and hissed at him. 'How could you? You deliberately took a confidence I shared with you and used it to your advantage.'

She only realised she was too close when his distinctive scent reached her nostrils, impacting on her starved hormones. But she wouldn't back away now and show him that he affected her at all. She lifted her chin, challenging him.

'I take it that you didn't let your father explain everything I said, then?'

Now Lia blinked. Her father *had* been saying something when she'd cut him off. She ignored the dart of doubt. 'I heard all I needed to. What possible other explanation could there be for your presence here in England?'

Ben's eyes glittered. 'What, indeed?'

Lia became aware that people were walking through the foyer and trying desperately not to look as if they were eavesdropping.

Ben obviously realised the same and cursed. 'We can't have this conversation here.'

He'd taken her by the arm and was walking towards a set of lifts before Lia could respond. She started to try to pull free. 'I think we've said all we need to say,' she hissed. 'You need to leave me and my father alone—you're not going to get what you want.'

But in spite of her words and efforts she was in the lift with him now, and he was pressing a button and they were ascending.

He let her go once they were moving and said grimly, 'You're not leaving until you hear what I have to say.'

Lia glared at him, struck temporarily mute as she was bombarded with memories of what had happened in a lift before. Mutual combustion. As if he were remembering the same thing Ben's eyes darkened, and his gaze dropped to her breasts under her silk shirt before lazily coming back up again. Lia could feel damp heat bloom between her legs, mere seconds after meeting the man again. She wanted to scream at the control he still had over her body.

But now the doors were opening and she could see they were on the top floor. Ben all but pulled her out of the lift and marched her down a long corridor with glass cube offices either side. People tried frantically to look uninterested as they passed by. Lia debated screaming, but then imagined Ben putting his mouth on hers to keep her quiet...

He took her to an office at the end—the largest one—with wraparound views of London and the dark brown Thames snaking through the iconic buildings on either side. It was impressive.

But not as impressive as the man who shut the door behind him and planted himself in front of it, his powerful body blocking her exit. Damn him.

Lia backed away. 'What the hell do you want, Mr Carter? I don't have time for this.'

He smiled mirthlessly as he leant back against the door, hands in his trouser pockets. 'I see we've gone back to Mr Carter.'

Lia folded her arms, feeling vulnerable in this enclosed space, even if it was all windows. 'Well, what did you expect?'

A look of something like self-recrimination passed over Ben's face, and then he pushed off the door and went to stand at the window, looking out. His back was broad, and Lia couldn't help remembering that day in Bahia, when he'd been working on the roof of the villa, laughing and joking with Esmé's husband.

She scowled. That man had never existed.

Ben spoke then, cutting through her acid recriminations. 'I was once told by a colleague that my buildings had more heart than me, and he was right. I believed that buildings weren't fallible and that my structures would keep standing even if I fell. They're not weakened by emotions and human frailty, or greed and corruption. Except...that's not true.'

Feeling a little disorientated, Lia said, 'What do you mean?'

After a long moment Ben turned around to face her. There was something bleak in his eyes. 'I was wrong to believe that my redemption lay in the structures I created and built.'

Lia shook her head, resisting the desire to understand him. 'I really couldn't care less about what you think of your buildings.'

Ben cursed softly and ran a hand through his hair, leaving it mussed up. He pinpointed her with that blue gaze.

'I'm trying to tell you...' He stopped. And then he

spoke more forcibly. 'I did come to see your father to talk about the business, and to ask for your hand in marriage.'

Lia felt pain lance her. 'I know. Which is why—'

'But not in the way you think.'

She stopped talking and something started beating inside her. Butterflies again. Or her heart. Or something more dangerous...hope. Damn hope. It would survive a nuclear apocalypse.

'What, then?'

Ben's gaze seemed to be burning all the way into her. 'I came to tell him that I want to marry his daughter because...I love her.' He waited a beat, as if to let her absorb that, and then he said, watching her carefully, 'But I told him that she wouldn't believe me after what I did to her and so I had to somehow prove it to her. And the only way I knew how to do that was by asking your father to take *me* over. I want to prove to you that you're more important to me than everything I've built up, because it all means nothing without you.'

Lia wasn't sure if she was still standing. She struggled to understand, shaking her head faintly, 'But...you let me leave. And you've been dating...that woman.'

Ben grimaced. 'I was too proud to admit that you'd got to me on an emotional level. My life was never about emotions—it was about building structures that affirmed my place in the world. Rooting my security in something solid. I was in denial, determined to put you out of my mind and get on with my life.'

A rueful look flashed across his face then. 'I was also terrified... Suddenly nothing felt relevant or important any more. I felt as if I was going mad. I'd only ever trusted myself, and yet I couldn't trust my own instincts any more because every instinct was telling me to come back to you, to admit that my priorities had changed...

completely. And nothing happened with that woman. She bored me to tears, and she wasn't you.'

Lia felt breathless, as if a huge fist was squeezing around her heart. The pressure was enormous. 'Even if I believed what you say about handing everything over to my father...even if I was to agree to marry you...ultimately you'd have everything anyway—you'd still have achieved what you wanted.'

His eyes were so blue it almost hurt to look at them. He was willing her to believe him—she could see that. But something was holding her back. *Fear.*

All she could see in her mind's eye was how her father had slowly diminished more and more as the years had passed and it had become less and less likely that Lia's mother would ever return. And now someone was standing in front of her, asking for her heart...and she was filled with terror.

She backed away, panic galvanising her. Emotion constricted her voice. 'I can't...do this.'

She whirled around, away from that too penetrating gaze, and made it to the door. She opened it just as her vision started to blur, but then it was slammed shut again and Ben was behind her, his hands above her head. Capturing her.

She turned around and looked up. He was too close. 'Let me *go.*'

He shook his head, looking fierce. 'Never.'

'I don't trust you—how can I?' Her heart was pumping nearly out of her chest.

Ben shook his head, caging her in. 'It's not me you don't trust—it's yourself. Because you're too afraid to reach out and grab what you've always denied yourself: the chance of the happiness you deserve. Just because your father denied it to himself his whole life, it doesn't mean you have to.'

His words struck deep into the very heart of her and Lia lashed out defensively. 'Since when did you become a psychologist?'

Ben's mouth quirked. 'Since a beautiful, bright, brave woman stalked away from our first date and turned my world upside down and inside out, showing me that everything I thought was important *wasn't*.'

Lia felt tears threaten. '*You* turned *my* world upside down and inside out.'

Ben's expression changed. Became serious. 'I know,' he said. 'Because from the moment I saw you I wanted you more than anything I've ever wanted before. Yes, I knew who you were, and, yes, I had an agenda. But in all honesty they were the last things on my mind. I had to keep reminding myself of my objective; that's why I let you go. I realised how far off course I'd come. I'd lost track of everything that I'd believed was important.'

His mouth tightened.

'When you walked away I told myself the last thing I needed was a wife who actually made me *feel* anything. I told you the truth when I told you I wanted you from first sight…as soon as I saw your photo I was done for. The fact that you were who you were…that made it justifiable for me to go after you. I will do whatever it takes to make you believe me, Lia. I will sign over Carter Construction to you, to your favourite charity, to Santa Claus…whoever you want. Trust me on this. My solicitor is just down the hall. Say the word and I'll have contracts drawn up. And I will never ask you to marry me if you're afraid that's still my endgame. If you can tell me that you truly don't want this, that you don't feel anything for me, then I'll let you go and you'll never hear from me again.'

Lia looked up into those blue eyes that had sent shockwaves through her as soon as she'd seen them. And all she could see was blazing determination, truth and…

her heart hitched...*love*. This man was ready to destroy everything he'd built up—for her. And he hadn't lied about wanting her from the moment he'd seen her photo.

But there was still something holding her back.

Her voice was little more than a whisper. 'But how can I trust that you won't leave eventually? Or that you won't hurt me?'

Lia had literally nowhere to hide. She was laid bare, exposing her deepest fears.

Ben looked so fierce for a second that she sucked in a breath.

'I would never leave you. *Ever*. You have just as much power to hurt me—more.'

Lia felt something fierce rush through her at the thought of this man being hurt...of leaving him behind. 'I could never hurt you.'

Some expression crossed Ben's face, something almost like satisfaction, and then he said, 'Not everyone is like our parents, Lia. Some people do find happiness. Security. Do you love me?'

Without an atom left in her body capable of keeping up her high walls of defence, Lia just nodded.

'Well, then,' Ben said softly, his eyes turning suspiciously shiny, 'we're already different to them. Because I love you too, and I pledge here and now to do everything in my power to make you happy for as long as we live.'

Lia absorbed that.

And then Ben said, 'They didn't love each other, Lia, not really. Not your parents, nor my parents. And that's where they failed.'

She looked at him and her chest expanded. Was he right? Could things really be different for them because they loved each other? Could it really be that simple?

But she already knew the answer, deep in her core, because it was spreading outwards and infusing her whole body with a lightness she'd never felt before. It could be that simple...and that hard...because loving Benjamin Carter was the scariest thing she'd ever done in her life. And the easiest.

And so she did the only thing she could. She reached up and pulled Ben's face down to hers and kissed him, until all the doubts and fears had fled and there was only love left behind.

Much later, in a hotel room around the corner from Ben's offices, Lia lay sated and blissfully drowsy after reuniting with Ben in a very comprehensive and convincing manner. She was tucked close in to his side, his arm around her. He was not letting her escape—not that she had any intention of doing that.

She trailed her finger up and down his chest, lazily, and after a while lifted her head to look at him. He looked back at her with slumberous blue eyes, a sexy smile making his mouth quirk.

'You know how you said you'd never ask me to marry you...?'

Now he looked wary. 'Yes...and I meant it. If that's what it takes to prove to you that—'

Lia put a finger over his lips, stopping him. She felt suddenly unsure, but forged on. 'The thing is...I appreciate that...but I'm just...that is, I'm just wondering... if you didn't feel you had to do that would you *want* to marry me?'

A look that Lia couldn't decipher came into Ben's eyes and then he was putting his hands on her arms and pushing her away from him so he could slip out of the bed. Lia sat up, feeling cold, not liking the insecurity she felt. Maybe it was too soon...

Gloriously naked, Ben was rummaging around in his pockets for something, and then he came back to the bed. He knelt in front of her and she pulled the sheet up over her chest.

He held a black box in his hands. Velvet. She looked from it to him, her throat going dry.

He said carefully, 'I didn't show this to you because I didn't want to push you.'

He opened the box then, and Lia looked down, eyes widening. Nestled against black silk was the most beautiful ring she'd ever seen. A rectangular-shaped sapphire flanked by rows of diamonds.

'The thing is,' Ben said, sounding uncharacteristically nervous, 'if you don't like it we can change it. But I'd like to ask if you'd accept this ring and consent to be my fiancée—for as long as you like. And if you ever decide you'd like to get married, then I'll be waiting.'

Lia felt emotion rise up to squeeze her throat. Happiness fizzed through her veins. And something else. A sense of freedom from the weight of the past.

She looked at Ben but he was blurry through her tears. She said, half-crying, half-laughing, 'I love it—and, yes. I accept. Now. I'll marry you, Ben Carter, if you'll have me.'

He looked at her for a long moment, stunned, and then Lia threw her arms around him, tumbling their two naked bodies back onto the bed, limbs entwining.

She was soon sprawled over his chest and Ben took her left hand. He looked at her as he pushed the ring down onto her finger, saying huskily, 'I love you, Juli-anna Ford.'

The ring nestled on her finger, fitting like a glove, and she wrapped her arms around his neck, love cracking her wide open. 'I love you too, Benjamin Carter... now, where were we?'

EPILOGUE

'THE TEAM ARE on the ground in India now, Lia. We can't thank you enough for what you're doing. You and Ben. Your charity has been invaluable in restoring order to the chaos.'

Lia looked out of the window of her office. 'I'm just sorry I can't be with you all at the moment.'

The man on the other end of the phone huffed a chuckle. 'Don't worry—your expertise is invaluable even from there, and I don't think that husband of yours will be letting you out of his sight any time soon.'

Lia's hand automatically went to her distended belly, and she glanced through the glass wall separating her office from her husband's in his London building, where they were now based.

Ben had agreed to relocate to the UK so that they could be near her father, who appeared to be undergoing a renaissance since Ben and he had merged companies, turning them into a formidable transatlantic company called CarterFord Construction. Her father had taken a long-overdue step back and was currently on a cruise with his new love—his long-serving secretary. For years Lia had suspected her of being in love with her father. They were very sweet together.

She frowned when she couldn't see her husband in his office and sat up straight, saying distractedly,

'Okay, Philip, please keep us updated on the development anyway.'

Lia put down the phone and stood up—and then smiled when she realised why he hadn't been able to see her husband. She went out of her office and into his, leaning on the doorframe, her hand on her eight months pregnant belly.

Ben looked up at her from his vantage point sprawled on the floor, shirtsleeves rolled up and hair mussed. His eyes gleamed and he put a finger to his mouth.

Their three-year-old daughter, Lucy, hadn't seen Lia yet, and she was saying in a very familiar authoritative voice, '*No*, Daddy—see? We have to build a room for the fire truck 'n all the animals.'

Fierce love and joy bloomed inside Lia—so much so it nearly took her breath away. She blinked away sudden tears, cursing her pregnancy hormones.

Ben sat up and reached a hand up to her, and then Lucy turned around and squealed excitedly, 'Mummy! Come see what we're making!'

Lia came in and knelt on the ground carefully, mindful of her extra cargo, and Ben pulled her into his embrace, his arms wrapping possessively around her belly.

Lucy, a dark-haired, blue-eyed imp who kept them very busy, jumped up. 'Can I listen to my little brother?'

Ben and Lia opened their arms and Lucy nestled in close to Lia's belly, face turned to one side, brow etched with fierce concentration, her little arms spread out to encompass Lia's expanded waist.

Lia leaned back into Ben's broad chest and felt him pull her hair to one side so he could kiss her neck. She shivered deliciously, and just then the baby kicked. Lucy giggled.

Lia felt Ben's smile against her skin and smiled in response.

He spoke against her neck. *'I love you...'*

And she turned her head and whispered back. *'I love you too...'*

* * * * *

The BRIDES FOR BILLIONAIRES *series
continues with
MARRIED FOR THE ITALIAN'S HEIR
by Rachael Thomas
Available November 2016*

*If you enjoyed this story, check out
these other great reads from Abby Green
AWAKENED BY HER DESERT CAPTOR
AN HEIR FIT FOR A KING
THE BRIDE FONSECA NEEDS
FONSECA'S FURY
Available now!*

'There is a price for my assistance.'

Of course there was. This was Nairo Moreno she was dealing with. A man who had somehow built himself up from the shabby, broken beginnings of their lives when they had first met and who was now this powerful, wealthy man. There had to be a price on anything he did.

'A price?' Rose queried.

'Oh, don't look so panicked,' he mocked as she turned uncertain eyes on him. 'I'm not going to demand your body in return for my favours in some odd modern version of *droit du seigneur*.'

He paused just long enough for her skin to smart under the bite of his mockery.

'There wouldn't be much point, would there? After all, we've already been there—haven't we, *querida*?'

The pointed reminder that they had once been lovers, that he had been the one to take her virginity all those years before, drained the strength from her muscles, making her grab at a nearby chair for support. It was an innocence that then she had relinquished happily and unhesitatingly, because she had been so much under the sway of the heated hunger she had known for this man, blinded to anything but her need for him.

He might have stepped in to save her business earlier this evening, but what he had decided so surprisingly to give her he could take away in the space of a heartbeat. She must not forget that she was no longer dealing with the boy she'd met ten years before. *This* man was a very different sort of male.

Kate Walker was born in Nottingham, in the UK, but grew up in West Yorkshire. She met her husband at university in Wales and originally worked as a children's librarian. After the birth of her son she returned to her childhood love of writing. Her first book was published in 1984. She now lives in Lincolnshire with her husband—also a writer—and two cats who think they rule her life.

Books by Kate Walker

Mills & Boon Modern Romance

Destined for the Desert King
Olivero's Outrageous Proposal
A Question of Honour

Royal & Ruthless

A Throne for the Taking

Return of the Rebels

The Devil and Miss Jones

The Powerful and the Pure

The Return of the Stranger

Italian Temptation!

The Proud Wife

The Greek Tycoons

The Greek Tycoon's Unwilling Wife
The Good Greek Wife?

Visit the Author Profile page at
millsandboon.co.uk for more titles.

INDEBTED
TO MORENO

BY
KATE WALKER

MILLS & BOON

First Published in Great Britain 2016
By Mills & Boon, an imprint of HarperCollins*Publishers*
1 London Bridge Street, London, SE1 9GF

ISBN: 978-0-263-92132-8

Our policy is to use papers that are natural, renewable and recyclable
products and made from wood grown in sustainable forests. The logging
and manufacturing processes conform to the legal environmental
regulations of the country of origin.

Printed and bound in Spain
by CPI, Barcelona

INDEBTED
TO MORENO

For Alison and Malcolm, aka Malison—a fine poet
and my favourite Tech Support guy. With many
happy memories of Writers' Holidays and other events.

PROLOGUE

THE ALMOST FULL moon was burning cold and high in the darkness of the sky as Rose slipped out of the door, shutting it cautiously behind her. She winced inwardly as the battered wood creaked on rusted hinges, the sound seeming appallingly loud in the stillness of the night, and froze in a panic, waiting for someone to stir upstairs, to come after her as her stepfather had done on that day almost three months ago. But the house remained silent and still, apparently empty, though she knew that there were half a dozen or so figures hidden behind the filthy, cracked windows on the upper floors.

She had to be grateful for the moonlight that illuminated her way down the weed-clogged path towards the street. It helped make sure that she didn't stumble over the beer cans or plastic bags of rubbish that littered her way. But for the few minutes it took her to reach the road and scurry out of sight, panic screamed a need to run along her nerves fighting a vicious battle with the need to move carefully and avoid making a sound. At any moment she expected to hear movement behind her, the sound of a shout waking and alerting everyone in the squat.

And one dangerous person in particular.

Rose's heart clenched as she tried to pull her thoughts away from the man she was leaving behind. A man she

had once seen as her rescuer, coming to her aid when she
needed help most. The man she now had to leave behind
or lose herself once and for all.

It was a bitter irony that she had once seen this squat
in the abandoned shell of a once elegant town house as
a sanctuary as she'd fled the unwanted attentions of her
hated stepfather, only to find that she had well and truly
jumped from the frying pan into the fire.

'Oh, Jett...'

The name slipped past her lips, and, despite everything
she did to push them away, images slid into her mind. The
picture of his long, powerful body lying on the dusty floor
of the bedroom they had claimed as their own, his head
with the overlong jet-black mess of hair pillowed on the
olive-skinned arms in which he hid his face. He had always
slept like that, even after they had made burning, passionate love, tumbling deep into sleep as if at the press of a
button. But she knew that the appearance of deep slum-
ber was a false impression. One awkward move, the faintest sound and he would jolt awake in a moment, coming
upright and alert in the space of a heartbeat, every wary
sense on high alert.

He'd stirred in his sleep as she'd left his side and only by
murmuring something about needing to use the toilet had
she persuaded him to let his head drop back onto his arms.

'Don't be long' had been the curt, brief command and
although she'd known he couldn't see her she had shaken
her head, letting the long fall of her bright red hair conceal her face.

'I won't be a minute,' she'd managed, knowing that he
wouldn't take that the way she meant it. She was not going
to be absent from his side for just a minute but for ever.
This would be her one and only chance to get out of here

before all hell broke out and she was going to snatch at that chance and run with it.

Yet even as she ran down the road there was a terrible tearing sensation inside her, in the region of her heart. A sense of loss and yearning for what she had thought she had, for what she'd dreamed of, that now, with a bitter realisation, she knew to have been a fake all the time.

If only... But there was no room, no time for 'if only'. There was no future for her with this man, the man she had been foolish enough to fall head over heels for, to give herself body and soul to until she had realised the truth about the sort of person he was.

She should have known he was no knight on a white charger when he'd, literally, picked her up off the street. But then she'd been so lost and alone that she'd been grateful for any help, caught up in the dark spell he had woven around her from the start. Now she could no longer ignore the evidence that told her that Jett was involved in the abominable trade of dealing illegal drugs. A trade that had resulted in the horror of the death of one of the other squatters. She shuddered fearfully just thinking of it.

Which was why she had to get out of here right now. She had to go as far and as fast as she could and never once look back.

The sound of cars coming down the road caught her ears. She knew why they were there. The police had acted on her information, and their approach meant that time really had run out for her.

Speeding up, she dashed away from the house that had been the only thing she could call home for the last few months, breath catching in her lungs as, skidding slightly, she whirled around the corner. Behind her, the convoy of police cars came into the street and pulled up sharply outside the door to the squat.

It was over. But the real truth was that it had never truly begun and her naïve foolishness had blinded her to the reality until it was almost too late.

CHAPTER ONE

NAIRO ROJA MORENO stepped out of the door of his private jet and frowned savagely as the icy blast of air and rain crashed into his face, making him blink hard against the cold.

'*Perdición!*' he swore, pulling up the collar of his jacket, the wind whipping the word from his lips and whirling it up into the steel-grey sky. 'It's raining!'

Of course it was raining. This was England, and it seemed that the weather had conspired to remind him just how much he loathed the place.

London, where he'd once thought his life might start afresh only to find that what was left of his heart had been taken and carelessly discarded without a second thought.

'*No.*'

He made his way down the steps, tossing back his hair in defiance at the weather. The memories that swirled in his thoughts had nothing to do with the temperatures, except for the fact that it had always been cold in that damn house. Cold and miserable except for the times that he had been able to persuade Red to join him in the tatty, inadequate sleeping bag.

Be honest. It wasn't the weather or the house that had got to him. It was the coldness of betrayal. The coldness of a heart he had once thought was warm and giving. Until she had left him with nothing when she had vanished out of his life and into the night.

Well, good riddance to her, he told himself, shaking off his memories in the same moment as he slid into the car that was waiting for him. He had had no inclination to go after her, and there had been no time to even consider it. He had been so occupied turning his life around and making his way back to his family—a reconciliation that she had almost destroyed by her actions—that she had been the last thing on his mind. He'd managed a second chance and he wasn't going to stuff it up. This trip to London would be the final part of the task he had set himself.

'Dacre Street,' he told the driver in response to the man's request for a destination. He could only hope the driver knew where the damn place was; it was in no part of the London he usually frequented.

Nairo settled back on the seat, frowning darkly as he raked his wet hair back from his face. He had to get into the city, do the job he'd come to do, keep his promise to Esmeralda. He had so much to make up to his sister and this one last thing to make her happy was what mattered. After this, his duty was done.

If there ever was a day when it was the worst possible moment for Louise to need to go home sick, then it had to be today, Rose told herself, sighing as she pushed back a floating strand of bright auburn hair that had escaped from the neat braid for the nth time. Obviously her normally efficient and organised assistant had been feeling worse than she had let on the previous day, if the state of the reception area was anything to go by. Everything needed tidying, and the diary that detailed today's appointments had been splashed with coffee, blurring the details.

Not that Rose needed any reminders. The appointment

had been made a week ago, the first contact being with a heavily accented voice on the other end of the phone. Nairo Roja Moreno's PA as she declared herself to be.

'Nairo Roja Moreno...' Rose murmured to herself as she considered the blurred words in the diary. The eldest son of an aristocratic Spanish family, his PA had informed her. And he wanted to talk to her about a wedding dress?

She'd meant to look up this Spaniard on the Internet last night, but her mother had been so unwell that it had taken all of her time and attention to get them both through the evening.

When she'd got the confirmation email she'd been overjoyed. It had seemed like a rescue mission arriving just in time. Caring for her mother through her illness had drained her resources, taken all her energy, mental and physical. She'd had no new commissions in an age. The mess of her marriage that had never been and the scandal that had followed it had seen to that. She was behind with the rent on the boutique, had barely been able to meet the costs of her flat. But if this Nairo Moreno really did want her to design his sister's wedding dress together with the bridesmaids' outfits, the flower girls and pageboys of which there seemed to be dozens, well, it might just save her from going under. Save her reputation publicly, save her life financially and perhaps even save her mother's life in reality.

Joy had endured a long and difficult battle with the cancer that had assailed her. She was weak and drained by chemotherapy, the operation, and was only just starting to recover. Any new shock, any extra stress might be dangerous, and, after all the time it had taken to rebuild their relationship from a perilously rocky point ten years before, Rose hated to think that everything could be destroyed now.

Her aristocratic visitor would be here any moment. Tapping her pen in a restless tattoo on the appointment book, Rose frowned as she looked out at the lashing rain that was splattering the plate-glass window of her design rooms. Not the best day to imagine a summer wedding.

Jett had hated the rain, particularly in the unheated squat. As a result, so many rainy days had been spent cuddled up together...

A rush of dark memories swamped her mind, loosening her grip so that the pen dropped from her hand, falling to the floor and rolling away under a display cabinet.

'Darn it!'

Getting down on her hands and knees, she groped in the darkness, fumbling for the pen just out of reach. It was then that she heard the door open behind her, the rush of cold damp air telling her that someone had come into the building from the street.

'Sorry! Just a moment.'

'De nada.'

It was the sexiest voice, deep and dark and so beautifully accented.

Of course! The Spanish aristocrat—what was his name? Nairo something. Suddenly becoming aware of the way she must look, bottom in the air, narrow skirt stretched tight, she made one final lurch, banging her head on the shelf before grabbing the pen, then turning to push herself upwards.

It *was* no problem to wait, Nairo reflected. He was perfectly happy to stay here and enjoy the spectacle of a deliciously rounded bottom stuck up in the air as its owner groped for something under the shelving. Folding his arms across his chest, he leaned back against the door feeling his pulse kick up and thud hard and heavy in his veins as he enjoyed the view before him.

If there was one thing he hadn't anticipated on this unwanted trip to England, then it was the possibility of indulging in a little sensual pleasure. There was so much to be planned and organised back in Spain, with the demands of his sister's soon-to-be in-laws to take into consideration, that he had allowed himself only the freedom of a couple of days away from the chaos and uproar that The Wedding of the Century had created.

Now, with this tantalising display of female charms on display before him, he allowed himself to reconsider.

It had been a long time—too long—since he had had the pleasures of a woman in his bed. His father's final illness, the need for ferocious commitment to work on the family estates, restoring the Moreno fallen fortunes, and now, of course, Esmeralda's engagement and upcoming wedding had ensured that he had had little time to breathe.

Suddenly the prospect of a few days' relaxation, even in the grey, rainy city of London, had infinitely more appeal.

'Got it!'

The triumph in the woman's voice made him smile, but it was a smile that leached from his lips as he saw her lift her head.

Red hair. His personal curse. A bronze, auburn red it was true, not the bright red that had been one of the glories that he had so loved in the woman who had once filled his days, haunted his dreams.

Red...

The echo of his own voice sounded inside his head as memories threatened to surface. He had fought against those memories, pushing them behind him as he set about restoring his life to some degree of order and rebuilding it from the mess it had become. The last thing he wanted was the resurfacing of anything that connected him to the time when he had lived in London in such very different circumstances.

Scarlett. It was the name of this shop—the designer that Esmeralda had sent him to find—that had put these thoughts in his mind.

'I'm sorry— I— Ouch!' The sharp cry of pain broke into his thoughts.

She had lifted her head rather too quickly in her triumph at having found whatever it was she was looking for and so had caught her face on the side of the shelf. Immediately he moved forward, holding out his hand to her.

'Allow me...'

That voice was designed to turn any woman to mush, Rose told herself. And the firm, warm grip of his hand was like touching a live wire, sizzling reaction sparking all along her arm.

'Th-thank you.'

The sharp bang on her forehead had brought tears to her eyes so that she was blinking hard to clear them as he swung her to her feet, the strength of the movement bringing her up and close to him. So close that she almost fell against him as she rocked on her toes before she managed to snatch back her balance and settle her feet on the floor.

She was assailed by a rush of heat from the closeness of a powerful male body, her senses tantalised by the heady combination of the musky scent of clean male skin, a sensual tang of some citrusy aftershave, all topped off with the fresh, wild trace of rain and wind that he had brought in from the street outside.

Suddenly, shockingly, all she could think of was one word, one man, one memory.

Jett... The word slammed into her mind without thought, without control.

No!

Why was she thinking of him? It was almost ten years since the night she had fled from the squat. A decade in which she had picked herself up, dusted herself off and built her life back up again. To the stage where this Spanish aristocrat was here today to discuss a commission to design a wedding dress for his sister.

A commission that she desperately needed. It would be the first time ever she had been asked to design a dress outside the small spread of the local area, unless you counted the dress that her friend Marina Marriot had worn just last month at her wedding to an up-and-coming actor.

'I'm fine now...'

She wished she didn't sound quite so breathless. Wished she had let go of his hand before this so that it didn't look quite so embarrassing as she had to ease her fingers from his.

'De nada.'

Again the sound of that sexy accent coiled around her, bringing memories of another man who had spoken with just that hint of an exotic pronunciation.

But there was no way that Jett would wear a suit like this one that made this man look so sleek and powerful and magnificent. That had to have been custom-made to flatter the powerful straight shoulders, the width of his chest and the lean length of his legs down to where his feet in polished handmade shoes were firmly planted on the tiled floor. Jett had never owned a suit. Like her, he had barely had a change of clothes. The tee shirt and jeans she wore as she fled from the house where the unwanted attentions of her stepfather had made sure it had never felt like a home being the only items that she'd had to drape over the door to what was laughingly called their bedroom.

Her eyes had cleared now and she was looking up into the carved, hard features of the most stunning man she had ever seen. Amber eyes framed with impossibly lush, black lashes burned down into hers. Hard bones shaped the lean cheeks, touched with a darkness of stubble even this early in the day. That mouth was an invitation to sin, warm, sensual, full lips slightly parted over sharp white teeth.

And she knew how that mouth felt, how it tasted...

She felt the world tilt on its axis, the room swinging round her.

'Jett...'

There was no holding it back this time. She didn't even try. It escaped on a breath that was all she could manage as she realised just who this man was.

A man who had once filled her days and haunted her nights. Even when she had run from him she had still taken him with her in her thoughts, her nights filled with memories that jolted her awake, left her drenched in sweat, her heart pounding. A man she had had to hand over to the police when she had learned the source of the money he had suddenly come into, then left to face the repercussions of his actions.

'Jett?' She heard him echo her response sharply, a frown snapping the black, straight brows together, cold eyes looking down into her upturned face.

Those amazing eyes narrowed, the beautiful mouth tightening as his head came up and he took a step back, away from her.

'*Red*... I didn't know *you* worked here.'

Worked here. Perhaps that was a score one to the fact that he really was here by accident. That he hadn't sought her out—because why would he do that after all this time? The thought didn't help with the thumping of her heart, the feeling like the beating of a thousand butterfly wings in the pit of her stomach. He hadn't come looking for her and it was all just a terrible misstep of fate.

But that dark emphasis on the word *you* twisted something in her guts, bringing home an awareness of the fact that she was all alone, not even Louise in the office, within call. Tension stiffened her back, tightened her shoulders.

'And I didn't know *you* worked for Nairo Moreno.'

That brought an unexpected twist to his mouth, the sensual lips twitching into something that could have been described as a smile but was totally without any warmth in it. His eyes seemed to impale her where she stood.

'Not worked...I *am* Nairo Moreno. I came here to see Ms Cavalliero. Oh—what, my darling Red...?'

The smile grew wider, darker.

'Did you think I was here to see you? That I would have hunted you down after all this time, determined to find you?'

She had actually considered that fact, Nairo told himself. It was written all over her beautiful face. The young girl he had once known as 'Red' had always held the promise of being a looker, but he had never anticipated her growing into the sleek, sexy vision who stood before him.

That pert bottom that had caught his attention from the start was only a small part of a slim, shapely figure displayed to full advantage in the cream lace blouse and navy blue, clinging skirt. The hair that had once been the vivid, vibrant colour that gave her her nickname was now a more subtle auburn shade, still with the glint of red blending in with the glossy darker tones. Those almond-shaped, slightly slanting hazel eyes were even more feline than before when accentuated with the subtle use of cosmetics that she would never have been able to afford back then.

A swift, sharp inward shake of his head broke the train of his thoughts, dragging them back from the path down which they had wandered.

She was the last thing he wanted in his world right now.

Hadn't she come close to ruining his life all those years before? Ten years younger, and a lifetime more naïve, he had risked losing everything for the sake of a few short nights of heedless passion. He had even, foolishly, blindly, come close to giving her a piece of his heart. Only to discover that he had been nothing to her when the promise of a reward for information had more appeal instead.

'It's taken me rather a long time—don't you think? Ten years. So why should I suddenly turn round and want to see you again? You can relax about that, *Red*—I am not looking for you but for your boss.'

'My boss?'

'*Sí*. Ms Rose Cavalliero. The owner of this business, and the designer of...'

An autocratic wave of his hand indicated the two beautiful dresses displayed on mannequins in the corner of the room. Of course, Rose realised, he was here to discuss the design of his sister's wedding dress. But the realisation that he still thought she was only the receptionist, that he hadn't put two and two together to recognise that the 'Scarlett' in her business name was in fact her, was in no way eased by the thought of that commission he'd come to discuss.

Oh, no, no! She couldn't work for him. She wouldn't do it. OK, so it might mean a real coup for her business. A boost to her reputation that would be of immeasurable value. But would it be worth it?

All the money in the world couldn't compensate for spending time with Jett—with this Nairo Moreno as he now called himself. Even if he hadn't come looking for revenge, it was obvious that he could barely bring himself to be polite to her.

But how could she get out of it?

'So where is she?'

The question came coldly, curtly, and seeing the hard set of his face Rose was swamped by a rush of cold unease.

To see the smoulder of dark anger in his eyes made her feet feel unsafe on the floor, her mouth drying sharply. If only she had known who this Nairo Moreno really was, then she would never have agreed to meet him today.

But of course he didn't realise exactly who she was. He still believed that she was only the receptionist. For a second the desire to put him in his place by pointing out that she owned the whole establishment and was the designer he had said he so wanted to meet warred with a sense of self-preservation. What she really wanted was to get rid of him before he brought his malign influence back into her present as he had done to her past.

'She couldn't be here. Her mother isn't well.'

Well, that was true enough. And the closer she could get to the truth with this man, the less likely she was to give herself away.

'She didn't think to send a message to let me know?' The anger was there now, in a frigid form. 'That's hardly good business practice.'

'It—it was an emergency. She got called away unexpectedly.'

'I see.'

His tone said the exact opposite as he pushed back the immaculate white cuff of his shirt and checked the time. On the sort of platinum watch that the man she had once known could never have afforded.

Unless of course… The coldness at her spine turned into a slow, icy creeping sensation that made her remember just why she had had to run out on him, the darkness of the world that she had discovered she had fallen into.

'I'm sure she'll be in touch…'

When she had some excuse ready. Some reason why

she couldn't take on his commission. She'd think of something when she wasn't faced with telling it to him in person. Right now, all she wanted was for him to get out of
her life and stay out. For good this time.

'I'll be waiting for her message.'

The dark thread of anger that laced the statement turned
it into an unspoken threat, making her heart clench painfully so that she had to struggle to draw her next breath.

'I'll tell her.' Embarrassingly it was a revealing squeak.

Unable to meet those coldly assessing eyes, Rose hurried to the door, deliberately moving so as not to risk touching him, or come within reach of one of those long-fingered
hands that now rested lightly on the smooth leather belt that
encircled his narrow waist. She didn't want to remember
anything about the touch of those hands, and the thought
of them coming anywhere near her again set the butterflies
fluttering wildly in her stomach all over again.

'You do that.'

This was not at all how he had expected the day to go,
Nairo reflected as he watched this new Red march to the
door and yank it open, standing there stiff and taut, rejection in every inch of her slender body. The meeting with
some society designer he had anticipated had not happened
and instead he had found himself confronted by memories from his past stirring the silt in which he'd believed
they were buried.

Forcing him to remember how this one slip of a girl
had turned his life upside down, blackening his name just
when he was fighting to win back his father's respect, and
then walked out on him.

To remember how soft her skin had felt, the warmth
of her body as she had curled up to him on the rough and
ready 'bed' that had been all the furniture their room had
possessed. He could still catch her unique, individual scent

even if now it was hidden under some crisp fresh perfume and it awoke a hunger he had thought he'd forgotten. A hunger that he had spent the last ten years trying to obliterate. He'd indulged his masculine needs indiscriminately but never, it seemed, managed to wipe it out. Not if it could be woken again so fast and so easily.

'As soon as I see her,' Red came back at him with what was clearly a pointed reminder that she wanted him to leave. And it was because she so obviously wanted him gone that, perversely, he found himself lingering.

She felt it too, this disturbing hot flood of memories and awareness. It was there in her face, in the wide darkness of her eyes, the pupils distended until they almost obliterated the mossy softness of her irises. Her breathing was tight and unnatural and he could see the faint blue tinge under the pale skin at the base of her neck where a pulse beat, rapid and uneven. A kick of reaction hit him in the gut, keeping him where he was instead of leaving as she clearly intended he should.

'Is she always this unprofessional?' he asked icily, watching as her mouth quivered, then tightened again.

How was it possible that after all this time he could remember how that soft mouth had tasted, the warm yielding of those pink lips against his own?

'She...has so many demands on her time. More than she can cope with sometimes.'

'She's so busy she can risk losing an important commission?'

Rose flinched inside at the sharp stab of the challenge. Just moments ago she had thought of the Moreno commission as the chance of a lifetime, a rescue package that had landed on her desk wrapped in beautiful paper and tied with golden ribbon. But now it was as if she had opened that magical parcel only to find it filled with black, stinking ashes, with a deadly poisonous snake lurking at the bottom just waiting to strike.

She had to get out of this contract somehow, but for now she would settle for having Jett—or Nairo as it seemed she must call him—out of the shop, out of her space, to give her time to think about the way she could possibly deal with this without ruining her professional reputation once and for all.

'I can't tell you about that.' The fact that it was actually the most honest thing she had said gave a new strength to her voice. 'So, if you don't mind…I'd like you to leave now.'

His smile was dark, devilish enough to send shivers down her spine.

'But we've only just found each other again.' The mockery that lifted his tone had the sting of poison.

'Well, you obviously haven't missed me in the past ten years.'

No, that sounded too much as if she regretted it. The last thing she wanted was for him to think that *she* had missed *him*, even if it was true. But all her courage had seeped away, leaving her feeling weak and empty, genuinely afraid of what she might spark off if she challenged him too strongly.

'I wish I could say it's been a pleasure to see you again, but I'm afraid that just wouldn't be true. And I really must ask you to leave now. We have this event—a bridal fashion show—tonight. I have to get ready for that.'

That she wanted him to go wriggled under his skin and stayed there, irritating him furiously. She'd got under his skin in a very different way in the past. He had let her do things to his heart that he had never allowed any other woman—any other human being except perhaps Esmeralda—to do to him before or since. But now that they had met up again, all that she wanted was to be rid of him as soon as possible.

The temptation to dig his heels in and refuse to move at all almost overwhelmed him. But a moment's thought left him realising that he didn't have to tackle this right now. Not yet. He knew where Red was; she wasn't going anywhere. He could afford the time to wait and discover rather more about her, and then he would act in the way that would give him the best satisfaction possible.

Shaking her life right to the roots just as she had done to his when she'd walked out on him, leaving behind a mess it had taken years to sort out.

A curt nod was his only response to her pointed remark. It amused him to see the way her shoulders dropped slightly in relief, the easing of the tension about her mouth as she believed that she had got rid of him.

'You'll tell Ms Cavalliero that *I* kept our appointment? And I expect to meet up with her at her earliest convenience.'

Left to himself he'd dispense with the designer and her frills and fancies and go straight to the result he most wanted—the settling of the score he had with the woman he'd only ever known as Red. But he'd promised Esmeralda and he wasn't prepared to take any risks with his sister's health that not keeping that promise might result in.

So he'd see to this damn dress—the dress of his sister's dreams—first. And then he'd deal with Red. He'd waited nearly ten long years already. He reckoned he could wait a little while longer.

The burn of his memories suddenly flamed up again, hot and hard, as he saw the way that she stood at the door, stiff-shouldered, taut-backed, her chin lifted in a sign of defiance. There was a flare of awareness in those mossy-golden eyes that pushed him just too close to the edge of the restraint he was holding so tight.

His feet came to a sudden halt, not letting him move forward. He caught her swiftly indrawn breath, noted the extra tension in every muscle that held her slim frame tight, drew in her stomach and lifted the swell of her pert breasts above the embroidered belt that circled her waist.

'Red...'

If only he knew how much she hated that once affectionate nickname! That focussed stare held her transfixed, unable to look away in spite of the fact that she felt as if his gaze were searing through her skin, burning her eyes to dust. Slowly he lifted a hand, touched her face, the blunt tips of his long fingers resting so lightly on the cheekbone under her right eye.

'I never thought I'd see you again,' he said flatly. 'It's been...interesting...meeting up like this.'

'*Interesting*—that isn't the word I'd use to describe it.'

Devastating, earth-shaking, came closer. So many times in the past she'd dreamed of just this meeting happening—and dreaded it in the same moment.

'But I need to tell you. I am not the man that I was.'

'I can see that. That is, if Moreno is really your name,' she challenged.

'Jett was only ever a nickname. Moreno is my family name, though I didn't use it then—before.'

Abruptly his mood changed, his eyes becoming darker.

'They let me go, you know,' he said. 'There was no evidence against me.'

The conversational tone of his voice was at odds with what she read in the taut muscles of his face. Just how had Jett become this Nairo Moreno?

The man who stood before her was light years away from the wild, rough-haired youth she had once known.

The one who had stolen her heart only to break it just a few weeks later, crushing it brutally under his booted foot. Was he the member of a Spanish aristocratic family he claimed to be or—that nasty slimy feeling slithered down her spine again, making her shiver—had his obvious wealth and position been bought with the proceeds of other activities in the years since they had known each other? There might have been no evidence of the crime she'd suspected him of, but he had clearly come a long way in ten years and that spoke of a ruthlessness and focus that few men possessed.

Something she didn't want to dig into too deeply. And a very good reason to get out of the contract to design a dress for anyone in his family if she possibly could.

'You will not tell anyone about the time we knew each other.'

It was a cold-blooded command, laced through with a powerful seam of threat, a warning as to what would happen if she was fool enough to reveal anything he wanted kept hidden.

'Not even Ms Cavalliero.'

'I doubt if she'd need to know.' Not when she already knew every dark detail about Nairo Roja Moreno. And wished she didn't. 'I certainly won't be telling.'

'Make sure you don't.'

The finger that rested on her cheek traced a slow, gentle path down the line of her jaw, to rest against the corner of her mouth, hooded eyes watching every flicker of expression across her face.

It was all that Rose could do not to turn her head sharply, pull away from that small, lingering touch. She wanted to move, desperately longed to back away, and yet at the same time that simple touch was so familiar, bringing back memories of the feel of his hands on her skin, the taste of his mouth...

She couldn't go there. She *mustn't* go there!

'Take your hand off my face.' She hissed the words out as much against the feelings that were stinging her as at him. 'I didn't give you permission to touch me and I...'

She couldn't continue in the face of his unexpected soft laugh and the way that he deliberately twisted his hand so that the backs of his fingers were now against her skin. Deliberately he stroked his fingers down her cheek again.

'I said don't do that!' This time she couldn't hold back and jerked her head away in angry rejection.

His laughter scoured her spine, but he lifted his hand slowly, bronze eyes gleaming with wicked mockery.

'My, you do have a tendency to overreact, *querida*. It didn't use to be that way. I can recall a time when you would beg for my touch.'

'Then you must have an amazing memory. It was a very long time ago.'

'Not long enough,' Nairo drawled, the smile evaporating fast. 'Some things you just don't forget.'

'Really? Well, I'm afraid my recollection isn't as good as yours—and it's certainly not something I want to revive.'

Making the movement look as if she were only wanting to ease his departure, she slipped away from him, holding open the door again.

'I'll pass on your messages.'

The words showed every trace of the effort she was making to get them out, fighting against giving in to the burning response even that most gentle of touches was sparking off all over her skin. One flick of a glance up at him was more than she could cope with. She could see herself reflected in those burnished eyes, small and diminished in a way that made her legs feel weak as cotton wool.

'I'll tell her—everything you said.'

'Except that you knew me before.'

How did he manage to inject such deadly poison into six simple words? The stepfather she had run from in a flight that had ended up with her living in the squat might have ranted and roared, bellowing threats, but he had never managed to make her quail inside in the way that this quietly spoken command could do.

'Except for that,' she managed jerkily.

For another dangerous moment his fingers still lingered too close to her face, but then, just as she thought that she couldn't keep control any longer, he lifted his hand away and let it drop to his side. The smile that he flashed on and off was like burning ice, no emotion at all in it.

'See you around, Red.'

'Not if I see you first.'

The words were muttered to an empty space. He'd gone, striding out into the darkness and the rain without a single glance back. It was as if defiance of his presence was all that had been holding her upright as she sagged back against the wall and let the door slam back into place.

He was gone. And she was free, safe—for now.

But it was only a temporary reprieve. There was no way she could hold off having Jett—in the form of Nairo Moreno—back in her life while he still wanted to see Rose Cavalliero. Right now he had no idea that *she was* the Rose he'd come to talk to, but she couldn't hope to let that last for very much longer. He would put two and two together, and when he did, then he would be back.

She had to get rid of him; she couldn't cope with him intruding into her life. Not just because of the past but because of the shocking effect he still had on her today.

Slowly her hand crept up to her face, covering the spot where Nairo's fingertip had touched her. She almost expected it to have etched a brand into her skin, marking her as his. He had done that long ago, hadn't he? He had touched her life and encircled her with bands of emotional and sexual steel so that she had never been able to break free. Even now, all these years later, he could still invade her life and if she wasn't careful he would leave it in ruins all over again.

CHAPTER TWO

HE SHOULD NEVER have let himself touch her.

Nairo slid his car into the nearest empty parking space, stamped on the brakes with uncharacteristic lack of care and switched off the engine. His concentration had been shot all afternoon, in a way so untypical of him that it felt as if he was teetering on the edge of a form of madness. The tips of his fingers still seemed to burn with the imprint of that touch, the connection of skin on skin, even though it was hours since he had walked out of the shop and left Red behind. He was sure that if he brought his hand close to his face he would still inhale the perfume of her skin, the fresh, unique combination that was this woman mixed with the light floral scent she had worn.

Or perhaps that was because the cloud of her personal body perfume seemed to enclose him ever since he had realised just who she was. It had been like that after they had first become lovers. In the squat she had always washed every day, even in the freezing water that was all they had available, and the scent of her skin had been the only thing that was fresh or clean in the grubby little room that they had called 'home'.

Waking up each morning to find her curled against him, the soft hair, longer and redder than she wore it now, falling over her face, had made him feel as if life was worth living at a time when he had had serious doubts on that matter.

She'd had her own problems too. Running from an aggressive and abusive stepfather, a mother who had been too weak to protect her, she had still given him a reason to wake up—if only because waking up usually meant another opportunity to take her in his arms, and give in to the heated passion that burned into his soul every time he touched her.

He had even thought about changing his life for her.

'Change—for her—hah!'

The words punched into the air as he pushed open the door to the hall where the wedding fayre was being held, the violence of the movement expressing the way the memories burned like acid.

He had thought about change—had even taken the first steps towards it—and she...she had just walked out on him, never looking back. She'd also added an extra little sting to her departure that had come close to ruining every chance he had had of rebuilding what was left of his relationship with his family.

The burn of that memory almost had him turning and marching right back out again. He wanted nothing to do with Red—and yet he couldn't get her out of his mind. Her betrayal, her desertion, demanded some sort of retribution and yet he had no wish to tangle himself up with her all over again. He had just about found peace after ten years' hard work. Did he really want to stick his head right back in the lion's mouth and risk it all over again?

But the promise he had made to Esmeralda held him prisoner. He had sworn he would bring her this designer she had set her heart on, and he was not going back on his word. Only with that contract secured and his sister happy would he consider just how he would deal with Red.

The sound of the buzz of many voices from the end of the corridor told him just where the event was being held and had him heading towards the glass-paned door.

The noise of conversation hit him along with a strong wave of perfume—a heady mixture of so many different fragrances. The room was full of women of all ages, shapes and sizes. There were flowers everywhere too, and a small runway set up in the centre of the hall with a white floor, leading to a fall of heavy velvet curtains in rich red. The colours of the flowers, the curtains, the women's dresses and suits whirled and blurred into a kaleidoscopic haze.

'And now, ladies, we have a special treat for you...'

The voice was immediately familiar and Nairo cursed under his breath. Because there she was again. The woman he had known as Red.

If he had felt that she had grown into a beautiful woman when he had first seen her in the boutique, then this was even worse. Now she was groomed, and sleek, elegant in a silky peacock-blue shift dress, simple and sleeveless, that clung lovingly all the way from the softly scooped neck, over the curves of breasts and hips to end just above her knees and reveal a heart-jolting slender length of leg. The ridiculously high-heeled shoes were exactly the same colour as the dress, except for a perky little white bow at the toe. The whole effect had him clenching his hands into tight fists and pushing them deep into the pockets of his trousers as he fought with his immediate and primitive response.

He'd thought he'd put her out of his mind. He'd tried his damnedest to do just that, but it had taken only one look, one touch, and it had become obvious just why he'd been hooked in that way. She'd had the power to entrance him as a skinny girl and now she'd grown up, matured, he was swamped by a hunger he hadn't felt before or since. Then he'd been naïve enough to label it with a softer emotion because then he'd been fool enough to believe that emotion existed. He'd soon learned his lesson.

Now was not the time he wanted to remember how he had once been able to hold one slender foot in his hand, lift it to his mouth and kiss it from the long, delicate toes all the way up to where her legs disappeared under her skirt...

...and beyond.

Infierno! He could feel an unwanted heat flooding his body, hardening him and making his heart pulse in a hungry response to the erotic memory that had him in its grip. Violently he shook his head to drive it away and only succeeded in drawing the attention of the women closest to him. Their expressions of surprise and the widening of their eyes a sure giveaway of how unexpected his presence was, here in this ultra-feminine environment.

Nairo ruthlessly determined to ignore them—he had no interest in any woman here except for Red—and the important designer, wherever she was. He pointedly directed his gaze towards the runway, and the woman on it, her auburn hair gleaming glossily under the spotlight.

He watched Red lift the microphone again and announce, 'As I said—a real treat—for the first time ever an exclusive preview of my brand-new designs for spring.'

My.

The word exploded inside Nairo's head, battering at his thoughts. *My brand-new designs...*

Of course—he'd been a complete fool. How could he have not realised? It had all been there in front of him, but he had been so set on his mission for Esmeralda—and so stunned to find himself face-to-face with Red after all these years—that his intelligence had failed him and he hadn't made the connections that he should have done.

Red. *Scarlett.* The name written above the window of

the small boutique. And the designer's name was Rose
Cavalliero.

Rose red. *Scarlett.*

The velvet curtains had opened and a model had
emerged from behind them, walking up the runway, her
progress marked by gasps of delight and admiration. She
was a willow-slim beauty, and the dress she was wearing was a masterpiece of lace and silk, a fairy-tale wedding gown.

But he spared it only one brief glance. There was no
space in his mind to focus on anything but the woman who
stood on the side of the runway, microphone in hand, talking about trains, beading, boned bodices...

All he could think was that *she*—Red—was also Rose
Cavalliero—

Scarlett's talented designer—the one his sister dreamed
of having to create a dress for her upcoming wedding.

The woman he had once known as Red was the woman
he had come to London to meet—and to persuade her to
come back to Spain with him.

Suddenly the room that had already felt so alien to him
in its total focus on femininity, the overwhelming reek of
clashing perfumes, seemed to constrict around him, the
lights dimming. It couldn't be any further from the rooms
in his father's home where he had lived as a boy. The old-
fashioned high-walled castle so wrongly named Castillo
Corazón—the castle of the heart! But the feeling of being
trapped was just the same.

As an adolescent, he had felt this sensation of being cornered when his new stepmother had insisted that he meet
all her female friends—the wives or daughters of acquaintances, some of whom had once been or still were his father's mistresses. They had almost mobbed him, circling
round him like brightly painted predators. He had learned

fast and young to recognise when someone was genuine
and when they were fake.

Or he'd thought he had.

He hadn't recognised the secrets behind Red's green
eyes. And he had known the slash of betrayal when he
had found out the truth.

'And perhaps for an older bride, this elegant look...'

The clear, confident voice carried perfectly, no real need
for the microphone, but it was not the woman on the runway whom Nairo was seeing. Instead it was the woman
he had met in the boutique that morning.

Hell, she'd still deceived him even then. She had known
who he was, known that he had come to see *her*, and yet
she had let him linger in his belief that she was just the
receptionist and that Rose Cavalliero was someone else
entirely.

She had had the opportunity to tell him the truth then,
but she hadn't taken it. Instead she had dodged the issue,
kept it to herself, and then she'd dismissed him once again
in a brief and curt email.

Scowling, Nairo remembered the message that had
reached him in his suite just an hour and a half ago. Rose
Cavalliero was sorry, but she was afraid that she couldn't
manage to fit in a meeting with him after all. She apol-
ogised for the inconvenience, but the truth was that she
wasn't taking on any more commissions at the moment.
She was sorry that he had been inconvenienced in coming to London for nothing, but she needed to take time to
care for her mother...

Coldly polite but dismissive. All of which could only
mean that she had something to hide.

'And this is the highlight of the Spring Collection. I've
named it the Princess Bride.'

Perhaps it was the name, perhaps it was the sound of the

murmurs of appreciation that flowed around the room, but something made Nairo look up to see yet another model emerging from behind the scarlet curtains.

In that instant he knew just why Esmeralda had been so insistent that this particular designer should create her dress. If she could make these women—every one of them—look so stunning, then what would she do for his sister? She would turn his shy, uncertain sibling into a glorious beauty—the princess she was meant to be—and surely that would give Esmeralda the confidence to face up to Duke Oscar's critical and demanding family without making herself ill again. And that was what he owed to his sister.

A memory stirred in his mind. The image of Esmeralda when he had come back from Argentina, where his father had sent him as penance for his adolescent rebellion. His sister had always been slim, but then she had been frail and delicate as a tiny bird. He'd even been afraid to hug her in case she might break. It had torn at his conscience to realise that the truth was that she was suffering from anorexia. It had taken him months to encourage her to let go her hold on her appetite and eat.

There and then he'd vowed that he would never let her down again. That he would do whatever it took to make her happy—keep her healthy and strong. To do that he now had to bring Rose Cavalliero back with him. Even if she had turned out to be the woman he had known all those years ago.

And when he had Red—or Rose or whatever her name was—in the castle in Andalusia, then he could tie up all the loose ends that were left hanging from when they had been together before. He would get rid of this unwelcome desire that still made him burn for her and he would teach her how it had felt to be the one cast aside when something better presented itself.

Leaning back against the wall, he folded his arms and prepared to wait and watch until it was time to talk to her.

Rose had been so focussed on the fashion show and making sure that everything ran smoothly that she had had no time at any point to actually look up and take notice of the crowd. But now, with the last dress displayed and the final parade of models down the runway, she could relax and look up, take a breath, glance out across the room...

And that was when she saw him.

Apart from the fact that Nairo Moreno was the only male in the room, it was impossible to miss him. He was leaning against the wall, arms folded, dressed all in black, with his shirt open loose at the neck. Like a big dark bird of prey amongst a flock of gaudy, chattering parrots. The burn of his golden-eyed stare was like a laser beam coming across the room.

He must have read the email she'd sent trying to get out of the commission he wanted. She'd asked for a receipt, so she knew he'd opened it. But he had determined to ignore it. She'd tried to avoid telling him who she was—who the designer Rose Cavalliero really was—but it seemed she'd failed miserably. Because now he was here—waiting, watching like some dark sentinel at the door.

'Rose!'

'Ms Cavalliero!'

Belatedly becoming aware of the way that she had been standing, silent and stunned, while her audience grew restless, Rose blinked hard, clearing her eyes of the haze of panic that had blurred her vision and forced herself to focus. At the front of the audience were the special guests, the reporters who had been invited specially in the hope of giving the new collection a great opening. That even more hopefully would lead to the sort of sales that would save her business, pay the rent for another twelve months. Give her mother a place to live and rest as she recovered from the draining bouts of chemotherapy. They'd only just found each other again properly; she couldn't bear it if their time together was so short.

Dragging her gaze away from the dark figure at the door, she switched on what she hoped was a convincing smile as she turned her attention to the first reporter to get to her feet—a well-known fashion writer for a luxury magazine.

'Do you have a question?' she managed. 'I'm happy to answer...'

'I'm glad to hear that.'

It wasn't the fashion reporter who spoke but another woman, a blonde she hadn't spotted before. Rose's heart sank. She knew this woman and so what was coming.

'Don't you think it's something of an irony, the fact that you are publicising your new collection now—with images of love and happy-ever-afters—when your own story is so very different?'

The bite in her voice was unmistakeable, sharp as acid. Rose recognised her as Geraldine Somerset, a person she had seen at one of Andrew's parties. The woman everyone had expected to be his fiancée before he'd met Rose.

'I don't know what you mean.'

'Oh, I'm sure you do.'

Geraldine lifted a newspaper that had been lying on her chair. Rose had no need to see it to know that it was a notorious scandal rag. She also knew just what headline the woman wanted everyone to see. Geraldine unfolded the sheet to its full length, waved it above her head, turning so that everyone could read the banner headline: *'Dream-maker or dream-breaker?'*

Rose even knew what pictures went with that story. How could she not when a copy of just that paper had been pushed through her letter box less than a week ago? On one side of the text was a picture of Andrew, head down, frowning and glum. The other was a picture of Rose herself, striding into her boutique—the name Scarlett perfectly clear and in focus. It had been taken shortly after the news of the broken engagement, the cancelled wedding, had hit the fan.

'Would you want to buy your wedding dress from a woman who only cancelled her own marriage just three days before the ceremony?' Geraldine was demanding now. 'Would you entrust the most important day of your life—or your daughter's—to someone who had so little care about her fiancé that she left him broken-hearted practically at the altar?'

'That isn't the way it was…' Rose protested, only to have the newspaper waved even more violently in rejection of her words.

'"Dream-maker or dream-breaker?"' Geraldine declared, clearly very proud of the headline it was obvious she had created.

It was equally apparent that she was having the effect she wanted. The whole mood of the evening had changed. The murmurs of appreciation and approval that had marked the end of the fashion show had now changed to darker, more critical comments. Already people were pushing back their chairs, getting to their feet.

'This has nothing to do with my work!' Rose tried, but it was like Canute asking the sea to go back. Everything had changed and Geraldine, with her emotive headline, the carefully slanted photographs, had turned the tide of opinion.

Rose had forgotten that Nairo Moreno was here. That he was watching all this.

The moment the thought had crossed her mind she lost her concentration as she flicked a hasty, nervous glance to where Nairo leaned against the wall by the door. Or rather, where Nairo had been leaning. Even as she watched she saw his eyes narrow sharply, the beautiful, sensual mouth tighten until it was just a thin, hard line. The frown that snapped his black brows frankly terrified her.

Not meeting her eyes, his gaze fixed on the scene before him, he levered himself up from his position and stood tall and dark and powerful as he surveyed the room.

'The woman's bad luck—she taints everything she touches.' Geraldine was getting into full flow again, her voice rising to almost a screech, the newspaper flapping wildly as she waved it high. 'I mean—who would want *her* to design a dress…?'

'I would.'

Cold and clear, the response cut through the buzz of outrage and comment that had filled the room. The silence that fell was as if a huge blanket had been dropped over everyone, stifling any sound. The audience stilled too, as Nairo moved forward, his movements the dangerous prowl of a predatory wild cat. A path opened up to let him through and even Geraldine froze to the spot, her words deserting her as he came closer.

Rose couldn't blame her. Seen like this, Nairo Moreno was the sort of man who could suck all the air out of a room simply by existing. She found herself struggling to breathe, waiting and watching…

'I said *I would*.'

Nairo had reached Geraldine's side now and he snatched the newspaper away from her, sparing it only the briefest, iciest glance before he crushed it brutally in one hand

and tossed it aside, contempt in every inch of his powerful body.

'I would have Miss Cavalliero design a dress for someone I loved. Anyone with eyes to see would do the same—wouldn't you?' he challenged, his fierce gaze raking over the rest of the audience. 'Anyone but a fool could see that as a designer Miss Cavalliero is hugely skilled. As a man, I'm no expert in fashion...'

Rose watched in amazement as he actually shrugged his shoulders in a gesture of assumed self-deprecation.

It had to be assumed, didn't it? Even as the Jett she'd known he wouldn't willingly admit to any sort of weakness in his own make-up. But the gesture had worked. The women surrounding him had actually smiled. Some of them were nodding.

'But even I can see that these dresses are works of art.'

He had the room in the palm of his hand, Rose realised. He was turning the tide of disapproval that Geraldine had threatened to direct against her.

'Miss Cavalliero...'

Nairo had moved closer, was holding out a hand to her. For the space of a dazed heartbeat she stared at it, only realising after a moment that he meant to help her down from the runway, onto the floor of the main ballroom.

She needed that help. Needed the support of his strength and the warm power of that hand. But even as his grip closed over her fingers, she knew a sudden stunning change, felt the sting of burning electricity fizz through her so that the hold she took on him was more than to get down the steps to the floor. It was like being taken back in years, to the days when she had been just a stupid, crazy, hormone-ridden teenager and she had first met Jett. Back to the days when she had given him her heart, her soul, her virginity. And he had only to touch her to send her up in flames.

From being cold with shock, she was now burning with response and could feel the colour heating her cheeks.

'Now can we talk about the dress you will create for my sister?'

Rose knew that everyone was watching, that she was the focus of all eyes, and she knew there was only one answer she could give. He had saved her reputation, her business, and the slam of the door told its own story: that Geraldine had conceded defeat and was on her way out of the room, out of the building—please heaven, out of her life.

She had caught that firm and deliberate emphasis on the word *now* even if no one else had. He knew she had tried so hard to get out of the commission he had proposed. The commission that would mean she would have to work with him, for him, all the time she was planning the dress for his sister. At least it was not for his *bride*.

But she'd been here once before, when Nairo had seemed to be her saviour and turned out to be a threat of danger she had barely escaped. So now had she been rescued or entrapped? Was he offering her freedom and a new security or had he actually caught her tight in some carefully planned and deliberately achieved spider's web? Did he really just want her to design a dress for his sister or was there more to his intervention than that?

Right now it seemed that he was her saviour—at least that was what everyone else would think. And because of everyone else, all those eyes on her, she knew she had no option but to give him the response he wanted.

'Miss Cavalliero?'

The prompt sounded easy, almost gentle, but she had regained enough composure to look into his eyes and easy and gentle were not what she saw there.

What she saw was ice, resolve and the sort of ruthless determination that warned her that if she didn't do as he wanted, then he was more than capable of turning this apparent rescue mission into one of total, devastating destruction.

She had been offered a lifeline as long as she went along with what Nairo Moreno wanted. Her life had been full of problems before, but now it seemed that by escaping one set of difficulties she had landed herself with a whole new adversary. One who she suspected was much more formidable than anyone she'd come up against before.

Out of the frying pan and into the fire. But what else could she do?

'Of course, Señor Moreno...' She forced her stiff lips into what must have looked like the most wooden and unbelievable of smiles. 'I'd be happy to discuss your commission with you.'

CHAPTER THREE

NAIRO MIGHT HAVE said that he wanted to discuss the design for his sister's wedding dress, but he showed no inclination to deal with that business right then and there. Instead he waited, smiling, courteous—apparently patient—while Rose spoke to the women who wanted to talk to her about designing their dresses, or their daughters'. The endorsement that Nairo Moreno had given her was apparently enough to convince them that Scarlett was the designer that everyone wanted now.

Which was not surprising really, Rose admitted to herself. After all, as she had discovered earlier in a quick, mind-blowing search on the Internet, the wedding that he was organising for his sister was to be the society event of the year. Esmeralda Roja Moreno was to marry into powerful Austrian aristocracy, it seemed. Duke Oscar Schlieburg was the eldest son of Prince Leopold of Magstein and his wedding was to be almost a state occasion. Her head was spinning simply at the thought of the boost of publicity and the prestige that would come to her business as a result of her involvement with such an event.

A boost that had already started, it seemed, as she collected up the lists of names and addresses of all the potential new customers she'd gained.

'That seemed to be a success,' Nairo's cool voice drawled as the last customer went out the door.

'Success is an understatement.'

Her response came faintly. She had been so absorbed in the matter in hand that she hadn't really been aware of the fact that he had been there all the time, a silent observer, sitting on the edge of the runway, his long black-clad frame standing out so starkly from the white and silver décor. She'd been fooling herself, of course, if she'd let herself think that he had gone. He had set this response in progress with his intervention for his own personal reasons, and now he was going to claim what he felt he was owed.

A chill breeze seemed to blow across Rose's skin as he dropped down from his place on the runway and started towards her and she wished everyone hadn't left her quite so alone.

'Th-thank you for your help. I really appreciate it.'

His dark head nodded, bronze eyes hooded to hide any emotion he might feel.

'There is a price for my assistance.'

Of course there was. This was Nairo Moreno she was dealing with now. A man who had somehow built himself up from the shabby, broken beginnings of their lives when they had first met and who now was this powerful, wealthy man. There had to be a price on anything he did. He was no longer Jett, the youth she had run out on so long ago.

'A price?'

'Oh, don't look so panicked,' he mocked as she turned uncertain eyes on him. 'I'm not going to demand your body in return for my favours in some odd modern version of *droit du seigneur*.'

He paused just long enough for her skin to smart under the bite of his mockery.

'There wouldn't be much point, would there? After all, *we've* already been there, haven't we, *querida*?'

The pointed reminder that they had once been lovers, that he had been the one to take her virginity all those years before, drained the strength from her muscles, making her grab at a nearby chair for support. An innocence that then she had relinquished happily and unhesitatingly, she had been so much under the sway of the heated hunger she had known for this man, blinded to anything but her need for him.

'Been there, done that—didn't bother to stay around to get the tee shirt,' she flashed at him, then immediately regretted her too-aggressive tone.

He might have stepped in to save her business earlier this evening, but what he had decided so surprisingly to give her, he could take away in the blink of an eye. Just as so many new customers had followed his lead to want to use her services, they could easily follow him *away* from her again if he chose to reject her after all.

She must not forget that she was no longer dealing with the Jett of ten years before. This man was a very different sort of male. Tall and powerful, his broad frame had filled out and strengthened where Jett had had a whipcord leanness that had been defined even further by the fact that there was never quite enough to eat in the squat.

Added to that he was someone else entirely—a man of status, with power and money no object. He had a sister who was marrying into the aristocracy and an estate which, if the Internet reports were to be believed, was more than the equal of his prospective in-laws. How he had come by that she had no idea; she didn't want to think about it too closely. She had bitter memories of the appalling ways he had planned on acquiring more money ten years before. But it all added up to someone who was light years away from the scrawny, long-haired Jett she had once believed herself in love with.

Thank heaven she was well over that particular nasty infection! But the scars the past had left on her soul reminded her that she would do best to play this particular game very carefully. Every instinct warned her that Nairo Moreno played to win and that he would prove a spectacular opponent if she was foolish enough to challenge him too far.

'*Querida...*' she echoed cynically. 'How come you're suddenly living in Spain and tossing about Spanish endearments?'

'Not suddenly,' Nairo corrected flatly. 'I always did live in Spain—or, rather, my family home was in Andalusia. And so, naturally, I grew up speaking Spanish.'

'You never used Spanish when we— In the squat.'

'No.' There was even less emotion in the response this time if it was possible. 'I didn't. But then I didn't want anyone there to know who I was.'

Shockingly the fact that he included her in the 'anyone' he hadn't wanted to know the truth about his background, combined with the fact that he had only ever used his native language to her in the brutally sarcastic way he had said *querida* just now, stung at her deep inside.

'And obviously neither did you. So tell me, when did "Red Brown" become the much more exotically named Rose Cavalliero?'

The room suddenly felt chill, as if the heating had been turned off, as from a shadowy corner of her mind came the echo of her mother's voice on the day she had been called to the hospital to find Joy recovering from a brutal beating that Fred Brown had given her.

'My own fault, darling,' Joy had admitted. 'I was a

sucker for a handsome face, a sexy body, a promise of support…and I thought he'd change.'

Wasn't that how it had been with her daughter when Rose had met Nairo?

'Rose was always my given name,' she responded stiffly. 'It's just that Brown was the name I'd been going by—my stepfather's name. You know why I was more than happy to change that when I found I could. It was only when I reunited with my mother and we started talking—really talking—that she told me my father had been an Italian artist she met on holiday—his name was Enzo Cavalliero.'

Another of the good-looking men her mother had fallen for, only to find herself abandoned when things got tougher. Joy had tried to contact him when she'd found herself pregnant, but he'd never responded.

'I've used it ever since. But I don't think that you should throw stones, Señor Moreno. You weren't exactly forthcoming about your true background either.'

A slight inclination of his head was all the acknowledgement of the hit she'd made he was prepared to give.

'Jett was a nickname the gang in the house gave me. It was easier to stick with that.'

But Rose didn't want to linger on the past. The present had enough complications of its own to be dealt with.

'So what exactly is your help going to cost me?' she asked now, determined not to let him see that anything he'd said had had any effect on her.

She was sure that he had expected she would want to know why he had never told anyone the truth about his background and that by deliberately not asking any such thing she had frustrated and irritated him in equal measure.

'More than designing a dress for your sister, I mean.'

A lot more, the hard twist to his mouth warned. But his answer was not what she'd expected.

'I expect you to come and live with me for a month— Oh, not in that way...'

That twist became more pronounced, mocking the startled reaction he had deliberately provoked and that she had been fool enough to give him.

'I doubt that either of us would care to go back to the way things used to be. No—you will come to Spain with me, meet Esmeralda, get to know her properly. You'll work with her on the details of the wedding—the bridesmaids' dresses, the pages' outfits... Everything.'

'I can't manage that,' Rose put in hastily, thankful that there was at least a real excuse for her not to fit in with his plans. She had no wish to spend any more time with him than she absolutely had to. If she had to design his sister's dress, then she would—she had too much to lose if she didn't. But the swirl of personal memories threatened to put her completely off balance and she desperately wanted to get this back onto a purely business level.

'I was telling the truth when I said that my mother is unwell.'

The way his dark brows snapped together warned her of what was coming and she knew the question was one she would have wanted answering for herself. Nairo had been the only other person she'd confided in about her stepfather's abuse and, worse, he also knew that Joy had sided with her husband in the face of Rose's accusations. That was why she had run away, a desperate move that had ended by throwing her into the arms of the man who had called himself Jett.

At that time Nairo had understood unquestioningly. That was one of the reasons she'd fallen head over heels for him, wildly, crazily, until she'd learned her lesson. She was secretly stunned that he even remembered, never mind felt some of the anger he had showed then.

'And you'd put your life on hold, ruin your business for her?'

When she had done nothing of the sort for her daughter. The implication was there and Rose knew she couldn't deny it. It was the way she had felt herself and it had taken long years of distance and slow, painful reconciliation before she had managed to reach the place she was in now.

'She's my mother.'

He was obviously not convinced.

'And did she act like a mother when she took your step-father's side against you?' There was something new and shockingly savage in his tone so that Rose had to hurry to reassure him.

'She regretted that deeply. She was scared—terrified. She'd been a single mother once and found it so hard. No money, no support.'

So Joy had thought her salvation lay in the support of a man, any man. And she was, as she had admitted, a sucker for a handsome face. Fred Brown had been a very good-looking man. A handsome face that hid a personality as black as pitch. But admitting that took Rose down paths she didn't want to follow as they reminded her that at one point—more than one—she had found herself to be very much her mother's daughter.

'But when I found her again she was in a real mess. Brown had been treating her as a punchbag because he was so angry I'd got away from him.'

'Is that what's wrong with her now?'

'No—she had breast cancer. She had the operation and now she's recovering from treatment. She's getting better every day, but I wouldn't feel right about leaving her even...'

'Then I'll make sure that she has the very best care.' Nairo dismissed her objection with a wave of his hand. 'A live-in nurse—anything and everything she needs.'

Just the thought of Joy having professional care, the attention that Rose hadn't been able to devote to her and run the wedding boutique as well, brought such a rush of relief that she almost grabbed the offer right out of his hands. She'd felt so guilty at the way she'd had to neglect her mother recently, leaving her in the tiny flat for far too many hours on her own. The demands of just scraping a living, finding the money to keep a roof over their heads, had forced her to focus on her work far more than she'd liked and it had given her an insight into why her mother had been prepared to grasp at anything—anyone—who seemed to offer an alternative. But the uneasy, apprehensive feeling that came with wondering why he was offering—and demanding—so much forced her to hesitate.

'I don't usually work this way!'

Everything was happening too fast. Only yesterday she had been barely aware that Nairo Moreno even existed, let alone that he was actually the boy she had once given her naïve foolish heart to, all grown up and turned into this unstoppable masculine force.

'It's this way or no way,' Nairo retorted.

'And if I don't agree?'

'I reckon Geraldine would be able to point me in the direction of another designer.'

It was said so lightly, even carelessly, that she couldn't believe he meant it. But meeting his stony eyes told a very different story. He meant every word and if he did go elsewhere, with Geraldine's recommendation, then her business was dead in the water. Her reputation would be shredded for ever if it got out that Nairo Moreno had withdrawn his commission from her.

'But why can't your sister come here and talk things over with me? That's how I usually work—how it would be with any other client.'

'Esmeralda is not just any other client. This wedding has to be perfect, and my sister has to have everything she wants.'

She sounded like a spoiled little princess and already Rose was regretting having anything to do with this wedding. Yet how could she regret taking on the commission that might turn her life around? If the response to Nairo's announcement that she was to design Esmeralda's dress was anything to go by, once this commission was completed, then surely everyone would forget the cancelled wedding, the 'broken-hearted' groom left almost at the altar? She would put her heart and soul into creating the most beautiful gown for Nairo's sister so that the wedding would be the perfect showcase for what she could design in the future.

How long would it take? A month, he'd said. Maybe less? She could cope with that, couldn't she? After all, she probably wouldn't have to see Nairo himself for any real amount of that time. He was a man, and from her experience the males involved in weddings, even the most doting grooms, stayed well back for as much of the time as they could.

'You'd really make sure that my mother has a nurse?'

'If that is what it takes. A live-in carer in attendance twenty-four hours a day. I know of an agency...'

Nairo named an exclusive and highly rated agency, the sort of establishment with fees that Rose couldn't even dream of being able to afford.

'You can choose her yourself—I'll set up the interviews for tomorrow if that will suit you.'

It would more than suit. It was far more than she could

ever have anticipated. If only it hadn't been Nairo who was behind it all. Surely he couldn't want her that much.

But of course. She almost laughed aloud. *He* didn't want *her*. He was here at the bidding of his sister. That demanding little princess.

'I understand how you feel about leaving your mother,' Nairo put in unexpectedly. 'My sister has been ill too. That is why she is not here with me.'

'Oh. I'm sorry to hear that.'

A kick of guilt left Rose feeling uncomfortable. She should be grateful to Esmeralda; because of his sister Nairo was offering her a lifeline that she had never anticipated.

'I'll look forward to working with her on the designs for her wedding—to make her dream dress, for a perfect day.'

'I'd appreciate that, thank you,' he said, his voice unexpectedly rough at the edges, and something had changed in Nairo's face. A relaxation of the muscles in his jaw, an unexpected light in his eyes, turning Rose's feelings upside down. She didn't care if the concern was all for his sister, only knew that the sudden rush of release from the tensions of the past year or more had gone to her head like the prosecco she had served earlier that evening.

'No, thank *you*!'

Her head spun with such relief it pushed into an unguarded response and before she had quite realised what she was doing she had come up close and pressed her lips against his cheek.

A kiss of thanks. That was all it was meant to be. Just a peck on the cheek. There and gone again in a minute. But as soon as her lips touched his skin, felt its warmth and the hardness of bone beneath her mouth, the moment the taste of him touched her lips she knew that it wouldn't stay that way. It couldn't end there.

It was like putting a match to a drift of dried tinder deep

inside her, setting everything burning, making her control crack dangerously. She remembered what that taste had been like before, what a simple kiss had led to. Something so wild, so passionate that it had been impossible to control. It was reaching out to grab hold of her already, turning her blood white-hot, melting her bones so that she swayed on her feet. She would have fallen if Nairo hadn't reached out and grabbed both her arms, holding her upright. Holding her close.

'Red...' Nairo said roughly, and the rawness in his voice told its own story. One she wanted and yet feared to hear.

It was still there. The sparks that flashed like lightning when they looked at each other, the flames that flared if they touched. She'd felt it in that moment when he had touched her cheek in the shop doorway and it was bubbling up inside her now like lava in a volcano, threatening to spill out and swamp her in a scalding flood.

'Rose...'

The fact that he had corrected her name only seemed to make matters worse. His tone was tight, constricted as if he was having trouble getting words out of his throat. But then he gave up on even trying. The proud dark head bent swiftly, his mouth coming down on hers in a hard, bruising kiss. It crushed her lips back against her teeth, opening them to allow the stroke of his tongue, tasting her, tantalising her. She could barely snatch in a breath under the pressure of his kiss as she let her head fall back, opening to him so that he could plunder her mouth. Time evaporated, sweeping all memories before it, and in her thoughts she was once more back in the scruffy darkness of the squat, alone with this man who had come to her rescue when she had most needed him, and who had stolen her naïve heart as a result.

The ten years in between had vanished. She was once

more the girl she had been then, young, innocent, lost in a world of sensation that she had never known existed.

Something she hadn't experienced since in all the time between.

It was like opening a door and letting in the sunshine. Nairo's strength was a powerful support, one she still needed as she swayed against him again. Her arms came up, reaching for him once more...

'*No!*' he said harshly, wrenching his mouth away, shocking her out of her dream world.

It had been a dream then too. Like the sort of fairy tale her mother had been looking for. She had thought him her rescuer, but she hadn't known the truth.

The long body so close to hers had frozen, stiff and taut. She could feel him staring down at her even though she couldn't see it, and she had to force her eyes open to meet his.

The darkness of desire had changed his eyes, distending his pupils so that there was only the faintest gold at their rim, and yet, in spite of that one betraying reaction, he couldn't have been further from her if he had been on the opposite side of the world.

His hands clamped hard and tight around her shoulders, pushing her away, the ferocity of rejection in his movements.

'*No!*' He didn't need the extra emphasis. His feelings were perfectly clear. 'This isn't going to happen. It isn't what I want.'

Liar! The word sounded in Rose's head and she wanted to throw it at him, to challenge him with it. The way her body was stinging in response to that kiss screamed at her to defy his hard-voiced declaration. How could he say that when she had felt his reaction in the tightness of his body, could still see it shadowing his eyes?

But even as her mouth opened to speak she caught the word back, swallowed it down, knowing that it was safer that way. But she wasn't going to let him get away unchallenged.

'My, you do have a tendency to overreact, don't you?' she tossed at him. 'It was just a little kiss.'

'Some *little* kiss.'

Nairo couldn't stop his mouth from quirking up into a smile at her response as he recognised her repetition of the comment he had turned on her in the boutique earlier. She had spirit, he'd give her that. But 'a little kiss' went no way towards describing what they'd just shared. A little kiss wasn't possible between them.

The taste of her was still on his tongue, his lips. His senses burned and every nerve still throbbed from the response that had blazed its way through him. The heat and hardness below his belt made it impossible to think straight. But when he looked into her eyes he knew he *had* to think straight. Hell, someone had to or he would give in to the primitive demands of his body that screamed for appeasement, throwing her down on the thickly carpeted floor, crushing her under his weight.

She would let him, he knew that without a doubt. She might scratch and hiss like an angry kitten, but she could not deny the enticement, the welcome that had been there in her eyes, in her touch—in that far from *little* kiss.

'However little it was, it's not what I want from you.'

'I should hope not, because that's not what I want from you either.'

She might try to disguise the flinch away from his words, bring her head up a little bit higher to declare defiance and rejection, but she was still fighting a disappointment that was every bit as strong as the one that was biting at him. The wide, blurred pupils gave away the fact that she was as turned on as he was. Even after ten years he still remembered how she looked when she was aroused and hungry for the pleasure he could give her.

'I might sign up to design your sister's dress—but that's all. It's a business deal, nothing more.'

'A business deal suits me fine,' Nairo echoed with a curt nod, holding out his hand to her.

She took it, even clasped it firmly and shook it in a very businesslike manner, but not before he'd noted the hesitation, the tiny jerk of her fingers as his palm touched hers. He knew just what that meant. Hell, wasn't he feeling it too? How could he miss the way her tongue slipped out, slicked across dry lips, the forced way she swallowed against an obviously tight throat?

He could have her right now if he wanted, and—*querido Dios*—he *wanted*. The need was like a searing brand on his body. He wanted her and he could have her if he just pressed a little more…kissed her again…caressed her…

He could have her, but what good would this be if, after all this time, after ten years' waiting, it was fast and furious, totally uncontrolled?

The demanding pulse that had taken prisoner of his senses insisted that it would be worth it—*right now*. But the little part of his brain that was still rational told another story. One that offered a fuller, deeper satisfaction.

Waiting would be worth it. Waiting would build the hunger, the sense of need, in her as well as himself. If he kept her waiting, then he would keep her hungry. The hungrier she became, the more complete his triumph would be when he finally made her his. This time she wouldn't be able to walk away from him.

This time he would be the one doing the walking.

'Can I give you a lift home?' It wasn't easy to make it sound careless, relaxed.

Her head came up, eyes wary at even that simple question.

'No, thank you. I still have some tidying up to do here. And I have a taxi coming...'

'Then I'll see you tomorrow—for the interviews. I'll call the agency and set them up.'

'That would be perfect.'

Her smile was a fake flash on and off, not meeting her eyes, not warming her face in the slightest. She might think that she was showing nothing, but he knew Rose Cavalliero, as he must now call her, of old. The harder she worked to project the fact that she was feeling nothing, the more she had to conceal.

It wouldn't be a problem keeping her wanting. He'd seen the disappointment in her eyes when he'd pulled back. It had almost been worth the difficulty he'd had to wrench his lips away from the warm, soft invitation of hers just to see the way those mossy-green eyes clouded with disbelief and frustration. The fire that had flamed between them all those years ago was still there, totally undimmed by ten years' absence. If anything, it was stronger now. The desire of a grown man for a woman rather than the adolescent rush of hormones he had known before. He had thought that he had wanted her then, but it was nothing compared to what he felt now.

'Tomorrow, then.'

Not a man to let grass grow under his feet, this Nairo Moreno, Rose reflected as she made herself take the business card he passed her. He had come prepared for this and would allow for no other possible outcome.

If anything should tell her just what his trip to England was really all about, it was that. All her earlier fears, the secret thrill of dread that he might actually have come looking for her after all this time, evaporated in a hiss that almost sounded like laughter at her own stupidity.

She couldn't have been more deluded.

He didn't want her. He couldn't have made that any plainer if he'd tried. The flat, emphatic statement left no room for doubt. He didn't want her and that should have made things so much easier. She should feel relieved, because she was going to have to travel to Spain with him, to stay there for a month while she worked on his sister's dress, and it would be so much easier knowing that she meant nothing to him, that he didn't want her in any way.

So why, instead of the relief she should feel, the soar of elation and freedom, was the emotion that filled her built on the sort of disappointment that shrivelled her heart?

CHAPTER FOUR

'You need to tell me about the wedding.'

'What?'

Rose lifted her head from the sketches she was concentrating on to see Nairo standing in the doorway of the workroom that had been set apart for her in the Castillo Corazón. This was the first time that he had approached her since they had arrived at his magnificent family home, and she'd been grateful for his absence as she tried to get her head round what had happened to her.

It seemed that in the time since Nairo Moreno had appeared in her life her world had been turned upside down. Was it really possible that it was less than a week since that moment and yet she seemed to have lost control of her life as surely as if someone—Nairo obviously—had wrenched the reins from her hands and was directing things the way that *he* wanted.

Nairo didn't wait for anything, it seemed. He wanted a carer for Rose's mother—one had been selected, appointed, moved into the tiny flat that she and her daughter shared, while Rose was whisked off to the airport in a chauffeured car, escorted onto a sleek private jet and transported here to Andalusia, where the luxurious golden-walled *castillo* was to be her base for the next four weeks or so. It felt as if she had been transported into a different world instead of just to another part of Europe. Her work-room alone, opening out onto a Moorish-style patio, would have swallowed up more than half of the shabby little flat that she had struggled to pay rent on and the suite she had been installed in with its tiled floors and decorated ceiling was almost twice the size of her London boutique.

When she had first seen her room, it had been like going back in time, with the huge canopied bed and the rather old-fashioned furnishings giving the place a formal, rather stiff, dark look. The most wonderful aspect of the room was the wide balcony overlooking the gardens and the river below. But she didn't have time to explore, to enjoy the beauty of her surroundings or even have a swim in the large outdoor pool. She was here to do a job and it was so much easier if she focussed on that and nothing else. It would also mean that she could get out of here as soon as possible.

'I didn't think that you'd be interested. But here...'

'Not that.'

Nairo waved away the pages covered with designs and colour swatches she held out to him.

'Not Esmeralda's wedding—I understand that that is going fine. No, I meant the wedding that never was— the one you were supposed to have with Lord what's-his-name...'

'Andrew,' Rose supplied flatly.

'Yes, Lord Andrew Holden. The man you supposedly left at the altar on the day of the wedding.'

'Three days before the wedding, actually.'

Rose knew she sounded snappy when really she was fighting with the rush of tension that stretched each muscle tight as she answered him. The thought of the day she had realised she couldn't go through with her wedding was particularly uncomfortable with Nairo before her, reminding her of the memories that had driven her to make that decision.

'Why do you want to know?'

'Because Oscar and his parents are getting concerned.'

Rose had seen Nairo's prospective in-laws, the Prince and Grand Duchess, only once, but that was enough to make her understand exactly why he was so insistent that things would be perfect for them. Their emphasis on propriety and social esteem meant that they would expect nothing less. And it was obvious that Nairo's sister was very much in awe of them.

From the moment that she had met Esmeralda Moreno she'd understood even more. Nairo's sister was almost nine years younger than him and, while she shared his black-haired, golden-eyed colouring, she had nothing of his powerful build and strength. Instead she was tiny, delicate, finely built. Too thin and nervy, speaking too quickly, worrying about too much. Rose suspected that she showed signs of suffering from some sort of eating disorder in the past, which made it clear why Nairo was so concerned and protective.

Esmeralda was definitely not the spoiled princess she had anticipated but a vulnerable woman who desperately wanted people to like her. And Rose did like her, very much.

'Oh, come on, I'm only the dress designer!' she protested. 'When the big day arrives, I'll be out of here and gone.'

She sincerely hoped that would be the case. Living here like this with Nairo likely to appear at any moment was stretching her nerves so tight she felt they might actually snap. It should have been an easy matter to avoid him in the huge *castillo*, but somehow she always seemed to bump into him when she least expected it. She was beginning to feel like a hunted animal, on high alert at every moment, while Nairo was perfectly polite but totally indifferent and businesslike.

This isn't going to happen, he had said and it seemed that he was determined to keep to that.

Still she found herself tensing up whenever Nairo walked into a room, focussing so hard on what she was doing that it was almost a discomfort. She was so aware of him, of the lean length of his tall dark figure, the glint of the sun on the rich darkness of his hair, the beautifully accented sound of his voice, the scent of his skin blended with a tempting citrus cologne. It was only then that she realised how deep she had dug a gaping hole at her feet and foolishly allowed herself to fall into it. She had fallen back into the bonds of his physical spell as badly as she had done all those years before, when she had been just an adolescent, and every day she spent at the Castillo Corazón pulled those bonds tighter and harder around her, stopping her from thinking straight and from sleeping at night.

She couldn't even use her mother as an excuse. The nurse that Nairo had provided for Joy had proved to be perfection in a human form. 'My guardian angel' her mother called her and under the woman's gentle care Rose's mother had not only been more comfortable than she had ever been when Rose had struggled with her care as well as running the boutique, she had actually thrived. The two women had become great friends so that as well as providing her medical care, Margaret also gave Joy the sort of female companionship she had been longing for. The sort of friendship that, try as she might, Rose had never been able to really have with her parent. There were too many shadows between them. Margaret and Joy shared knitting patterns, read books, enjoyed cooking together and Rose knew that she would be going a long way towards risking the steady progress of her convalescence if she was to take Margaret away.

There was more to it too. The last time she'd spoken to her mother there had been a new, very different note in Joy's voice. One she hadn't heard in so long—if ever at all. Pushed to describe it, she'd have had to say that there was a lack of the guilt that had always been just under the surface ever since they had reunited when Rose had gone to visit her in the hospital after Fred's last attack on her.

They'd determined to put the past behind them, made a home together, but Rose knew that her mother's conscience always troubled her when she looked back, particularly when she'd seen how hard her daughter worked to keep the roof over their heads. So now the relief and delight at what she saw as Rose's newfound success lightened every word, every phrase. After all the time it had taken them to rebuild their relationship, could she really risk going back on that?

'It's not as simple as that,' Nairo said now. 'There has already been a lot of interest in the fact that you're here— and involved in Esmeralda's wedding. I need to know how to handle it if the paparazzi come hanging round the gates, trying to take photographs. There's a risk that they're becoming more interested in *you* than the bride and groom and they're starting to demand to know whether you're a curse on any wedding you're involved with.'

'Oh, that's just stupid and you know it.'

Rose used the need to put the papers back into order and down onto the table as a defence against the rush of colour she knew had heated her cheeks.

'I saw the effect just the mention of the story had on the audience at your fashion show,' Nairo stated coolly. 'It could have turned pretty nasty.'

'Because Geraldine stirred it up. She won't be here at Esmeralda's wedding.'

'But you will be, and if you come trailing the shadows of your past life behind you and bring the paparazzi to our door, then it will turn this whole thing into an ordeal for my sister instead of the happiest day of her life.'

'Well, you should have thought of that when you asked me to design the dress for her and made sure that I would do it.'

You have a nerve to talk about past scandals, Rose wanted to fling in his face, but the memories of how she too was connected to that past dried the words on her tongue. Combining those memories with the thought of her mother's happiness and health now made sure that she didn't dare risk opening another can of worms. She couldn't forget the unspoken threat that had been in his warning that she was not to talk to anyone about the time when they had met before.

Echoes of that time had surfaced on the first day when they had reached the *castillo*. As she had got out of the car, Rose had stared up at the huge, beautiful golden building, with the darkening rays of the setting sun vividly reflected in the glass of every wide-paned window.

'Is all this yours?' she'd gasped, unable to believe it. Unable to connect this glorious, elegant building with the man she had first known to be living in a squat, no job, no money of his own.

'It is now,' Nairo had responded flatly. 'I inherited from my father. What?'

He'd looked down at her sharply.

'You don't think all this is bought with the profits from my dirty dealing?'

It was the first time he had breached the wall of silence they had built around the past. The wall she had had to build around it in order to be able to go on with this 'business arrangement'.

'I never…' she'd begun, but at that moment the great wooden door of the *castillo* had opened and a tiny whirlwind in the shape of his sister, Esmeralda, had rushed out to meet them, flinging herself into Nairo's arms and hugging him tightly so that there had been no chance of continuing the conversation.

It still hung there between them now, unspoken, not dealt with, and Rose knew that one day it would have to be faced or it would blight the rest of her life.

'You saw enough to realise that I have a "past",' she flung at him. 'That was the time to get out of things if you'd wanted to keep this squeaky clean so as not to offend your in-laws. Instead you made sure that I got this commission and that everyone there knew it. Why?'

It was a question he'd asked himself so many times, Nairo acknowledged. If he'd had any sense, he should have turned and left her to the ruin of her fledgling business. He'd have found another designer to please Esmeralda. He'd have appeased his sister somehow and not jumped, feet first, into the murky puddle of complications and memories that this woman brought with her. But, Esmeralda or not, he had known from the start that he couldn't just turn and walk away from her. Not until he'd got her well and truly out of his system.

'You were the designer Esmeralda wanted. And I hate bullies. Geraldine was a born bully, anyone could see that. She wanted the attention to herself and she was determined to do anything to win it. I enjoyed making sure she didn't succeed.'

It was true he hated bullies, and he had no trouble recognising an emotional tormenter when he saw one. Hadn't he seen enough with the way his young stepmother had treated Esmeralda, whom she'd considered a rival for her husband's affections? Though he'd never reckoned that she would start on him as well. That was why he had moved forward to act when Geraldine had been trying to stir up trouble. But there was more to it than that. In spite of everything, the memory of the way Rose had walked away from him, in spite of the fact that the tall, elegant woman who stood on the runway in that clinging peacock-blue dress was light years from the girl he'd befriended and protected in the squat, he had still seen some faint and unexpected traces of the Red he had known back then. He'd seen the stress lines round her eyes, the way she was biting her lower lip. The memory had disturbed his responses so sharply that he had moved forward, acted, spoken, before he had even realised what he was doing.

'She was supposed to be marrying Andrew before he met me. She wanted her revenge.'

'I would have thought she'd have been happier to have him back on the market.'

'Mmm.' Rose looked uncomfortable about that. 'The problem was that he didn't want her back. He'd been looking for an excuse to break off with her and—well, I provided it.'

'Are you saying he didn't love you?'

'No.' Bright auburn hair caught the blaze of the sun as she shook her head, sending it flying in the air. It also sent the aroma of her perfume, light and delicate, wafting towards him, threatening to scramble his thoughts so that he had to drag them back into focus. 'The opposite. He was crazy about me.'

The emphasis on the word *crazy* warned him there was more to this story than she was happy to acknowledge.

'So what happened? Why did you call the wedding off? He was too "crazy"?'

And Nairo was too aware, Rose reflected secretly. He'd caught on some betraying note in her voice, a look in her eyes, and seen part of what she would have liked to have kept hidden from him.

'He was…rather obsessed,' she managed, finding it embarrassing to say any such thing to this man. Why would he believe that Andrew had been so over the top in his avowals of devotion and adoration when Nairo himself had found her so totally forgettable? 'I—I realised that I didn't feel the way that he did. He took it badly.'

'Three days before the wedding,' Nairo murmured darkly.

'I know! I know! You can't make me feel any worse than I do already.' She'd lived with the guilt ever since.

Her voice sounded too uneven, too raw, and she had to move away, riffling through the papers in her hand as if looking for something special amongst them. There was no way she was going to admit that she had tried so hard to care for Andrew as he'd wanted. She knew there was no great passion between them; they hadn't even made love. But she had thought that would all come in time. Until the day when, sorting out her belongings, ready for the move to the elegant apartment that was to be her new home, she'd come across a dusty, faded box at the back of a cupboard.

In that box had been the one and only photograph of herself with Nairo she had ever owned. Creased and battered, it was one of a set they had taken in a cheap photo booth on an afternoon when they had actually had a few pounds to spare. A joyful, laughter-filled day that she had wanted to record for ever and so had dragged Nairo into the booth with her in spite of his protests.

The sketches in front of her blurred now just as that photograph had done then and she blinked hard. How could she have married Andrew—married anyone—when she knew she didn't feel anything like the overwhelming power of emotion that had swept over her when she had been with the man she had known as Jett? She couldn't have given herself to anyone else unless she had felt something that had at least come close to what she had felt then. The man she still felt that way about, she realised with a feeling that left her fighting for breath.

Even worse, she knew she had proved herself to be her mother's daughter when she'd rushed in without thought, just as Joy had plunged into marriage to Fred Brown. She'd believed she'd found someone who would care for her, someone who would take the burdens from the shoulders that had supported them since she'd promised to help her mother escape from her stepfather's brutal influence. In a weak moment she'd seen hope and so she'd said yes, only to realise that she'd done so for the worst possible reasons.

'I should never have said yes to his proposal. Our engagement was a terrible mistake.'

'Why such a mistake?' Nairo questioned. 'Looking at it from the outside, I would have thought that Andrew Holden was the perfect choice.'

'Oh, really? And why was that?'

He'd caught her on the raw there, he could hear it in her voice as she tossed the question over her shoulder at him, the muscles in her face stiff and tight with rejection.

'Good-looking, tall, successful, with a great position in society. Wealthy...'

That brought her spinning round to face him. Her eyes were unusually bright as she turned them on his face.

'And you think that his money was the answer to everything? The reason why I wanted to marry him in the first place?'

Nairo shrugged indifferently, brushing off her challenge to him.

'Isn't that what women want in a marriage?'

It was what his mother and stepmother had wanted from his father. The old man had always been a sucker for a pretty face, a sexy body. He had been so convinced that he was 'in love' that the thought of a prenup had never entered his head. Between them, his two wives had drained almost everything the old man had to offer and then headed for pastures new when there was nothing left. The first Señora Moreno had been happy to leave her children behind, not wanting her pleasurable lifestyle with her new partner to be restricted by a son and daughter, then just nine and one year old. The second, Carmen, had even tried to take Raoul's son from him in the end.

He'd vowed that he would never leave himself as vulnerable to any woman as his father had done, and for most of his life he had kept to that vow. The only reason he had ever come close to breaking it was standing before him now. He'd had a lucky escape there. One that had taught him a much-needed lesson on the risks of weakening. At least he had had the sense to keep the truth about his family from her, though he'd come close to telling her that Christmas when he'd tried for a reconciliation with his father. She'd still found a way to make money out of their relationship when she'd gone to the police.

'Not me!'

The fury of her indignation clashed with his own challenging stare so that he could almost see the spark where they met in the air between them.

'But your business was in difficulties—you're oceans deep in debt.'

That made her head go back, green eyes widening in shock.

'How do you know that?'

The smile he couldn't hold back wouldn't have looked

friendly. It wasn't meant to. It was just an on-off twitch of muscles, an uncontrolled response to the realisation that even now she still didn't recognise the difference between the raw youth he'd been and the man he was now.

'I make it my business to know everything about anyone I'm dealing with. If I want the information, it's easy enough to get it. So wouldn't marriage to him have solved all your money problems?'

'Maybe—yes. But shouldn't the fact that I *didn't* marry him show you that that wasn't what I was looking for from him?'

He had to concede that, Nairo acknowledged. But if that was not the reason she'd been prepared to marry this Andrew, then why had she backed out so late? For an uncomfortable moment he was back at the fashion show, watching the woman called Geraldine brandishing the newspaper with the scandalous headline right in Rose's face. He'd stepped forward to stop the obvious attack right then and there, but he'd never actually really challenged himself on *why* he'd done that. He'd claimed that he hated bullies— and he did—and the sight of her pale, strained face had taken him back ten years to the moment when he'd first set eyes on her looking lost and alone on a London street.

But there was more to it than that.

'Wouldn't I be much more comfortable, more settled, as Lady Holden?'

'As I recall, you always dreamed of marriage and a happy-ever-after...'

He let the rest of the sentence fade off into a dark growl, not liking the memories that came pushing to the surface as he spoke.

I don't do love. I don't do commitment... Through the years his own voice came back to haunt him. He'd been so sure, looking at the ruins of his father's two marriages, the destruction they'd left behind—particularly for Esmeralda. *I certainly don't do marriage. If you want those, then you'd better find yourself someone who does.*

But the irony was that in the moment that Geraldine's announcement had made him realise Rose had done exactly that—found someone else, agreed to marry him—then his world had rocked off balance and he'd found himself moving forward, taking action without really thinking things through.

It hadn't even been the fact that he wanted to please Esmeralda. This went deeper, was more personal than that. He didn't want Rose being with anyone else. He wanted this woman back in his life, in his bed.

He hadn't had enough of her ten years ago and he didn't intend letting her be with anyone else until he'd got her out of his system.

'Perhaps I did,' Rose acknowledged. 'But there would have been no happy-ever-after. I was very fond of him, but I could never give him what he needed from me. My timing was really really bad, but it would have been far worse if I'd married him and then realised my mistake.'

It all sounded so perfectly rational, so believeable. At least, it would have been if it hadn't been for the way that her eyes wouldn't quite meet his. She was holding something back, hiding something from him. But before he could try to drag out of her just what it was, the door opened and his sister hurried into the room.

'So have you finished your sketches, Rose?' she asked, her voice bubbling with excitement. 'Have you got something to show me?'

'Yes, I have them here...'

Rose reached for the sketches from the table once again and it was only now that he saw how much her grip on them had been crumpling the paper so that she had to smooth them out to show Esmeralda her designs.

'If we've finished...'

Her hazel eyes went to Nairo's face, her eyebrows lifting in question. He knew what she was asking, what put that faint frown of concern between her fine dark brows. Was he going to leave things there, with whatever she'd kept hidden still unsaid?

It seemed he was going to have to because her question, the look she turned on him, alerted his sister to his presence in the room.

'I didn't see you there, big brother! Don't tell me you've suddenly developed an interest in bridesmaids' dresses—because that's all we're going to let you have a peek at! No one but Rose and I will see *the* dress before the big day. It's our secret.'

'And that's how you must keep it.'

Rose could only blink in astonishment as she heard the change in Nairo's tone as he addressed his sister. The cold stiffness had melted away, leaving a warmth that flowed over her like liquid honey. But only for Esmeralda. When he turned back to her his eyes were opaque and hooded, hiding any emotion.

'Would I dare to get in Esmeralda's way?' he drawled. 'We're finished here—for now. We can carry on this converation at another time.'

So was that a promise or a threat? Rose had no way of knowing because as he finished speaking Nairo moved to drop a quick, affectionate kiss on his sister's head, then strolled out the door. The gentle gesture wrenched at her heart, reminding her of how she had once believed that he had cared for her too.

No—bitter realism made her add it as the door began to swing to behind Nairo's tall figure. Gentleness and warmth were not what there had ever been between the two of them. Their relationship had been based on a searing sexual passion that had caught them up in a conflagration too wild, too ferocious to be resisted. She might have thought there was concern at first, when he had come up to her when she had been sitting on the stone steps in Trafalgar Square, cold and miserable, too tired to go any further. One of her shoes had split, letting in the wet, and her hair had hung in damp rat's tails around her face and shoulders. Perhaps then he'd felt a touch of concern for her. He couldn't have felt anything else.

Quite frankly, then she'd been a mess.

'So—Rose—do you have the designs—the dress...?' Esmeralda's excited voice broke into her thoughts as she tugged the sheets of paper from her hand. 'Let me see.'

Rose could only be thankful that the younger girl's enthusiasm and excitement meant that she didn't notice her own distraction, the way that her mind was far from focussing on anything like the plans for the wedding dress but instead had followed Nairo out the door and back into the past they had once shared.

'Oh, but these are *gorgeous*! *Maravilloso!* Perhaps we should have let my brother stay and see these. Then he'd understand why I insisted that it had to be you designing my dress and he should fetch you for me.'

She sounded so determined, so resolute that for a moment Rose remembered once again the way she had dismissed Nairo's sister as a spoiled, demanding little princess. But she'd seen with her own eyes since she had come to stay at the *castillo* that Esmeralda was a charmer, a delight. She could easily wind anyone round her delicate fingers, but she only used that appeal on her obviously besotted brother. No one could have missed the way he watched his little sister so closely, a faint frown deepening the lines around his stunning eyes. There was more than just brotherly affection behind that watchfulness. Some memory that it seemed only the two of them shared.

'Surely they would impress even him,' Esmeralda was chattering on, unaware of the way that Rose's thoughts had drifted away. 'They might even convince him that romance really does exist.'

'Your brother is not a romantic?'

By imposing enough control over her voice she managed to make it sound relaxed, even light.

'Surely someone living here amongst all this beauty...' The wave of her hand took in the high decorated ceiling, the tiled floor that led out onto the patio, the sun streaming through the wooden blinds from the garden, where the sound of the river below in the valley was a gentle background song to the formal beauty of the *castillo*. There was so much to the place that she still hadn't seen.

'Oh, *no*...' Esmeralda shook her dark head sharply. 'He has no time for looking at his surroundings, not even to bring this place up to date really. He's had to work too hard to make sure that the estate was saved and that we could still live here.'

'The estate was in danger?'

Seeing the elegant luxury that surrounded her when contrasted with her own small flat, Rose found it hard to believe any such thing.

'We almost lost everything,' Esmeralda assured her. '*Papá* was ill and he let things slide. That was when he brought Nairo back from Argentina after seeing the great job he did there.'

'Argentina?' It was a strangled sound of surprise.

So Nairo had lived abroad for some—how much?— of the time since they had been together in the squat. No wonder he'd seemed to have disappeared off the face of the earth and she had never seen or heard anything of him since that fateful night.

Esmeralda nodded. 'We have an *estancia*. That was almost derelict too. But my brother, he knows how to work—and work.' Her endearing, bright smile quirked her mouth up at the corners. 'Even if *Papá* didn't approve of so much he did out there.'

'No time for romance?' The uncomfortable fluttering of her heart made it a struggle to speak.

'No time—and no *heart* for romance. I'm not quite sure what happened, but I know that when he was in England he met someone.'

Esmeralda shook her head as if in disbelief.

'Some cold, cruel little witch who stamped on his heart and then betrayed him without a care. She got off unscathed, but my brother... Pah! If I could get my hands on her...'

Rose's head was spinning. *When he was in England...* Could Esmeralda mean *her* as the 'cold, cruel little witch'? But that was not how it had been. Nairo had been the one who deserved those accusations. He must have told the story differently.

Nairo had once told her why he was in London, living in the squat. A huge row with his father, so he had just walked out, taking no money with him. 'A woman' had been behind it was all he would say. So did Esmeralda have it wrong and the woman who had hurt her brother was actually someone he'd left behind in Spain?

Or perhaps Rose was too sensitive to this account of things? Perhaps there had been some other woman in England... Unfortunately that version of things didn't bring any sense of relief, only a tangled mess of complicated feelings that twisted and burned at the thought of Nairo being so involved with someone else that the other woman had left him feeling that she had 'stamped on his heart'.

Stamped on his heart! That made it obvious that *Rose* couldn't be the woman Esmeralda had meant. The Nairo she had known had had no heart to be stamped on.

From the depths of her thoughts a flash of dark memory came back to haunt her. Nairo holding Julie, the girl-friend of Jason, an older man who also shared the squat, the blonde woman's head on his shoulder. The burn of jealousy she had felt had been like nothing she'd ever known.

A faint noise out in the hallway made Rose glance up. Reflected in the mirror on one wall, she could see the tall dark figure of Nairo just beyond the doorway almost blending into the shadows of the wooden-panelled corridor beyond. He hadn't walked away at all but must have heard every word of the last conversation. As her head came up, she saw the heavy lids that hooded his eyes lift so that he was staring straight at her.

Just for a moment their eyes locked in the reflection in the glass, the intensity of his stare making her blood run cold in her veins. Then he turned on his heel and strode away.

CHAPTER FIVE

Rose was out on the patio, at work on her designs, the sun gilding her arms exposed by the sleeveless white cotton top. She had pulled her chair right to the edge of the swimming pool and let her bare feet fall into it so that the water lapped against her lightly tanned toes as her head was bent over the sketch pad on her knees. Her pencil moved swiftly and confidently over the paper, adding a flurry of lace here, a waterfall of a train there. Her auburn hair tumbled forward over her face as she concentrated, the copper strands in it caught and illuminated by the setting sun until they glowed a fiery red, much closer to the colour they had been when Nairo had first seen her.

He had been away from the *castillo* for only four days and yet coming back to her now was like seeing her anew.

It had been the red of her hair that he had first seen, spotting her slumped wearily against a wall, the brilliant glow shining out in the dull grey of a wintry afternoon in spite of the fact that it had been raining heavily and her corkscrew curls were limp around her head. Long, thin legs in faded black leggings had been splayed out on the steps she was sitting on as if she didn't have the energy to place them any other way, and her head was down-bent then as it was now, but then it had been a sign of depression and withdrawal, not the current focus on creativity.

He had easily picked her up from the pavement where she sat and carried her when she had swayed against him in obvious weakness. She hadn't eaten for two days, she'd told him later. She'd left home in a frantic rush, running from her abusive stepfather, no time to collect more than her handbag. But her purse had had so little cash in it, and that stepfather had put a stop on the bank card he had once let her have.

A card he had later expected her to pay for with sexual favours.

A red haze burned before his eyes and he cleared his throat to ease some constriction that had unexpectedly closed it off.

'Buenas noches,' he said hastily as Rose started at his approach, scrambling to her feet, her eyes wide as she turned towards him.

'How long have you been there?' Her tone was stiff with tension, warning him to stay away. A warning he had every intention of ignoring.

'Not long. But you seemed so absorbed, I didn't want to disturb you. '

He gestured with his hand towards the sketches that lay open on the table, a dress in a swirl of pink lace, the one she had been working on, uppermost.

'Aren't you supposed to hide those from me? Some ancient superstition about no one seeing The Dress until the big day.'

A wash of colour swept up into her cheeks at his teasing tone, and she moved the sketches around, fanning them out and then back again before answering him.

'Oh, no—that's just the bride's dress—Esmeralda's gown. And I'm past the point of drawing sketches for that. We've already had a couple of fittings and it's almost ready. These are some other designs—suggestions for the weddings of other clients. Women who were at the fashion show that night…'

She let the sentence trail away, but there was no mistaking which night she meant. Deliberately he waited and watched the struggle that went on behind her eyes before she opened her mouth again.

'I really am very grateful to you for what you did to help me.'

Grateful was fine. Even if she made it sound like something that was the exact opposite. He could use 'grateful'. He would have preferred something much more passionate, but at least it was better than the frozen mask that she slapped on her face whenever she was forced to be alone with him. She managed that as fast as she could, but he had still been able to catch the glint of awareness in her eyes, the way her white teeth had dug into the rosy softness of her bottom lip when she had thought he hadn't noticed her. But of course he'd noticed her. How could he do anything else?

His resolve to wait was coming back to bite him and bite him hard. Being with her and not being able to touch her in a sensual way was a torment, all the more so because it was self-inflicted.

He could sense where she was in the *castillo* even in the silence of the night, imagining her up in her suite, asleep on the high canopied bed or lingering in the deep roll-top bath, the water scented with some floral oil. Every instinct seemed to home in on her even when he tried to focus on something else. He could tell if she had been in a room and had left it just before he'd entered by the whisper of her soft slippers in a corridor, the trace of her perfume that drifted on the air. And to sit in a room with her, hear her voice, the bubble of laughter that seemed to well up so often when she was sharing something with Esmeralda, made his skin feel too tightly stretched across his body, pulling painfully taut across his scalp.

Just to watch her move across a room, see the sway of her breasts and hips, the smooth curve of her behind, the length of her legs, made his blood pound, his groin ache. This was why he had never been able to forget her. It was the reason for the burningly erotic dreams that had plagued his nights, forcing him to wake in a knot of sheets, with sweat sheening his skin. He had thought he'd suppressed those dreams after all this time, but from the moment she had come back into his life he'd been tormented all over again.

Being with her and not having her made him curse his blind stupidity in ever starting out on this idea. And now, when she had no trace of make-up on her porcelain skin, lush black lashes framing those mossy-green eyes, it was all he could do not to lean forward and crush the soft pink lips under his demanding mouth. Her long, fine hands were slightly stained with a wash of colour from the water-colours she was using on the designs, making a memory twist in his guts. Those fingers had once been smudged heavily with coal dust as she had tried to light a fire in the grate in their room in the squat, using a few battered, damp pieces of coal that had fallen from a passing delivery lorry in the week before Christmas.

'Perhaps I should save this for the big day itself,' she'd said, holding her grimy fingers out towards the weak, spluttering flame. 'Then we'd have something special to celebrate. But I can't wait…'

He hadn't encouraged her to wait either. Because it had been in that moment that he had resolved to make a move to change his life for her and with her. He'd known his father would demand a high price before he'd allow the prodigal son to return home, but it would be a price he was prepared to pay if it meant that he could offer Rose a better future. But he hadn't reckoned on her desertion, the betrayal that meant his Christmas Eve had begun with a visit from the police and had continued to go downhill from there.

It had almost lost him his honour, his family. And the damage it had done to Esmeralda was something he could hardly bear to remember even now.

'I've just been talking to my mother,' Rose said. 'I ring her every night and Maggie—the carer who is looking after her—has been a godsend. She and Mum are getting on so well, it's like having her best friend come to stay.'

He knew how that felt. When his father had been in his final illness, just four years before, the trained care of the professional nurses brought in to help him had been invaluable. He couldn't imagine having to cope with the round-the-clock care the old man had needed, and the business of dragging the estate into the twenty-first century without knowing that they were dealing with everything that was needed in his sickroom. They had also been able to keep an eye on Esmeralda too when he couldn't be there. But Rose had had to manage on her own. And her mother...

Her smile, the light in her face caught on a raw nerve. With the memory of that miserable winter day in the squat so clear in his mind, it was impossible not to contrast the way she looked now talking about her mother, and the bleakness that had dulled her hazel eyes when she had thought about not being able to be home at Christmas. *Infierno*, hadn't that given him the final push to hold out an olive branch to his father?

'I'm pleased for you.'

'For me?' She had obviously caught the distance in his voice and it made her frown. 'But you've been really kind to my mother and I'm glad to see her happy.'

'You can forgive her that easily?'

'Forgive—but she's my mother.'

'You ran away from her.' The memory made his voice hard.

'No!' Rose shook her head, sending her hair flying, the softness of it and scent of floral shampoo tormenting his senses. 'Not from her—from her husband.'

'She married him—her choice,' he dismissed. 'And she didn't protect you from him.'

'No,' Rose admitted with obvious reluctance. 'But she was scared.'

'And you weren't?'

'Nairo—I saw what he did to her. Her face—the bruises all over her body. Broken ribs.'

Her earnest tone, the expression on her face made it plain that it was important to her that he understood. And now, perhaps he did as he couldn't have done back then.

Her mother had been little or no help to her, he recalled, remembering the anger that had tightened his muscles, burned in his veins at the thought that in her own way Joy Brown had been as much of a waste of space as his own vindictive stepmother. That was why he'd been astounded to find that mother and daughter were now living together, with Rose doing everything she could to support her ailing mother. With a generosity he hadn't expected, she had obviously forgiven the older woman's neglect even before Joy had been taken ill. But then hadn't he been able to reconcile with his father once the old man, recognising how ill he was, had asked for his help after finally acknowledging the foolishness of believing Carmen's selfish lies?

I only wanted to give you and Meralda a new mamá... Raoul's voice, rough with the after-effects of too much wine, too many cigarettes, came down through the years to haunt him. That would have been so much easier to believe if that 'new *mamá*' hadn't been an ex-showgirl who'd worked in the casino where Raoul regularly lost more than he could afford—and no more than six years older than his adolescent son.

'Is it any wonder that I detest bullies?' he murmured, seeing some of the tension leave her body as he spoke. 'In that case, I'm glad that I could help. So how is your mother?'

'Making great progress. She's feeling stronger every day and she sounds so relaxed. There's a new lightness in her. It was like hearing her coming back to life. Really I don't know how to thank you!'

'Ah, well, I can think of a way. I came to ask you something. Esmeralda has gone to spend the evening with her fiancé and his parents, so I came to see if you wanted to have dinner with me.'

'Oh—there's no need.' Rose placed her hands flat on the top of the table in order to control the way that they had started to shake nervously. 'I was looking forward to a quiet night on my own. Perhaps a bowl of soup.'

'We can do better than that.' His smile burned through the defences she had struggled to build around herself. 'I know that you've come here to work, but I'm no slave driver. Surely you can give me a chance to say thank you.'

'Th-thank you?' Her tongue stuttered over the words in the face of the unexpected warmth of that smile. 'No, really, I am the one who should be thanking you.'

Nerves twisted into knots in her stomach, forcing her to face the fact that she had no alternative but to agree to his invitation. It would look so ungracious to refuse it now.

Besides, when he smiled like that, he made her forget all about the man he had once been, the cold manipulator who had been hidden behind the sexy, whipcord-lean youth with unkempt black hair and gleaming eyes. But where had that youth gone—if in fact he had gone anywhere? Wasn't he just hidden under the sophisticated veneer that Nairo Moreno presented to the world? She had been deceived by him once and it had shattered her heart. Was she going to risk letting that happen to her all over again?

But it was only dinner, and here in this house. It wasn't even a *date*.

'It's only dinner,' Nairo said, echoing her thoughts with unnerving accuracy. 'Nothing to be scared of.'

'I'm not scared. Of anything.'

But it was too fierce, too emphatic to be fully convincing. As she watched that smile deepen in his eyes she suddenly knew that she was in big trouble. There was no way she could back out without making it obvious just what she had been dreading and so risking even further humiliation if she had this all wrong.

'Dinner, then.' She started packing away the sketches carefully in her portfolio. 'I hope you'll forgive me if I don't change my outfit. It's been a long day and…'

She let the sentence drift when he actually laughed at her concern.

'I'm only offering a casual meal, Rose. I'm not like my soon-to-be in-laws insisting on everyone dressing for dinner. I thought this would be an opportunity to escape all the formalities and relax.'

'Oh, that sounds great!'

Her relief was genuine. The past weeks had been something of a strain when she had found that she was expected to change for dinner every night. The formal meals around the highly polished table in the huge ornate dining room had been something of an endurance test and she'd already worn the few smarter dresses she'd brought with her at least twice. Her blue linen trousers and white sleeveless shirt were cool in the heat but hardly the sort of dressing up she had had to become used to.

'To be honest, I'm just in the mood for something simple like an omelette or cheese on toast.'

'Or fish and chips?' Nairo inserted lightly, taking the breath from her lungs with an instant vivid memory of just what had provoked that comment.

They had both managed to get temporary jobs in the run up to Christmas and to celebrate their first income in weeks had indulged in fish and chips, fresh from the paper, with fingers prickling from the icy cold. That cold now seemed to reach out from the past and encircle her heart. In spite of having so few comforts, and nowhere secure to live, she had thought that she was happier then than she'd ever been in her life before. Head over heels in love with the man she called Jett, she had adored and trusted him so much that she had given him her body, her virginity without fear or hesitation.

It had been less than twenty-four hours later when the bitter truth began to dawn on her as Nairo had started to talk about a way of making sure they had more money, a plan to secure their future.

'I don't eat chips any more,' she managed. 'Too much fat.' She regretted that comment as she saw the way it drew his burning gaze to her body, drifting slowly and deliberately over her shape, lingering blatantly at her waist and hips.

'You know you have no need to worry about that, Red,' he drawled, golden eyes challenging her to find an insult in his obvious admiration. 'And you don't have to fish for compliments.'

'I'm not fishing! And my name is Rose. No one ever calls me Red any more.'

'You'll always be Red to me.'

It was impossible to interpret just how he meant that comment and he didn't give her time to think about it as he turned to go back indoors.

'I can't offer you fish and chips, but I reckon I could rise to an omelette if that's really your choice.'

'*You* could...' Rose gave up on trying to hide her confusion as she was forced to trot in his wake.

That confusion grew even worse as she followed him, not towards the elegant dining room, where she had had all her meals so far, but across the tiled floor of the spacious hall and...out the main door?

'No—hang on a minute.' She hoped he'd believe her breathlessness was caused by her efforts to keep up with him. 'Where are we? I thought...'

'I invited you to dinner. You accepted.'

'Yes—but...' Unnerved, she looked back into the house, then turned again in time to see the amusement grow in his eyes.

'I thought you wanted a rest from the formality.'

'I did—but...'

'This way.'

He caught hold of her hand, leading her out into the still, soft warmth of the evening. Unable to break free without an awkward struggle, Rose let him take her with him along the gravel path towards another door set into the wall of the *castillo*.

'What is this?' she asked as he paused to slide a key into the lock.

'My home—my apartment.'

He flung the door open and stood back to let her past him.

'*Mi casa es su casa.*'

Rose stepped onto polished wooden floors, stared up at the high white-painted ceilings that soared above the hall-

way and the wide, curving staircase. Through the doorway
she could see a living room, with more wooden floors,
huge multicoloured rugs and large squashy sofas in a rich
deep red. The walls were lined with bookshelves and, even
at this point in the evening, the whole room was flooded
with light. As soon as she stepped into it, the room spoke
to her of comfort and relaxation more than any of the huge,
formal rooms in the main *castillo*. It had the same elegant
proportions of course as anywhere in the rest of the main
building, but it was so much more of a home than those
rooms with their old-fashioned, stiff furnishings.

This explained something that had puzzled her before.
She had assumed that Nairo had been out and about when
he didn't eat with his sister and her. That he had work to
do or he might have been wining and dining—and more—
one of the beautiful women he was so often seen with ac-
cording to the gossip magazines. She had never thought
that he might have this separate section of the *castillo* to
himself. Something about the room tugged on a memory
but one she couldn't bring to mind as it hovered on the
edge of her thoughts.

Nairo watched Rose stand in the centre of the room,
staring round at her surroundings, her confusion evident
on her face. He'd aimed for that and obviously he'd more
than succeeded. It gave him a grim sense of satisfaction
to see that this separate section of the *castillo*, his private
home, had surprised her as much as this.

It would surprise Esmeralda too if she had known that
he had brought Rose here tonight. He never brought anyone
to this apartment, least of all any woman he was seeing.
Those sorts of relationships were conducted away from
the *castillo*, in the woman's home, or the privacy of a suite
in a luxury hotel. The apartment was his, and only his. It
had been his refuge from the time he had come back from

Argentina, a place where he had the privacy and isolation that had never been his while his stepmother, or one of his father's more recent conquests, had been in residence in the main building.

His personal apartment had been a place of retreat when he returned to try to drag the value of the estate back from the brink of bankruptcy. A place that was his alone. Much as he loved his sister, and, towards the end, he'd rediscovered a connection with his father, he'd needed privacy for his own thoughts and a space to relax in.

Though relaxed was exactly the opposite of the way he felt right now. He didn't know what had possessed him to invite Rose here, to bring her into his private sanctum. He hadn't thought beyond the fact that he was tired of waiting, that he couldn't hold back any longer.

Seeing her in the main rooms of the *castillo*, with Esmeralda or perhaps Oscar and his family around, was becoming totally intolerable. He wanted Rose on her own. Just the two of them. The feelings she inspired in him were not for public times, for the company of anyone else. They were hot thoughts, burning desires that were just for the privacy of his own apartment. And ultimately for his bedroom.

But for now, he would play things casually; they had the whole night ahead of them.

'Pour yourself a glass of wine and come and talk to me while I cook.'

'You cook? You really meant it?'

'Of course—simple meals at least. An omelette, wasn't it?'

If he had offered anything else, she might have tensed up, decided this was a very bad idea, but this was so relaxed, so simple that it felt like coming home.

No! She couldn't let herself—wouldn't allow herself

to think like that. There was no way this apartment was anything like home to her even if the warm colours of the furnishings and the polished wooden floors were so very different from the formality of the main part of the main house, which had made her feel as if she were living in a museum most of the time.

'Pour one for me too.'

Nairo had headed through a door at the far side of the room, into the kitchen, Rose assumed. Spotting the bottle of rich red wine on the table, opened and left to breathe, she felt her heart hiccup once again.

Had he been so sure that she would join him? For a moment her steps turned towards the door, then she caught herself up, refusing to give in to the twist of nerves in her stomach.

She had told Nairo she wasn't afraid and she wasn't going to let him prove her wrong. Not when she had the chance of facing up to the mess their past had been and dealing with it once and for all. Determinedly she turned back, reached for the bottle of wine. She was lucky that she had already launched her steps towards the kitchen when the realisation of just why this apartment had seemed strangely familiar hit home with a head-spinning rush.

One night when the wind had rattled the window panes in the squat and they'd huddled together against the cold, she had spilled out some of her secrets, her fears, her unhappiness. Not just in her stepfather's home but before that, when her mother had struggled to find them anywhere to live, when one room had often been all they'd had to share together. Fred Brown's comfortable semi had seemed like heaven in contrast to that. At first. When they hadn't known the fear and distress that had hidden behind that safe suburban door.

In order to distract her, Nairo had set her to imagining what a real home would be like, creating the rooms in her imagination. Then he'd done the same. The place she was in now, she realised, was one of the rooms he had described to her then.

In the kitchen Nairo was already at work; he had pulled onions and peppers from the huge fridge and was busy slicing into them with a brutally sharp knife, his movements quick and efficient.

'Wine…'

It was all she could manage as she placed the glass beside him on the huge central island and then leaned back against the nearest worktop, sipping at her own wine as she did so. She couldn't take her eyes off his hands, lean and strong, and the speed and neatness with which he sliced and chopped. He had rolled the sleeves of his crisp white shirt back from his wrists to just above his elbows, exposing a long stretch of tanned olive skin liberally shadowed with crisp black hair. The way that the hard muscles bunched and moved under the satin skin transfixed her and she took another hasty swallow of the delicious wine.

Her whole body tingled under the memory of how it had felt to have those powerful, long-fingered hands stroke over her, making her quiver in uncontrolled delight.

'What is it, Rose?' Nairo had noticed her abstraction, and he paused in his preparations, dark head coming up, deep bronze eyes fixing on her face. He followed the track of her stare, glancing down at his arms, then flashing back up again to clash with her green ones. 'Not seeing what you wanted to see?'

There was danger in his question and in the darkness of the eyes that watched her intently.

'I—'

Straightening up, he stretched his arms out, flexing those elegant muscles all over again, as he waved his hands in her face. The burn from the acid onion juice on his skin made her eyes sting as she blinked in shock.

'No needle tracks, no scars, no trace of drug abuse. Not the arms of a junkie—hmm, *querida*?'

The hiss with which it was tossed in her direction made frightening nonsense of the term of affection so that her shocked and startled eyes lifted sharply, locked with his, unable to look away.

'Or do you think it all went up my nose?'

'No! Oh, no, no!'

She didn't even have time to rationalise her response, it was instinctive, escaping without a thought. Not this Nairo, the hard-working businessman, respected by so many, devoted to his sister...

But this Nairo was the same man as the Jett she'd known all those years ago. She'd been so *sure*.

No. It hit hard as a blow. She'd been so *scared*.

She'd thought she should fear him then, but the cold rage in his eyes told her that she had more reason to be afraid right now. And yet scared was not what she felt—not in the same way. Because she knew that right now that icy rage was justified.

'I never thought...I mean, I spent all those weeks with you. We lived together—I saw you night and day. Saw you dressed and...and...' her voice shuddered on the word '...undressed. I knew there was nothing like that. I knew that you were not an *addict*!'

She didn't know how she expected him to react. She only knew that it wasn't with the cynical laughter that made him throw back his head in a dark travesty of amusement. Disturbingly all she could think of was the way it had felt to lie in the sleeping bag with him, her head on his shoulder, nose pressed close against the bronzed skin of that strong neck, feeling the muscles move underneath it, breathing in the scent of his body. Even after ten years the memory still had an intensity that slashed at her heart.

'But you thought that I was prepared to feed others' addictions—for profit.'

If he'd raised his voice, shouted at her, then she knew she would have backed away, heading for the door. But his tone was flat and low, almost gentle, as if this were a casual conversation and not an exhumation of the darkness of the past that still lingered between them. Yet, for all that soft, steady tone, there was no hiding the ruthless control that went into keeping it that way. That had always been the difference between him and her heartless stepfather. But now she had to face the fear that that ruthlessness had blinded her to differences that went so much deeper.

She'd known this had to come sometime. At some point the silt that had gathered around their time together would have to be brought to the surface, exposed to the cold light of day. It was inevitable. But life had been so peaceful, so easy for the weeks she had been here that she had actually allowed herself to think that perhaps it didn't matter. That maybe she could complete her commission and get away again, unscathed…

Oh, who was she kidding? She hadn't been unscathed from the moment he had walked into her boutique and back into her life. The truth was that the past had left its scars, heart deep, and his return had shown that those wounds were still only barely healed. One word, one touch, one kiss like the one at the fashion show, and the delicate covering behind which she'd hidden them was ripped away, leaving her emotions raw and exposed.

The only surprising thing was that he'd waited so long. Why had he held back until now?

But then he said, 'And yet you were prepared to put up

with vile—my criminal past—in order to get this wedding dress commission?' And it all became so obvious.

It was for Esmeralda, of course. He'd wanted to make sure his sister got the dress of her dreams. Nothing was to come between that and the wedding. But now it seemed he was satisfied with how that had turned out and he'd decided to challenge her.

'You thought so little of me.'

She'd thought the world of him once and that was why disillusionment had hit so hard.

'I saw you.'

Nairo tossed the knife down onto the chopping board, clearly dismissing all idea of preparing any sort of meal for them.

'You saw what?'

'You—and Julie…'

'Julie?'

He could barely remember the name, but slowly the image came back to his mind. The bosomy blonde who had been the latest to warm Jason's sleeping bag, but who had made it more than plain she had an interest in him. Whenever Jason had been out of the squat she had tried to flirt with him, stroking his face, pressing unwanted kisses on his lips. But she'd usually waited until Rose was out too. Had Rose seen her…?

'Julie meant nothing to me.'

'Nothing?' Her wide eyes challenged that statement, but the sheen of tears that glistened in them told a different story. 'I saw you kissing her.'

'*Infierno*, you saw no such thing.'

Nairo reached for the knife again, pulling a pepper towards him and starting to slice into it, his movements hard and vicious. It was either that or reach for her— and he didn't know just *how* he would do that. Right now to touch her for any reason would blow this whole thing apart.

'You saw nothing. You saw *her* kissing *me*.'

'Oh, and you were fighting to get away from her, were you?'

Scorn and disbelief rang in Rose's voice and in that moment he knew just what kiss she had seen. The time when he had tried to convince Julie to get out of the squat—get away from Jason and his dirty deals. She had said that she would go if he went with her, her eyes even filling with tears when he had said no. He had tried to let her down gently, telling her that he was already committed. That had been the one and only time that he had admitted to anyone the way he had felt about Rose. He hadn't even told Red herself—something for which he was to be so very grateful later.

'No, I was not. But at least she didn't betray me.'

'Do you really think I could stand by and…?'

'And what, Red? And *what*?'

The knife slashed through the firm red skin of the pepper, hacking into the wood of the chopping board and leaving a cut so deep that he almost had to wrench it free.

'Fine—I kissed her—if that's the worst that you can accuse me of, then…'

Had she really just walked out on him because she had seen him comforting Julie? Had what they had meant so little to her that she could just turn her back and walk away? The slices of pepper dropped into rough, shapeless pieces, any attempt to dissect them carefully abandoned completely.

'So you didn't give her heroin?'

'What?'

Once more the point of the knife hit the chopping board and stuck, his fingers clenching so tight around the handle that his knuckles showed white. He couldn't make himself look at her, knowing that he would lose what little was left of his control if he did. Had she really thought him capable of that?

'You gave her drugs.'

His mind was back in the darkness of the squat, after that one lingering kiss. Lingering on Julie's part, never on his. He had tried one last time to make her stop, change the path she was on. A path that would lead all the way down to hell if she didn't get off it.

'Get out of here,' he'd told her. 'Get away and start again. That's what I'm going to do. I can't stay here any longer.'

He'd unpeeled her fingers from around the tiny wrap of drugs she'd clutched in her hand and held it up.

'No more, Julie,' he'd said. 'No more… If you leave it, you can come with me if you like.'

Was it possible? Could it be that Rose had actually seen that as him encouraging Julie in her habit, but, cold and controlling, he had told her she could have no more that day?

He knew—hell, he'd always known—that Rose had had good reason to go to the police. That the poisonous atmosphere in the squat had to be exposed and dealt with. Hadn't that been the reason he had wanted to get her out of there? The one thing that he had never ever been able to come to terms with was that she actually believed *he* was capable of being behind it all. So convinced that she hadn't even stopped to ask, to give him a chance to put his side of things. She had just turned and walked, leaving him behind without a backward glance.

Now it seemed that she had added other imaginary crimes to the list. But the ultimate betrayal was that, like his father, she had gone with what she had thought she'd seen, believing in the way things had looked rather than actually asking him for the truth.

'I gave her nothing.' The knife moved again, the sharp blade chopping faster and faster, dicing the pepper into tiny pieces. 'Not drugs. Not a thing.'

Absolutely nothing. Not a thing. How could he when at that time the only part of his heart that he had allowed to open was given to someone else entirely? To the woman who was standing at the other side of the island accusing him of...

His head came up, eyes blurred as he tried to focus on her face. The face that had once meant so much to him. Still so beautiful, but no longer the Red he had thought she was. The Red he had never ever really truly known. For such a short time she had made everything make sense— given him a path to follow, when all the while she had believed that he was lower than the grubby floorboards of the squat beneath her feet.

'Did you really think that *I* was the dealer in that place? That *I* was the one selling heroin?'

CHAPTER SIX

'TELL ME THE TRUTH. Is that what you thought?'

The expression on her face gave him his answer. But it was obvious that she couldn't hold back any longer.

'You had it in your hand that day and you suddenly had money. You said— You told me…'

I have a plan—a way of getting us out of here. The words hung between them in the stillness of the night, dark and determined and—as he now saw—so easily interpreted in a totally different way. By her at least. *But I need to get more cash together. Just give me a few more days.*

'I said I would get us out of there. I was working on it—but you didn't wait. You walked—you *ran*… You told the police that I…'

'I had to, Jett…'

Impossibly, she had reverted to the old familiar name, the one she had once used with warmth, he had believed, with love, he had deluded himself.

'I couldn't just sit back and let that happen.'

'Let what happen?' His voice sounded raw and cracked. 'Let *what* happen, Ms Cavalliero?'

'Jett—Toby *died* from an overdose, from a bad batch of that stuff. I couldn't let that happen again.'

'You couldn't— You— Oh, *infierno*!'

The curse broke from him as an unwary, unthinking

movement had lifted the knife again, bringing it down onto one of his fingers, slicing in deeply.

'Hell…'

For a moment it was all he could say as the pain shook him out of the daze of anger and denial that had held him.

'Oh, Nairo…'

Suddenly she was beside him, hands coming out, reaching for him. She took his fingers in hers, letting the knife drop back onto the work surface with a clatter as she turned towards the sink, taking him with her.

She turned on the taps, splashing water onto the cut finger, letting it wash away the blood that had sprung to the surface as she reached for a paper towel, folded it into a pad and clamped it down onto the wicked-looking cut, pressing it hard to stop the bleeding.

'Hold that—tight!' she said, her voice trying for authority but threaded through with a quiver of concern. 'I'll find something—do you have a first-aid box?'

'That cupboard over there.' He indicated with a nod of his head. 'Second drawer.'

Rose found the sterile dressings easily, even though her hands were shaking as she grabbed at them. Ripping off the protective plastic, she was back at his side in a moment, seizing his injured hand with a roughness that betrayed the way she was feeling. The sight of the ugly cut under the stained paper pad made her stomach roil and she almost slapped the dressing down onto it, needing to hide it. Stretching the fabric, she fastened it tight, then added another one on top of it, making sure it was secure.

'*Gracias.*' It was raw, husky, and it made her keep her head bent, her eyes fixed on his fingers.

The job was done; it was time to let go. And yet somehow she couldn't pull her hand away. Her fingers curled around Nairo's, twisting, smoothing. She was stunned by how passively he let his own hand lie in her grasp.

'Thank you,' he said again, his voice deep and rough-edged in a new way that brought her gaze to his face. 'Rose...'

She felt she could drown in the fathomless pools that were his eyes. Her own face was reflected there, eyes wide, skin pale. Her hands still held, his but now it was for a very different reason. She felt the burn of his skin against hers like the sizzle of wild electricity, singeing her nerves.

'Rose, listen to me, damn you...'

His words seemed to scrape along her senses, making her breath catch and snag in her throat. She had to listen. She couldn't let go, couldn't move away.

'I did *not* sell any drugs to Julie or to anyone. You can believe me or not, but that is the truth. I was not dealing. I would rather die.'

He'd offered no proof, but the shock was that she didn't need any. The fact that he hadn't even tried to produce anything to convince her but had simply stated the facts hit her like a slap in the face, making her thoughts reel. How had she got it so wrong? How had she let herself be deceived so easily?

The full realisation came like a dagger out of the darkness, slashing at her in a way that wounded more brutally than the chopping knife had sliced into Nairo's finger. It had been there in the moment just now when she had realised how scared she had been when she'd been in the squat. Not just scared of Jett—but everyone. Anyone.

Her mother, her stepfather—they'd all let her down in their own way. Deep inside, wasn't the truth that she'd believed everyone would act that way? Particularly the men.

Even Nairo.

She'd thought she'd loved him, but had she truly trusted

him? Could you really say you loved someone without the deepest, most absolute trust?

The thought of the cruel wound she had just bandaged still made her shiver deep inside and now this new thought made the shudders colder, crueller. Had she let herself lose someone she had once cared for so deeply in the biggest mistake of her life?

Even as she asked herself the question there came a low, icy little thought at the back of her mind. Someone *she* had once cared for so deeply—but who had never actually said that he cared about her. She thought she'd loved him, but she hadn't trusted him to love her back.

'But the police…'

His grip on her hand tightened until she winced under the pressure.

'Oh, yeah, the police came—they had to, after you called them, didn't they?'

Molten bronze eyes burned down into hers, but Rose was back in the past, in the dark and the cold of that Christmas Eve. She had been unable to leave, to run as far and as fast as she should have done, and she had crept back to hide in the shadows across the street. She had seen the police raid the house, bringing out everyone inside. And she had seen Nairo bundled into a waiting car, speeding off towards the police station. Arrested, she had believed.

'No.' Nairo had seen the look on her face, watched the thought processes that changed her expression flit through her eyes. 'No, they didn't arrest me. Nothing to arrest me for. They searched the place, took everyone in for questioning—you should have stayed around longer. You might have learned a truth or two.'

That caught her on the raw, had her biting her lip hard, teeth digging deep into the softness of her flesh. There had been one moment when he had looked out from the back of the car, staring into the darkness. She had flinched back into the shadows, but...

'You saw...'

'I saw.' The confirmation was dark, brutally cold.

He'd seen her. He'd known she was the one who had reported him to the police. Who had had them raid the squat and arrest everyone they found there.

'I had to—surely you could see that? I couldn't have such a thing on my conscience...'

'And you thought that I had offended that delicate conscience? What was it, Rose—was it that, after your vile stepfather, you were seeing villains everywhere? So you thought I was one too? Or was it really something else?'

'What else could it be?' The way he'd come so close to her own disturbed thoughts earlier, the fear of what might be coming, made her voice tremble, her hands tighten on his.

'They found nothing on me, Red.'

Somehow he managed to imbue the once affectionate name with the burn of acid so that it seared over her skin, taking a much-needed protective layer along with it.

'Not a trace of powder, not a single syringe. There was nothing on *my* conscience, then or any other night. But there was plenty to find on Jason. It was Jason who was the dealer in that squat. So you see, you didn't earn your money—not really.'

'My money?' This was new, and unexpected. 'What money?'

She watched his beautiful mouth twist into a cynical sneer and in a sudden panic tried to pull her hands from his only to feel his fingers tighten around hers, holding her prisoner. She couldn't have moved away anyway. Her legs were numb, unfeeling as the shock of what he was saying punched into her chest, taking her breath from her.

'The reward that Toby's parents offered to anyone who
could help them find who sold him the drugs that killed
him. Wasn't that what stirred your *conscience* so that you
just had to act?'

'No—no way!'

Once more she tried to wrench her hands from his,
only to have those strong fingers curl around hers again,
twisting so that he could pull her closer to him, her breasts
crushed up against the hardness of his chest, his breath
warm on her skin as he bent his head to stare straight into
her eyes, searching deep as if to find the truth he wanted
there.

'It wasn't— I couldn't...'

'Do you know, *querida*?' Nairo's drawl was slow and
lazy, totally belying the intensity of his stare. 'If I wanted
to, I could almost believe you.'

If I wanted to.

'But you don't—do you?' Rose snapped, fighting
against the sharpness of the stab of that careless response.
'You want to believe that I only betrayed you to the police
because it would profit me.'

His shrug was a masterpiece of indifference, brushing
aside her protests effortlessly.

'It was a long time ago, a third of a lifetime—I've put it
all behind me. And betrayed?' It came with a deadly softness. 'You might think that, my dear Red, but let me tell
you that before I could feel betrayed, I'd have had to care.'

The poisonous bite of his words tore at her inside,
though she was determined not to let it show. It was a
fight to find more defiance against him, but she dragged
it up from deep inside, tilted her chin higher, tightened
her mouth.

'So you think that the only reason I could leave you
was for money?' she flung at him. 'That otherwise you

were so irresistible I wouldn't have been able to tear myself away? Did you ever consider that perhaps I'd realised that I wanted—*needed*—more?'

That memory slashed at her now, the one that had tormented her when she'd first come into this apartment and recognised it as the home that Nairo had described to her. He'd wanted her to respond with her own dream home, but she hadn't been able to do that. She'd had no idea what a real home looked like. Only that it was safe. With people she trusted.

'That I wanted what *Rose* wanted, what I have now—not to exist, as Red did, in a place like that, with a man like you?'

'If you did, then you were lying to yourself,' Nairo returned harshly, squashing her protest. 'And you've been lying for the past ten years with your Lord Andrew and your non-marriage.'

His dark head bent, came so close that his mouth was just inches away from hers. If she was to lift her head, then their lips would meet—and she shivered inside at the thought of the conflagration that would sweep through her if that happened. She feared it and yet she wanted it so much.

'You couldn't put anything in place of what we had—the passion that burned so hot and hard from the moment we met. That made me pick you up from the street where I found you. That made you give yourself—your virginity—to me without a second thought. You couldn't find anything to match it.'

There were no words to deny his accusation. She had wanted it then and, no matter how hard she tried to deny it now, she still felt exactly the same way.

No, not exactly. In the past she had fallen into his arms in the throes of her first, her only, blaze of naïve passion.

Nairo had come to her rescue when she had been lost and alone, homeless and helpless on the streets of London. She had thought that he was her knight in shining armour, her saviour. But he'd had nothing more than that passion to give her, and, needing so much more, she had let her fears grow until she'd convinced herself that she had no alternative but to run. But she'd been running from the lack of love, never from a man who dealt in drugs.

But the hellish thing was that even knowing that didn't change anything.

From the moment that she had seen the knife slice into his finger and had felt the shock of horror at the thought of his beautiful hand being damaged in that way, she had known she was in deeper than she dared to admit. Once long ago, in the squat, she had caught her hand on an exposed nail, just a graze, far less damaging than the knife cut, and instinctively he had reached for her, bringing her hand to his mouth, to kiss away the soreness of the shallow graze, looking straight into her eyes as he did so. She had loved the slow smile that had curved his lips, felt herself drawn irresistibly into the darkness of his eyes, and he had pulled her to him and crushed her mouth with his. They had ended up in bed—if the battered sleeping bag could be called a bed—that night, coming together again and again, only having to reluctantly put a check on the passion that burned between them when they had run out of the small supply of condoms that had been all Nairo could afford to buy.

She had been prepared to make love one more time without, she recalled, heat rushing over her body at the thought of how naïve she had been. She had never been able to impose any control on herself where he was concerned, as irresponsible as her mother, who'd been only the same age when she'd fallen pregnant. Nairo had always been the one to insist on a degree of sanity—out of consideration for her, she had always thought. She'd believed it was because he didn't want her to have to deal with unwanted consequences of their relationship so young. She had seen it as evidence of how much he cared, but later she had been forced to consider the possibility that it was really to protect himself. To ensure that he wouldn't be burdened with any responsibilities that might tie him to her for a future he had no desire to face.

Now she knew where he disappeared to at night, to this private apartment, she was again confronted with all the thoughts that had filled her mind when he hadn't joined them for meals, of Nairo being out on the town with a succession of beautiful women. In her imagination he had escorted them home, taken them to bed...

But perhaps if he had been here all the time... If he had spent the evenings in his apartment—alone?

Was she a fool to imagine that that was possible? To allow herself to think that Nairo had no one special in his life right now—no one, full stop?

The passion that burned so hot and hard from the moment we met. You couldn't find anything to match it.

Was it possible that that passion was the way he felt— had felt—still felt—too?

'You still can't, can you?'

'No?' She tried to make it into a challenge, bringing her chin up defiantly, but that only brought her lips even closer to his, the warmth of his breath on her skin, the taste of him so close that she could almost sense it on her tongue. 'You think not?'

She was teetering on the edge of a dangerous cliff, balanced so precariously that the tiniest puff of a breeze would send her flying, tumbling head over heels into the pit of molten need that was already threatening to enclose her.

She didn't want to say no, didn't want to put a stop to this. The need to acknowledge the reality of what he said was a burn in her veins, the tiny connection between their hands like putting her fingers into a live electric socket. She knew it was safer to let go—but at the same time she knew that it was the last thing she could do. She wanted this touch, needed more of it, as common sense fought a nasty little war with the hungry sexuality that was making her pulse thunder hard against her temples.

She wished he would make the first move, but deep down she knew that was just cowardice. She *wanted* this, she should own it, acknowledge it. If she chickened out now, she would only regret it so hard tomorrow.

But if she acted, would she regret it even more?

'I know not,' Nairo declared. 'If you'd found someone else to give you what we shared, then you would be with him now. But no, no one—definitely not your Lord Andrew. So can you face the truth—or can you actually claim that what I say is a lie?'

The danger was that he was talking to himself, Nairo knew. He wasn't just challenging Rose to admit how it had been, how it still was, for her, but forcing himself to look the truth in the face and review his own life in the ten years that had passed since they had been together. There had been no one else who had affected *him* so strongly, no other woman who had trapped him in her searing appeal, since the day Rose had walked out on him on that dark December night. Oh, there had been other women—too many—who had warmed his bed and eased the appetites of his body. But none of them had made him yearn as she had done. None of them had truly satisfied him.

They had been enough to stave off the hunger of his most basic needs, but he had left every bed with a feeling of emptiness and discontent so that in the end he had simply given up. He had nothing to give these women and they did nothing to fill the emptiness inside him. He had focussed instead on the work of the estate, the business deals that kept his mind from straying onto other, more sensual paths. In the beginning he had told himself that he was doing this only to rebuild his relationship with his father, to regain Raoul's respect, but the truth was that he was still trapped by the memory of how it had been with Red.

That was why he had had to keep her with him now. Why he couldn't let her go until he had gorged himself on her warm and willing body, to wipe away all the hunger she had left him with and know that at last he was done with the blind, foolish obsession he still had with her, sated and fulfilled so that he was at last ready to move on.

'No,' Rose said softly.

The single syllable was so unexpected that he felt it like a start inside his head, his gaze going to her face in shock, searching her eyes.

'Is that no, you don't want…?'

'No, I can't claim that what you say is a lie.'

If her voice had had the slightest shake in it, any sort of hesitancy, then he would have let her go, stepped away from her, forcing his attention back onto the preparation of the simple meal he'd been planning, though it would kill him to do so. He wanted her. *Infierno*, but he ached to possess her, to taste her mouth, feel the warmth of her skin under his touch, the softness of her body yielding to him.

But it was that *yielding* that he wanted. He wanted her willing and he wanted her as eager for his touch, his kiss, as she had been all those years before. Nothing else would give him the satisfaction he craved. He had been through every form of hell keeping his hands off Rose since she had come to live at the *castillo*, and now his blood was thundering in his veins so that he was hard and hot as hell, aching with need, unable to believe what she was saying.

'I'd like to be able to say that I don't feel that way about you, but I'd be lying...'

Nairo's only reaction was a long, slow blink, but she knew she'd stunned him.

'So?' Nairo questioned very softly. 'Rose, what are you saying?'

Could he bring his face, his mouth, any closer, without touching her? Did he know how much it tormented her to be this close and not to reach out to him? To be surrounded by the warmth of his body, the scent of his skin, feel his breath on her cheek? Her mouth had dried painfully and she had to slick her tongue over her parched lips in order to be able to speak. The way that his darkened eyes dropped to follow the betraying movement, the brush of the rich dark arcs of his lashes over the bronzed high cheekbones almost destroyed her.

'I—I...' she tried, failing to find any words to express the denial that self-preservation demanded she turned on him. The denial that would be every sort of a lie. 'I... Oh, Nairo...'

It could not be held back any longer.

'Kiss me! Kiss me now!'

CHAPTER SEVEN

WHO MOVED FIRST she had no idea. Had she lifted her face so that the tiny gap between their waiting lips was obliterated, bringing their mouths together in a clash of wild and searing passion? Or had he brought his lips down on hers in response to her wild-voiced demand? Or perhaps to silence any attempt she might make to deny what she'd said, to retract the command she had been unable to hold back?

He needn't have worried. There was no way that she could even consider denying the hunger that had been eating at her from the moment that he had walked into her boutique, back into her life. It was as if she had been asleep for the past ten years and like Sleeping Beauty had only been waiting for that one kiss from a very special prince.

A prince? Oh, who was she kidding? Certainly not herself. Nairo was no fairy-tale prince now just as he had never been that knight in shining armour she had dreamed of when she had first met him. He had promised her nothing, no happy-ever-after, but the truth was that now she didn't care.

All she wanted was Nairo the man, right here, right now. His brutally devastating kiss forcing her mouth open under his to taste the innermost essence of him, to let her tongue dance against his in intimate passion. The caress of his hard fingers on her skin, pushing under her blouse

at the waist of her jeans, skating over her nerves so that
she shivered in urgent response, pressing herself against
the heat of his long body. Her breasts were crushed against
the powerful wall of his ribcage, against her hips the hotly
swollen arousal that told her he was feeling every bit of
the hunger that seared its way through her.

In a burning haze of need, she felt her feet leave the
floor as he lifted her, holding her in arms as strong as steel
bands. With a moan of surrender against his demanding
mouth, she flung her arms up around his neck, laced her
fingers in the silk darkness of his hair and gave herself
up to the feelings that were sweeping like a tidal wave
through every inch of her.

'*This* could never be denied, never forgotten,' Nairo
muttered against her lips, tugging at her blouse so roughly
that buttons pulled off and fell to the floor with a soft rattle.

'Never…' she echoed him, unable to find any other
words in the flames that took her mind out of reality and
into a world where there were only the two of them and
the heat that melted every barrier between them.

Her hands were shaking as they slid from his hair, tracing the powerful lines of his face, fingertips catching on
the day's dark growth of stubble that shaded his chin. She
couldn't believe that she had the freedom to touch him, to
kiss him once again as she'd been able to do in the past. It
seemed that if she opened her eyes she might find that the
immaculate modern kitchen had disappeared and they had
been transported back to the squat. Dusty and dull and cold
it might have been, but to her it had been a special place.
Because she had been there with Jett and because she had
already lost her heart to him, all her illusions still in place,
no thought of the way they were soon to be shattered.

'Never, never, never…' she whispered, cradling his chin
in her hands so as to draw him closer, tracing the shape of

his lips with her tongue so that she tasted his mouth, the faint salt of his skin.

But suddenly Nairo snatched his hands from under her blouse, bringing them out to close around her arms, as he lifted her from the worktop where she had been sitting, let her slide down the hot hard length of his body.

'*No.*'

It was rough and hard and unbelievable.

'No,' he said again. 'Not like this—not here...'

'*Yes*—here—now...'

Here, now, anywhere, any time. He surely couldn't be thinking of stopping.

But then to her relief Nairo moved again, swinging her up into his arms as he turned, taking her towards the door.

'I swore to myself that the next time I did this, I would have a bed to take you to,' he murmured into the fall of auburn hair. 'A proper bed—not some damn shabby sleeping bag on a cold hard floor.'

She had been perfectly content in a shabby sleeping bag on a cold hard floor, Rose told herself as he carried her across the room. Because then it had meant so much to her. She had been lost in the way she felt about this man; she'd never paused to have second thoughts about it. All her thoughts had been of him.

So when he laid her down on the softness of a wide, wide bed, the fine cotton smooth and cool under her heated body, she knew a tiny hiccup of hesitation, a needlepoint of doubt puncturing her need. It lasted all of the space of a couple of uneven heartbeats, only surviving until Nairo came down beside her, his hands caressing the need back into her body, his mouth exploring her face, her lips, the skin that those hands exposed as he pushed aside her blouse, unhooked the delicate lacy bra underneath.

Within moments Rose was adrift again, throwing her

head back so that he could kiss his way down the lines of her throat, across her shoulders. The warm, tantalising path his lips and tongue traced over the slopes of her breasts had her catching her breath in delight, arching her body up to meet his touch, increase the pressure of his kisses as the fire stoked up higher and higher inside her, throbbing at the hungry spot between her legs. When those tormenting lips curved over one pouting nipple, drawing it into his mouth where his teeth scraped gently over her skin before the swirl of his tongue soothed the faint sting in the same moment, it set up a whole new burn of need along every nerve.

'Nairo…'

His name was a choking sound of hunger as her hands held him closer, clutching at the powerful shoulders above her, and then, impatient at the unwanted barrier of his clothes, pushed their way between them to tug at the buttons on his shirt with as little care as he had shown hers earlier.

'I want…I *want*…'

'I know, *querida*…'

His voice had an edge of raw laughter at the urgency of her response, the words muffled against her skin as his wicked mouth teased her to even further heights of need, hunger burning out of control.

She didn't care that she showed it. Didn't mind what he thought when her own hands joined his at the waistband of her trousers as he eased the zip down, helping him to slide the garment down to her ankles, where she kicked it aside impatiently. She wanted to be naked with him, touched by him—oh, dear heaven, possessed by him! In her naïve foolishness she had lost all this ten years before and having rediscovered it now she could barely wait until Nairo made her his all over again.

Now she knew exactly why she had had to break off her engagement to Andrew. Why she had known all along that their marriage would have been the biggest mistake she had ever made. She had never felt like this, never known this all-consuming need with anyone but Nairo. And knowing that the mild affection she had only ever felt for anyone else, it was no wonder she had never been able to go through with taking their relationship any further.

'Red—Rose...*momento.*' The roughness of Nairo's voice betrayed the battle he was having with his self-control. Control that Rose didn't want him to hold on to.

'No...' She pouted her protests, her hands finding the buckle of his belt and flipping it open, sliding down the heated, swollen bulge of his erection, a smile curling her lips as she heard his groan of near surrender. But when she eased down his zip, sliding her cool hands into the heat underneath and feeling his long body buck in fierce response, she couldn't believe it when his hard fingers came down, closing over her wrist and holding her still.

'*Rose!*' It was a sound of reproach, the tightness of his jaw, his gritted teeth betraying the fight he was having with himself. 'We have to... We need...protection.'

Of course. If there was one thing Nairo had always considered whenever they had made love in the squat, it had been the need for protection. Somehow, in spite of the little money they had had, he had always made sure they had the condoms they needed, had never taken her to bed without them.

But there was something she needed him to know.

'Andrew...and I,' she managed as he levered himself up on one elbow, pulling out the drawer in the bedside table and reaching inside. 'I want you to know—we never...'

She couldn't complete the sentence. That tiny move

he'd made away from her let in a drift of air that cooled the mindless hunger just for a second.

But a moment later the heat and the need were there again as Nairo rolled back over her, covering her face with kisses that seemed even more ardent than before and that soon obliterated that moment of uncertainty. He tugged open the foil packet he'd grabbed, fingers uncharacteristically clumsy as he slanted his body away from her just for a moment.

'*Socorro*. Help me...'

It was a raw mutter of command, his hands reaching for hers as she aided him in sheathing the hardness of his erection, her fingers shaking as she felt his heat against her skin.

'Now...'

His impatience showing in the lack of finesse with which he pushed her back down onto the bed, Nairo's long body came over her, powerful, hair-roughened legs coming between hers, pushing them wide, coming so close to the hungry heart of her. Rose's eyes closed in anticipation, her head going back against the pillow, but even as she did so she heard his breath hiss in a sound of impatient dissatisfaction.

'No—*querida*—open your eyes. Look at me!'

His face was so close to hers when she obeyed him. His eyes glazed with passion, the high cheekbones streaked with red.

'I want you to remember this—to know who I am.'

'I know. And I remember...'

Her words broke off on a high wild cry of fulfilment as he thrust, hard and fierce, between her legs and up into the waiting, moist and yearning core of her body, making her close her hands over the powerful shoulders above her, her nails digging into the rigid muscles of his back.

When he began to move, she had no choice but to go with him. She rose to meet each thrust, sighed a release as he eased away, breath catching in her throat as she opened up more and more each time, giving everything she could, taking as much as she could get from him. It was hard and fast and ferocious as if the missing years had been stored up in the sexual hunger that now brought them both together in the wildness of their need. She welcomed the almost roughness of his passion, welcomed it and matched it as it took her higher and higher, pressure building and building until there was nothing left, nowhere to go but into the starburst eruption of total completion as they reached an explosive climax together.

Nairo woke early in the morning, as the dawn crept over the horizon and began to lighten the room, revealing the figure of the sleeping woman at his side, her auburn hair spread out across the pillow, her cheek cushioned on her hand.

His whole body ached in satisfaction in the same moment that just looking at her, at the soft swell of her breasts against the white linen of the sheets, the curve of her hips, the dark triangle of hair at the juncture of her thighs, sent a pulse thudding through him all over again. It roused a hunger that had been ten years building and from which nothing, not even the deep sleep of fulfilment that had finally swept over him, could distance him. He had Rose in his bed again after all this time and it had felt incredible.

It had been the best sex of his life, the sort of physical connection that he had been looking for all these years. It was what he had wanted ever since he had been with Red back in those days in the squat. Inexperienced as she had been then, she had been just a promise of what he now knew he had been searching for and why. Once he had found her again, he had had to keep her with him to anticipate just a moment such as this. To wake with her beside him, having taken her again and again until they had both tumbled into exhausted and satiated sleep.

At some point in the night, he had gone into the kitchen and fetched fruit and wine, a very belated replacement for the omelette that had never materialised. He had fed her grapes and peaches, licked the juice from her kiss-swollen lips. Then, when the shivering response of her body had made her spill some of the wine down onto her naked breasts he had lapped that up too, delighting in the way that her skin quivered under his tongue, the soft moan that escaped her mouth.

'So what happened to you after you left the squat,' he had asked at one point in the night when the darkness in the room hid their faces from each other, the expressions that might have betrayed more than their words could ever do. 'Where did you go? Surely not back to that bastard of a stepfather?'

He knew she'd reconciled with her mother, but surely she couldn't have gone back there. This time the shiver was far less sensual, far more a gesture of distress.

'Never! I couldn't have gone back there to save my life. But I got in touch with my mother—rang her when I knew he wouldn't be at home.' Her voice sounded bruised with the memories she was so reluctant to unearth. 'She was so unhappy—she realised just what this man she'd married was like and, like me, she was desperate to escape. We arranged to meet. But then she ended up in hospital.'

She paused, took a deep swallow of her wine as if finding strength to go on.

'She was bruised and battered. Broken ribs. We planned to get away together—leave him behind and make a new life for ourselves wherever we could. We had no money—

Mum wouldn't take anything from him and he'd controlled all the finances—but we didn't care. We contacted social services—they found a flat in another town, and we took whatever jobs we could find.'

Nairo levered himself up at her side, looking into her shadowed face. She had some courage, he had to give her that.

'And how did you end up with the designer's job?'

Rose tapped the edge of the glass against her teeth, gathering her thoughts.

'I found a job shelf-stacking in a supermarket—Mum and I worked in the same place. When I could, I started with evening classes—art and design—found I had a flair for that. When Mum found a better job I tried for college—won a scholarship. I worked in the evenings doing repairs and alterations at first, then I made a few dresses for people locally and I was lucky. People loved what I made. From that I got a place in a fashion house. I started at the very bottom, trained, worked hard...'

Her teeth flashed white in the shadows as she gave a slightly forced smile.

'I was lucky that I found some premises at an unbelievably low rent, and I seemed to get a reputation just by word of mouth. Then Mum found out she had cancer—and I met Andrew...and it all went downhill from there.'

'You never slept with him?'

He sounded as if he couldn't quite believe it.

'Never.' Suddenly she looked up at him, eyes shadowed in the moonlight. 'I never wanted to.'

Nairo's head went back sharply as he frowned his disbelief.

'But you wanted to marry him.'

'I said yes to his proposal.' Somehow she made it sound so very different from 'wanted to marry him'. 'I thought

Andrew offered me safety.' Her breath hiccupped on the word. 'But safety wasn't what I really wanted.'

It was supposed to reassure, but somehow it had a shockingly opposite effect.

'Safety,' Nairo repeated. 'As opposed to...'

Suddenly he slammed his wine glass down onto the cabinet at the side of the bed. Did she still think he was the dangerous one—the lawbreaker?

'If you wanted the bad boy...'

'Nairo, no! I had it all wrong. I was wrong. I should never...'

He couldn't stop himself from responding even though he knew his furious nod of his head had shocked her rigid.

'Yes, you should,' he growled. 'If you truly suspected that anyone—that I was involved with that filth, then of course you had to do something about it.'

'If I suspected...' She reached out, took hold of his hand as she leaned towards him. 'I did—but I was *wrong*. About you. And if you must know, I was wrong about Andrew as well.'

But that new mention of the man whose ring she'd worn was too much. He didn't want any thought of her past fiancé intruding into this night with her.

'Forget that man. He has no place here. All that matters is you and me.'

He'd taken the glass from her hand, placed it on the bedside table next to his own. Then he'd leaned over her, pressing his mouth against hers, kissing away the regretful words. As he'd known she would, Rose had returned his kisses, softly at first, then more hungrily, passionately, her mouth opening under his, her hands coming up to lace around his neck, pulling him down to her. She'd slid down on the pillows, taking him with her, the stroke of her hands turning from gentle to teasing to demanding in the space of a couple of heartbeats.

The next moment they had forgotten all about talking, or thinking, and had lost themselves in the wild, blazing passion that totally consumed them.

And now she was still here, beside him, naked and warm. All he had to do was to waken her...

But something stayed the hand he reached out to touch her, held it hovering over her body, so close that when she breathed in and out, slow and deep, the warm, flushed flesh of her breasts almost brushed against his palm.

If that happened, then he knew that so much else would happen too. He would not be able to control his response. Already his body was hardening in fierce anticipation of the pleasure it had known during the night and hungered to know again.

But know with *who*? Who was this Rose who had welcomed him into her warm and willing body so often in the night, and who lay there now, an open invitation to the heated oblivion he had known?

Was this the woman who had walked out on him without a backward glance, leaving him to face the police? They'd had nothing to convict him on, obviously, but the scandal of that raid on the squat and subsequent arrests had damn near destroyed every chance he had had of a reconciliation with his father.

Rose stirred, sighing softly, and Nairo pulled his hand back further, away from the temptation she offered.

Had she truly not known about the payment for information about the drugs that had taken Toby to his death? He had always believed that that had been her motivation for going to the police, and Jason, spitting fury at being found out, had vowed vengeance on her for exactly that.

Roughly he pushed himself up and out of the bed,

the jerky movement echoing the disturbed nature of his thoughts.

So what if Rose hadn't known about the reward? She'd claimed she loved him, but she hadn't trusted him. Like his father before her, she hadn't believed in him enough even to *ask* for the truth, going by what she'd seen, not by what she should have known of him. Then she'd seduced him into staying in the squat that night when he had planned to leave, to meet his father, to start the peace process that he had hoped might see him back in the family home.

But 'No—don't go...' Rose had pleaded, stroking his hair, his face, and pressing her gorgeous body softly against his, curling around him and doing that amazing little shimmy of her hips that had him hard and hungry in a moment, totally unable to resist her.

He was already burning erect now, just remembering it. So much so that it was uncomfortable and difficult to pull the zip of his jeans closed over his straining hardness. Every nerve in his body urged him to stop the crazy behaviour of pulling on his clothes—to throw them off and get back into that bed with Rose once again...

'Nairo...'

For a moment he wasn't sure if the soft voice he heard was in the past or behind him until the repetition of his name brought his head round to see where she had stirred in his bed, sleepy eyes only half open, a faint frown drawing her brows together.

'Where are you going?'

She levered herself up on the pillows, pale skin flushed from the warmth of the bed, the marks of his touch, the tumbled auburn hair falling over her face. Her mouth was still swollen from the passionate kisses he had pressed on her through the night.

'Don't...' was all she said and it was enough to stop him dead in his tracks.

'Come back here.' She held out a hand to him, regarding him through those half-closed eyes. 'Please.'

It was too much, and, with a groan of surrender that came close to a sound of despair, he tossed aside the tee shirt he had been about to pull on and threw himself down on the bed beside her. Gathering her slender naked body to him, he kissed her hard and let the waves of sensuality break over his head, taking him down, deep down under the surface until he was lost to the world.

CHAPTER EIGHT

IT HAPPENED AS she left Nairo's apartment.

That last time had been so very special, their lovemaking holding such an intensity, a sultry passion such as she had never known. Nairo's kisses seemed to draw her soul from her body, his touch leaving a trail of fire wherever it had caressed her skin until once again they had both fallen into a deep pit of exhaustion from which Rose had only just managed to wake before it was too late. After snatching at her clothes and pulling them on hastily, she made for the door.

She thought that she had slipped from the bed quietly enough not to be noticed, her bare feet silent on the thickly carpeted floor, but it was as she reached the door that she heard Nairo stir in the bed behind her.

'What are you doing?'

His voice was muffled by the pillow, but there was no mistaking the sharpness of the question.

'I have to go! You know I do. If I stay, I might be seen by one of the staff, perhaps even Esmeralda. Or, worst of all, one of Oscar's family, particularly Grand Duchess Marguerite. She always wakes early. Do you want people to know about…us?'

Was there an 'us'? Or had their time together just been

a one-night thing? Never to be repeated? To be kept hidden like a dirty little secret.

If she'd done this before—all those years ago on the night when she'd crept away from him in the squat. If she'd stayed, curled back beside him—or just *asked* him what was going on—might she have discovered then how different things had been, rather than the way she'd believed them to be? If she'd asked him, would he have told her...?

'Jett...'

The old name was just a whisper, a sliver of sound barely escaping her lips, and she was convinced he hadn't heard it. She heard him shift in the bed, turning his face on the pillow so that he was looking straight at her.

'No—you're right.' It was curt, dismissive. 'That would be a bad mistake. You have to go...'

A heavily indrawn breath signalled a darker change of mood.

'And the name is *Nairo*,' he said with brutal emphasis. 'Jett never existed in the same way that Red was just a fantasy.'

'Of course...'

Now she really did have to go—and not just for fear that someone in the main house might see her. She had completely lost control of her emotions and the burn of despair inside her was something she would do anything to conceal from him.

She had thought that she'd learned from the past. That she should talk to Nairo, ask him what he felt, what was happening, rather than just running away. So she'd asked. And the answer he'd given had made it plain that there was nothing special between them. Only the wild, blazing passion that had raged through them last night and killed rational thought. The hunger of desire that needed no explanations, no feeling, no *caring*.

That was all that Nairo had to offer her, and if she was going to be strong enough to take what he had to offer for as long as he offered it and not ask for more, then she had to hold herself in and never let anything of the true way she was feeling show. If he had wanted more than they had already, then he would have made it plain. She didn't dare to push it any further.

To do so was to risk blowing even this 'relationship' wide open and destroying it completely.

'I'll see you back in the house...'

Where she would show him the calmest, most unemotional face he could want. If this was all he had to offer her, then she'd take that and not ask for more.

Somehow she made it down the stairs, gripping onto the bannister with tight fingers, blinking hard to drive the tears away.

But still they blurred her vision, blending with the hazy light of the dawn to create a cloudiness that meant she could barely see as she made her way onto the path around to the main door of the *castillo*. So when a sudden bright, vivid flash came out of nowhere, blinding her, she thought it was more of the same distortion of her vision that resulted from the stinging moisture in her eyes.

Until it came again. And again, suddenly becoming a fusillade of sparks and flares blazing out around her into the silence of the morning.

It might have been ten years before, Nairo told himself as he watched the door settle back into its frame behind her. With Rose creeping from his bed to leave him without a word. Except that then he had barely stirred as she had slipped away from his side. He had never even suspected that she had gone for good.

Would she be back this time? Did he want her to stay?

Hell, he wasn't finished with her yet, that much was sure. The side of the bed where she had lain was cooling rapidly, but that wasn't the only reason why that space felt empty. He didn't want this night to end, didn't want Rose to leave. And not because he was concerned that the Schlieburgs would see her, though that seemed to be what disturbed Rose—what she seemed to expect that he would be troubled by.

Oh, he was quite sure that Marguerite wouldn't be too happy to find that he was sleeping with the hired help! But she would come round to it. Unless of course it affected the preparations for the wedding if the news got out, which, with what he'd seen of the reactions to Rose's past, it well might.

It was obvious that Rose wanted to keep it hidden, and expected that he'd feel the same way. He'd let her think that. Because the truth was that he wasn't ready to share this change in their relationship with the world. He knew that she believed that was because of a concern for the in-laws. That the prim and proper Schlieburgs were always in his mind whenever he acted right now. But the real truth was that it was less Esmeralda's new family that concerned him, but his sister herself. If he came out into the open about that fact that Rose was his mistress, then Esmeralda would read so much more into it. She would look into his face and see things that he didn't want her to see.

Or was there something more to it than that? The uncomfortable twist in his guts had him sitting up sharply, staring into the mirror on the wall, meeting his own eyes, searching to see just what was in the face he presented to the world now. He knew what had been there ten years before. The anger, the sense of betrayal, the loss.

Don't be long, he'd said and she'd promised him that she wouldn't be. But then she was gone and that was the last time he had seen her for ten years. Ten long, hollow years, he admitted now, acknowledging deep inside the emptiness he'd endured when she'd left him. He had been so sure that everything was going to be right. She had reached for him, had loved him—or so he'd believed—opening to him so warmly, so willingly, so generously, so heartfully.

But the truth was that she had used his desire for her to keep him right there in the squat until it was too late for anything else, until she had known that the police must have been on their way, and then she'd tossed that cool 'I won't be a minute...' at him and walked out of his life.

Or had she? Raking both hands through his hair, he forced himself to face the new thoughts that had intruded into his mind as he had come awake. There had been a difference, something close to desperation, in the way she had reached for him that long-ago night. Something that, recalling it now, had jarred so badly that he had reacted angrily when she had called him Jett. It had not been a comfortable experience being reminded of the man he had been then.

He'd still been smarting from his father's brutal dismissal of him, the way he'd been thrown out of the family home on the word of his lying stepmother. His judgement had been way off. He'd seen Rose as just another deceitful female who'd come between him and his family, ruining his good name all over again in his parent's eyes. That had been the final slash of the emotional knife that she had used to cut away every last trace of the connection they had shared, destroying the chance he'd thought he'd had of taking it further, making it work.

But he hadn't shared his plans with her. If he had asked her to stay that Christmas, told her about his plans to reconcile with his father, what would she have done?

He pushed himself upwards, throwing back the sheets as he reached for his jeans, pulled them on, dragging a black tee shirt over his head. This time there had been something else in her voice. A muffled, thickened sound that had made it seem as if she was upset.

Was it possible that there was more to it than he had suspected? he asked himself as he dashed down the stairs, out the door. Perhaps if he caught her up, made her talk to him... Perhaps there was something they could salvage...

He came to a violent, abrupt halt, the shaken, devastated realisation of just what was happening stopping him dead as he saw Rose some way off across the lawn...and the sudden frenzy of brilliant camera flashes filling the silence of the morning.

'Señorita Cavalliero...'

'Miss Cavalliero... Rose...'

The chorus of voices, some English, some speaking in Spanish, came at Rose out of the half-darkness, all firing questions at her. All the time the barrage of camera flashes went off right in her eyes until she threw up her hands to shield her face from their glare.

'Hey, come on, Rosie, give us a smile! Talk to us!'

'What do you want?'

She'd been through something like this when she'd broken off her engagement to Andrew, and that she'd understood. She'd left things to the very last minute and the plans for the wedding had been in the public eye for a few weeks. So she'd felt she deserved it when the paparazzi had descended on her shop, firing cameras in her direction, hurling questions she couldn't answer.

But now...

'When did this all start up, then, Rose? Been going on long?'

'How does it feel to be another notch on Nairo Moreno's bedpost—or is he a notch on yours? Is this why you dumped Andrew?'

'Will you be showing Señorita Moreno how to run out on her wedding at the last minute as you did?'

'No! Nothing like that!'

Rose kept her hands in front of her face as she tried to move forward, struggling to see her way along the uneven path. The reporters and cameramen were closing in on her on all sides, pushing and shoving, setting her off balance so that she stumbled awkwardly.

And would have fallen if strong arms hadn't suddenly come out to grab hold of her, haul her upright again and hold her tight against something warm and hard and supportive.

Nairo. Nairo's hands holding her. His arms keeping her upright, his powerful chest and long body providing the support she needed to stay on her feet. The heat and scent of his skin surrounded her and made her feel warm and safe, enclosed in a protective shell. She heard the buzz of excitement from the pestering reporters but couldn't bring herself to respond to it.

Luckily she didn't have to. She felt Nairo draw in a deep breath, then heard his voice, calm and strong, coming over her head to reach her tormentors.

'Gentlemen…'

She could hear the irony in his tone, feel the fight he was having with his own forceful nature to keep the control he clearly believed was necessary.

'Stop harassing my fiancée.'

No, she had to have heard that wrong, He couldn't have said… But even as the sense of shock reverberated through her she saw the same effect hit the reporters as they stilled, silenced, stared.

'I—' she tried, only to have Nairo squeeze hard where he held her. Then he bent his head to brush his lips against the side of her face.

'Let me get rid of them.' It was soft enough to be inaudible, especially when another thunderstorm of camera clicks and flashes drowned every other sound.

'Nairo...' Rose tried to protest, but he silenced her with another kiss, longer and more lingering this time, right on the lips she had parted to protest, creating a new frenzy of interest and making her mind whirl in confusion. Then he spoke over her head as he addressed the paparazzi.

Yes, the engagement was a recent thing—very recent. But not unexpected. Nairo had fallen for Rose from the moment he saw her, but he'd wanted to wait so as not to interrupt his sister's wedding and take the attention away from the bride-to-be. No, they hadn't even chosen a ring yet, though, in his family, tradition usually decided on that.

Rose heard his answers through what sounded like a thousand bees buzzing inside her head. The shock of the ambush by the reporters, the unexpectedness of Nairo's arrival, the solution he had adopted to explain their situation and that kiss had all combined to scramble her thoughts so completely that she couldn't be sure she was hearing anything right. The one thing she was sure of was that the reporters seemed happy with the story they'd been given. If she interfered now, contradicted anything Nairo said, then it would only make things so much worse.

So she managed to stand at Nairo's side, his arm around her waist, her body pressed close to his, and watch and listen as he appeased the scandal hunters by giving them what they obviously thought was a story worth a banner headline and a couple of the photographs they were still busy snapping as fast as they could.

'*Spanish aristocrat to marry designer who ran out on her own wedding!*' She could imagine the headlines now, and that made it a struggle to obey the hissed command

of 'Smile!' that Nairo gave her with a swift tightening of
the arm that held her.

She knew what he was doing and why he was doing it
even if the reporters didn't suspect. She recognised the
defensive mode that Nairo had slipped into from the moment he had caught up with them and found her hounded
by the pack of reporters. He was making the best of a bad
job, putting a new spin on the fact that she had been caught
sneaking from his apartment after what had obviously
been a long night spent there with him. The very last thing
that he would have wanted to happen before Esmeralda
was married to her duke. This was his personal nightmare
come true—the one he'd warned her he would be furious
if it materialised. He was making sure that at least when
his sister's soon-to-be in-laws heard about this—as now
inevitably they must—they would not be appalled at the
thought of a raging sexual affair but hopefully more tol-
erant of a couple who were secretly engaged but had held
back from announcing it in consideration of the fast-ap-
proaching wedding.

'*Gracias, señores...*'

Nairo had obviously defused the problem for now because the reporters were packing up equipment, turning
away, the story ready for filing for tomorrow's news.

Clearly Nairo thought so too because he grabbed hold
of Rose's hand and almost dragged her in the direction of
the main house. Yanking open the huge carved wooden
doors, he pulled her into the tiled hallway and leaned
back against the wall, letting his breath escape in a hiss of
forceful relief blending with a sound of barely repressed
fury.

'Hopefully that will hold them,' he muttered, releas-
ing her at last.

'Hold them!' Rose spluttered, not knowing how to express the mixture of feelings that were curdling inside her. 'How can it hold them when you've just delivered a story that will run and run? They'll want more and more of this fiction...'

'I only said that we were engaged.'

Nairo looked down at her with an expression that made her wonder if she had suddenly grown an extra head. No wonder when the emotional battle going on inside her had made her voice tight and constricted like the control she was struggling to impose on the sudden rush of sadness that had swamped her at that 'I only said...'

Only. There was nothing only about this where she was concerned. The casual way that Nairo had dismissed the idea of an engagement between them—even a pretend one—as having any importance made it only too clear the size of the chasm between them on this.

It meant nothing to him but a pragmatic way of dealing with an unexpected problem and it didn't matter who else was involved or whether they agreed to his approach or not. While for her, the word *engaged* burned like a branding iron.

Add to that the fact that Nairo had only decided to bring their relationship out into the open because it had been forced on him. He'd used this way of explaining it because of the impact it might have on his beloved little sister. Rose might find herself on the pages of the gossip columns, Nairo might now have to tell his family about their relationship, but the truth was that she was really nothing more than his dark little secret, something he would have preferred never to let anyone know about.

'But *engaged*!' Rose echoed. 'Why did you have to say that?'

'It's the only thing the Schlieburg family will understand,' Nairo returned, his expression making it clear that she should have known that. 'If we are planning on getting married, they'll accept that. But a casual hook-up...'

His mouth twisted wryly and he shook his head.

'Not so good.'

'And what when this thing is over and we go our separate ways?' There was an awkward crack of her voice on the words.

A shrug of his powerful shoulders dismissed her question carelessly.

'Engagements break up.'

'But it will be too...complicated.'

It was the only word she could find. *Complicated* came nowhere near what she really meant. She had broken away from this man once before and it had been hell living with the memories. Those memories had even pushed her into the total mistake of her relationship with Andrew and got her the reputation as a heartbreaker when the truth was that it was her own heart that had been breaking at the thought that she seemed incapable of loving anyone else after losing Nairo.

So what did that mean for the way she felt about him now? She had ached with the loss of him even when she had believed that he was the drug dealer she had felt morally obliged to hand over to the police. Now that she knew more about that situation, recognising deep in her soul that she had made a bigger mistake in even suspecting him than giving him her heart, how did she feel about the man himself? She wanted him like hell, that much was obvious, but more than that?

Oh, it was pointless even questioning herself about it. He had made it plain that she was nothing more than a sexual fling for him. This affair was the leftover embers of the carnal passion that had flamed between them so powerfully all those years ago. They had never had a chance to allow that fire to burn itself out, and the bonds of passion that had tied them together had only frayed, not actually been broken. They were still there, still tangling round them, refusing to set them free until they allowed this hunger to burn itself out. The young, foolish adolescent love she'd once known for Nairo had never vanished. Now it had grown into a powerful full-blown adult passion. The love of a woman for a man.

But was Nairo only set on indulging the physical hunger he felt for her until at last, sooner or later, he was sated and could turn and walk away?

The cruel ache deep inside told Rose that she strongly suspected that would be sooner rather than later. He had only actually acknowledged her this morning because the paparazzi had forced his hand. Left to himself, wasn't it more likely he would have kept her hidden away?

'Complicated is not really what you mean,' he said now.

'Of course it is.'

Nairo shook his head, golden eyes locking with hers.

'I told you that you couldn't lie to save your life.'

Which lie did he mean? It caught on raw nerves that he might have guessed something of her feelings, reading too much from her face.

'You're afraid that when we split up they'll think you've done it again—run out on your husband-to-be so close to the wedding day.'

Rose hadn't been aware of holding her breath tight in her lungs, but the sudden inward rush of air snatched in a moment of release made her head swim.

'You're right. That's it.'

She grabbed at the chance to hide the whole truth. Surely there was enough of it in that to convince him on this at least.

Shockingly gently, Nairo reached out a hand, traced a

single fingertip down the side of her face until it came to rest along her jawbone. This time he actually did let the control over his expression melt into a sort of a smile.

'Don't worry, *querida*—I'll take the blame. When the time comes, I'll give you plenty of cause to break it off. Everyone knows I'm not the marrying kind, and you're unlikely to change that. All you'll have to do is to look like the broken-hearted fiancée. Everyone will be on your side in this.'

Even you. Rose dropped her eyes to the floor for fear he might see something she wanted to hide. So now he would be considerate when his thoughts were all of breaking up with her. Did he have to make it so blatantly clear that he just wanted to get her out of his system?

But then she should have expected this, shouldn't she? This was the same man who all those years ago had sent her running with his cold-blooded declaration of *I don't do love. I don't do commitment...I certainly don't do marriage.* And now he'd just reinforced that statement every bit as strongly, if perhaps a little less harshly.

Nairo Moreno or Jett, it didn't matter which incarnation of this man she was with, he'd stated openly that commitment was not in his vocabulary. While she seemed to fall in deeper with every breath she took.

'Great.'

She could have tried harder to make it sound convincing, Nairo told himself, but she hadn't even bothered to inject a note of resolution into her response. He had offered her a way out of the mess in which they'd suddenly found themselves, but she didn't appear to give a damn about it.

He'd come hurrying after her, wanting to talk. Willing to admit that the past had been full of mistakes, marked by emotional scars they'd both carried. That perhaps the present could be different. That had all been shattered in

the moment he had seen her beset by the gang of reporters. He hadn't paused to think. Had only known that he
couldn't let her be exposed to the scorn and ridicule that
had been directed at her before by Geraldine and her type.

'Well, at least we won't have to get divorced or anything
messy like that,' Rose said carelessly. 'That would really
upset your prospective in-laws.'

The flippant response set his teeth on edge; the muscles
in his jaw tightened so hard they actually ached.

'That is not going to happen.'

Things weren't going any further; he would just settle
for what they had. Like a fool he'd tried to push things ten
years ago, wanting to hold on to everything he thought he
could have. So he'd rushed into telling his father that his
life had moved onto a very different path. That he'd found
the woman who would make him change. He'd wanted
to show Raoul that he could settle down, become part of
the family again, and he'd thought that Rose would come
with him. But he'd moved too fast, assumed too much.
He'd learned the hard way how wrong those assumptions
had been.

Not this time.

'Our relationship is to be a tragic mistake. One we
rushed into but then realised we couldn't live with. If the
family ever think it was anything else...'

She actually recoiled from the intensity in his voice, her
mossy-green eyes opening wide to reveal the dark shadows swirling inside them. She had looked like that once
before. In the squat when he had told her that he had a way
of getting them out of there, with money to support them
both. At the time he hadn't realised that, believing so ill
of him, she'd been horrified at the thought of any sort of
future together. Just as now she couldn't make it plainer
that all she wanted was a sexual fling. Time to—what was

it she had said?—get this thing out of her system. *This thing!* Little Red had grown up—she had no fear of saying exactly how she felt.

'You're really over the top about looking after Esmeralda, aren't you? What created this obsession?'

She was getting uncomfortably close to memories he didn't want to probe.

'Is it an obsession to want your sister to be happy and cared for?' he growled. 'Surely that's a normal brotherly feeling.'

'Happy, maybe,' Rose acknowledged. 'But you seem prepared to do anything for her.' Even tie himself into a fake relationship he didn't want so that her in-laws would be happy. 'Don't you think it's OTT?'

Something flared in those amber eyes. Anger? Rejection? Or something else?

'She was only a kid when I left home—and she needed me. When I went back—when my father finally let me in—I promised myself I'd never let her down again.'

'Let her down?'

She'd seen the way he looked at his young sister—and, more importantly, the way that Esmeralda looked at him. Those weren't the looks between someone who had been let down and the person who'd upset her badly. The truth was that Rose had envied Esmeralda's close connection with her brother, the obvious complete trust she had in him.

'How did you do that?'

But that was obviously a question too far. His jaw set tighter, his face seeming carved from granite. Hardly surprising when she had touched on that all-important word *trust*. The one thing he had wanted from her—and the way she had failed him. The bitter twist of her conscience was nasty and sharp, making her suddenly need to sidestep this particular subject.

'So what do you mean, when your father let you back in? I was the one who had to get away—escape from having anything to do with my stepfather. So I couldn't risk going back home. You told me you were the one who just walked out. So, presumably you could walk back in?'

No response. Not a word or a change in his set, taut features. Suddenly she wanted to provoke him. Wanted the truth from him.

'It was OK for you, surely. You had a comfortable home, a business, family wealth just there for you.'

'Walk back in! Hah!' His tone was so cynical it could have flayed a layer of her skin away. 'You have to be joking.'

'Why? Wasn't it like that?'

'In my dreams. How could it be with—'

'With what?' Rose questioned when he broke off, turning his head sharply to stare out across the garden, where the sun was now beginning to burn through the dawn mist, refusing to meet her eyes. 'What happened? Nairo—tell me.'

CHAPTER NINE

'NOTHING TO TELL.'

The face he turned back to her was bleak and so ruthlessly controlled that it seemed as if his cheekbones might slice through the skin where it was pulled taut and white against them.

'It no longer matters. It's done with.' He bit the words off with a brutal snap. 'In the past.'

If he expected her to believe that, then he needed to be more convincing. All that his expression conveyed right now was the fact that he was cutting himself off from whatever had happened, and his body was so rigid that it made her want to ease some of the tension away from his muscles.

'It might be in the past, but it's pretty obviously not done with. Not when it makes you look like this.'

With careful fingers she traced the drawn shape of his cheeks and jaw, feeling the muscles bunch under her touch. She wanted to soften it even more, perhaps risk a kiss, but she didn't dare. Every instinct told her that if she pressed her lips to his, then he would respond with that searing hunger that flared between them so fast. Light the blue touch paper and stand well back.

Even if she welcomed the thought of being taken to his bed again, of giving herself up to the passion that stormed her body, sent her brain spinning, she knew that if she did so, if she let him take her out of the here and now and throw her into the wildness of pleasure he could give her, then he would never let her go this way again. He would snatch at the opportunity to distract her totally, and so never tell her the truth, never let her into this particular dark space inside his mind.

'Tell me,' she urged softly.

'I told you. Back then.'

'Oh, come on!' Rose mocked. 'You told me only as much as you wanted me to know. Why do you think...?'

But that was treading on dangerous ground, going back to the confrontation they'd had the previous night. She hadn't trusted him. She'd been a naïve fool to think she could say she loved him when she had never really known him. But the man she was getting to know now, the man who cared for his sister, had worked so hard to regain his father's respect... Who, face it, had come to her rescue just now even if he had used his own pragmatic way of dealing with things, and so had trapped them both in a situation that he must hate. One that tore at her heart for the lie that it was.

'You told me that you had a row with your father and walked out.'

He'd made so little of it then that she had believed it had been nothing like the fear she had fled from in her own home. It seemed that in that, as well, she'd been badly mistaken.

'He threw me out.'

Suddenly he flung up his hands in a gesture of surrender and it was as if she had pressed the right button, and the stream of words couldn't be held back.

'My parents' marriage was toxic. She married him for his money and thought her duty done when she provided one heir—me. Two children were not in the contract, so she didn't stay around after Esmeralda was born.'

'She left when you were—what—nine?'

The sharp nod of his dark head held all the anger he wasn't prepared to express.

And his sister just a baby. It was no wonder that he had always felt so protective to Esmeralda as her big brother.

'We had nannies of course—and my father had plenty of women, but none of them stayed around very long. They just helped him spend his money and then moved on. But later *Papá* married again. My stepmother—my *much* younger stepmother—tried to seduce me. She came on to me one night, hot and heavy. I'd had a drink and, stupidly, didn't quite realise just what she was up to. But then when we were found in a compromising situation—she had half her clothes off and was starting on mine—she claimed I'd been the one who had started it all. My father told me to get out.'

The stark control was back, giving away only the most basic of facts. That in itself told Rose more than she wanted to know about what had actually happened.

'He cut off my allowance, threatened to disinherit me totally, said he never wanted to see me again. I can't say I wanted to see him either if he believed her word against mine.'

Rose flinched away from the flat coldness of that statement, knowing how much lay behind it. No wonder he had been so darkly angry at the way she hadn't trusted him either. With his father's betrayal behind him—both his parents' really—he would find that so very hard to forgive.

She wanted to reach for him again, bridge the gap between them with a touch, but even though they were barely inches apart the emotional chasm seemed too great to overcome.

'So I came to London, ended up in the squat.'

The look he turned on her actually had a glint of dark humour in it, an unbelievable smile tugging at his mouth.

'It wasn't just any old squat—it was actually once my family's London house. One my father had let become so run-down because he'd been spending all his money on women. To tell you the truth I quite enjoyed the thought of squatting in the family home. After all, *Papá* had left it to go to rack and ruin. At first it gave me some satisfaction to know my father would hate my being there—but later I had a crazy idea of standing guard over the property, making sure it wasn't totally destroyed by the others.'

His bark of laughter was cold and brutal so that she winced inside just to hear it.

'I should have realised then how bad things had got—how fast my father had gone through his fortune—and that was before Carmen divorced him and took half of what was left. But then, that Christmas, I decided it was time to try to build bridges. I contacted my father—offered an olive branch. He was hard work—I almost didn't make it.'

Another shrug of those powerful shoulders, another controlled, obvious understatement, hiding so much more. And her behaviour must have made it so much worse. She didn't need to be told; she could fill in the blanks for herself. His father had heard about the drugs bust and the police raid. He'd also learned that someone had died and had blamed Nairo for that.

'I'm sorry.' What else could she say? 'So sorry.'

His eyes were dark, shuttered as he looked down at her, but astonishingly he shook his head in rejection of her apology.

'What else were you supposed to do if you wanted to stop that awful trade that Jason was involved in? It was what I was going to do as soon as I got you out of there.'

For a moment she'd been so rocked by that 'what else were you supposed to do?' that she almost missed the final throwaway sentence. But even as she registered it, he was speaking again and that dreadful, flat, controlled tone allowed for no interruptions.

'When I was allowed back home, I found that the stepmother had left. She'd abandoned Esmeralda—who was only nine. That was the second time she'd lost a mother.'

Bitterness twisted the word into an appalling sound.

'The woman who gave birth to us walked out when she was only a baby. Now this one. And my father was busy with a new woman. I promised myself I'd take care of Esmeralda, but he said he wouldn't have me in the house unless I went to work on the *estancia* in Argentina—to "earn my place in the family".'

'Esmeralda told me you revived the *estancia*. You proved yourself with a vengeance.'

Nairo nodded sombrely.

'What did you do there?'

For the first time his face lightened. There was even a curve to his lips, a light in his eyes.

'I turned the place into a profitable venture by making it a popular holiday destination—horse riding, wine tasting. I even set up an arts trail—there are some brilliant new painters out there. My father must have hated the way it had become so commercial—but he couldn't deny how it started paying its own way. Especially when it ended up out of the red and completely into profit.'

'He'd have had to admit you did the right thing. And he must have let you come back home.'

'Yeah—but when I did Esmeralda had changed out of all recognition. She'd felt so out of control for too long. There was nothing she could do about the family situation, so she started to impose a ruthless control on something she could govern—herself.'

'I wondered if she'd had an eating disorder,' Rose put in on a gasp of shock. 'Was she anorexic?'

It was obvious when she thought about it. Esmeralda was so delicate, so bird-like. She almost looked as if a touch would snap her in two. And if this was what she was like now, some time since the events Nairo was describing, then what must it have been like back then?

'She almost died.' Again, the flat, toneless voice expressed the horror of that time.

'I understand,' Rose said, knowing she meant more than his sister's story. It was no wonder he was now so totally focussed on propriety and the family's reputation. That he wanted Esmeralda to be happy.

But he had lost his mother too. When she'd walked out she'd left both of her children, and Nairo, at nine, had to have been more aware of her abandonment than his baby sister.

No wonder he'd reacted with such ferocity when she'd told him her story, declaring that her mother should have been there for her, to defend her. That she hadn't deserved the—in *his* mind—too easy forgiveness Rose had given her. But for Esmeralda's sake *he* had been prepared to hold out an olive branch to his father, to work his 'penance' in Argentina.

And not just for his sister, a sad little voice in her thoughts reminded her. *As soon as I got you out of there.* He had thought of her too then, but she had let her fears swamp her and had run into the night. Had she really been fool enough to lose something that could have been so valuable because she'd been afraid she was like her mother?

Some cold, cruel little witch who stamped on his heart and then betrayed him without a care.

Esmeralda's words sounded over and over in her head, making her feel worse with every repetition. What if Nairo's sister had really not been mistaken? What if *she* was the one who had betrayed Nairo in this way?

What if he had once truly cared for her—all those years ago? And she had destroyed that caring by not trusting him so that now all he wanted was the blazing physical passion that had brought them together this time.

A passion that he had felt obliged to cover up by announcing their fake 'engagement' to the world. So that now he was tied into a relationship with her that he had never chosen or wanted.

'I can't do this,' she muttered, knowing from the sharp turn of his head, the dark, assessing glance down at her, that he had caught her words and knew exactly what she meant.

'You have to.'

'No, I don't—I can admit the truth, tell everyone that this engagement is a lie. Move out...'

At least that would free him. So why didn't he look pleased—relieved even?

'But that would break our contract.' His frown darkened dangerously. 'I can still take this commission from you, get someone else in to finish the dress.'

'You wouldn't!' Stark horror rang in Rose's voice. 'Not when Esmeralda's wedding is so close.'

'I would,' he returned, hard and sharp. 'If it meant stopping you from ruining her day by letting her know that what I've just told the press is a lie and so opening up a new sort of scandal that will have the paparazzi feasting on it like vultures for weeks.'

He would too, Rose realised. There was no doubt on that. He felt he had to make up to his sister for her losses—for what he saw as his abandonment of her when she needed him—and to do that he would pay any price. Even letting himself be bound into a fake relationship that he hated the idea of.

'I can't let you do that to her.'

And she couldn't do it either. She had grown so fond of Esmeralda over the past weeks, come to care for her.

'All right, then,' she agreed heavily.

It was only—what? Another couple of weeks and then she could...

Her mind flinched sharply away from the thought of what would happen then.

'Be assured you will still have the wedding commission and all that goes with it.'

He made it sound as if that were all that mattered, but then that was how he believed she felt. It was what she had set out to make him think she felt. The twist of pain in her gut had to be ignored if she was to go on. And she had to go on.

'OK,' she said slowly. 'I'll do it.'

'For Esmeralda?'

Of course, in his mind it could only be for Esmeralda. There was no one else who mattered.

'Of course for Esmeralda,' she said sharply. 'She and Oscar make a lovely couple and, like you, I'd hate it if anything prevented them from having their perfect day.'

Now what had she said that made his jaw clamp tight like that, the muscle at the side of his mouth clenching in uncontrolled response?

'Don't you believe me?' she asked uncomfortably.

For a long moment he looked down into her face.

Then, 'Oh, yes,' he said slowly. 'Yes, I believe you.'

It was the answer she wanted, but somehow it didn't give the reassurance she was looking for. There seemed to be so much behind the simple comment. With a brusque nod of agreement he turned and walked away down the hall, leaving her staring after him wondering why, when he'd said he believed her, he had left her feeling that he actually felt the exact opposite.

'And for you,' she suddenly found herself saying, the words escaping before she had time to think.

She would have caught them back if she could, but then she saw the way his long back stiffened as if a bullet had hit him between the shoulder blades and he came to an abrupt halt. Slowly he swivelled on his heels to turn round to face her.

'What?'

Too late to go back now, and, besides, she didn't want to withdraw the declaration even if he was glaring at her from beneath black brows drawn sharply together.

'Just what does that mean?'

'That I hope that when you've seen Esmeralda married to the man she loves, you'll finally feel that you've done your duty. That you'll have repaid whatever debt you feel you owed your sister—and even your father...'

'You think that's what all this is about?'

'I know it is.'

Though she had to admit that the deepening of that frown made that certainty falter badly.

'And I hope that maybe my part in all this will make up for the mistake I made in believing that you were involved in dealing drugs. I thought that was where you were getting the money you said would change our lives.'

'You didn't trust me enough to ask!'

There was something in his voice that tore into her heart and ripped it open. She deserved it, she knew, and she stiffened her spine to take the accusation that should have been made all those years ago.

'But I didn't trust you enough to tell you.' Nairo supplied the words she had hesitated to say.

'No, you didn't.' It was just a sigh. 'I thought I loved you, but I didn't know what loving someone really meant.'

She did now, and it was tearing her apart not to be able to say it. This time it was not a matter of trust, but knowing that this was not what he wanted from her. That the blazing heat of passion that they shared in bed was all that she meant to him.

'You can't really love where you don't really trust.'

'We were young—foolish—' Nairo's tone almost threw the words away. 'We had a lot of growing up to do.'

Rose could only nod mutely as she clamped her mouth shut on any thoughtless words she might let spill out and ruin the emotional truce they had reached. If this was the best she could have with Nairo, then she would take it.

'Now all we have to do is to see Esmeralda married,' Rose blurted out. Anything to remove that dark frown from between his eyes, lift the tension that held his jaw so tight. 'And then break off our fake engagement. That can't come soon enough.'

She couldn't keep him trapped longer than she was absolutely forced to.

'You promised…'

'I promised that no one would blame you for our break-up,' Nairo inserted, cold and steely. 'And you needn't worry—I'll keep that promise.'

'Good.' She even managed a smile to go with the word, though she prayed it didn't look as unconvincing as it felt. 'And then we can go our separate ways, knowing we owe each other nothing.'

Say no, she begged him in the privacy of her thoughts. *Tell me, just this once, that you don't want it to end this way.* If he even offered her an affair, for as long as it took to burn itself out between them, she would take that. She'd take anything if he'd just make her feel that she mattered to him, in this way at least.

Nairo's silence seemed to drag on and on, drawing out and out until she felt as if her already overstretched nerves might actually snap under the strain. But then at last he moved, nodding slowly.

'That would be the best way to handle this.'

'Then we'll keep to that business deal.'

Rose forced a smile onto stiff lips, though agreement was the last thing she felt. She even held out her hand as if she were still making the business deal he had first proposed to her. Her throat closed tight as Nairo took her fingers in his, her eyes blurring so that she missed the sudden change in his expression.

'No,' he shocked her by declaring sharply, his hand clenching around hers, holding tight as he whirled her towards him, right up against the warm, hard wall of his chest.

'There's more to it than that and you know it. There's this…'

His kiss plundered her mouth, crushing her lips back against her teeth, his tongue sliding along the space he had opened to him, tasting her, tormenting her.

'We've locked ourselves into this fake engagement now, the least we can do is to take advantage of it,' he muttered, rough and raw. 'I want you, and if you try to say that you don't want me, then I'll out you for the liar you are.'

'I— You…'

She tried to speak, but there was nothing to say. She'd told herself that if he had nothing to offer other than his passion, then that was what she would take for as long as it lasted. She wouldn't ask for anything more, knowing he had nothing to give.

So she gave up all attempts to think or to speak and sank into the warmth and strength of his embrace with a sound that was a sigh of acceptance and surrender and encouragement all in one.

'Yes,' she managed. 'Yes—I want you. I want this.'

For as long as it lasted.

CHAPTER TEN

'THAT LOOKS BEAUTIFUL...'

The voice in her ear made Rose start in surprise. With her head bent over the soft pink silk, her hands busy folding and pinning to get the perfect length for the skirt, she hadn't even been aware of the fact that Nairo had come into the room where she was working on the fitting for one of the bridesmaids' dresses. She didn't notice his arrival until he bent his head down to hers and pressed a kiss against her cheek.

Unable to look up at him, or find any words to respond, she simply nodded her head and focussed even more intently on the material in front of her, even though she knew that was not what was supposed to happen. Not when she was meant to be greeting her fiancé on his return after too long an absence away on business.

The feelings were there, it was just that she found it impossible to show them. He'd been away from the *castillo* for some days and she'd missed him more than she could imagine. It was a feeling that had been made all the worse by the knowledge that as the time drew closer to the actual date of Esmeralda's wedding, then so too the days of their 'engagement' must be counting down until the moment when the need for the pretence would be over and the break-up Nairo had promised he would choreograph would have to be set in motion.

When that happened she would have to pack her bags and leave. For good.

'Don't you agree, Marguerite?'

Nairo stunned her even more by turning nonchalantly away towards Oscar's stern matron of a mother, who had taken to supervising the preparations for the wedding, making sure that everything had her seal of approval before it was finalised, smiling easily.

'The dress is spectacular, isn't it? Your daughter will look wonderful in it.'

It was impossible not to contrast that easy question—and the duchess's equally relaxed agreement—with the way things had been just ten days ago. Before Nairo had announced their fake relationship to his family. After that, it had been as if the heating had been turned on in the house and the atmosphere had warmed steadily, even when Nairo wasn't there. Esmeralda, of course, had been overjoyed that her adored brother and her newfound friend had apparently fallen head over heels in love, and the Schlieburg family, even Duchess Marguerite, had thawed noticeably.

Not that this had made life any easier for Rose herself. Quite the opposite. The truth was that every moment was more uncomfortable, every glance, every smile, a torment when she knew they were all based on a lie, one she had to maintain because of her promise to Nairo. She was supposed to pretend that she was madly in love with him, a pretence that, deep inside, was frighteningly easy. Too easy, so that she felt she was in real danger of giving herself away to him while she knew that the softening of his voice when he spoke to her, the gentle touches on her arm or her waist and, worst of all, the softly lingering kisses that he drifted across her cheek or her lips, were just part of the act he had determined to play. One that he seemed better at playing, when there was nothing real in his feelings, than she was when her emotions were tearing her to pieces inside, making her feel as if she were bleeding to death from a thousand little cuts.

What made matters worse was the fact that she couldn't talk to anyone about their relationship.

Relationship! Hah! Rose let the pink silk drop from her hands as she lifted her finger to suck at the spot where a pin had gone in sharply and a tiny bead of blood had risen to the surface.

This was no *relationship*. The real truth was hidden away like a dark and dirty secret while every day she was treated with growing affection and welcomed into the family as if she really belonged there. But only for as long as Nairo would allow that to last.

'Careful! You don't want to mark it.'

He had seen the tiny damage she had inflicted on herself and he moved swiftly to ease the silk away so that there was no risk of her staining the beautiful material. But at the same time there was the touch of his other hand at the back of her neck, tracing over the knots of her spine where it was exposed by the way her head was bent over her work. The warmth of those strong fingers lingered, moving softly, stroking, circling over the bone at the nape of her neck, sending delicious shivers of response through her whole body.

'Come to me tonight,' he murmured against her ear, soft and low. 'Eleven o'clock...'

Another whisper meant for her alone and already Nairo was moving away, taking his caressing hand from her so that she felt a cold sense of loss that was a shadow over her heart. One that she couldn't help but contrast with Esmeralda's glowing happiness. Nairo's sister could bring her love for Oscar right out into the open for everyone to see, while Rose could only hide the truth of hers away. Holding it close to her heart while Nairo thought the way she was behaving was as much an act as his own performance.

It was a bitter irony that in those past days, when she had thought that she'd loved him, she had run away from revealing that love, not having the strength to hold on to it for better or worse. Now she knew how hard real love was to handle, she was strong enough—or did she mean weak enough?—to hold on as hard as she could until the day that this dream would come crashing down around her.

Perhaps it was that thought that made all the difference, or the days of his absence on a business trip were what made Nairo particularly passionate that night. She had barely arrived in the apartment before he snatched her up in his arms and carried her into the bedroom, dropping her down onto the bed with little ceremony. Then he proceeded to strip every item of clothing from her, giving her no time to feel the chill of the night air on her exposed flesh as he kissed and caressed his way down her, leaving her burning and tingling where his lips had touched.

By the time his hard body slid into her welcoming warmth she had been floating on a heated tide of hunger, yearning and open to him. The pulse that throbbed at her temples made her head swim so uncontrollably that she was thankful to be supported by the soft downy pillows. Her whole body felt as if it had dissolved into a pool of molten wax, lost, adrift, blind with her need for him.

That night her orgasm was so sharp, so overwhelmingly powerful that it seemed to split her mind in two, sending her spinning into the wildness of a world where nothing existed but herself, this powerful, passionate man and the exquisitely raw sensations they had created between them.

It took a long, long time for her to come back to reality. She had no idea how long she lay there, oblivious to everything but the man whose hard, warm chest cushioned her head, his ragged breathing slowly easing and his heart slowing from its frenzied race under her ear.

'That was special.' She couldn't hold it back even if it was the least she could tell him. 'So special.'

She felt the change in his mood in the way it affected the long, lean body lying beside her. From a sweat-sheened relaxation that came with intense sexual fulfilment, every muscle suddenly tightened, holding taut against her in a disturbing silence that pushed her to defiance.

'Oh, I know I would be a fool to think that you agreed with me.'

'It was special to me,' he said at last, his voice slow and dark. 'How could it not be? I've known the best sex I've ever had with you.'

If it was meant to be a compliment—and obviously that was the way that he intended she should take it—then it didn't have the desired effect. If sex was all it was, then it meant too little, nothing like the feelings she found herself longing for. Besides, it couldn't be true. No matter how she might long for even that little satisfaction.

'That's not really true,' she managed, unable to hold the words back.

'What?'

This time he pulled away from her, lifting himself up until he was propped against the carved wooden bedhead. Coldly searching eyes raked over her face.

'Just what the hell are you talking about?'

Could she, like him, tell the difference? Nairo wondered. The very thought rocked his sense of reality. *Noth-*

ing could ever match the way he had once felt about her. The searing burn of that long-ago innocence he had thought they had shared. From the first time, she had made everything make sense, made him want to change his direction in life, to change his world.

For her.

His head spun at the thought that she might even have sensed any feeling like that. Was there something in what he had done—the way he had kissed her, touched her, taken her body—that had risked exposing that hidden part of him to her? A part that not even his father, nor Esmeralda, had ever seen.

'Tell me,' he demanded. 'What the devil is that supposed to mean?'

She shifted in the bed beside him, lifting herself up till she was kneeling close, sitting back on her legs. She pulled the sheet with her, covering the pink-flushed delights of her body from him. It was that change in her mood, the need for concealment, that alerted him to the fact there was no room for dreams in what they had now. She still held her essential self apart from him, even when she had given him her body so willingly and openly.

'That there was someone very special once... No?' Rose questioned as she saw his head move in adamant denial.

'No one.'

'But Esmeralda said...'

The beautiful mouth that had just given her so much pleasure twisted sharply, giving her his response without him having to speak.

'My sister is a hopeless romantic. Besides, she was only a child at the time and she knew nothing. And now, all wrapped up in the fairy-tale details of her upcoming wedding, she still knows nothing of the truth of the basic facts of how it can be between a man and a woman.'

His tone formed the words into ice, making Rose shiver as they landed on her exposed skin, pulling the sheet closer round her for protection from their impact.

'And how is that?'

'Do you have to ask? You were there. You know what it was like.'

'Tell me,' she said, needing to know exactly what she was dealing with. 'How was it?'

That was almost a smile, she noted. But a smile that did nothing to warm the chills that had shuddered over her skin. Instead it made her shiver even more, deeply and inwardly.

'Couldn't be simpler,' Nairo stated. 'I had the hots for you and you had the hots for me.'

He reached out a hand, let his fingers trail across her shoulders and down to where the white sheet formed a tight but impossibly fragile barrier against his touch, his eyes darkening noticeably as they locked on to hers. She managed to control her response but only just.

'I still do—more so now you've grown up.'

Something in Nairo's face changed, sharpening that stare till it felt like the scrape of a blade across her skin.

'That was how it was for you too, wasn't it?'

Somewhere in the back of her mind, Rose acknowledged the death of the wild, foolish hope she had let half form.

'Oh, yes...'

Fearful that that probing gaze might discover more than was safe, she affected a tone of total nonchalance, even managing a sort of a smile, though it couldn't have been as careless as she had hoped for.

She'd prayed he'd forgive her for going to the police and that wish had been fulfilled. It was a long time ago he'd said, a third of a lifetime. So he'd shrugged off her foolishness, her naïveté in suspecting him. But behind that was the real, darker truth that he could shrug it off so easily, not because it hadn't mattered but because *she* hadn't mattered. Because he had never cared about her as she had cared about him.

'That was exactly how it was for me,' she managed even though the lie burned on her tongue like acid, threatening to make her stumble over the words.

Needing to protect herself from the way he made her feel, the way she was tempted to lay her soul open to him, she pushed herself out of the bed, wrapping the sheet round her and taking it with her.

'I'm starving,' she tossed over her shoulder at him, knowing she meant a very different form of hunger than the one that could be appeased with any amount of food. 'Want anything?'

'You know what I want,' he growled behind her, but to her surprise he snatched up his black towelling robe and followed her into the kitchen.

'So where did you go this time?' she asked a short while later, curled up on the settee and nibbling on the edge of some slices of apple, which were all that she could manage to prove her claim of hunger without them choking her.

'London. I had business there.'

Nairo fetched a glass of wine for them both, placing hers on the table before her while he lounged in one of the big dark red chairs, stretching his long legs out in front of him.

'Your mother's looking better,' he added unexpectedly.

'You went to see her?' Rose found it hard to believe, but he nodded easily.

'It seemed wrong to be so close and not check she was OK. And yes, she's doing fine. And she and Margaret are even better friends than before. She sends you her love.'

'Thank you! That means so much!'

It meant even more that he had put aside his own belief that she had forgiven her mother too easily in order to do this.

'I never thought...' she began, but Nairo was shaking his head, anticipating what she was about to say.

'I would never have been able to live with myself if I hadn't made peace with my father before he died,' he said, his voice rough and low. 'All I wanted was to be part of the family again. That's why I swallowed my pride...'

The way he tilted his glass, swallowed down some wine, revealed his feelings more than any words.

'Me too.' Rose dropped the apple slice down onto her plate, unable even to make a pretence at eating it. 'And I think I should say that's what Mum was looking for all her life—a sense of belonging.'

Something changed in Nairo's face, not exactly a softening, but his muscles lost some of their tension, the tautness of his jaw easing just a little.

'I brought you something.' He indicated with his glass, waving it in the direction of the dresser near the door. 'A gift.'

'You didn't need to...'

'Now what sort of a fiancé would I be if I didn't bring my betrothed a present to compensate for being away from her for so long? It's over there...'

Getting to her feet, the sheet wrapped round her trailing along in her wake, Rose moved as he directed.

'Here?' She let her fingers rest on the top of the briefcase he'd obviously deposited there as he arrived back home.

'Open it. It's not locked!' he added as she hesitated. 'Look inside.'

'I'm looking—' Rose stared into the open case. 'But what...?'

'In the bag—from the art gallery.'

He was watching intently as she picked up the cream paper bag with the name of a London art gallery on it in an elegant script. It was thin and flat as if there were nothing in it.

'This?' She frowned her confusion. 'But...'

There was just a single sheet of card inside the bag, a glossy postcard that shook in her grip as she tried to focus on it. It was an abstract design, glowing with colour. A splash of scarlet and gold and a deep clear turquoise that was her favourite colour ever.

'Lovely!' she managed, knowing there was something she was missing. 'It's gorgeous, but...'

When had he got up and come close to her? She hadn't seen him move and yet suddenly he was behind her, the heat of his body reaching her through the thin covering of the sheet.

'Turn it over.'

As he spoke he reached out to capture the fingers clasped on the edge of the card, lifting her hand to turn it over as he instructed, so that she could see the words written on the back: *Rosa in tramonta*.

'It means rose in sunset,' Nairo was explaining when she saw the rest of the inscription and knew exactly what he'd done. Why he'd done it. The room seemed to spin round her, everything blurring wildly.

'Enzo Cavalliero...' she managed through the tears that were streaming down her face. 'Enzo... My father...'

Twisting in his arms, she could only rest her damp face against his chest and weep out the tidal wave of emotions that had overwhelmed her.

'Hey...' His voice sounded odd, shaken. 'It was meant to please you.'

'And it does…' Rose drew in her breath on an unsteady hiccup. 'So much.'

'Bueno' was all he said. And then he just held her loosely, supporting her until the storm of emotion was over. At last, dashing a hand across her eyes and sniffing inelegantly, she regained some control and lifted her head to smile up into his watchful dark eyes.

'Thank you.' It was low and heartfelt. But she was surprised to see that no answering smile lit his face.

'I'm only sorry…'

Gently he lifted the card again, pointed to the dates. It took a moment, but then she realised what he was trying to tell her. Enzo Cavalliero had died very young.

Before she'd been born.

It took some long moments and a lot of hard swallowing before she could respond, nodding her head and managing at last to say in a whisper, 'No wonder my mother could never find him.' Her voice strengthened as she swallowed again. 'But at least she can know that he didn't abandon her…and me. Did you tell her?'

His rough shake of his head dismissed that idea.

'I thought you'd want to do that.'

He was so right about that. She couldn't wait to tell Joy, show her the postcard.

How different would her mother's life had been—and her own—if Enzo hadn't died so young? Perhaps she would never have run away from Nairo as she had if she'd had a family of her own, more reason to trust. But then there came the inevitable realisation that she would never have had to run from Fred Brown and so she'd never have met Nairo at all and that splintered her thought processes completely. All she could do was hold on to his hand, and the beautifully coloured card, and repeat sincerely, 'Thank you for this.'

It was when her mind and her eyes cleared as she turned back to close the briefcase that she stopped in astonishment as she saw what now lay on the top of it that had been hidden under the gallery bag at the start.

'What's— This is the house,' she said, picking up the photograph. 'The squat.'

It was no longer a squat. The large town house had been renovated, fully restored to its original elegance.

'What's this?' There was a large plaque at the side of the door. The words on it set her mind reeling again.

'Esmeralda House—a clinic...?'

'For anorexic girls,' Nairo supplied with obvious reluctance.

He didn't look at her but kept his gaze fixed on the photograph. Was he, like her, looking at that first-floor window as if it were possible that the ghosts of the people they had been ten years before might appear behind the glass?

'I didn't want the house for myself and I wanted to put it to good use. They can get medical and psychological help there. They can even live there under supervision until they get well.'

'What a wonderful idea!'

This time when she flung her arms round him it was with real delight and enthusiasm and she felt the stiffness of his long body hold for a moment, then slowly ease against her.

'I'm glad you think so.'

It was another moment before his hand came up to rest on her back, long fingers splayed out against her shoulder blades. The warmth of his touch set a whole new rush of sensations flooding through her. Not sexual but that sense of belonging that she had enjoyed since she had come to be part of the household here. The feeling of being part of a family in a way she'd never known before.

'Nairo,' she said quietly. 'Do you have a photo of her?'

She didn't explain who she meant and she knew she didn't have to. Already Nairo was reaching for his phone, scrolling through photographs until at last he held it out to her.

'That's Esmeralda?' She couldn't believe it—could barely recognise the bird-like creature she knew in the small, sturdy little girl with the huge dark eyes and the curling black hair. 'How old…?'

'Nine. Just before…'

Before he'd been driven out of the house by his lying stepmother, his angry father.

She knew what she wanted to say and suddenly, in this new atmosphere, she felt she could say it.

'Did that woman—Carmen—tell her she was fat?' She read the answer in the set of his face, the way that his jaw had clenched tight. 'How dare she?'

But he didn't want her to go any further, that much was obvious. So instead she took his hand and led him back to the big settee, pulling him down beside her, and leaning against him softly.

Taking his hand in hers, she stroked along his fingers, tracing the muscles, the veins.

'You can't blame yourself for Esmeralda's illness, you know.'

His hand jerked under hers, but she tightened her grip, holding him still.

'Your parents, your stepmother—they all did their part.'

'If I'd been here…'

'If your father had believed you, you would have been here.' Her voice rang with the confidence of knowing that was the truth. 'Nothing else would have stopped you.'

For a long, long moment he was silent and still, but when he spoke his lips were just against her temple.

'Gracias,' he said. *'Muchas gracias.'*

He didn't need to thank her, Rose thought. It was enough that he was here, holding her like this. She could stay here all night. But even as the thought crossed her mind she felt Nairo stir and he turned her hand so that now he was the one holding her fingers in his, the one stroking her hand.

Until he stopped dead, his touch and his focus resting on just one spot. At the bottom of the third finger of her left hand. Instantly she knew what was on his mind.

'No! I don't need a ring—I don't *want* a ring.' She prayed it sounded definite rather than desperate.

'Esmeralda asked about it. It's expected,' Nairo growled.

She couldn't bear it if he went any further. She already felt bad enough, fighting the urge to turn tail and run.

'It might be expected, it might be tradition, but this is a *lie*!'

Twisting in his hold, she came halfway across him, almost on his lap, as she set about distracting him the only way she knew how.

'An engagement ring should be about commitment,' she managed, pressing a kiss against his stubble-shadowed jaw and then moving up, one kiss at a time, towards his beautiful, sensual mouth, feeling the instant reaction in him and breathing a silent prayer of thanks for it. 'About togetherness—about love. But there's none of that here.'

Her hands stroked over his skin, caressing, teasing, awakening the need she wanted him to feel. His groan was a sound of surrender, one that told her she'd succeeded, even if deep down that was the last thing she wanted. She welcomed the hunger and demand of his response in the same moment that it tore her heart in two.

With only the slightest tug he released the derisory protection of the fine cotton sheet, letting it fall to the side, exposing her nakedness to him once more.

Nairo's hand smoothed over her skin, along the curve of her hip and sliding upwards over her ribcage to curl around and cup the heaviness of one breast. He let one finger trail over the darker-toned nipple and watched as if hypnotised the way that the skin puckered and pouted under his touch. His smile was a slow, lazy curl of his lips before he bent his head and let his tongue circle the raised bud. The warm breath of his laughter made her draw in her own air on a gasp of delight before he took the sensitised skin into the heat and moisture of his mouth, tugging on it softly in a way that sent the burn of desire flashing along every nerve in her body.

'I've never known love,' he murmured against her, making her quiver and squirm against the softness of the white linen sheet. 'Never wanted it, but, *infierno*, *querida*, when things are this damn good, then who needs love?'

'No...one,' Rose managed on a gasp. 'No one could want anything more.'

Even the deep-down knowledge that she was lying, that she desperately longed for so much more, couldn't enforce the restraint she knew she should impose on herself. Restraint had nothing to do with this—it was all sensuality. The glorious wild storm of passion that was swamping her, driving away every other thought from her mind.

She wanted so much more than this. Needed more from this man than the feelings he had brusquely described as 'the hots'. She wanted things that were a lifetime, an eternity, away from what he was prepared to give her. But she wanted *him* so much that she couldn't bear to drag herself away and turn her back on the little he did have to offer her.

So she let him pull her down beside him, felt the rest of the sheet torn away and tossed aside, her pulse thundering rough and raw as he moved to come over her, the heat and hardness of his body searing over hers. His mouth took hers, his hair-roughened legs coming between hers, nudging them aside to let the blunt heat of his erection push at the moist core of her being that so longed for him.

She was open to him already. Lost to herself, given up entirely to him and oblivious of anything else. She was all sensation, all heat. All longing, all need. And that was all that mattered right now.

'Oh, yes,' she told herself, whispered against his ear as she pulled him closer, adjusted her body so that he could feel the need she had for him. 'Yes!'

Tomorrow would come soon enough and she would have to face what tomorrow would bring. But for here and now, for tonight—if only for tonight—as Nairo had said, when things were this damn good, then who needed love?

If she said it often enough, then she might just come to believe it.

CHAPTER ELEVEN

'I'VE HAD A wonderful time, Rosalita! Everyone said how absolutely beautiful my dress was.'

Esmeralda accompanied her joyful words with an enthusiastic hug, squeezing all the breath out of Rose and taking away her ability to answer at the same time.

'Just think—next time it will be your big day!'

But that was a step too far. With its scenes of joy and promise, the declarations of love and commitment, it had been inevitable that Esmeralda's wedding day would be an ordeal, but two things had combined to make it even worse than she had anticipated.

The fake engagement was bad enough and she had struggled to accept the congratulations of so many of the guests at today's event. Her head had pounded, her jaw muscles had ached from the effort of forcing a fake smile onto her lips. But the last twist of the knife had arrived in the shape of a letter that had been delivered to her room only that morning. She had discovered it lying on her dressing table when she had crept back into the house from Nairo's apartment, just in time to help Esmeralda prepare for her wedding, and the memory of its contents had haunted her all through the day.

She couldn't meet Esmeralda's wide brown eyes, knowing the questioning look that would be in them. So she stared fixedly over to the side of the room to avoid it. But that only made matters so much worse when she spotted the tall, darkly elegant figure of Nairo making his way towards them.

Knowing that he believed she couldn't lie to save her life, she had hoped that she would be able to keep away from him today, at least until she got some control over her face and her thoughts. But she had forgotten that Esmeralda had wanted her to be waiting at the door of the cathedral, ready to make any last-minute adjustments to the dress before she began her walk up the aisle.

'I can't wait for you to become my sister!' she had said.

Rose had hated having to lie to Esmeralda and the knowledge that very soon she would have to disillusion the girl who had become such a close friend to her was more than she could bear. Now that Esmeralda was happily married, and Nairo had achieved his stated aim, then surely the end couldn't be long in coming, and the report in the newspaper cutting that had been in that envelope, with the photograph that brought such bittersweet memories along with it, must surely mean that she was already living on borrowed time.

'We don't want to rush into anything,' she managed painfully, aware of the fact that Nairo was prowling nearer.

'Don't want to rush!' Esmeralda laughed up into her brother's watchful face. 'Oh, come on, Nairo—what do you call rushing? I mean, you haven't even given dear Rose a ring.'

This time Rose couldn't hold her feelings in check as her gaze flew to Nairo's face, clashing with the hard stare of his bronze eyes with a sensation like slamming into a brick wall. Were his thoughts too filled with the memories of the night she'd told him she couldn't bear to wear such a symbol of the lie they were living?

'I don't need a ring,' she put in hastily. 'Really I don't…'

But Esmeralda was not to be diverted. 'I don't understand you, *hermano*…' She shook her head at her brother. 'Now that you've finally found someone you can love, wouldn't you want to let the world know about it? I know I would!'

'But you, little sister, just want everyone to share in all the fripperies and the fancies that make up your idea of a romantic wedding.'

As always when he spoke to his sister, Nairo's tone was warm and indulgent, making Rose struggle against the bitterness of knowing that she would only ever share in that warmth as an act put on to present a false image of their relationship.

Desperately she lifted the beautiful crystal glass she was holding to her lips, hoping that a swallow of champagne would at least ease the painful dryness in her throat. She felt as if she had been struggling to breathe through the tightness in her heart since the moment she had watched Nairo take his sister's arm in order to lead her down the aisle to her groom.

This might be his sister's wedding, but that image of Nairo, sleekly elegant in the fitted formal wear, was the way that he would look at his own marriage, with the slender figure of a bride at his side in a dress of beautiful white lace, with a delicate veil cascading down from her head. She had no idea who that future bride might be. She only knew that it would never be her.

'But I came to tell you that your new husband is looking for you—and I need to claim my fiancée. Rose and I need to talk.'

He hadn't needed to add the second half of his comment; the mention of Oscar had been more than enough to have Esmeralda turning and setting off in his direction before Nairo had even finished speaking. Leaving Rose alone with the man whose looming presence sent uncomfortable shivers of nerves skittering up and down her spine.

'Talk about what?' she asked sharply, knowing immediately it was the wrong thing to say and the wrong way to say it.

'Not here,' he responded, his voice as flat and expressionless as his face. 'Come with me.'

His grip on her hand was hard and tight, and he set off in the opposite direction to his sister without looking back to see if Rose was following him. Of course she was; it was either that or be dragged along in his wake.

How many difficult and life-changing conversations had begun with the words *we need to talk*? Rose asked herself as she stumbled after Nairo. Once out in the hall, with the doors closed behind them, the buzz of conversation died away to just a low hum and the house seemed suddenly cold and silent, alien somehow. Only now did Rose realise how much she had come to love living at the *castillo*. Not because of its size and luxuriousness but because over the past weeks it had felt like home to her too, she realised, living there in security and peace for perhaps the first time in her life. The nights she had spent with Nairo had been the glorious icing on the cake that was the sense of coming home, so much so that she had pushed away to the back of her mind the realisation of the fact that before too long, she would no longer belong here.

But wasn't the truth that she had never actually *belonged* here?

The time with Nairo was ticking away too, and she'd known this moment had to come. She just hadn't expected it to come quite this fast. The ink was barely dry on Esmeralda's wedding certificate, but it seemed her brother was already looking for his freedom. Well, she wasn't going to beg for more time. She'd gone into this with her eyes open, and if this was what had to be, then she'd face it with as much dignity as possible.

Don't worry—I'll take the blame... All you'll have to do is to look like the broken-hearted fiancée.

There would be no hardship there. When she left here she wouldn't need to pretend that her heart was shattered. She would leave it behind her, in Nairo's keeping, and would have to try to find a way to live without it.

'In here...'

The library was as far as possible away from the ball-room, and it had a door that locked. Perhaps that would guarantee them the privacy he needed, Nairo told himself as he led her into the room he'd decided was the best place for this. If there was such a thing as a 'best place' for this. Just as there was never going to be a 'best time' for it either.

The truth was that this was probably going to be the worst possible time to have this confrontation with Rose. But he had been living a lie for too long now and he couldn't let the situation continue a moment longer.

Today had been the last straw. He had had to watch Esmeralda light up like a brilliant star, her joy blazing in her eyes. He had felt the tremors of emotion run through the fingers that rested on his arm as he walked her down the aisle. Tremors that had vanished in an instant as she had seen Oscar turn to face her, his own smile mirroring hers.

It had been that smile that had shaken him out of the reverie he had slipped into. Just for a moment, wildly, crazily, dangerously, he had actually found himself imagining that *he* had been the one heading for the altar—with Rose as his bride...

Coming back to reality had been like being slapped hard

in the face, and it had forced him to acknowledge there
was no way he could let this situation continue as it was.

He was in danger of finding himself back in the same
sort of mess as he'd faced ten years before if he wasn't
careful. Had he really learned so little in the intervening
time? That was when he had known that he had to speak
to Rose, and as soon as possible.

But now that he was here, in this quiet room, turning
the key in the door against intruders, it seemed that all
words had deserted him.

'Is this going to be so bad that you have to lock me in?'

Rose's voice was high and rather tremulous, though she
flashed a smile that was clearly meant to make him think
she had used the line as a joke.

'I'm keeping others out, rather than locking us in.'

Though he didn't think she'd stay around long once he'd
told her what he had to say. She'd been reluctant to come
here from the start and now it seemed that she was positively itching to get away.

When all he wanted to do was to keep her with him.

He'd known he was in trouble in the moment that she
had moved forward to help Esmeralda arrange her dress
when they had stepped out of the limousine onto the stone
steps of the cathedral. Everyone who had seen his sister in
her wedding finery had exclaimed in delight at the vision
she presented. But for Nairo there was only one woman
in the whole of Spain in that moment.

Her dress was an old gold colour, silky and close-fit-
ting, with touches of lace at the shoulders and hem. Her
auburn hair had been gathered up under a ridiculous
frivolity of a hat, nothing more than a couple of feathers in
a colour that exactly matched that dress, and just the way
those feathers nodded and danced in the breeze made his
heart clench on a clutch of need. He had rarely seen her

wearing much make-up at any time, but today the subtle use of shadow made her hazel eyes seem huge and dark, and her lips looked full and soft, touched with a shimmer of colour. How he had stopped himself from giving in to the hunger that burned through him, tilting up that determined little chin and planting a hard, demanding kiss on that luscious mouth, he would never know. He'd had an ugly fight with his most primitive needs right there in the porch of the cathedral and he was having exactly the same battle right now.

Especially when she reached up and unpinned the perky little hat, tossing it onto a nearby table and shaking back her hair in a gesture that spoke of relief and freedom. One that almost broke his resolve to hold on to his control.

'I know what this is all about,' she said, her voice sounding as uneven and jerky as the pulse that was battering at his temples.

'You do?'

He had thought he had managed to hide his true feelings throughout the day.

But then he realised that she had opened the small boxy clutch bag she carried and was pulling something out of it. A creased piece of newspaper.

She unfolded the paper, slapped it down on the table in front of him. But he didn't need to see it. He knew exactly what she was trying to show him. It was the same photograph that had hit him right between the eyes when he had opened the paper that morning.

'Ah...' he said flatly. 'That.'

'Yes—that.'

Narrow fingers tipped with soft rose-pink polish reached for the paper again, and, intriguingly, he noticed that they shook a little as they did so.

She touched the photograph briefly, then looked up at

him, green-brown eyes dark like the water in the depths of a bottomless, shadowed pool.

'That was what you wanted to *talk about*, wasn't it?'

The emphasis on the two words made him wince inwardly. She was sounding altogether more challenging than he had expected. Had he got this all wrong?

'Partly.'

He wasn't giving anything away, Rose reflected. The single-syllable answers told her nothing, and surprisingly she couldn't see the anger she'd expected in his face. Or was he just better at hiding it than she'd imagined?

She flattened the newspaper again, so that the face in the picture stared up at her from the photograph.

Her own face.

It was a tiny, tatty old passport-style photograph. The sort that was taken in a photograph booth, four prints for a few pounds. It showed every day of its ten years of age, and she knew that age to the exact day. It was one copy of the photograph that she and Nairo had taken in a rare moment of indulgence. Nairo was laughing into the camera while she had her lips pressed tight against his cheek in a playful kiss.

The photo had been published in the UK papers as well as the Spanish ones and the headline in the copy she had read: 'Hola de Nuevo! *Long-Lost Lovers Reunited.*'

The story below it told how 'billionaire Spanish entrepreneur Nairo Moreno knew his beautiful fiancée, designer Rose Cavalliero, many years ago'. The whole story of their life in the squat had been dragged up again, even with a photograph of the once near-derelict building as it was now repaired and restored to its former glory. But no mention of the use to which it was now being put.

The story of the drugs raid had been excavated too, the report of the police investigation repeated over again. Only right at the bottom did it say that Nairo had been found completely innocent.

She knew what seeing this report must have done to Nairo, the anger he must have felt. Surely he would believe there could only be one person who had provided the information to the press. All day she'd been expecting the volcano to explode at any moment; she was just stunned to find that his anger was such an icy, controlled response rather than the eruption she'd been expecting.

'Tell me about it,' Nairo said, and there was a subtle change in his voice. No anger. No recrimination. Instead she might almost have said that he sounded as if he had lost something very important. It was strange because that was the exact way she was feeling too.

Swallowing hard, she had to draw on all the courage she could find inside. She'd sold him short ten years before by not talking to him openly; she wasn't going to do it this time.

'The photo—' she began, her mouth so dry that she found it hard to form the words. 'I didn't…'

'No—you didn't. But I kind of wish you had.'

'You—what…?'

Coherent thought deserted her. She could only stand and stare into the clouded golden eyes that had turned opaque and hidden.

'You didn't give the photo, the report, to the papers. I know you didn't. You couldn't. You would never hurt someone you love that way.'

A rush of relief was blended with another very different strain of emotion. How did he know? How had he guessed? What had she done to give herself away? And how was she supposed to cope with the fact that he'd guessed and yet he looked so uninvolved—so *disappointed*?

'You would never do that to Esmeralda on her wedding day.'

Now her head was really spinning. She had come in here expecting the outbreak of war, to be told to pack her bags and get out, but instead she was confronted by this deadly quiet man with the almost colourless face, the deep dark eyes, and suddenly she didn't know who Nairo was or what he wanted from her.

'I don't understand.'

Her legs felt weak as cotton wool so that suddenly she plumped down into the nearest chair, grabbing hold of the arms for support. But that just made things so much worse. Nairo's dark figure towered over her, making her feel very small and vulnerable.

'What has Esmeralda to do with this?'

That made his face change at least, but the way it brought the frown back to between his dark brows didn't help at all.

'Surely it's obvious. I've seen you with Esmeralda. I know that you care for her. You wouldn't do this to her.'

She wanted to smile, she wanted to laugh, she wanted to break down and bury her head in the cushions on the chair, weeping her heart out. She wanted to do all three at once. Shockingly, it was laughter that won and she heard the strangled, slightly hysterical sound echo round the elegant room.

'You know I didn't do this—for Esmeralda?'

His frown this time was one of genuine confusion.

'Of course—who else?'

'Oh, Nairo, don't you know?'

As soon as she asked the question the stab of a shard of ice right in her heart gave her her answer. Of course he didn't know. He could see the way she felt about his sister, but to the way she felt about him he was totally blind.

Either because he just couldn't see, or because he didn't *want* to.

It was then that something hit her like a light bulb going on inside her head. Of course! She was the one who couldn't see. He had promised to give her a reason to break off their engagement. One that everyone would understand, and this…

'Look. I know you want this over and done with!'

She pushed herself to her feet again, unable to hold back, not caring if she let him into the way she was really feeling. It was too late to worry about that.

'But really, don't you think you could have waited—that you could have had a bit more consideration? Today was supposed to be Esmeralda's perfect day. She's so happy… What do you think she'll feel when she realises that our engagement has broken up—today of all days?'

'It has to be today,' Nairo flung at her, his voice raw with emphasis. 'There's no other way. Because I can't live like this. I can't live this lie any longer.'

CHAPTER TWELVE

SHE COULDN'T KNOW what it had done to him to lie all this time, Nairo admitted inwardly. To fake the feelings or, rather, to show the feelings and know that she believed they were faked, put on for show to convince everyone else and meaning nothing.

What was that saying 'fake it till you make it'? Hadn't the last weeks been such hell because he had been *making* it for so many days now while all the time the person he most wanted to persuade was convinced that he was doing the perfect job of faking it as they'd agreed? That was what he couldn't bear to live with any longer.

The truth was that he'd hoped for something else, he admitted bitterly. He'd hoped that when he let Rose know that he trusted her, totally sure that she hadn't been the person who had sent the photograph and the story to the press, then things would change. He strongly suspected he knew who had done that and it wasn't her. It had all the hallmarks of Jason's nasty-minded tricks and schemes to make a profit out of someone else's upset. Though how he'd got hold of the photo in the squat he had no idea.

But the real culprit didn't matter. What mattered was the fact that he believed in Rose. For perhaps the first time in his life he had put all his trust in a person—a woman— who wasn't part of his family. He had brought her here to demonstrate that trust and deep down he'd hoped that when he'd done so she might rethink the idea of breaking off this false engagement, going their separate ways.

That had failed miserably. Bitter laughter caught in his throat, making him cough, and he was grateful for the way that needing to cover his mouth with his hand gave him a chance to hide what he was feeling, to hold back the words that he came so dangerously close to letting slip. The ones she clearly didn't want to hear.

'No more lies!' he managed, forcing the words out so that they sounded as cold and as brutal as her *I know you want this over and done with!* Anything else would have stuck in his throat.

No more lies. Rose had to struggle to catch the words because they seemed to get tangled up in the cough that shook Nairo's throat—or was it a laugh? She couldn't see what there was to laugh about.

But then she remembered how just a few minutes before, she had let go and laughed herself, when laughing was the last thing she felt like doing. When she really wanted to just break down and weep.

Thinking back, she knew he had said something…but she couldn't make it make any sense.

She didn't give the photograph to the press, she had said, and he had replied…

'No—you didn't. But I kind of wish you had.'

She only realised that she had repeated the words out loud when she saw him nodding along with them, a strange little smile curling at the corners of his mouth as he raked both his hands through the darkness of his hair, ruffling it impossibly.

'I'm a fool, aren't I?' he stunned her by responding. 'A blind, crazy fool. But I did hope.'

The tousled effect of his hair falling softly over his forehead gave him an impossibly young and boyish look that tugged on something vulnerable in her heart. She hardly dared to ask, but she had to take the risk because if she missed this chance it might be the only one she would ever get.

'Why would you...?' Her voice shook with disbelief. 'How could you ever *hope* that I'd sent the photo to the papers?'

Nairo sank back against the huge polished oak table in the middle of the room, staring down at his feet, shaking his head as if in disbelief at his own behaviour.

'So that then I'd know you kept the photo.'

'Do you *still* want proof?'

Had she been a fool to let herself hope? She couldn't believe how close she had come to letting him in and now it seemed that she had been blindly led along by what she most wanted rather than what he had actually meant.

'Rose—no...'

His movement towards her was rough, almost desperate, his hand coming out to her. But she was already reaching into her purse, yanking out the small photograph and tossing it down onto the table. That would show him she hadn't parted with her copy of the picture to any reporter.

'I don't need any proof at all. I know exactly what you mean.'

'You do?'

It was meant to sound unconvinced, totally sceptical. But there was something in his tone and in his face that shook the conviction she needed so that instead her words were only questioning, suddenly uncertain.

'I do. Because of this...'

Nairo's hand slid into his pocket, pulled out a black leather wallet and opened it. The small piece of paper he took out and placed on the table beside the one she'd just tossed down had a black-and-white image on it just the same.

Except that on this one it was Rose who was looking straight into the camera, her mouth stretched wide in a smile. And Nairo was the one who had his lips pressed against her cheek.

'You...' It was all that Rose could manage, the sight of the two photographs side by side taking any other words away.

It was the fact that he waited, silent and still, that got to her in the end. It gave her a strange sort of hope, one that she would never have found in any words he might say.

'You kept the photograph—but why?'

'Because I never wanted to forget you.'

Forget her or forget what she'd done? The way she'd treated him.

'When I saw the photo in the paper I hoped that was what it meant to you too. That you had kept your copy, perhaps for the same reason.'

Shockingly, Rose saw that the fingers that reached for her copy of the photograph were not quite steady.

'But I knew you would never have done that. You just couldn't.'

The revelation of his total trust was so huge, so important, that it rocked her mind and for a moment she had to turn off onto a mental siding, another topic, while she gathered her thoughts.

'Who do you think did that?'

'Who gave it to the press?' Nairo asked. 'Jason, I expect. That night he vowed he'd have his revenge on you— on both of us. He must have decided this was worth a try to come between us.'

'Come between us,' Rose echoed. 'But was there ever an "us" to divide?'

'Can you doubt it? Look at those pictures—'

A long forefinger dropped onto the one he had pulled from his wallet. The one where he was kissing her cheek, his eyes closed in an expression of absolute happiness.

'The day we took those felt like a whole new beginning for me. That was the day I first contacted my father, told him I was prepared to apologise.'

That rocked Rose's sense of reality.

'But you'd done nothing wrong—why apologise?'

'If that was what it took. I wanted to turn my life around—make a fresh start. I wanted to have more to offer you than a dreadful room in a scruffy squat. I wanted to take you to Spain—bring you here. Give you a home—with me.'

'Instead I messed it all up for you.'

And for herself. She'd lost her chance to make that new start in life with Nairo. The pictures of the two of them blurred through the film of bitter tears.

'It was my fault as much as—more than—yours,' Nairo said urgently. 'I didn't trust you enough to tell you. Didn't trust you with my real name or my hopes to reunite with my family. I was never honest with you about my feelings. I haven't been even now.'

'Even now?' What did she take from that? Rose had no idea at all and she was afraid to hope.

'When I saw how the paparazzi were hounding you, I thought it would be too much for you. You wouldn't be able to take the press attention all over again and you'd leave.'

'You came to my rescue.'

'No.' It was hard, forceful. 'I couldn't let you go, but I was a coward and didn't tell you why. So I pushed you into an engagement, hung it on the importance of Esmeralda's big day. I had to keep you here until we had a chance to try again. But why would you want to try again if I was never honest with you about my feelings?'

'And what are those feelings?'

It was the question she had to ask, but he would never know how much courage it took her to make it. A direct question demanded a direct answer, but what if the response was not the one she longed for?

Nairo drew in a long, ragged breath, reached out to touch the photographs again as if they were some sort of talisman.

'I wanted to get the wedding out of the way so that then maybe we could have our own time.'

Our own time sounded wonderful, but what she needed was a future. She'd tried to tell herself that she would accept what they had for as long as he let her, but watching Esmeralda today she had known that just wasn't enough. It was all or nothing. She couldn't accept anything else.

'Nairo—we agreed.'

'I know we agreed.' It was dark, raw, vehement. 'And I'll keep to that if I have to. If you still want me to give you an excuse to break us apart and let everyone know this engagement is over, then I promised and I'll keep that promise. But don't ask me to make it look as if I want someone else—as if I love someone else. I can't do that. I once told you that you couldn't lie to save your life and on this neither can I. It would be a lie to make it look as if I care for anyone else. Even for you.'

This time his shake of the head was more violent, sending his already impossibly tumbled hair flying until it fell back in even more disarray than before.

'I can't lie like that even to give the one person I really love her freedom.'

The one person I really love. Rose's heart was thundering, her pulse racing. Had she heard right? Had he really said…?

'In fact I can't let you go at all.'

Again he pushed both hands through the now wildly ruffled black hair, the gesture expressing so much more than his carefully controlled words.

'I know you stayed for Esmeralda…'

'It wasn't just for Esmeralda. How could it be when I—'

'You love her,' he inserted, and the odd shake in his voice did more to convince her than anything else he had done or said.

'I love her—for herself of course,' Rose told him softly. 'But perhaps even more than that I love her because she's a part of the family of someone who means the world to me. Because she loves and is loved by someone I love more than life.'

'Who?'

It rasped from a throat that sounded constricted as if he was having to fight to get it out. But there was no fight left in his eyes. Their bronze depths were clear and unshadowed, totally open to her, hiding nothing of the way he was feeling. That feeling gave her heart such a lift that she felt almost as if her feet had left the floor as she smiled at him, straight into those eyes, everything she dreamed of sharing showing in her own face.

'Oh, Nairo—do you have to ask? I love you with all my heart.'

She needed to make the first move now, stepping forward, reaching out to him. But he met her more than halfway, gathering her up into his arms and crushing her against him as his mouth came down hard on hers.

It was all that Rose had ever dreamed of. All she had hoped for but never believed it would come true. She was here, in Nairo's arms, and to him she was *the one person I really love*. She couldn't ask for anything more.

But Nairo, it seemed, had one more thing he needed to say. Slowly, softly, reluctantly he released her, searching in his jacket pocket for something. The leather box he pulled out was obviously old, worn, slightly battered.

'Esmeralda said I'd never given you a ring. I know how you feel about that—but this is different.'

'How *I felt*,' Rose inserted gently, needing to put every last misunderstanding behind them.

He looked down at the box in his hand, closed his fingers around it, then opened them again.

'I brought this with me because I wanted to ask you to marry me properly. To do me the greatest honour of being my wife—but now...'

He frowned, tightened his hold on the box again and shook his head.

'This is the ring I'm supposed to offer. It's tradition— the family ring—one handed down from generation to generation and so it's the ring I'd want you to have. But my father gave it to my mother—and look how that worked out. I didn't think you'd want something that came with that shadow over its history.'

'Oh, Nairo...'

The fact that he cared, that he'd even stopped to consider that, told her more about his feelings than any more flowery declarations of love and devotion. He wanted her to have his family ring—but he wanted it to be right for her. He didn't want them to end up at war, separated like his parents, who had scarred the family so badly.

'But there were others who wore it, weren't there?' she said softly.

He nodded slowly, dark eyes locked with hers.

'My grandfather gave it to my grandmother and he and

Abuela were married for almost sixty years. And their parents before them.'

Rose couldn't hold back her smile. He needed that and she wanted to give it to him.

'So its history is not all bad, my love. There was just that one blip—and we can break away from that. We can make it a ring of love and happiness all over again.'

It was as if a light had been switched on behind his eyes. His head came up, his long body straightening as if a huge weight had been lifted from his shoulders. His own lips curved into an echoing smile as he flipped open the box, displaying the magnificent diamond ring it enclosed.

'We can—and we will, *mi amor*,' he declared in a voice that resonated with confidence and, more importantly, with a newfound happiness. 'I could ask for nothing more than to spend the rest of my life making you, my beautiful wife, the happiest woman in the world, if you'll let me.'

'Oh, yes—yes, please!' was all that Rose could manage before he caught her to him again and crushed her lips in a kiss that sealed his promise for the rest of their days together.

* * * * *

MILLS & BOON®

MODERN™

POWER, PASSION AND IRRESISTIBLE TEMPTATION

A sneak peek at next month's titles...

In stores from 20th October 2016:

- **Di Sione's Virgin Mistress** – Sharon Kendrick *and*
  A Diamond for Del Rio's Housekeeper –
  Susan Stephens
- **The Italian's Christmas Child** – Lynne Graham *and*
  Snowbound with His Innocent Temptation –
  Cathy Williams

In stores from 3rd November 2016:

- **Claiming His Christmas Consequence** – Michelle Smart
  and **Married for the Italian's Heir** – Rachael Thomas
- **One Night with Gael** – Maya Blake *and*
  Unwrapping His Convenient Fiancée – Melanie Milburne

MILLS & BOON®

EXCLUSIVE EXCERPT

Dante Di Sione can't believe the beautiful blonde
who 'accidentally' stole his family's tiara is black-
mailing him – for a date to her sister's wedding!
If Willow wants to be his fake fiancée, she'll
have to play the part to the full. Only Willow's
confidence is fake…and she's a virgin!

Read on for a sneak preview of
DI SIONE'S VIRGIN MISTRESS
the fifth in the unmissable new eight book Modern series
THE BILLIONAIRE'S LEGACY

"I'm sorry. I'm out of here."

"Dante…"

"No. Listen to me, Willow." There was a pause while
he seemed to be composing himself, and when he
started speaking, his words sounded very controlled.
"For what it's worth, I think you're lovely. Very lovely.
A beautiful butterfly of a woman. But I'm not going
to have sex with you."

She swallowed. "Because you don't want me?"

His voice grew rough. "You know damned well I
want you."

She lifted her eyes to his. "Then why?"

He seemed to hesitate and Willow got the distinct
feeling that he was going to say something dismissive,
or tell her that he didn't owe her any kind of explanation.

But to her surprise, he didn't. His expression took on that almost gentle look again and she found herself wanting to hurl something at him...preferably herself. To tell him not to wrap her up in cotton wool the way everyone else did. To treat her like she was made of flesh and blood instead of something fragile and breakable. To make her feel like that passionate woman he'd brought to life in his arms.

"Because I'm the kind of man who brings women pain, and you've probably had enough of that in your life. Don't make yourself the willing recipient of any more." He met the question in her eyes. "I'm incapable of giving women what they want and I'm not talking about sex. I don't do emotion, or love, or commitment, because I don't really know how those things work. When people tell me that I'm cold and unfeeling, I don't get offended—because I know it's true. There's nothing deep about me, Willow—and there never will be."

Don't miss
DI SIONE'S VIRGIN MISTRESS
by Sharon Kendrick

Available November 2016

www.millsandboon.co.uk

Give a 12 month subscription to a friend today!

Call Customer Services
0844 844 1358*

or visit
hillsandboon.co.uk/subscriptions

MILLS & BOON®

Why shop at millsandboon.co.uk?

Each year, thousands of romance readers find their perfect read at millsandboon.co.uk. That's because we're passionate about bringing you the very best romantic fiction. Here are some of the advantages of shopping at www.millsandboon.co.uk:

* **Get new books first**—you'll be able to buy your favourite books one month before they hit the shops

* **Get exclusive discounts**—you'll also be able to buy our specially created monthly collections, with up to 50% off the RRP

* **Find your favourite authors**—latest news, interviews and new releases for all your favourite authors and series on our website, plus ideas for what to try next

* **Join in**—once you've bought your favourite books, don't forget to register with us to rate, review and join in the discussions

Visit **www.millsandboon.co.uk**
for all this and more today!

MILLS_WEB